PAY FOR PLAY

PAY FOR
PLAY

Bill Gannon

Copyright © 2023 by William Arthur Gannon

All rights reserved. This book or any portion thereof may not be reproduced or used in any manner whatsoever without the express written permission of the publisher except for the use of brief quotations in a book review.

Library of Congress Registration Number: TXu 2-362-664

ISBN: 979-8-9910051-0-4 Trade Paperback
ISBN: 979-8-9910051-1-1 eBook
ISBN: 979-8-9910051-2-8 Audiobook

Printed in the United States of America

First Printing, 2024

Book design by Glen M. Edelstein, Hudson Valley Book Design

For Lisa,

You made sure I didn't spend my retirement binge-watching cartoons, playing golf, and crushing beers after men's hockey. Your support and constant nudges (I didn't say nagging) got me to finally sit down and write this book after years of rough outlines and story development. You believed in me even when I was convinced napping was a more productive pastime. This novel is a testament to your patience, your love, and your ability to hound me when I most needed it.

CHAPTER 1
Predators Are Hunted

Before the two men reached the back door, Marcus knew he'd kill the fat one first.

Hiding in the shadows of the second-floor bedroom, he watched their approach. The larger man lumbered forward, through knee-deep snow, without caution. The other man walked differently, like a predator, head pivoting from side to side. His eyes scanned left, center, right. Back and forth. Up and down. He was the leader.

Unlike the heavier man in front of him, the leader's weapon was drawn. Marcus watched him goad the larger man forward as protective cover, following in his footsteps to keep his own feet dry and warmer. Smart. He needed to live long enough to answer some questions.

Marcus remained motionless, surveilling them from the darkness above, holding back a smile. The conditions were perfect. The bitter cold was jarring. At this temperature, the air bit as it hit the back of the nasal cavity and throat. The eerie quiet was menacing. Heavy snow muffled the sounds around them. The sun was low and dimmed, more white than yellow. Frozen. Lifeless. Hushed.

Marcus knew nothing here was familiar to the leader. Not the cold; not the smell of northern pines in winter; not the sound of lake ice settling and cracking under its own weight. It would be strange and uncomfortable. Marcus wanted him off balance.

He watched as the leader reached out and pushed on the back of the larger man, spurring him to move forward faster. The larger man slipped and fell to his knees. He shuddered as snow filled his shoes and rose up his pant legs. Marcus leaned forward and tilted his head, looking down at a sharper angle as they approached the stairs. The leader's eyes focused on getting to the back door unseen and unheard in the fading daylight before the cold numbed their hands and feet. Marcus made sure that there was nothing in their path, other than snow, to block their entrance or to raise their levels of caution. No other footprints, no security system, no lights, and no signs of movement.

Marcus estimated the man in front was a hundred pounds overweight. His leather loafers and light jacket were useless in the ten-degree temperature and deep snow. He wasn't smart, he wasn't prepared, and he wasn't in charge. But his size deserved respect. The other one, the one following behind, was more dangerous. Choosing the order in which they'd die was simple calculus.

The kitchen looked out to the back deck and was open to the dining room. The pantry and laundry were adjacent. An impressive master bedroom and expansive vaulted great room were down the first-floor hall. Upstairs were five more bedrooms, a media room, and Marcus's office. The largest upstairs bedroom had an internal balcony looking down onto the great room below. The real estate agent must have said, "It has a magnificent floor plan for entertaining," ten times. But since Marcus purchased it, he'd had exactly one guest. Unlike her, the two men creeping onto the back deck weren't guests. They were prey. He'd bought the cabin four years ago for its serenity. Tonight it will be a scene of extreme violence.

Stepping back, deeper into the shadows behind the second story window, Marcus opened the music app on his iPhone and tapped "Recently Played" and "Everywhere." He descended the stairwell and crept down the hall to the great room, where he'd wait.

The silence surrendered to the music. A haunting guitar riff, heavy on reverb, blended with the beat from a drum machine, and an eerie synthesizer. The rhythm was slow and determined. The vocals hit the mark perfectly the moment the window of the kitchen door was broken.

The bigger man shattered one of the small panes of glass with the grip of his handgun and used the barrel to clear the remaining shards so he could reach through and unlock the handle. All he had to do was turn the knob and they'd be in. He didn't notice the dead bolt was already unlocked. He didn't know Marcus wanted them inside the house.

The men entered the kitchen cautiously, scanning the room for threats. The room had light oak cabinets with dark wrought iron handles. Granite counters had tans, browns, and blacks in streaks and the island had a veneer of fieldstone. The larger man nodded approvingly, recognizing the expensive Viking stainless appliances. The whole place smelled like pine and varnish. A rush of frigid air entered the kitchen through the broken glass and whistled in harmony with the music. Newspaper circulars rustled on the counter.

Twenty-five wireless speakers in the cabin enabled Marcus to stream music to every room, all controlled by the iPhone in his back pocket. The music was cavernous and gently echoed off all the hard surfaces. The exposed beams, notched walls, soaring ceilings, and wide-plank wood floors all reflected sound. It was low and soft, but immersive. It came from everywhere. If the two men weren't there to kill Marcus, it would have been a perfect volume for a dinner party.

Hidden in the great room, Marcus used his iPhone to nudge up the volume slightly.

"Stephen, find out where the music is coming from," Javier commanded in a monotone barely louder than a whisper. There was no question who was running this operation.

Javier looked around the kitchen, running his hand across an unread Sunday edition of the *New York Times* on the table. "Escalating US-China Trade War Puts GDP at Risk." The house appeared empty, but the increasing volume of music proved otherwise. Javier allowed a wry smile, knowing it was a mistake for their target to think a bit of music would be anything more than a mild and extremely temporary distraction.

Stephen turned and grinned at Javier, his confidence growing. "This will only take a few minutes."

Javier turned to Stephen. "He is probably unarmed, but be careful."

"I'll go upstairs," Stephen replied with a frown as he bent over to look into the wine refrigerator. It was empty.

"No, you look on this floor. I'll go upstairs. Find him and turn this fucking music off." Javier spoke to him like he was talking to an adolescent.

Stephen stood, stiffened and straight, clearly annoyed.

Javier didn't appreciate Stephen's glare and repeated, "Find him, Stephen, and be careful," as if Stephen needed even simpler instructions.

They split up, Javier moving quietly up the back staircase while Stephen worked his way toward the first-floor hallway. Neither of them noticed the small cube camera on the counter opposite the door they'd smashed. Marcus hid several more in rooms and hallways. All streamed to the same iPhone now controlling the music. Nobody could get close to Marcus, crouched in waiting in the great room, without their approach being seen.

Marcus pressed the volume button up and up again. Now it was loud. Verging on uncomfortable.

The rising volume made communications difficult between Javier and Stephen, especially when they searched on different floors. When they could not immediately find the source of the music or turn down the volume, the atmosphere changed from annoying to unnerving.

As Marcus turned the volume up again, his face hardened. He wanted them to have no doubt. He was waiting.

CHAPTER 2
Ground and Pound

The heavy man didn't like being called Stephen. He'd always been Stevie as a kid or Big Stevie now. Javier was a prick, but orders are orders, and for today Stevie would take his orders from Javier. Swallowing his pride, he'd do what he was told.

Stevie had worked for them before. In fact, it was the third time he'd taken a job from the Mexicans in the last two months. But he'd never worked with Javier. He didn't expect to again after today. It was how they handled these things. He was told Javier would lead the mission. Stevie was OK with it because the money was four times what he typically got paid and twice what he got for cleaning up their mess at the Quincy marina last week. So, he'd do whatever Javier told him to do, but he didn't like being treated unprofessionally. He was big and slow, but he wasn't stupid.

"Fuck, it's loud," Stevie mumbled. When he'd scoped the area a few days earlier he noticed the nearest cabin was over a mile away. He wasn't worried about neighbors hearing anything. Plus, there was no snow on the ground last week. The thick blanket helped deaden sound, but he should have worn better shoes. The snow inside his pant cuffs was melting, his socks were soaking wet, and his feet were cold from the quarter-mile trudge through the woods to the back of the cabin. His toes, numb and tingly, radiated pinpricks up his calves, clear signs of mild frostbite.

The pantry on the left was mostly barren. A jar of peanut butter, some dried pasta, and a few cans of soup scattered on the shelves. He tapped the five-gallon gas can on the floor, checking to see if it was full. It drew a smile. "I'll need that later."

Stevie scanned the laundry room on the right. It looked like it had never been used. No bottles of detergent. No dryer sheets. No lint in the trash can.

He sensed the music resonating and reverberating even louder as he pressed forward down the hallway. It was disorienting. Wood floors flowed into wood walls into wood ceilings. In the low light it was hard to tell where the edges of one met the other. Shadowed browns and yellows bled into each other. It was claustrophobic. Stevie paused, taking a deep breath, and refocused. He repeated his orders aloud. "Find the guy. Get the hard drives. Kill him. Burn the house to the ground." The Mexicans needed the data returned and Marcus dead. They demanded a clear message be sent. With luck, Stevie would get a chance to take care of the girl next, without Javier's supervision. Stevie would have fun with that. She was a real looker, and it would be a great payday.

The plan was simple enough, but Stevie still had to be cautious. The guy could have a gun. He was hiding, which was smart. It would have been smarter if he'd run. Stevie would be careful. He was always careful. But the damn music was so loud, and his feet were frozen. It was all so distracting.

Stevie worked his way toward the great room trying to be quiet. At 325 pounds, he was moving more quickly and directly than he should have been, leaving size-fourteen wet footprints in the hallway headed toward the great room.

Upstairs, Javier passed by the last bedroom on his way toward the office. He paused to scan the space, noticing a gi with several patches and some colorful canvas belts hanging in the closet. Blue, purple, brown, black, and black with several stripes. Javier gave them a dismissive inspection. He was only interested in pulling the hard drives from the computers, not how the guy stayed in shape. The office was his target. It doubled as a workout space, with a large desk, a couple of computer monitors, a heavy bag, kettlebells, and a large gym mat. Javier's frustration grew, irritated that he had already been in the house too long. He wanted to finish the job and fly home to where it was much warmer. "Where is the fucking music coming from?" he growled.

Downstairs, Marcus crouched low in the corner to the right of the doorway to the great room, looking at his phone. Stevie was within ten feet of the entrance. Javier was upstairs in the office. Marcus raised the volume again, then slid the iPhone into his back pocket. He backed tightly into the corner, inside the doorway. He was out of sight from the balcony above and shielded from the view of anybody entering from the hall.

When Stevie broke the threshold of the great room, his walk was wobbly and uneven from numb feet, wet shoes, and snow-filled pant cuffs. A moose head, mounted on the two-story fieldstone chimney, stared at him from across the room. A darkened chandelier, made of deer antlers, which Stevie mistook for a pile of pointed sticks, hung twenty-five feet above his head. Stevie's ears rang from the music. He turned to look back down the hallway at the wet footprints he was making on the wide pine floorboards. Twisting back forward and rotating his eyes toward the bear-hide rug on the floor in front of him, the blow dropped him to his knees. Stevie didn't have time to raise his weapon. It fell from his hand, bounced off his gut, and landed on the floor.

It was strange. The gun was right there, but Stevie couldn't reach it. Even on all fours, he struggled to keep balance, unable to shuffle forward. It happened so fast and with such force there was little pain. He couldn't yell, and breathing was difficult. Stevie was overwhelmed with confusion and panic.

Internally, the impact caused acute trauma. He had a partial obstruction of his trachea, severely limiting oxygen intake. Stevie's fourth cervical vertebrae was fractured. Vascular tears and internal hemorrhaging exuded fluid down his esophagus into his stomach and lungs. His legs and arms worked but would not move. He was frozen on the floor. Stevie had killed more than two dozen people and he never understood why they became paralyzed before he shot them. Now he knew. Terror petrified them, and Stevie was terrified.

The fist, thrown as a right cross to the windpipe, was as fast as it was brutal. Marcus had never thrown one in a match on purpose, but accidents happen. An accidental throat strike got him disqualified once during a fight two years ago and put his opponent in the hospital with a crushed larynx. Marcus didn't mind being ejected. He'd seen the fighter hit his girlfriend at a restaurant the day before the match, so Marcus didn't care that the asshole had to be fed through a tube for a month. Marcus didn't need the $10,000 in prize money anyway.

Here, the punch was purposeful and it did what Marcus knew it would. It was vicious and violent. Stevie went straight to his knees with a look of fear in his eyes. Or was it confusion? Marcus hoped it was fear, like the fear Marcus's friends must have felt. Crouching over Stevie, Marcus whispered in his ear, "You made a big mistake when you laid your fat hands on her." Before Stevie could regain his balance, Marcus stepped behind him, bent over, and locked a rear-naked choke. It was perfectly braced and ferociously tight.

A rear-naked choke is not a choke in the way most people think. It's not strangulation and it does not crush the trachea. Those could take minutes to incapacitate the victim, giving them a chance to fight back. A rear-naked choke compresses the carotid artery along the side of the neck, starving the brain of blood. Stevie was unconscious in less than eight seconds. He had no time to scramble for his Glock, or fight back, or cry out.

Stevie gradually slumped over on his side. Marcus didn't check if Stevie was breathing or for a pulse. He checked his own phone. The camera in the office showed the other guy unscrewing the back of his computer and ripping out the hard drives. Javier hadn't heard anything over the blaring music.

Marcus picked up Stevie's gun and tucked it under his shirt in the small of his back at the waistline. He grabbed Stevie by the shirt collar and waistband and dragged him to the opposite corner of the great room. The smooth pine floors and Marcus's adrenaline-fueled strength made repositioning Stevie easy.

Stevie was still breathing but it was a struggle, gasping and gurgling, and slowing. Marcus sat Stevie down with his fat legs in front of him, facing away from the corner and toward the doorway Stevie had just walked through. Marcus shimmied down and sat behind him, his back up against the exterior wall. Marcus put his left arm around Stevie's neck. In this position, they were both partially obscured from the view of the upstairs balcony. Stevie's girth hid Marcus's entire body but allowed Marcus to spy over Stevie's shoulder through the doorway and down the hall. It was the only way the leader could enter.

Stevie was rapidly losing the battle to breathe. His weight, the strike to his throat, and the choke were becoming mortally effective. Marcus hunkered in and pulled out his iPhone from his pocket and pressed the down volume button several times. Everywhere the music lowered to a softer level. Immediately, footsteps quietly echoed above him on the balcony overlooking the great room.

"Come downstairs, please."

Javier was startled. The voice was not Stephen's, and it wasn't wavering, forced, or panicked. It sounded like how a father might speak to a young boy who left a mess in the kitchen. Marcus's tone was direct and even a little condescending. Javier thought, *¿Quién cree este tipo que es?* (*Who is this guy?*)

Javier hugged the wall of the upstairs balcony trying to see below. Stevie's big gut and outstretched legs were barely visible in the corner, but he could not see Stevie's face or who was talking. Javier knew, based on where the voice was coming from, that the man was using Stevie as a shield. "Clever," Javier whispered through clenched teeth. Javier had underestimated his target twice. The distraction of the music and Marcus's ability to subdue Stevie were two missteps Javier would have to reassess when he got back home.

Javier turned slowly from the balcony above the great room and muttered, "*Hijo de puta*," ("son of a bitch") under his breath. It was directed at the man who sent him here, not Marcus.

Marcus placed the iPhone on the floor next to his right hip so he could watch Javier, on camera, creeping down the stairs and approaching the doorway of the great room.

Unlike Stevie, Javier was silent and precise. He used the walls and shadows from the failing daylight to provide cover. He abruptly stopped, just on the other side of the threshold. The only thing Marcus could see was the muzzle of Javier's handgun, emerging from the shadows, pointed right at him.

CHAPTER 3
Message Sent

At fifty-five, Carlos was two years older than Alejandro. He was thicker. Not overweight, just stockier than his younger brother. His round face and full cheeks sat beneath a head of thick black hair.

Alejandro was younger but looked older. He was taller, thin, and wiry with a lean and well-defined muscle structure. Alejandro's dramatically receding hairline had more gray in it than black. His face was pointed and sharp, almost rodent-like, with yellow and crooked teeth from years of smoking and infrequent dental care.

They lived and worked together in a large hacienda in the foothills twenty miles northwest of their current location. All their family business decisions were agreed to by both of them, together. Major meetings were attended by both Banderas brothers. They rarely disagreed on anything important, and they never fought. They were best friends and ruled the cartel as equal partners.

"Shall you go first, or shall I?" Carlos was in a playful mood.

"By all means, *hermano*." Alejandro chuckled. He bent at the waist, bowed his head, and motioned downrange. "You first."

They were taking turns shooting at beer bottles placed on the ground next to the heads of two men, buried in sand and stone up to their necks, approximately twenty yards away. Alejandro leaned against the customized Hummer pickup watching Carlos aim, shoot, and miss. It was a ridiculous truck with a five-hundred-horsepower engine, eight-inch lift kit, and thirty-inch custom off-road wheels. The matte-black paint, tinted windows, black trim, and black leather interior gave it a menacing military stance. The bed of the pickup was lined with hard plastic and was used to haul live victims. Never dead bodies. Those were left in the desert for the crows.

The truck had enough rack-mounted halogen lights to illuminate a soccer field. It was after midnight, but the whole scene was a glowing, high-definition landscape of scrub brush, cactuses, and stark rocky outcroppings. Flies and moths were swarming the lights. A ten-thousand-watt sound system boomed cumbia music into the nighttime desert.

The brothers were enjoying themselves. Hysterical laughing and friendly insults rang out as shots were taken and shots were missed.

"Ha, not even close!"

"Maybe you should move closer."

"You shoot like our sister."

"Why don't you throw rocks at them instead?"

"Are you sure you are not left-handed?"

The brothers went back and forth. They tried quick draws, gangster holds, and behind-the-back shots. The Ruger looked like an Old West six-shooter but packed a much bigger punch.

Had Carlos and Alejandro not been drinking all day it might have been more immediately dangerous for their intended victims. The brothers had been deep into the Don Julio 1942 since 11:00 a.m. But as it was, somebody was not leaving the desert tonight. The two men used as target practice were here as a message to everybody else in their organization who might be too lazy or too comfortable. It was a warning for those not providing their full effort, or worse, planning some form of betrayal. Be it by gunshot to the head or prolonged exposure to the 120-degree heat tomorrow, *los socios*, the lowest-level workers of the Banderas cartel, would learn their loyalty was nonnegotiable. For Carlos and Alejandro, it was entertainment.

Carlos turned his glance back toward the truck where his son was in the driver's seat. Carlos cared deeply for Enrique. He'd grown into a formidable man. He had Carlos's full head of hair, though it was more brown than black. Enrique was tall and muscular. His lean athletic build was more similar to Alejandro's than Carlos's. Carlos knew Enrique was destined for greatness.

"Son, turn the music down a little. I want to talk with our guests." Carlos said it like he was about to welcome a close friend into his home for a visit. He was calm and smiling, with his arms wide open toward the two men Alejandro and his henchman had buried shortly after sunset. The difference between a nice chat with a friend and what was happening here was that, in this case, one of Carlos's hands held a .45-caliber pistol.

Enrique observed his father and uncle from the truck. When he was a boy, they frequently invited him to participate in fieldwork. It was a chance for a father to reinforce to his son an important lesson: Sending clear messages is critical. There are times to be incredibly charitable and times to be ruthless. Carlos and Alejandro taught him it is essential to show your subordinates the benefits of good work and loyalty, as well as the seriousness of poor performance and betrayal. Both Carlos and Alejandro sensed disloyalty from the two men crying in the desert.

Tonight, Enrique was a bit bored, but he knew not to interrupt his father and uncle when they were at work. He'd seen them enforce their will on villagers, government officials, local police, and even the military. Now he was in his mid-twenties and violence neither disturbed nor repulsed him. It was his family's profession. Farmers reap fields for grain. Cattle ranchers slaughter cows for food. Loggers clear virgin forests for lumber. Cartel bosses kill people who interfere in their business.

"Fuck around, find out," Enrique muttered, barely loud enough for the man seated next to him to hear. Enrique lowered the volume further just as another of his father's shots ricocheted off the stones wide of its target. With the music lowered, the groveling and begging of the two men was clearly audible. Another loud crack from the Ruger echoed into the darkness.

"Carlos, I thought you wanted to talk to our guests." Alejandro laughed. "I'm sure they have a lot to tell us." He grinned that awful grin.

Enrique and his uncle Alejandro were close. Their family often spoke of how much they looked alike. But even after seeing his father and uncle in action at dozens of these kinds of meetings, his uncle's smile still unnerved him. The way Alejandro tilted his chin down, raised his eyes and eyebrows, and let a tight narrow toothy grin slowly expand made Enrique uncomfortable. It was Alejandro's tell. He did it every time he and Carlos had somebody cornered and were about to end them.

"I know, brother, I know. I wanted to make sure I had their full attention." Carlos said it like he was seeking Alejandro's consent. "May I proceed?"

"By all means. Proceed." He was grinning.

Carlos walked over to the two men. The white-hot lights from the truck burned their eyes. They struggled with tears and dust and insects. They could only see when the shadow heading toward them stepped between their line of sight and the KC lights mounted on the roll bar of the Hummer.

The man on the right had vomited. Chunks of beef empanadas and cheese were drying in his beard. It smelled sour and rotten, like garbage on a hot day. The man on the left had lost his hat when he was dropped in his hole. Rock and dirt was shoveled around them both, pinning them in place five feet apart. Had they been able to turn and look behind them, they would have seen dozens of holes like the ones in which they were trapped, some filled in and some still empty. All had been excavated by backhoe, waiting for their chance to be part of sending a message from the Banderas cartel.

Carlos casually strolled over, reached down, and picked up the hat with reverence. He dusted off the brim, using his hands to bring it back into proper shape. He bent over and placed it squarely, but gently, on the police officer's head. The other officer watched, frozen in place.

Carlos crouched between them. His shadow stretched a hundred feet back into the darkness. In a singsongy voice he said, "Now, who would like to tell me how the border patrol was able to confiscate our last shipment?"

Neither of the two police officers made eye contact with him.

Carlos followed with, "The first one of you to tell me what I want to know lives."

The policeman with his newly placed hat said, "I, I, I don't . . ."

The blast of the Ruger was instant. This time it was not wide of its target. It entered above the left eye. There was no shock or surprise among those observing; neither Enrique nor Javier both seated in the truck, nor Alejandro leaning against the bumper, were startled. They all knew the message was coming. The sharp crack of the Ruger and the red spray as the officer's head snapped backward, hitting the sand and stone, was anticipated.

The victim's face was contorted in shock. There was a clean, neat, small hole where the bullet entered. Crimson leaked out the front. In the back, scoops of brain tissue and skull were melting out of a much larger crater.

"The scorpions will eat well tomorrow," mumbled Javier as he smiled. Enrique had no reaction and no interest in conversing with the hired help.

Carlos exhaled and sighed loudly, shaking his head slowly. It was a forced breath and made solely for effect to the remaining prisoner. He looked down at the bloody stump. "I said, the first one to tell me what I want to know lives. Telling me you don't know anything about what I need to know is not," he paused and inhaled slowly, "helpful." Big exhale.

Carlos shifted to his right and kneeled directly in front of the remaining cop, blocking him from the intensity of the halogen spotlights. He extended the reach of his gun hand, flipping his wrist, rolling the Ruger back and forth. "So. What. Can. You. Tell. Me?" Each word had one flip of the gun. Side to side. The sixth word ended with the Ruger pointed directly at the cop.

The remaining victim wanted to talk. But the gun in his face and the ringing in his ears, combined with the blood and tissue splattered on his cheeks short-circuited the connection between his brain and his mouth. All he could do was shudder and cry. Snot poured from his nose, making it hard for him to breath. He vomited again and began to choke. He could only gurgle unintelligible sounds and quiet sobs. He wanted to talk but he couldn't tell Carlos anything because he didn't know anything.

The murdered cop was the son of Carlos and Alejandro's sister and Enrique's cousin. He had been feeding Carlos and Alejandro information about troop movements, border security schedules, and drone flights for four years. He was family. The lack of emotion and regret at his murder by his uncles and cousin proved that family ties didn't matter when loyalty was in question. His death would send a clear message to everybody in the organization. "Nobody is safe. Not family and certainly not you."

The cartel demanded unquestioned allegiance. When one of the tips forwarded by the now-dead officer caused Carlos and Alejandro to reroute a shipment, which in turn was confiscated by the Federales, they immediately believed their nephew was working against them. "Ahh. Maybe he didn't know anything," Carlos said as he looked at the bloodied stump. It didn't matter. The power of the message was more important than finding the collaborator if there truly was one.

The cop who was still alive and buried in front of Carlos had been on the cartel's payroll for a decade. He'd always done as he was told. He was slow and sloppy at times, but he got the job done. Now he was sobbing next to his dead friend, terrified, confused, and incoherent.

Carlos rose and used a piece of dried wood to wipe chunks of his nephew's skull off his shoe. He didn't look up when he said to the other officer, "You don't know anything, do you?"

The surviving cop, unable to form the words through his sobbing, weakly shook his head, "No."

The plan was always to keep one of them alive. It would ensure the message from Carlos and Alejandro would spread. The survivor would tell the story to everybody in the cartel. Keeping this last man alive would amplify fear and compliance across the organization.

"Javier, get out of the truck and dig up our friend here," ordered Carlos.

"Yes, Javier. Dig him up. The shovel is in the back." Enrique laughed. It was intended as an insult, and it was interpreted that way by Javier, who had greater ambitions than to dig holes and clean up messes for the brothers.

When Javier didn't immediately move, Enrique barked, "Go on. Get to it."

Carlos headed back to the truck, ready to return to the hacienda. "Son, tell me more about your plan."

CHAPTER 4
Dark Vision

Enrique, Carlos, and Alejandro climbed into the cab of the pickup. Javier and the disoriented survivor, covered in dirt, dust, and vomit, hauled themselves into the bed of the truck for the forty-minute ride home. It would not be enough time for Enrique to share his entire vision for the future of the family business, but it would be long enough to get his father and uncle hooked on an idea.

The Banderas cartel felt different for Enrique now. Growing up in the US, he was not connected to it like his father and uncle. He knew how it operated, but he didn't wake up in the morning thinking about grinding locals under his boots or blackmailing politicians. Enrique wasn't interested in finding better trafficking routes to smuggle refugees or new ways to conceal narcotics from the authorities. He didn't want to spend every day worried about turf battles and gang wars with the other cartels. His vision was much bigger, more international, and more legitimate.

His father and uncle ran the business the way they'd been taught by their father. They were good at it. Enrique was sent to the US by his father to get the education and experience to be useful in other ways. That was why Enrique came home to visit.

He had a plan to radically change how the cartel earned revenue.

"What you and Uncle Alejandro have done is impressive." The compliment belied a more lackluster tone of appreciation from Enrique. "You've done incredibly well by staying in your lane." His words cut sharply, slicing his father's pride. Enrique had transformed what his father had seen was a strength, namely their focus, and made it seem narrow and limited. Enrique made it a shortcoming.

"You are swift and agile. You are big enough to protect your territory, but small enough to evade unwanted attention. You've grown steadily, while remaining off the radar of the military and the politicians. But the future has significant risk for us."

Alejandro kept his eyes on the terrain as he drove, but he stiffened at the dismissive tone Enrique was conveying.

Carlos winced as well at the nicely wrapped criticism from his son. Enrique's analysis of their business stung, but Carlos knew it was true. He and his brother were concerned for their future. Political changes were coming. A year earlier, the US government launched the Kanasin Project, offering increased funds and personnel to help the Mexican government combat drug cartels. This included funding for intelligence gathering, surveillance equipment, drones and helicopters, and training for Mexican security forces. The treaty hadn't delivered any significant results yet, but eventually it would put the entire drug trade at greater risk. The cartels would inevitably fight among themselves as governmental pressure, interference, and interdiction efforts increased. Carlos was concerned how Kanasin and all the technology changes on the horizon would change his competitive dynamic.

The Banderas cartel was smaller than the cartels to their south and west. It was getting squeezed, and pressures from the US and Mexican military would incentivize larger cartels to invade Banderas's territory as a way to maintain their revenues.

Enrique continued, "The first thing we need to do is reinforce and protect our current business. I have ideas to make us stronger and to fortify our supply of narcotics. This will protect our current business." Enrique wanted them both to know he would never abandon their legacy. He needed to make this clear before he shared his true reason for returning home.

"I have the solution to our supply problem. A way to ensure we can produce all the product we need." Carlos and Alejandro nodded. "I'm ready to finalize an agreement with the Chinese." The Banderas cartel had been working with a group of Chinese nationals who had access to large supplies of the base chemicals, precursors, and raw materials needed for drug production. Recently, Enrique negotiated an extension to their agreement to purchase counterfeit Chinese drugs, which the cartel was now smuggling into the US.

"You've always had the skill of a politician," said Alejandro. It wasn't a compliment. Alejandro hated government officials, though he admired his nephew. He thought Enrique was a bit too soft.

"Our Chinese partners are looking for a single point of control. They are concerned working with each cartel separately is inefficient and risks incursion by our government. Too many possible points of failure. I've convinced them that we can be a distribution center for all the other cartels," explained Enrique. "They see our smaller size as an advantage. They believe they can control us more easily. As soon as I relay your approval to the Chinese, they will inform the other cartels." Enrique paused, waiting for the cartel bosses to nod their consent.

"That protects our supply and provides a shield against our rivals. They won't risk annoying the Chinese and their own supplies."

Carlos and Alejandro approved the plan and nodded support.

"Now we need to protect our money," Enrique continued.

"I've met with bankers, politicians, and businesspeople who can help us." The cartel was a cash business, and it was becoming increasingly difficult to mask, store, and transfer the cash they were generating. The challenge for the Banderas cartel was not making money. The challenge was depositing and withdrawing money. Without banking privileges, there was no way to spend their earnings.

"We will use international corporations and tax havens," Enrique stated matter-of-factly. His father and uncle listened. They were not uneducated men and knew the Mexican and US governments were working together to track illicit foreign financial activity and monitor suspicious transactions. The Financial Action Task Force was already causing problems. It analyzed banking data and financial records looking for criminal patterns and increased legal pressures on financial institutions to ensure cooperation. Carlos and Alejandro didn't know how FATF's technologies worked. Enrique did.

"The US is now sharing their investigations and information globally. This is going to get difficult for everybody. With the network I've created, I've solved that problem. They won't be able to track us." Enrique had their attention.

"But there is a bigger problem." Enrique addressed their immediate concerns. Now he was ready to pivot to his vision. "Our business is constrained by three forces. The first is the larger cartels. They only allow us to operate in restricted areas, even with Chinese protection. If we try to expand, we risk war. We would lose that war."

Carlos and Alejandro bristled, but it was true. The other cartels had more men, superior weapons, greater access to the military, and more robust political cover.

Enrique continued, "Our new relationship with the Chinese will provide some protection, but it doesn't mean our rivals will stop trying to carve out their own deals or look for other sources. We will need to constantly defend our traditional businesses."

"The second problem is cleaning our money. The other cartels will learn to do this as well. So, at most, we have a five-year window, and then we lose this advantage too." The bosses were becoming less comfortable.

"The final problem is our biggest one, and it is why I've come home. It is our product line." His father and uncle looked at each other across the cab of the truck, confused. Enrique clarified, "All the cartels have the same revenue streams. We all have the same model. We all do the same thing."

"It has always been good business for us," his uncle angrily protested.

"Yes, but the problem is that when revenue slows or governments interfere, profits fall for all of us. And when they fall, wars break out over territories, markets, and resources."

Carlos and Alejandro knew this to be true. They were in a time of relative quiet right now, but flare-ups between cartels were common and, once they erupted, a truce was hard to negotiate. "If government interference, banking restrictions, and product overlaps converged, the result will be a very brutal and bloody war," Enrique continued.

Lack of sleep made Carlos and Alejandro irritable. The portrait Enrique painted made them more so. Their grumbles were noticeable and increasing in volume, but they could not counter Enrique's arguments. "So what do we do?" Carlos growled.

Enrique started his pitch. "What if there was a way to grow our business ten- or twenty-fold in the next ten years, doing something our rivals cannot?" Carlos and Alejandro both snapped their attention to him, eyes wide with interest and skepticism.

Enrique continued, "I can show you how cash from our core business today can fund something new and generate billions of dollars in clean profits every year." As Enrique sat between his uncle and father on the drive, he could sense their fatigue. He saw the dark circles under his father's eyes and the heavy wrinkles on his uncle's forehead accentuated by the dirt, sweat, and grime of the past day. Enrique raised the tone and excitement in his voice to keep them focused. "We can be a $10 billion business in a few years." The change in their faces was immediate. With this spark of an idea, their weariness and frustration gave way to optimism and hope. They were ready to listen.

From the bed of the truck, through the open rear window, Javier strained to listen. He wanted to learn everything about the cartel, but all this talk of LLCs, tax havens, and non-extradition countries eluded him. He was a military leader, not a banker or an accountant.

Enrique looked directly at his father. "Today, our business generates about $500 million in revenue a year. It's time to expand."

"We are expanding," Alejandro rebuffed. "Our business grows every year."

"It does. Eight percent per year. At that rate and with our relationship with the Chinese, we will top out at $1 billion in five years." Enrique knew Carlos and Alejandro could be happy with $1 billion. He hurriedly interjected. "My plan would take us to $5 billion in that time and $10 billion in ten years." Their reaction was exactly what Enrique hoped he'd spur. Alejandro turned toward him instantly, almost swerving off the dirt road. Carlos smiled broadly. The numbers were astonishing.

"Go on." They said it nearly simultaneously.

"Last year, I launched a new business. It is a new path for us. It is a business model our rivals cannot imitate or copy." Enrique developed the business plan in college and refined it at graduate school with feedback from a wide array of players who worked at the edge of legitimacy. Lawyers, US bankers, and financiers his father had corrupted for the cartel. Politicians and masters of statecraft who were in the pockets of the cartel's Chinese partners. Tech entrepreneurs looking for sources of capital on their way to wildly profitable initial public offerings (IPOs) and willing to ignore where their seed money came from. Enrique bootstrapped this company with his own money and now had a compelling business in strong growth mode, ready for its own IPO. It was a business model he could manipulate and grow using his charm, charisma, and ruthlessness. These were the traits he'd learned as the son of a cartel boss.

"The revenue opportunity is staggering." Enrique made a passionate investor pitch to Carlos and Alejandro. In just a few minutes he gave them all they needed to know about his company and how it would change their future. Enrique outlined how it would tightly bind the cartel to the Chinese, well beyond their drug trade. He shared revenue projections and how he'd clean the cash for cartel use. He detailed their path to diversified revenue in areas not discussed in congressional hearings on human trafficking or covered in nightly news broadcasts reporting on rising drug US overdoses. Enrique's plan pivoted the Banderas cartel into a business not threatened by the US border patrol or the Mexican army. It was a business that did not compete against larger cartels.

Enrique was confident he'd get his father's and uncle's support. The challenge was the cartel alone didn't have the resources or capital to fully fund growth in his new venture. He needed the Chinese. This was the purpose of his visit. "I will need you to help me arrange a meeting with Mr. Huang. Give me one year to prepare everything we need. Could you make that happen?" Enrique looked first at his father then turned to his uncle. They'd just pulled into the driveway of the hacienda and the shaken police officer and Javier were climbing down from the bed of the truck.

"When you are ready, we will schedule it."

"I will need $500 million—$250 million from you," Enrique said, looking side to side at his father and uncle. "And $250 million from the Chinese."

"Prepare your plan," his uncle replied.

The sun appeared above the hills and dripped onto the lush back lawn of the hacienda. The horses were awakening and starting to gather in the paddock. A worker swept the patio while another skimmed leaves from the pool. The flowers were opening and extending toward the rising sun.

Carlos rubbed his eyes and stretched. He was ready for bed. Before he headed to sleep, he reinforced to Enrique the learnings from last night. "As you build this enterprise, I want you to remember what we have taught you. You will not have a strong brother at your side, as I do. It means you will need people around you who you can trust or intimidate. Reward them when you can. Show no mercy if they are disloyal."

Enrique nodded.

"My son, in the desert last night we were not looking for the lost drug shipments. We weren't really looking for the person who informed the authorities. We were telling everybody who works for us that we value devotion above all else."

Enrique understood.

CHAPTER 5
Galvanizing Deception

Carlos and Alejandro were second-generation leaders of the Banderas cartel and had never travelled more than one hundred miles from their hacienda in Central Mexico. It was a factor of personal safety and control. The US government was on one side, and larger cartels surrounded them on the other three. If they wanted to protect their modest empire, they needed to avoid incarceration, stay alive, and evolve.

Carlos saw changes coming he didn't fully understand. Technology was used for things he didn't anticipate. Mobile devices replaced pagers. Bank accounts and personal records were accessible via the internet. Digital currency replaced cash. All types of products and services, legal and illegal, were traded, sold, and bought on social media. Everything was moving fast, hard to understand, and impossible to predict. Alejandro was comfortable running the cartel the way their father did, but Carlos recognized the threat to their business and needed somebody he trusted to advise him on how to protect their domain. Enrique was their only hope to navigate new technologies in a new world.

This is why fifteen years ago Carlos packed up twelve-year-old Enrique for the US, sending him to a country on fire with the O. J. Simpson and Oklahoma City bombing trials underway. Carlos wondered if the US was any safer than his home, wedged between warring cartels and the US border. He was heartbroken to send Enrique away, but Enrique was not heartbroken to leave. Carlos remembered how eager he was. He watched Enrique practice his English, eventually eliminating his Spanish accent. He watched his son, with striking looks, a quick wit, gifted athleticism, and exceptional intelligence, excel at everything he attempted. His transition from Mexico to the US was surprisingly easy. Enrique did not lack confidence or drive and Carlos was deeply proud of him.

From the moment Enrique arrived in Connecticut to live with the family of a lawyer working for the cartel, Enrique was determined to belong and to fully integrate. He had an incredibly clear vision of what he needed to accomplish and how he needed to get there. Enrique took the hardest classes, studied long hours, captained the most competitive teams, and dated the most popular girls. He flourished and finished at the top of his class at a prestigious preparatory school.

Enrique's clock speed, the way his mind worked, and his creativity, impressed and even intimidated his professors. By his sophomore year in college, his teachers were turning to him for advice on system design and programming. He could speak with ease and total comfort about theoretical mathematics, physics, machine learning, and encryption like other students would talk about plotlines and characters from Harry Potter or Twilight.

America was good to him, and he was as much a full American as he was the son of Carlos Banderas. Even though he now acted and sounded exactly like an erudite academic from the Northeast, including the Connecticut accent, Enrique had no intention of walking away from the family business. He was always thinking about how to expand their enterprise.

In the year since the night in the desert, Carlos found sleep difficult. More holes in the desert were excavated, more were bodies buried, and more messages were sent, but still, more and more Banderas production and storage facilities were raided. Narcotics shipments were regularly confiscated by the Mexican army and US border control. Rival cartels openly trespassed on Banderas territory. Skirmishes were more common. Carlos called his son in the US after midnight. "It's time. Mr. Huang will meet us in Chihuahua in three weeks. Be ready."

Fifteen years after Enrique moved to the US, he was prepared to stand alongside his father and uncle as a representative of the Banderas cartel and ask a shadowy member of the Chinese government for funds to launch a new venture. It was his only chance to save the cartel.

"*Mi hijo*, I am so proud. What you have done is amazing. What you have accomplished in America is more than I could have dreamed for you."

"Thank you, Papa. I've worked to make you proud. To make our family proud."

"I was sad to see you go." Carlos remembered his fear and emptiness seeing his son in the helicopter headed toward Mexico City and on to JFK International Airport. His son had no such fear. "Now our future depends on what you've learned."

"I'm ready." Enrique said it with certainty and confidence. There was no hesitation or ambiguity or doubt.

Even so, Carlos felt it necessary to underscore the threat. "We've reached a point where squeezing more from our existing business is not impossible. Our market to the north is being flooded with increased doses. The margins aren't there anymore. It was a divisive midterm election in the US and their politicians are looking for a distraction. They are going to come after us all. Troops will be deployed on the border. It's time for your plan." Carlos made it clear what stakes were at play.

Enrique nodded.

"There are other problems too. Other cartels have been difficult in renegotiating the terms of their relationships with us. We have had several clashes recently as their squads have encroached on our territory. Tensions are high."

"How bad is it?" Enrique probed.

"We've done what we can. Our agreement with the Chinese helps, but Alejandro and I are especially concerned about Los Feroz."

Los Feroz (The Ferocious) was formed in the early 1990s by Mexican military deserters. It had a reputation for extreme brutality. Its members were once the muscle for other cartels, but its leaders realized they had the discipline to run their own criminal organization. They'd hang the decapitated bodies of rival cartel members, politicians, and police in public as a way to stake claim to any territory they sought to control. Los Feroz is one of the most powerful and violent criminal organizations in the world, generating billions of dollars from drug trafficking, human smuggling, extortion, kidnapping, and murder. Billions of dollars from basically the same business model as the much smaller Banderas cartel.

"We've been moderately useful to Los Feroz because of the relationship you established with the Chinese. We are a year into the new agreement and the flow of raw materials and precursors has enabled Los Feroz to manufacture a record tonnage of methamphetamines."

"That's good, though," proclaimed Enrique.

"Yes, but the peace with Los Feroz was tenuous. They are not happy about having to work through us. They are pushing back."

"There are issues with the government too," Alejandro interjected. "Shipments to the US are increasingly intercepted at the border and those making it through are being sold for lower street values." The Banderas cartel was in a vice. No matter how many people they dragged to the desert, Carlos and Alejandro couldn't stop the constriction. They needed the revenue Enrique had promised.

"Let's see how Huang reacts. I'm ready," Enrique assured Carlos and Alejandro, with Javier tagging along, as they headed into the office where Huang was waiting. The cartel could not bankroll everything Enrique needed for the launch. Generating $500 million a year, and with roughly $400 million in banks across Central America, the Banderas cartel could not underwrite the whole endeavor. His plan needed to be a joint venture, and China was the ideal partner.

Yichen Huang looked the part of mid-level bureaucrat: meek, unassuming, quiet, and attentive. But it was a costume. He was an ambitious man with substantial responsibilities in North and Central America, including the oversight of all cartel interactions and the infiltration of US businesses. Huang hid behind unassuming looks. Average height. Average weight. Dark black hair slicked back. Thin wireframe glasses. His dark suit, blue shirt, and blue patterned tie were not suited for the heat of Central Mexico, but they were elements of his disguise. He reveled in being underestimated. His emotions were always in check and difficult to read.

Sitting in Carlos's office, Huang was unimpressed. It was a foreign setting. To him, the bright and colorful textiles and artwork clashed with the earth tones of the floor tiles, archways, and walls. The high ceilings were adorned with tattered rotating fans. He was thankful for the artificial breeze since there was no air-conditioning. The late-June heat was already unbearable. Sweat dampened his shirt, and his tie felt like it was trapping heat within his body. He was broiling from the inside. It was already over thirty degrees centigrade and headed to forty (104 degrees Fahrenheit).

The office had a large heavy cedar conference table, adorned with intricate carvings and ten heavy wooden chairs, upholstered in dark leather. Huang looked around the room. It might have been used by a local mayor or politician fifty years ago. Nothing here would make you think this was the center of a $500 million business. The lamps on the desk and tables were old. They resembled clay pots painted in brown and yellow with blue geometric designs. Their dim light bulbs barely shined through their dark brown, heavy lampshades. There was nothing bright or modern here—no audio or visual equipment, no computers, no modern electronics of any type.

By contrast, Huang's office in Hong Kong was on the seventy-eighth floor and was vivid with chrome and neon and was fully wired. This was dusty, old, and unfamiliar. There was an unpleasant aroma of manure and earth, like a farm, wafting through the open window. Living with horses and cattle repulsed Huang.

The lands surrounding the hacienda were much hotter and drier than his home of Tianjin. He much preferred coastal cities to this flat, arid, and colorless panorama. Fourteen million people lived in Tianjin, making it one of the largest cities in China, but its land mass and population was dwarfed by Mexico City. Tianjin was vibrant and noisy with the relentless sounds and motion of ships, trucks, and train traffic emanating from Bohai Bay. It was nothing like what he saw out the window of his jet as it approached Mexico City.

Huang studied the terrain from ten thousand feet as the plane circled on approach. A sprawling metropolis unfurled beneath. It was a colossal expanse of humanity stretching in every direction. It was a mesmerizing mosaic of roads and alleys connecting tight-knit neighborhoods, expansive slums, ancient architectures, and modern skyscrapers. The city's pulse could almost be felt from above, a rhythmic heartbeat of movement and energy, success and despair. Descending lower, Huang could see mountains encircling the city, helping to retain an ever-present atmospheric shroud of haze and ozone, making Mexico City dirtier and less breathable than any major city in China.

Huang wanted to hear their plan, make his decision, and leave quickly. He hated Mexico. His relationship with the Banderas cartel was stable and profitable, but it was small and not strategic in terms of his global ambitions. Huang wanted more, a lot more. The potential of Enrique's plan was intriguing, however. Huang struggled to maintain his demeanor and to contain his enthusiasm in front of the Mexicans. This was so much more important than arranging the shipment of chemicals and precursors for the Banderas cartel through ports in Michoacán or Mazatlán.

The idea Enrique sketched for his father and uncle a year ago was now laid out in vivid detail for Huang. At its core, it was a venture capital play that would leverage cash from the Banderas cartel and an investment from the Chinese to invest in US companies. Enrique's plan was stunning in its simplicity. Their investments would be legitimate in some instances, and in others their stock selections would be manipulated with inside information.

Enrique's company would pick the winners they'd invest in and the losers they would short. Even though Carlos and Alejandro were seated at the head of the table and Javier was hovering in the corner, Enrique knew he was playing to an audience of one. The Chinese official in front of him had the ability and authority to approve their entire plan.

When Carlos first raised the idea with Huang three weeks ago, Huang insisted on reviewing Enrique's idea personally. He would not delegate the task to any of the twenty or so aides reporting to him in Hong Kong, China, or New York. This would be his choice, his decision, and, if it worked, his triumph. It would be his pathway to more influence and power within the party. It was an opportunity for Huang to control his own destiny.

Huang's current assignment was temporarily based in Hong Kong. He liked it better there than his home of Tianjin, and certainly more than Mexico. If Enrique's plan delivered on its promise, Huang would have the stature and authority to move permanently to Hong Kong. He'd never have to travel to Central Mexico again. He'd assign one of his subordinates to deal with the cartels. Huang could not understand how the Banderases lived in such a lifeless and empty countryside. The hacienda, while lush and green, was surrounded by hundreds of miles of grays and browns, sand and stone. The land was barren, desolate, dry, and dead.

"Gentlemen, here it is." Enrique handed each of them, except Javier, a leather-bound business plan. "This is the mechanism we will use to identify and invest in US tech firms."

Enrique's business plan forecasted mind-boggling returns from cartel and Chinese investments. "There are specific demands for each company in which we invest, ranging from preferred stock to convertible shares, to board seats, to participation in R & D efforts, to ownership and transfer of intellectual property if the companies fail."

The plan detailed a global network of financial institutions and venture capital funds that would aggregate and cleanse funds for Enrique's venture. "We will route money across US-based limited liability companies and through banks in Mexico City, the Cayman Islands, Southeast Asia, the Bahamas, Belize, and Africa. LLCs would own LLCs. Bank accounts would flow from and between tax havens and non-extradition countries," Enrique enthusiastically outlined.

"It is a very ambitious structure for money laundering, Mr. Banderas," Huang noted. "Quite thorough and complex."

"When you consider the sheer volume of banking transactions we will make and the billions of dollars we will be moving, the more complex, the better," Enrique responded. "It will keep us hidden, invisible, and safe from US agencies."

Carlos kept pace with Enrique, flipping pages as he did, making approving nods and snorts along the way. Alejandro fidgeted in his chair, shifting left, right, and back again. He tapped his left foot against the leg of the table, signaling his discomfort in his ignorance. The financial mechanics of the plan were above his understanding. The prospect of cleaning millions of dollars in profits was exciting, but Alejandro didn't understand or really appreciate the intricacies of how it would occur. Javier, in the corner away from the discussion, was unable to follow along with any of the details. His blank stare belied his utter cluelessness and ignorance of what was being discussed. Enrique ignored Javier, wondering why his father invited him to attend.

Huang, unlike the rest, fully grasped the intricacies and complexities. He appreciated the critical importance of privacy and secrecy when dealing with billions of dollars of investments in US tech companies. He possessed a deep understanding of what was needed, and he was certain Enrique did too.

"All of this will be wrapped in a politically correct veneer, where we promote our focus on leveling the playing field. To everyone, including US regulatory agencies, our venture will look like an affirmative action program for new technology companies in third-world economies." Enrique let the elegance of the deception sink in. "We will tell a compelling tale of the good we are doing in the world."

Enrique shared a draft press release outlining the benefits to entrepreneurs, new technology companies, and emerging countries. "We will make a promise, a pact, to share our gains, to invest in local economies, and to build educational and business connections between the third world and Western sources of capital," Enrique continued.

It was all marketing bullshit, but it would provide the cover his firm needed from SEC, IRS, and FBI investigators. The regulators would be unable to trace the source and flow of funds, and what they did discover about the firm would read like a fairytale of goodness and light.

Enrique flipped page by page, walking Huang through the

total assets he'd require and how all of it would be used. He was looking for any sign their partner was balking. "Mr. Huang, I've asked for a significant investment from your government. Does this raise any concerns?"

Huang didn't raise his eyes from the book. Enrique paused, turning to his father, looking for support. Huang was already reading ahead, reviewing pages well ahead of where Enrique was pointing. Enrique could not tell if Huang was paying attention, or if he was looking for a faster way to get to the ending and go home.

Huang lifted his glasses, rubbed his eyes, and mumbled something in Chinese. Enrique could not tell if it was a sound of approval or skepticism.

Enrique kept moving forward. "We will grow the investment from your government and my family into $5 billion in five years and $10 billion in ten years." Huang, with his glasses still perched on the top of his head, raised his eyes to meet Enrique's. It wasn't a glance of piqued interest. It was a look of, "Get to the point."

"The returns to you will be significant. We will start with individual investments in established firms. Then we will move into new growth companies and venture funding positions for start-ups. We will provide seed capital in the beginning, followed by early-stage and mezzanine investments. Our profits will grow as these firms expand and as their IPOs are launched. And all along the way we will be manipulating these firms. Magnifying them."

Huang's eyes returned to the business plan. He was waiting for something more interesting, something to justify his fourteen-hour flight to Mexico. Something more than insider trading. So far, Enrique was dancing around what Huang really wanted to hear. So far, this was of little interest to him and had nothing to do with Huang's role or responsibility to his government.

"On page forty-eight there is a comparison of our forecasted returns versus average venture capital returns last year. It shows the targeted investment returns by year."

"Mr. Banderas. You are predicting returns more than double

what the market has delivered historically. How is that achieved?" Huang's interest was mildly triggered.

"More than triple, actually. The returns are higher because we will make markets and move markets, not just passively invest in them. We not only take equity positions, but we also drive activity in those companies where we have holdings. By amplifying certain firms and obstructing others, we can outperform typical venture capital returns by three to five times." Enrique paused.

Huang remained expressionless.

"Mr. Huang, this venture will provide your government and my family with billions of dollars in clean US cash. It will generate massive profits every year." Enrique was looking for signs of approval and acceptance from Huang, but he saw nothing. No change in demeanor. No excitement.

"A return of over $9 billion on your initial investment in the next ten years is impressive, Mr. Banderas." Huang waived a skeptical hand. "But is it worth the risk?" He shook his head in skepticism as a way to strengthen his negotiating leverage. Huang wanted more from this partnership.

Enrique smiled and leaned forward. He welcomed Huang's gamesmanship. Enrique waited for this moment to lay out the real value for Huang. "But what if these magnificent returns weren't the most compelling benefit for you? What if the true value was to be measured in trillions of dollars?" Enrique smiled as *trillions* rolled from his mouth.

For the Banderas cartel to withstand threats and pressures from its rivals it needed unwavering Chinese support for their drug trade. For Enrique to bind Huang and the cartel together, he needed to be more than a distribution channel for Chinese pharmaceuticals, chemicals, precursors, and counterfeits. Trading shares in US equities was interesting, but it wasn't enough value for Huang, and Enrique knew it. What Enrique outlined next would be. It was what Huang was waiting to hear and the reason he came to this meeting in person.

"This venture will provide you covert access to hundreds of US technology firms, their intellectual property, their patents, their technologists, programmers, scientists, and engineers. You will be inside their walls and inside their products. Their data, algorithms, and code will be laid bare. It will all be accessible and open to you." Enrique watched for a change in Huang's posture. "It's worth trillions."

Huang's official role was to oversee a team that disrupts America's prestige in its own hemisphere. In some cases that meant helping the cartels undermine US borders and security. His team also focused on intellectual property theft, patent infringement, and corporate spying when it would distract or diminish US stature. What Enrique proposed was an incredibly bold, visionary, and transnational approach to cyber espionage. It was an irresistible opportunity.

"Tell me more, Mr. Banderas." Huang's glasses were back on the bridge of his nose as he listened intently. Huang stopped flipping pages and let slip a small grin, for the first time breaking his veneer. Huang was intrigued and he let it show.

"Our scout teams will identify the most critical and vulnerable tech firms to penetrate. Our capital resources will be used to gain access to their intellectual property. Our mesh of financial entities will shroud us from unwanted regulation or inspection," Enrique summed.

It was masterful. The fact that the cost for this access was paid through insider trading and stock manipulation was ingenious. And all the Banderas cartel wanted was an exclusive agreement on chemicals, narcotics, and counterfeits and a small investment in this new initiative. Two hundred fifty million dollars was a meaningless sum for Huang. It was an easy decision.

With this plan, Huang could deliver more to his superiors in a few years than his predecessors had in two decades of kickbacks, payoffs, and corporate bribes. Huang's operatives would be inside the firms they were spying on. They'd be part of their technical teams, standards committees, and financial operations. They'd enter Enrique's agreements with smiles on their faces and cash in their outstretched hands. They'd exit with backdoor access to systems, gateways for malicious Chinese code, and pathways to embed spyware into the final products delivered by US tech firms to their largest customers. No business would be safe. Huang's team wouldn't have to sneak in and steal anything—they'd own it.

Huang flipped the leather binder closed, raised his glasses, and rubbed his eyes. He'd heard enough and he liked it. The four men shook hands, ignoring Javier.

The sunlight entering the room was blinding, and Huang was ready to return home to inform his superiors he'd recommend support for the project. It would take time to secure the funding, but he committed his government to a $250 million investment. Combined, the initial seed money for year one was a half billion dollars with a commitment for another half billion in year two if Enrique met his promises. The cartel and the Chinese were fifty-fifty partners. The helicopter was idling on the back lawn, prepared for the thirty-minute ferry back to the airport and Mr. Huang's departure.

Carlos and Alejandro barely spoke in the meeting. It was Enrique's show and he delivered superbly. He'd negotiated an agreement to secure their exclusive access to Chinese precursors and chemicals for their narcotics business and he secured funding for the new venture. As Huang's helicopter disappeared over the rise, headed back to Benito Juárez International Airport, the three of them hugged and celebrated.

"Javier. Go tell Isabel, bring us tequila," Carlos said as he patted Enrique on the back.

"Yes, Javier. Bring the three of us a drink," Enrique said, reminding him who was family and who was a servant.

CHAPTER 6
Marcus's Induction

"Rich, stop. I've already moved to Back Bay. I don't need the sales pitch anymore. I'll be in the office for the new employee onboarding session tomorrow at 10:00 a.m. sharp."

"The session starts at 7:00 a.m., Marcus." Rich was not amused.

"What? No special considerations? I thought I was your best friend," Marcus needled. He enjoyed letting air out of Rich's balloon. Marcus was the "little brother" in this relationship. They'd been athletic rivals, teammates in the Olympic developmental programs, and now Marcus was going to work directly for Rich.

Rich Anderson had a tendency to keep pushing and pushing even when he'd gotten his way. And he could be a real son of a bitch when he didn't get his way. Tweaking him was Marcus's way to let him know it was OK to lighten up.

Rich sighed. "I'm sorry. I know. It's late. But I need your help. Wall Street loves the numbers we are delivering, but they are skeptical of me as CEO. Our investors are wondering if I can keep delivering. I need you to help me change our business and grow."

Marcus understood his new role in the company, but that didn't stop Rich from repeating it, again. "I hired you to set the tone, build the culture, and extend our delivery capacity."

"I got it," Marcus responded sincerely. He heard the exhaustion in his friend's voice.

Marcus's recruitment process was a long one. It was two years of phone calls, meetings, and gentle offers from Rich that steadily grew in intensity. The opportunity to run a team and a robust salary is why he left his job as the director of IT at a telecommunications firm to join his friend. Even so, Marcus had trouble deciding whether Rich had cracked the code with the job role and compensation, or if Rich just wore him down. "Did I win, or did I tap out?" Marcus wondered. Rich was tenaciousness.

Marcus admired Rich. Once he had an idea or vision, Rich never let it go. He'd attack it from all angles. He'd find weak spots in an opponent to exploit or find areas of strength and remove them. It felt that way to Marcus during his recruitment. Rich countered every objection Marcus raised and attacked all the advantages his current employer, HNPC Telecom, committed to Marcus. It was an approach Marcus had seen dozens of times on the wrestling mat against Rich when Marcus was at Penn State. Rich would make you think he was going to attack in one direction to draw you out, then he'd counter. Before you knew what was happening, you'd be on your back. Pinned. Rich was the one person Marcus couldn't overpower, outthink, outwit, outmaneuver, or overwhelm. Working for him would be a challenge.

"Marcus, all our teams are high-performing. But scalability is our number-one barrier. Hiring new analysts can't be the only way to increase our output. We need to find a way to deliver more to our clients without having to hire as many people."

Rich's problem was chronic in services firms. If you can't find a way to scale productivity, the sole way to grow revenues is to increase staff size. Wall Street hated a linear relationship between head count and revenues. They wanted to see increased billings and growing margins, which means that productivity and deliverable volumes needed to grow. The problem was, if you tried to ramp productivity alone, in a services business, you'd risk burning out the team. If you saddled the analysts with too many new clients, they wouldn't have the capacity to support existing clients, and you'd face staff and client retention problems. Rich needed Marcus's help to solve his problem. How could they get more output from the same people without killing them?

"We are about to hit a wall." Rich rubbed his temples.

Marcus listened, recognizing agitation in Rich's increased pace and rising voice.

"We release our quarterly earnings tomorrow. The numbers are good, but they could be better."

During the recruitment process, Rich had never been this sour.

"I want you do things we aren't doing today. I need you to challenge our current approaches. Find the barriers and overcome them."

"I understand," replied Marcus in a "yessir" kind of way.

Rich reinforced it. "I need you to think and operate like you have no limits."

"Ethically, right?" Marcus nervously filled the silence. He was joking.

"Yes." Rich was irritated.

"Well, I hope the team is ready. We have a lot of work to do." Marcus was eager to start.

"Push them. Drive them. Earn their respect."

Marcus was anxious about managing a team. At HNPC he'd been a sole contributor reporting to the CIO. Here he'd have three brilliant and driven technology experts under his command and no clear blueprint to follow.

"You'll meet Beth tomorrow in class. It's her first day as well. She is impressive; you'll see what I mean. Jeff and Deb have been with me for two years. They are already working on client projects. I'll bring them by at some point for introductions. Enjoy the onboarding session tomorrow."

"Ten a.m. sharp." Marcus hung up the phone.

"Asshole," Rich replied into dead air with a smile.

"Beth Rivera," Marcus repeated slowly as he typed her name into the search bar. She maintained an impressive social media presence and a detailed profile on LinkedIn. Beth had a strong academic pedigree and an impressive work history for somebody two years younger than Marcus. She'd already changed her job function online to reflect her new role on his team. Marcus was moments away from shutting down for the night when he slid his cursor to the top of the screen and clicked on images. He was hoping to see the face of the woman Rich was so enthusiastic about. There were images of her on vacation, running a road race, and eating at a beachside restaurant. But the headshot she used for her business profile made Marcus stiffen, almost knocking the breath out of him. She was gorgeous. But that wasn't what struck him.

It wasn't as much her face, but more the way her wavy dark blond hair framed it. It wasn't exactly her smile, but more the shape of her mouth. Mostly it was her eyes. He'd seen her eyes before. Those same almond-shaped, dark, beautiful, nearly black eyes. The similarity in her appearance, the angle of her head as she smiled, and her captivating eyes were unsettling.

Over his shoulder, the TV weatherman was pointing to a map of Massachusetts showing record highs expected tomorrow. "It is going to be an oppressive day."

Marcus's gaze swapped back and forth from the TV screen to the laptop perched on his thighs, distracted, not knowing which was more important. His eyes were drawn to the laptop. He was transfixed on the familiarity of her face and eyes.

"Stop. It's not her." Marcus said it out loud as a command. He still had trouble saying her name without starting to spiral. Her name led to her face and her eyes and her laugh and memories that he hadn't allowed to surface in years. Beth looked so much like her it was unnerving.

Marcus needed to jolt his mind back to the present and focus on something else. At 11:30 p.m., he went for a three-mile run along the Charles River, secretly hoping a drunk college kid would mouth off looking for a fight or a homeless guy might try to mug him. He sought confrontation. He needed someone or something to focus his anger. To dissipate it. But there was nothing and his sleep that night was shallow and restless. He knew his first day was going to be uncomfortable.

✯ ✯ ✯

As Marcus walked to the office early on day one, the air was already heavy and thick with moisture. A hot day in Boston was unlike anywhere else in the US, especially a hot day in Copley Square. The whole city was historic, but it was especially old in this area. The streets were narrow and many of the buildings dated back to the 1700s. Boston was not as populous as Chicago, LA, or Dallas, but people were jammed closer together. It was denser in this section than in Boston's financial district or near Government Center. There was never a breeze because the streets had no outlet or access to the harbor. On a hot August day, it was stifling, still, and humid. It was pungent, like New York City, but more stagnant. When temperatures exceeded ninety degrees Fahrenheit it was unbearable, and it would be ninety-six degrees by noon. Boylston Street was humming in the early morning. Stores and coffee shops were open. Cars were bumper to bumper as pedestrians ignored traffic lights and crosswalks in a hurry to get to their air-conditioned offices.

Marcus approached the lobby entrance envisioning how different it had been four months ago when thousands of spectators were lined up in front of the building watching the marathoners. Today, there were no signs of the explosions. The buildings were fully repaired. All the shattered windows had been replaced and the marble edifices, cracked and broken by shrapnel, were restored. It was a prime office location in the most expensive part of Boston. The surrounding buildings displayed the logos of the world's largest financial firms, investment houses, and insurance companies. Marcus would be working in close proximity to these firms, whose CIOs he hoped would be his clients.

Marcus's name tag was on a mahogany table outside the conference room. He put it in his pocket and dashed in while Beth's back was turned as she fixed a coffee. The executive briefing center could be adapted dynamically depending on the needs of the meeting. Twenty people could sit around a large modular U-shaped table for board meetings, or it could be arranged in classroom style, like today, using small desks.

There was lots of glass and chrome. All the systems, including their laptops and cell phones, were connected wirelessly to the network. Projectors hung from the ceiling projecting onto two screens so everybody could see.

Marcus took a seat in the front of the room. The instructor opened the onboarding session for thirty-two new hires on the fifteenth floor of the Boston headquarters for Lexington Advisory Group.

"This year, total global technology spend will be just shy of $3 trillion." His voice forcefully accentuated *trillion* to give it extra punch, as if the word *trillion* and its profound size wasn't enough. "Next year it will be well over $3 trillion." He karate chopped his right hand into his open left hand for added emphasis.

The company was bursting with growth. The conference room was typically used for strategic consulting sessions with clients. These were held for either buyers of technology products or the vendors of those products. Both lined up for advice and counsel from analysts on what they should buy, what they should build, and how to maximize investment returns from $3 trillion.

Of the thirty-two new hires, twenty-four were going to be research analysts, like Marcus. The others were going to work in sales or client services. But they were all one team, and everybody needed to learn the corporate way. Even so, the session was geared more toward those becoming analysts, because they were what set Lexington Advisory Group, or LAG, as everyone called it, apart from smaller rivals in the market. They were the technology experts whose advice LAG clients would pay hundreds of thousands of dollars to elicit.

"LAG has more analysts who have more real-world experience than any other advisory firm in the world. We have more expertise, in more technology markets, in more industries, than any of our competitors. This means our clients get the best advice." The presenter was sticking to his standard script.

"The problem for our clients is inefficiency. Half their spend for technology is wasted, but they don't know which half." The instructor chuckled, though he'd delivered that line at least ten times this year.

Marcus, in the front of the room, couldn't roll his eyes at the trite cliches and tongue-in-cheek humor peppering the keynote for the two-day new employee training session. As the only newly hired senior manager in the two-day session, he'd be expected to set a good example.

The presenter continued, "Half of nearly $3 trillion spent on hardware and software is not delivering full value. Their investments don't achieve their goals, don't deliver needed functionality, are delivered too late, or require costly unplanned change orders to make them work."

Most of the audience was frantically taking notes. Not Marcus.

"This puts our clients, the chief information officers and their senior business leaders, in a dangerous position with their boards of directors. Does anybody know why?" The presenter paused, waiting for a response.

Marcus sat forward and spoke up. "Waste and inefficiency gets noticed by their boards and investors. It gets them fired."

"Correct! And our job is to help these CIOs budget, plan, and deploy new technologies faster and cheaper while helping to avoid wasted spend on things that won't work." The presenter loved it when he had a willing shill in the audience.

Marcus supposed the "half the spend" example was a bit of bloviating, but he wasn't going to argue. It was his first day at LAG, and at his previous job he'd seen enough foolish IT projects not to split hairs over whether it was 30 or 50 percent.

He did wonder, however, why the presenter left out one major piece of the LAG puzzle. In addition to helping CIOs buy and deploy IT products and services, LAG also made a fortune helping IT vendors produce and sell those same solutions to CIOs. A third of LAG's revenues came from vendors. It intrigued Marcus that LAG was a trusted advisor on both sides of the buy/sell equation, and he was curious how it avoided conflicts of interest.

Balancing was a challenge. When Rich Anderson, CEO and chief of research, founded LAG it originally only serviced CIOs. But when vendors experienced LAG's influence firsthand, they clamored for access too. A positive whisper in the ear of a CIO from a LAG analyst could win a multimillion-dollar deal for a vendor. A negative appearance in LAG's research could obliterate tens of millions of dollars in sales opportunities and crash the vendor's earnings and stock price.

LAG was like a Roman emperor whose thumbs-up or thumbs-down sealed the fate of hundreds of IT vendors. At first, the vendors believed if they paid for services, LAG's coverage would be more favorable. LAG's research and corporate ethics teams kept blatant vendor favoritism in check. So, when vendors found they could not buy their way into positive coverage, they purchased the services so they wouldn't be surprised when LAG's opinions were published. IT vendors often placed senior LAG analysts on their advisory boards hoping to elicit valuable insights to help them build, price, and deliver solutions more effectively. LAG's revenues from CIOs were exploding. Its revenues from IT vendors were expanding even faster.

LAG's business model found a way to play both sides—buyers and suppliers—without compromising independence or ethics. But it was a struggle. The mythos of that conflict fascinated Marcus.

It was carefully constructed and forcefully communicated both inside and outside LAG. Vendor independence and client confidentiality were the two pillars on which LAG's brand rested. Without it, CIOs would never trust the advice they received from LAG and would stop spending. Without the CIOs, the vendors would not fear LAG's opinions and would stop spending. If LAG played it transparently and fairly, however, the cash machine would hum along nicely.

For now, the presenter kept on the path of the buy side. "A typical CIO will deploy two or three major data center, analytics, ERP, or infrastructure projects in their career." He paused, waiting for all the eyes in the room to look at him.

"In their entire career!" he screeched.

"These are multimillion-dollar investments. How can you be an expert at something you do two or three times in a career?" He channeled his best high school drama lessons, hands waving and voice cracking as he artificially strained to sound even more incredulous.

"How could they?" He didn't wait for a reply from the audience. "I'll tell you. They can't."

The speaker paused to catch his breath.

"Our analysts are involved with fifty major deals a week. We see fifty of these a week and a CIO sees two in a career."

Marcus looked out the window and stretched, holding back a yawn. OK, move along.

The presenter continued, "LAG knows what solutions are working and which are not. We know what functionality is necessary and which isn't. We know what vendors fulfill their promises and which don't. We know what prices are being paid and which vendors can be squeezed for discounts." He was gesticulating wildly, building volume and movement as he went. It was a choreographed dance across the front of the room. "CIOs are anxious to engage our analysts so they can avoid catastrophic mistakes and waste."

He paused. "But that isn't all we do," the instructor continued softly. "With our unique understanding of CIO needs and spending plans we can turn toward helping vendors design and build the best products for CIOs."

And there it is, thought Marcus.

Marcus raised his hand. "How do we keep our vendor business from influencing our CIO business? How do we prohibit analysts from personally profiting from their research?" Marcus knew that with trillions of dollars at stake, the temptation to break the rules and let data leak from one client to another, between rival CIOs, or between buyers and sellers would be seductive. LAG's analysts had access to highly sensitive and confidential information from both buyers of technology and sellers of technology. It would be easy to accept gratuities or secretly trade stocks on that knowledge. He wasn't sure if it was illegal, but it was dishonest.

"Our rules of engagement and our guidelines for ethical behavior are core to our culture. They are part of every client contract we write and are prominently displayed for all our associates, clients, and prospects." The presenter was delighted at Marcus's participation. He'd make sure Rich knew Marcus was actively participating.

"Our corporate governance teams report directly to the CEO. In cases where behaviors are in question, we have a zero-tolerance policy. Analysts are prohibited from trading stocks in any companies they cover." It was a rehearsed answer.

Growing murmurs and crosstalk among the attendees warned the presenter he was losing the room's attention. He made a note to get the team from corporate ethics to address the new recruits tomorrow. For now, he needed to get the session back on track.

"You have been asked to join LAG because you bring the expertise, experience, and credibility needed to support IT leaders with the strategic purchases they are making. We will equip you to engage, advise, and influence the largest and most strategic IT investments in the world." He hung on the *in the world* part like he was introducing fighters in the ring.

It triggered a thought. Marcus would have to find a good gym close by where he could spar early mornings before work. It had been a couple of weeks since he moved into his apartment in Back Bay, and he missed the camaraderie of sparring, rolling, and working out. It helped clear his mind. He put a mat in the guest room of his new apartment, but nothing was an adequate substitute for live drilling, strikes, and the coaching he needed to keep his technique sharp. Plus, the neighbors wouldn't appreciate the sounds of a heavy bag thumping before 6:00 a.m.

"The largest companies in the world and the technology vendors supporting them all crave our insights and opinions. You will be the face of LAG to these clients." The presenter kept selling them on the importance and dominance of LAG.

"You will publish research, develop evaluation tools, and build models for your practice areas. As you grow your brand and increase your coverage, you will manage client meetings and consulting sessions. Your work will enrich our collective expertise." The presenter knew he was dancing perilously close to a Borg reference. His voice mimicked a Star Trek–like tone.

"Resistance is futile," Marcus murmured.

"We are here to help you develop your brand in the market. We will promote you as a dominant expert in your field. Together we will grow LAG into a multibillion-dollar advisory services firm in the next five years." The presenter's sermon was thin on specifics.

It is an elegant value proposition, Marcus thought. He ran the math in his head. There was over $1 trillion in risky IT investments within LAG's target market, and LAG could drive a 20-30 percent improvement through cost reduction or better implementations. That translates into a $200 billion improvement for LAG's clients. Marcus's experience was that CIOs would readily pay a quarter of those savings to justify buying LAG services in perpetuity. Marcus spent more than that when he was a LAG client working at HNPC, with Rich and his team.

★ ★ ★

Rich visited Marcus in his HNPC office during his unofficial recruitment effort two years ago. Marcus ran the network infrastructure team at the large communications services firm. They'd had drinks every time Rich was in town, but this was different. "I'm not coming in for a social call, so wear a suit to work tomorrow," Rich chided his friend. "I have a surprise for you."

Rich was there to meet with Marcus's CEO. The HNPC board was hoping to leverage Marcus's personal relationship with Rich to elicit LAG's help with an alarming vendor implementation and contract problem. The board was bracing for a massive write-off that would likely tank their stock and cost the CIO and CEO their jobs.

LAG's contract negotiation support rescued the project and saved HNPC nearly $10 million. It cast a positive glow on Marcus as a result. In return, Marcus got to spend more money with LAG and more time with Rich and his team on other projects. It wasn't long after Marcus's first engagement with LAG that Rich had begun softly and not so softly recruiting him to jump ship and join him at LAG. Text messages with pictures from exotic locations. Emails with clippings of their earnings reports. Calls with reminders to watch cable news coverage where Rich was presenting to Congress. Hints at a massive salary increase and the chance to run a team. The promise of working with his best friend. Rich leveraged it all. He was unrelenting.

At HNPC, Marcus rode his relationship with Rich through two annual LAG contract renewals, and he got a promotion and raise after each one based on the savings LAG delivered back to Marcus's firm. There is a saying old-timers in IT used: "Nobody ever got fired for buying IBM." Today the saying was: "No CIO ever got fired for using LAG." Marcus benefitted greatly from

LAG's work. With each project HNPC gave to LAG, Rich would pay a visit to Marcus, which inevitably resulted in them sharing a ridiculously expensive meal and then closing a bar where they discussed Marcus's future. And every morning after, Marcus awoke to a massive headache and a bit of unease over what he'd promised his best friend.

"I've built a business model that Wall Street loves. They value the predictability of our revenues and our growth. We routinely retain 90 percent of our clients, and we are growing revenues 20 percent per year," Rich boasted to Marcus.

"Sounds like you have it all working perfectly," Marcus agreed.

"My problem is in the long term, because growing at 20 percent year after year gets harder when the total revenue number gets bigger. LAG always needs more clients and bigger clients to feed street expectations. It means a lot of analysts to hire, which drives huge cost increases. Investors are starting to question our long-term strategy. That is why I need you, Marcus."

★ ★ ★

That's why I need you, Marcus . . . Rich's plea still echoed with Marcus. His best friend asked him for help. Marcus would not refuse. He did not refuse. He owed Rich too much. Marcus shifted his eyes back to the speaker, but really, Marcus was stealing looks at a copy of LAG's press release from this morning outlining its quarterly earnings. Rich sounded worried last night, but the results, announced before the market opened, were fantastic. All the sequential quarter and annual comparisons were outstanding. Revenue growth was strong, cost of sales was in line, debt was low, free cash was high, and margins were nudging upward.

It was strange for Marcus to see Rich acting this vulnerable. Marcus reviewed LAG's performance compared to its rivals who announced earnings last week. LAG was larger, growing faster, commanding higher gross margins, supporting less debt, generating greater cash flow, and delivering higher client retention. All the dials and gauges were pointed in the right direction.

In the onboarding session today, the speaker was laying out an aggressive future for LAG. As a former client who saw exactly how powerful LAG can be, Marcus was thrilled to be there. The feeling was mutual because Marcus was the ideal analyst candidate for LAG. His undergraduate degree was in electrical engineering from Penn State followed by an MBA from MIT.

Marcus's resume landed on the desk of a recruiter at LAG two months ago. LAG was growing rapidly and would need to double the size of its team within the year. They needed bona fide technology experts who had peer-level experience working with CIOs. They were hiring candidates who had superb people skills, communications skills, and the executive gravitas to sit face-to-face with CIOs, CEOs, and corporate boards. LAG needed experts, like Marcus, who could be trusted to guide senior business leaders through highly complex, multimillion-dollar technology purchases, negotiations, and deployments.

Candidates for analyst positions had to thrive in environments where multitasking was normal. They had to produce deliverables in abundance. In a typical week they'd work forty to fifty hours publishing research, developing forecasts, and crafting vendor analyses and then spend another twenty to thirty hours in client meetings or face-to-face consulting sessions. On top of this, they were in charge of their own brand. The best analysts were engaged with providing quotes to the business press, providing expert commentary to cable news outlets, and speaking to business leaders at flagship industry events. It was a rigorous role, and the burnout rate was high, but the compensation plans were attractive.

Marcus wasn't even aware LAG's recruiting team was looking at his resume. Rich created it and sent a backgrounder on Marcus to LAG's human resources department. Later that week, when Rich asked HR to make him an offer, they didn't resist. They were beyond capacity trying to hire hundreds of new employees, and if the CEO wanted someone in particular they weren't going to argue. Marcus was honored his friend considered and endorsed him. He didn't have a chance to say no.

What caught the eye of HR, as much as his stellar academic and work pedigree, was his athletic resume. LAG liked athletes. Their competitiveness, drive, focus, and ability to work though distractions made them ideal. Per Rich's instructions, candidates who had wrestled were of special interest, and Marcus wasn't just a routine wrestler. He was a two-time all-American and a national champion at 157 pounds at Penn State. It was easy to see why Rich liked him. They had a lot in common.

Wrestlers, by the nature of their sport, are accustomed to making split-second decisions under pressure. They are trained to live with, and work through, the consequences. From the time they are youth wrestlers through college, they'd made millions of split-second choices in matches, which were blocked, countered, or reversed by their opponents. Their innate ability to push through was key.

The tiny and everyday obstacles that might derail, distract, and dishearten a typical analyst were simply challenges to overcome with new approaches, new attacks, or new tactics for a wrestler. The ability of wrestlers to embrace delayed gratification, to endure soul-crushing physical and mental stress, and to work long arduous hours while staying singularly focused on accomplishing an objective made them a compelling employee profile. Wrestlers don't second-guess their decisions. They don't go backward. They adapt and drive forward.

There was an inherent honor and loyalty to wrestlers too, making them worthy of a conversation regardless of academic pedigree. Around, over, and through. The physical and psychological training wrestlers endured mapped well to the fluid, moving, unstructured, and intense demands at LAG. Add an MIT graduate degree to the mix and HR knew Rich found somebody special.

There is a dilemma with wrestlers, though. All the things that make them incredible individual contributors, things like self-reliance, discipline, and boundless productivity, often make them less effective managers and team leaders. Wrestling is not a team sport. It is based totally on self-reliance, self-discipline, and an individual work ethic. Regardless, Rich appointed Marcus as the team leader for the new LAG research service focused on emerging technologies.

The role would report directly to Rich, and Marcus was his sole candidate. Rich knew what he wanted, and Marcus received an attractive offer from LAG before the end of May. Now he was sitting in the same onboarding session as the other analyst Rich hired. Marcus side-eyed her as she took her seat in the back, several rows behind him.

As the presenter began to wrap up day one of the onboarding session, a tingle spread down Marcus's neck. Small hairs rose and stiffened. He could feel Beth's stare. A momentary glance revealed she was even more beautiful than her social media pictures.

"Not yet. I'll talk to her tomorrow," he promised. There was no way he could introduce himself to Beth if he weren't totally on top of his game. As the speaker unplugged and closed his laptop, signaling the end of the day-one session, Marcus quietly exited the conference room through the side door to avoid getting trapped.

He needed to be better tomorrow.

CHAPTER 7
Beth's Initiation

"You're the cornerstone. You'll show them all how it's done." Rich knew Beth was on board, but there were still three months until her start date and he wanted to practice the sales pitch on her before he used it to close Marcus. He was meeting Marcus and his CEO at the HNPC offices in two days.

This wasn't an interview. He'd promised Beth a role at LAG years ago. Far earlier, even, than when he'd been preparing and softening Marcus to join him. Rich outlined a role for her while she was still in graduate school. Her joining LAG was never in question and this meeting in Boston was ceremonial.

Rich was supremely confident all the pieces would be in place for the August onboarding session. Beth was committed and Marcus would submit shortly. Jeff and Deb were already on board and fully engaged with LAG clients.

"It's hard *not* to be a cornerstone when there are only four of us." Beth laughed.

"Fair enough. You guys are my experiment. An agile group to whom I'm giving wide latitude. You will work differently, faster, and more strategically. You'll build new models and products for our clients." Rich made it clear the Emerging Tech Team would be treated differently from others within LAG and that Beth would be encouraged to experiment with new approaches, new revenue models, and new markets. "Eventually you'll have a totally different compensation plan from other teams," he finished. "See you in August."

☆ ☆ ☆

Beth was thrilled with the opportunity. She arrived early for the opening-day onboarding session, beating Marcus to the meeting. He slipped past her as she poured a cup of coffee. Her gray skirt was hemmed above the knee, but not too far above the knee, and her perfectly tailored white blouse was tight, but not too tight. Two of the male sales trainees loitering at the coffee station clumsily stopped talking and tried not to gawk as she thumbed through the name tags to find hers. She picked it up, nodded negatively, and put it in her purse. There was no way she would pin that tag to her expensive silk blouse. She bypassed the onlookers as if they weren't there. She was only interested in meeting Marcus. Beth opted for a seat in the back of the room. It was a better vantage point to see everybody in attendance.

"This year, total technology spend will be just shy of $3 trillion." The head of corporate training didn't impress Beth. He was struggling to appear casual, but his designer jeans, Ferragamo loafers, and purposefully tousled haircut were nothing more than a costume. He was playacting in front of the new hires and Beth hated actors. The way he emphasized *trillion*, to provide somber dramatic effect, made her eyes roll, and she didn't care if he noticed.

The man sitting front-row center with dark hair, in a tight cut, caught her attention. She liked the way he dressed. Business casual with worn jeans, polished but broken-in boots, clean and pressed white button-down shirt with cuffs flipped up. There was an edge of an arm tattoo peeking out below the right shirtsleeve. He was athletic. Sleek and muscular, but lean. A slight cauliflower ear on the left side was visible from behind. "That's him," Beth whispered. It was Marcus Shea, her new boss.

She restlessly shifted in her seat, staring at him, willing him to look back. Turn around. Turn around. Turn around. She was disappointed at her vain attempt at psychokinesis. At this point she didn't care if he caught her staring and could not hold back a frustrated grimace as he continued to avoid even as much as a distant glance.

Beth noticed that his eyes never left the speaker. At best he'd smile at the dumb jokes, but he never laughed. Her scowl softened to an approving smile, recognizing that he was not a political kiss-ass. She had done her homework on him and knew his academic chops, work history, and wrestling background. She knew why Rich liked him. They were alike in many ways. *He'll be a challenge*, she thought. She liked challenges.

Her modus operandi in meetings, like this onboarding session, was not to engage right away but to size up the attendees and listen. She judged all the new analysts in the room based on their body language, how they dressed, how they paid attention, and questions they asked. It was an immediate blot against them if they impulsively laughed at the presenter's inane jokes. She observed which analysts needed to take notes and knew they would have trouble keeping pace with her. Beth passed judgment on each attendee instantly. *Phony. Idiot. Fake. Acceptable.* She went row by row. So far, five of the twenty-four analysts in the room met her standard and only one of the five, Marcus, impressed her. He carried himself differently than the others, more strongly. His posture was relaxed, shoulders back, at ease. Everybody else looked like they were on trial.

Like Marcus, Beth was an athlete. She placed fifth in the NCAA indoor hurdles. Her master's in computer science rounded out impressive credentials and made her a high-value hire for LAG. She was personally selected by Rich Anderson to be a firebrand on the new Emerging Tech Team—to break rules. She'd force CIOs to rethink their strategies and she'd drive other analysts to change their approaches to their jobs. If nothing else, the CIOs would have trouble taking their eyes off her. But if that's all they saw, they'd do so at their own peril. Beth had a sharp tongue, a quick wit, a fast mind, and an incredible aptitude for deciphering complex data and building compelling plans of action. She was smart, fast, and fearless.

The speaker's increasingly shrill tone grated on Beth. "A typical CIO will deploy two or three major data center, analytics, ERP, or infrastructure projects in their career. In their entire career! These are multimillion-dollar investments. How can you be an expert at something you do two or three times in a career?" Beth found the presenter's screeching and arm flapping insufferable. He was reinforcing the most important aspect of LAG's value proposition and acting like a Saturday-morning cartoon character. His breathless indignation didn't work. It was artificial.

Beth watched Marcus, shifting in his chair, sitting back, and crossing his arms, and read it as a negative reaction to what they both were hearing.

The speaker regained his breath. "Our analysts are involved with fifty major deals a week. Fifty a week versus two in a career. LAG knows what solutions are working and which are not. We know what functionality is necessary and which isn't. We know what vendors fulfill their promises and which don't. We know what prices are being paid, and which vendors can be squeezed for discounts."

Beth could see the speaker was losing the crowd. The escalation of his tone, pace, and gestures were comical. Murmurs and whispers were increasing. The room settled in when he switched topics.

"But that isn't all we do. With our unique understanding of CIO needs and spending plans we can turn toward helping vendors design and build the best products for CIOs."

Rich had never shared this side of the LAG business model with her during the recruitment process. For the first time today, she was intrigued. She didn't realize LAG generated revenue from both buyers and sellers of technology products and was curious how Rich ensured one side didn't taint the other.

Beth smiled in agreement when Marcus raised his hand and asked for clarification. Unfortunately, the answers from the presenter were as canned as the rest of his session. Beth caught Marcus's skeptical tone. He was dissatisfied with the answers as well.

The presenter pulled the room back on track. "You have been asked to join LAG because you bring the expertise, experience, and credibility needed to support IT leaders and the strategic purchases they are making. We will equip you to engage, advise, and influence the largest and most strategic IT investments in the world." He bellowed, "In the world," and she stopped listening. She'd learned nothing important in today's session.

As the class disbursed at the end of day one, Beth headed for the lobby. She waited for Marcus to pass by, but he'd left through the side door.

CHAPTER 8
Hyenas on the Prowl

It was a mile walk from his new apartment to LAG's offices and Marcus headed out the morning of day two with plenty of time to grab a token of apology at Dunkin' along the way. "Two large coffees, please. One black and one with extra cream and four sugars." He noticed how Beth liked hers yesterday, and a cup of coffee was a more acceptable olive branch than groveling for forgiveness. It was a mistake when he didn't introduce himself yesterday. Today, he was ready. Old memories in check.

Marcus's morning walk from Marlborough Street, past the shops and restaurants on Newbury Street, and past the Old South Church would be even nicer in the fall when the heat and humidity was over. The main thoroughfare and side streets were teeming with movement. Cars, delivery trucks, panel vans, scooters, and people walking all competed for space. The temperature was heading toward being uncomfortable and it was only 6:30 a.m. The narrow sidewalks corralled pedestrians into tight packs. He could feel sweat building on his lower back. The odor of dirty water and last night's garbage wafted from the alleyways. The area made for a good run when it was cooler at 4:00 a.m. this morning, but it was much less pleasant now in a sport coat and slacks.

Marcus swiped his badge at the front desk for day two. He scanned the frenetic activity in the lobby as analysts scurried to their desks, hurried into meeting rooms, and darted into the elevators. His head was on a swivel. *I bet nobody in here had ever taken the CEO to his back with a blast double and pinned him with a crucifix.* Then Marcus caught himself. *Yeah, but it was in a practice.* Marcus and Rich wrestled each other twice in dual meets and twice in the NCAA tournament. By Marcus's recollection he was one and three against Rich. Not that he was counting, but Rich was a much better wrestler.

Even shielded with a peace offering, Marcus needed a few moments to mentally prepare for his first introduction with Beth. He stood at the front of the room and shook out his arms and legs, subtly bounced up and down from the balls of his feet to his toes, and deeply stretched his neck side to side. If anybody were paying attention, they'd have noticed a typical pre-bout warm-up routine and then laughed as the guy doing it was in pressed khakis, a light blue oxford shirt, and a blue sport coat.

Marcus heard her approach from behind him. "No thanks." Beth sidestepped one of the sales rep's offer of a bagel, never making eye contact. She strode defiantly toward the front of the conference room. Marcus pivoted toward her, coffee in hand. She was headed toward him with purpose. Seeing her stern face and determined walk, Marcus knew she wasn't going to leave the second chance for an introduction up to him. But now, looking at Beth more closely, he felt off balance. *It's hard enough to be on your game with such a beautiful woman. It's even harder when just looking at her triggers memories you've blocked for years.*

Marcus had game-planned the moment. He would fumble his way through an apology and extend the coffee and his "welcome." He was hoping for some light chitchat and to schedule time for them to meet tonight for dinner following the onboarding session. Marcus's plan was torpedoed before they got within ten feet of each other as Rich brashly walked into the room with two LAG analysts in tow.

"This is great. I'm so glad you guys had a chance to meet," Rich bellowed.

"Yeah, we're already fast friends," Beth interrupted, throwing a "you owe me" glance at Marcus.

Rich hurried toward them with arms open wide and a big smile on his face, leaving the two analysts behind. Where Beth's body language showed confidence during the training session, and even a bit of a chip on her shoulder as she approached Marcus, her demeanor changed with Rich. She gave him a hug, but it looked forced. Her beautiful eyes got noticeably bigger, but it was more of a startled reaction than an autonomic response associated with affection. It was like she was surprised he was there. A reaction like when you bump into an old flame, unexpectedly, in a foreign airport or at a small restaurant you'd never been to before. She didn't look ready for him to be there.

If he'd noticed it, Rich didn't acknowledge her uncomfortable reaction. He turned and introduced the two behind him. "This is Jeff and Deb. Marcus, they'll round out your team."

Jeff looked the part of a technology researcher with tousled salt-and-pepper hair in need of a combing and trim. His thin face and angular nose supported small bifocals. His slacks and a shirt were well past time for a donation to Goodwill. He was slim, but not fit. Nothing like the star college soccer player Marcus envisioned when he searched Jeff's social media accounts. Jeff's role was primarily back-office at LAG and not client facing, so Jeff didn't really care about his appearance, and neither did Marcus. Deb looked younger than Jeff but was, in reality, a year older. She had an understated beauty with graying flecks in her dark hair. She still had the body of a swimmer with broad shoulders. She was dressed in a proper skirt and jacket for client video calls with no makeup or jewelry. Deb wore flats, so as not to tower over Jeff. He really didn't care, but she was conscious of their height difference and didn't want to make her husband uncomfortable when meeting their new boss for the first time.

For the moment, Marcus ignored the two analysts, focusing more on the way Beth was reacting to Rich. Marcus knew Rich and Beth had some sort of history, but Rich didn't share the extent.

Marcus stood there foolishly holding two cups of coffee. Reflexively he gave Beth her cup and passed his cup to Rich. "Sorry," he said to Jeff and Deb. "Only have two hands." Marcus would drink the stale conference room brew. He stood in the middle wondering how to initiate the conversation. On his left was Beth trying to gain her composure in front of Rich, and on his right were two analysts who would report to Marcus, now trapped in a clumsy introduction.

Marcus was more comfortable talking to Jeff and Deb. Stepping toward them, he said, "It's great to meet you both. I've been reading your latest research. The analysis on internet security was really well done." It was directed at Jeff. "And the contract restructuring ideas for Alliance Bank was really creative." That was directed at Deb. Marcus didn't tell them he'd read all the research the two of them had ever written at LAG. There were dozens of research reports and hundreds of pages from the past two years. They were good analysts. He'd change their preparation and delivery discipline. They were a good tandem, but he'd make them better.

Beth's awkwardness only lasted a few moments. The way Rich angled away from her and the way she shifted backward to avoid touching him was odd. But if there was a weird reaction, she suppressed it. Her taut smile loosened. Her posture straightened, her shoulders relaxed, and she became more assertive.

"I was wondering when you'd climb down from on high and leave your executive suite to bless the peasants with your presence," Beth poked. It wasn't something a stranger would say to her boss's boss, so Marcus remained quiet, evaluating their connection.

"I've always been a man of the people, Beth. Even those of such low station and experience are thankful for the warmth of my presence." He laughed. He certainly wasn't mad at her.

"Hey, Rich," Marcus smiled.

"I was wondering if you'd both run away after day one." Rich had his hands over his heart feigning hurt feelings. "I didn't get a response to the email I sent you both."

Beth commented, "Haven't logged in yet."

"We start early here, Beth," Rich said. It was a friendly jab, but point made.

Rich spent the next few minutes small-talking with Marcus and Beth about their first day and how thrilled he was they'd joined the LAG family. He hit them with a flurry of ideas for new client engagements, upcoming travel, great local restaurants, and fun local attractions. Marcus had experienced the brain-dump avalanche from Rich before. Rich had a tendency to keep selling long after the buyer agreed. In this case, he was selling Marcus and Beth on the excellence of the LAG lifestyle.

It is not uncommon that people who are blessed with incredible gifts, such as music, scholastics, the arts, or athletics, are socially awkward. Solitary years pursuing excellence can stunt the natural maturation and the experience needed for robust socialization skills. That was not Rich. He was young, handsome, athletic, and the smartest person Marcus had ever met, and at total ease in a crowd. But it was strange how he ignored Jeff and Deb. It wasn't totally dismissive, but he didn't engage them in the conversation either. It was as if their role in the new Emerging Tech Team was utterly subordinate to Marcus and Beth. Marcus made a mental note to spend time with both Jeff and Deb to ensure they felt engaged and personally invested in his vision for the team. Marcus would treat them not like subordinates but as teammates.

"It was great meeting you both." Deb nodded toward Marcus and Beth. She was looking for an exit and Rich's tone annoyed her. "I'm booked all day with client calls, but I hope we can catch up soon." Marcus and Beth would soon learn how demanding LAG clients can be and how precious and incredibly rare free time can be. Deb didn't have any free time now.

"Yes." Jeff checked his watch. "I have to run as well. I've got to analyze some new benchmark data for a client. They've got a massive software implementation underway, and it is going superbly. We are going to feature their case study in an upcoming best practices report."

They exited with Rich close behind. Now Marcus was alone with Beth.

The moderator for day two watched the interplay between the new Emerging Tech Team and the CEO and was ready to call the room to attention. For day two, Beth and Marcus sat next to each other. They settled on seats closer to the middle of the room as a compromise without even discussing it. Neither had a notepad or pen. They looked at each other and subtly rolled their eyes when the presenters' schtick was too much and they began to press the presenters with questions when they were short on details or clarity. Marcus and Beth worked well together in the workshops and breakout sessions. Marcus was impressed. It was natural.

The end of the agenda for the two-day onboarding session arrived, but oddly, the presenters were not packing up. Three executives were added to the program. The session was supposed to end at 3:00 p.m., but Marcus had ruined that prospect with his questions yesterday regarding conflict of interest and compliance. Beth made sure to thank him with a sharp elbow to his ribs and a smile. One of the three executives said, "We stand here before you as the final presenters and the last speakers standing between you and the bar. We will try to be quick."

For the next two hours, the heads of corporate ethics, corporate governance, and corporate compliance outlined the dos and don'ts of being an analyst and the cans and cannots of being an advisory salesperson. They shared case studies and examples of what behaviors were right and wrong. In truth, all the presenters wanted to do was submit the room to the standard corporate certification test, give everybody their paper diploma, and go home. But since Marcus, a new research leader, had raised some very serious questions they were obliged to provide more meaty responses.

"Every year, on the anniversary of your hire date, each LAG associate attends a two-hour session reviewing and reinforcing our compliance, client confidentiality, and governance processes. At the completion of training, you will be tested on our policies and when you pass you will receive a certificate of completion. You will sign a copy and it will be placed in your employee file." The session moderator was determined to reinforce the process in case Marcus spoke separately with Rich.

Marcus felt Beth shifting impatiently in her seat, fidgeting, adjusting her posture.

"What are the penalties? There had to be repercussions," he whispered to her. She wasn't satisfied with their answers either.

"Is LAG's certification process designed to protect the associate or the client, or to shelter LAG from liability?" Beth asked the presenters. She was in sync with Marcus, and he could tell by their triple scowls the answer was the latter.

Marcus was not surprised when they stammered the reply. "We've built a strong ethical culture here and we have the systems and training in place to ensure it remains that way."

"When a group of analysts supports multiple CIOs competing in the same industries or engage CIOs, buyers, and vendors who are locked in a common buy-sell cycle, the potential for a breach in confidentiality is inevitable," Marcus offered as a way to help the presenters clarify their answer and for everyone in the room to understand the importance of confidentiality. He didn't add that any violation of trust could lead to massive legal and financial implications, but wanted to.

The whole scenario was a particularly acute problem for advisory firms where analysts collaborate, engage in joint client meetings, discuss sensitive client information, or have shared access to network drives where confidential client information is stored. Proprietary pricing, trade secrets, sensitive financial information, personnel data, or other types of restricted information from buyers and vendors resided on analyst laptops and LAG servers. Water cooler conversations between analysts and salespeople were common. It is easy to cross the line when the line is so dimly drawn. An analyst who wanted to do a little day trading on the side could access drafts of research reports and make stock trades prior to LAG publishing a major endorsement. It would be a quick capital gain, as long as they hid their identity. It was a scenario the three speakers ignored.

The tribunal attempted to deflect the discussion. "Our analysts are consummate professionals who understand our code of ethics. As such, we've never had a situation where client confidential information has been shared. We've never been sued." Marcus knew these situations would be exceedingly rare, but a lack of lawsuits was the wrong barometer. LAG would find any way to settle an investigation, then seal it and keep it private. The potential risk to client reputations and their businesses was real, and the impact could easily be in the tens of millions of dollars. LAG had such presence in the market, and its brand was so important, it would never let a confidentiality situation come to trial. LAG would settle quickly and quietly, bolstered by nondisclosure agreements all around.

Marcus knew the difficulty in protecting privacy and the complexity in proving or litigating damages. He was curious about a more direct scenario. "What about ways to spot pay-for-play?" he asked. The three presenters nervously looked at each other, none of them volunteering to go first.

Pay-for-play accusations could devastate an advisory firm's brand. It occurred when an analyst provided biased recommendations in exchange for payment or favors. This type of corruption was frequently charged but rarely substantiated in the advisory industry. It would require proof of an analyst receiving compensation from a company in exchange for publishing positive research reports or promoting the company's solutions via consulting. It would require proof that a company didn't deserve a particular, albeit totally subjective, rating or recommendation from an analyst. In other words, it was nearly impossible to prove.

"That goes straight to the credibility of the analyst, and we treat it exactly as we would a violation of client confidentiality in any form," the head of governance weakly chimed.

"All our analysts know it is critical to maintain a high level of integrity and transparency in their work and to avoid conflicts of interest or compromise their objectivity," added the corporate ethics officer.

Marcus was curious about pay-for-play because there where quiet accusations leveled against their entire industry by vendors who believed they were unfairly treated. The claims were not aimed at LAG specifically, but at the industry at large. With huge chunks of market share and billions of dollars in revenues riding on how positively analyst firms cover a vendor, a poor rating or even an absence of a vendor from a research report could be devastating.

In his previous job, Marcus had heard vendors griping to his CIO that, "Those analysts are compromised. They are getting paid to cover our rival. Anybody can see our product is better." Vendor suspicions were far more frequently lodged than ever proven, but poor ratings inevitably triggered grouchy murmurs about unfairness and allegations of analysts on the "take." All it took was for a vendor to lose a multimillion-dollar deal to a rival for accusations to fly.

Marcus sat back and took a breath. Beth could tell he was uneasy pressing the ethics, governance, and compliance leaders further, so she interrupted. "Is there any way to spot smoke before there is a fire? Is there a way to find out there is a risk before it becomes a real problem?" Both Beth and Marcus were looking for a formal policy or process to root out potential misconduct before it erupted publicly. The trio were stumbling over themselves to end this discussion.

"Hey, it's our second day on the job. Let's not make enemies just yet," he whispered to Beth with a grin. They both realized the presenters needed an off-ramp.

"I apologize. It feels like I'm taking the group down a rathole," Beth offered.

"LAG's reputation is impeccable. You've provided a great overview. Thank you," Marcus finished her sentence.

Marcus could see by the way they looked at each other that the discussion was finished. There was no benefit to push further. Both Marcus and Beth wondered if the meteoric rise of LAG, under Rich's leadership, might have outpaced its ability to enact the controls necessary to protect it from shifty employees looking to profit from LAG's brand and reputation, but they wouldn't get the answers today.

Marcus turned to Beth and whispered, "There is another problem. All three enforcement teams report into Rich. If he is busy or cannot engage, it's a single point of failure."

After the ethics discussion, all the new LAG employees took the annual online certification test. Everyone passed with a perfect score. Marcus and Beth were apprehensive. For something so crucial to the LAG brand, the test confirming their proficiency was too easy.

Beth proudly held her signed eight-by-eleven certificate by its corners. "Here you go, boss. I passed."

"Wow. A perfect score. It makes you perfectly average in today's class." He folded her certificate in thirds and placed it in the pocket of his blazer. "Do you want a pat on the head and a cookie, or do you want to grab a drink? I reserved at table at Bistecca at 8:00 p.m."

"Drinks, please." Beth smiled. It was the first time Marcus let down his guard with her.

Marcus's plan was they'd have a drink or two at a bar down the street before dinner. They'd discuss first impressions of LAG and, after a couple glasses of wine, learn more about each other over a perfectly grilled veal chop. Their workload was about to become intense, and they'd be spending a lot of time together. Better to find out now if she was a mayonnaise-on-french-fry type of person.

The bar, High Yield, was on the same side of the street as LAG's office and midway between LAG and Bistecca. Rich had recommended both and was especially effusive about the bar.

It was crowded at 6:00 p.m., but they found a couple of seats by the door next to an open window onto Boylston Street. The sun was setting, and it was becoming a comfortable night. The heatwave broke with some passing showers, and while still warm, the humidity had dropped. Waves of gray-haired executives stopped in for a drink before catching the commuter rail from Copley headed west to their four-bedroom, three-bath homes in the suburbs. Younger executives were traveling in packs barhopping before heading to dinner in the North End or their apartments in Southie.

"Did you find it odd they weren't going to spend any time on the confidentiality and compliance risks until I raised it yesterday?" Marcus couldn't help but keep pulling on that thread. He tried to think of other topics, but he was still too uncomfortable and nervous around Beth to start any intimate, personal sharing just yet.

"Yeah. And what do you think about the annual certification process? It's never going to stop deliberate violations. The training and testing helps analysts avoid making innocent mistakes, but what if an analyst does it on purpose? They could pass certification after certification and still willfully violate company policy," Beth added.

"I was thinking the same thing." He took a sip of wine.

"But I haven't heard of problems at LAG. Based on our first two days, I'd say there is a strong corporate culture to do what is right." Beth wasn't interested in any more talk about confidentiality, work, or Rich.

"I'm curious. Why didn't you introduce yourself yesterday?" she jumped right in.

It was more abrupt than Marcus expected. He'd been hoping for the effects of another glass of red to kick in first. "It was a little overwhelming yesterday. New surroundings. New culture. New people. I guess I wanted to get my bearings first," he lied. And even now, as he looked at her, he saw Kelly's face as if it were superimposed on Beth.

Behind them, it was getting louder as a group of four young men in expensive but ill-fitting suits was making a bit of a scene trying to outmaneuver each other to talk to two attractive women sharing a bottle of wine at the end of the bar. Marcus could not hear what they were saying, but their body language was clear. They were on the prowl. One would try a pickup line, and before the women could brush him off, another would jockey into position.

Beth noticed it too. She was becoming tense and rigid. He glanced down as her hands squeezed into fists and watched her pivot her head to the right, straining to hear more of their conversation, all telltale signs that she was going to interject. Beth was not going to sit still while the women were forced to fend off four men who were becoming increasingly rowdy and touchy.

"For Chrissake, it's Tuesday, not a Saturday night. Why do these assholes need to turn this into a meat market?" She kept her eyes on the women while talking to Marcus. She wasn't looking for his reply; she was narrating her growing disgust.

Marcus watched her as she watched them, happy her attention was off him. Before Marcus had a chance to ask her if she'd like him to go speak to the men about their behavior, she slid out of her seat and walked their way. She brushed past them and assumed a defensive position between the two women at the bar and the pack.

"Hey, Susie. Hey, Mary. I didn't know you guys were going out tonight. Marcus and I found a table by the window. You need to join us." Beth didn't know their real names and motioned toward the door. She was offering the two women a way out and away.

The four clowns were caught off guard and turned their gunsights to her. While the men were bumbling, trying to decide who would speak to Beth first, she mouthed, "Are you two OK?" The woman closest to Beth was rigid and gave Beth the "I'm not sure" face.

"Come on. Join us," she repeated to the women, who hurriedly closed their tab, grabbed their glasses, and prepared to separate themselves from the group of hyenas. "On our way," said the woman closest to her. The other pulled cash from her wallet and left it in the billfold.

The men didn't move, making the women shimmy between them toward their escape route and the door. "Very classy, gentlemen." Beth said it loud enough for them to hear. She followed behind as the caboose to the train, weaving between them and the door. The biggest and most slobbery of them reached forward and put his beefy left hand at the juncture of Beth's shoulder and neck. "They gotta leave, but maybe you can stay with us and have a drink." There was a chorus of, "Yes, you gotta stay," from his wingmen.

"Get your hands off me." She reached across her chest with her right hand and tried to pull his hand off her shoulder, forcing her to rotate into him. He gave her a slobbery grin.

None of them saw Marcus working his way toward the bar. As Beth spun for a fight, Marcus stood less than two feet away, off her left shoulder. In one move he gently placed his right forearm on her left hip and used her own momentum to glide her to her right. In the same move, he launched a crushing left hook. The body shot sent a shock wave through the man's ribcage and into his liver.

When most people watch boxing, they cheer for knockouts. An uppercut, hook, or cross striking anywhere from the jawline to the ear is the target. If the blow is hard enough, the brain will reverberate in the skull, causing a loss of motor skills and possibly unconsciousness. Marcus avoided that strike for a few reasons. First, a haymaker in the middle of a bar draws attention. It has a lot of motion and can be easily seen. It also makes a lot of noise. The sound of fist striking skull can be as loud as a bat hitting a baseball. Second, a punch to the head would immediately elicit a response from his three friends. They were already pretty boozy and unruly, and he didn't want a brawl that could put Beth and the two women at risk. What Marcus wanted to accomplish, relatively quietly, was to disable the largest of the four men so he could finish it outside.

The liver punch is a brutal attack. In June 1986, in a heavyweight championship battle, Mike Tyson knocked out Jesse Ferguson, a much bigger fighter, with a liver punch to retain the title. Jesse Ferguson was a trained professional who got punched for a living and Tyson's left hook to the area above the oblique and under the rib cage left him unable to stand. The guy Marcus just bundled had never been hit like this in his life.

The liver is one of the largest organs in the human body. It filters toxins from the bloodstream, produces bile, and regulates glucose levels in the body. When the liver is struck violently, the force of the blow can cause significant long-term damage to the tissue, but its short-term impacts were what Marcus wanted.

The blow set off a cascade of physiological responses. The thin layer of ribcage absorbed the brunt of the impact but transmitted an electrical signal to the surrounding nerves. These nerves, intertwined within the autonomic system, relayed messages to the brain, signaling the body's extreme state of distress. The force compressed and deformed the liver, momentarily disrupting its ability to function. The sudden trauma triggered a swift activation of pain receptors, sending signals along the electrical pathway connecting the liver to the spinal cord and brain. The brain interpreted these signals as excruciating pain, overwhelming the man's sensory perception with radiating and debilitating shock waves through his back, chest, and shoulder. He withered with immediate nausea and a loss of breath, losing control of his legs. He was dizzy and disoriented. Most importantly, he was unable to speak.

Biff, or Tad, or Benji or whatever his name was, could now be easily guided outside by Marcus, and his friends would follow.

"Beth, could you and the ladies head back to our table?" Beth was a few feet away and witnessed it all, but even so, the speed made it difficult to track. It was motion blur. Her eyes had trouble capturing enough visual information to recognize what happened. She wanted to knee the guy in the balls and leave. Marcus now had the guy's arm over his shoulder and was shuffling him out the front door with three confused buddies behind him. Nobody else in the bar noticed anything strange. Just another drunk kid bounced from a bar.

It took a minute to navigate the patrons who were heading in through the door and another couple of minutes for Marcus to walk the man two blocks to the right and into an alley. Marcus leaned him against a dumpster. The man was beginning to regain the use of his legs and his wits, but the pain was too intense for him to fight back or yell. All he could think about was he was going to piss blood tomorrow.

The three amigos rounded the corner of the ally a few seconds later, breathing heavily. They were slowly concluding that Marcus attacked their friend, leaving him unable to walk on his own. That made them mad. They were even more angry that Marcus had interrupted their efforts to convince Beth to have sex with all of them.

The first wingman stood at the entrance to the ally and barked, "What the fuck did you do to him?" He was hulking out his shoulders and chest trying to look bigger.

The second man was slightly crouched, looking more anxious for combat. "Teddy, you OK?"

All Teddy could do is moan. He still couldn't answer.

"What the fuck, man? What did you do?" The third friend was having trouble processing the situation. He stayed a few steps behind the other two. He was the smart one. Something did not look right to him, and he wasn't about to jump in without more information. He'd never seen Teddy in distress. Teddy was always the alpha male in their group. He was the one who never backed off. Whenever there was a loudmouth at a game or at a bar, it was Teddy who would bring order. His size and high school jock mentality would always make the other guy pull back.

"What did I do? What. Did. I. Do? That's the question, isn't it?" Marcus slowly took a step toward them shifting his position toward the center of the alley. He wanted room to fight.

"Well. Without going into the physiology of it all, I disrupted his liver function and broke two of his ribs." Marcus's tone wasn't violent or threatening. It was clinical. He waited for them to process his description.

They looked at each other and then at Teddy and then Marcus. Nothing here made sense. They were having a good time, drinking in a bar, and talking to two ladies. A hot chick came up and cockblocked them and now Teddy was bent over a dumpster looking like shit with drool leaking from his mouth and snot dripping from his nose.

"The asshole sucker punched me," Teddy rasped, barely able to stand.

They all looked at Marcus, preparing to attack.

"Now wait, guys. I don't think this is a good idea," Marcus lied. He loved the idea.

"He hit me." Teddy was barely able to talk above a whisper. "Kick his ass."

That was all it took. Three untrained and unprepared novices, who'd never been punched in the face, tried a bum-rush.

In any fight where it's multiple people against one, the perceived tough guy would go first. When he started to win, a couple of the other guys would jump in. Their strategy would be to share in the victory. There was a general flow and sequence to how these things went. The problem for the three guys at the entrance to the alley was that Teddy was their tough guy, and he wasn't going to help. He was a mess. Without any leadership, or real muscle, they had no plan and there would be no flow. Instead, they embraced the chaos of a group attack.

Marcus struck the first guy with a front kick as he stepped forward. It hit him right in the sternum. The celiac plexus, or solar plexus as it is known, is a network of nerves that control the muscles of the diaphragm. When struck, even with a small amount of force, it can cause nausea and vomiting, sweating, and a frightening sense of suffocation. He was doubled over and incapacitated.

The second one tried to attack at a tangent. Marcus slipped a wild overhead right and punched him square in his face, breaking his nose. His forward momentum was immediately thrown backward with the blow. Pain radiated through his sinus cavity and behind his eyes, which were engulfed in tears as a response to the broken ethmoid bone.

The third guy, looking at the other two on the ground and Teddy still unable to stand, put his hands up and slowly backed away from Marcus. He turned and sped down Boylston Street, hurrying past the bar as Beth was heading out the door. His face was ashen, and his eyes were watering. His walk was uneven and awkward as he tried to move as quickly as possible away without running. He looked at Beth, terrified, and said, "I'm really sorry." He was crying.

Beth sprinted in the other direction, toward the alley. Marcus was in trouble. *What happened? Do I call the police?* Her mind raced. He tried to save her and the two women at the bar and now he was hurt and bleeding in an alley. She had flashes of him being beaten up, stabbed, or even shot. She ran the last few yards, pulling out her phone and beginning to dial 9-1-1.

Marcus stepped out, looking like nothing had happened. It was getting dark, and his right hand looked like it had blood on it, but nothing else would indicate a problem. He was not hurt. He was not breathing hard. He didn't appear to be even mildly concerned. He was smiling.

Marcus hooked her arm, turned her around, and together they walked back toward the office. It was a slow, casual stroll. To any outsider, it would look like a romantic walk, with her arm holding his. They looked like two young professionals out on a date on a beautiful August Tuesday night in Boston.

Marcus remembered there was a diner next to the entrance of the parking garage for LAG's offices. They'd do Bistecca another time.

"What happened?" Beth was in disbelief.

"At this point, I should tell you about Kelly."

CHAPTER 9
Childhood Damage

"Coach Smith? Tom Almeida, Marcus's grandfather."

"How can I help you, Tom?"

"We've had an emergency. He needs to come home," Tom said in a numb and distant voice. He heard the words, but they didn't feel like they were coming from him.

"Immediately?" The coach was surprised.

"Yeah. There is a flight from Denver to Boston tonight at 10:00 p.m. Please make sure he's on it."

Tom gave the man a truncated version of events.

"God, Tom. I don't know what to say. He'll be there," the coach replied, stunned.

Marcus was in Colorado Springs at a two-week national development camp for U16 (under 16) wrestlers. His speed, strength, and mat intelligence were far above his competition. He was a standout.

The coach knocked on the door of his dorm room. "Marcus. Your grandfather called. They need you to fly back to Boston tonight."

Marcus protested. "We've got a match tomorrow! Why?"

The coach couldn't bring himself to break the news. "Your grandparents will meet you at Logan."

In less than ten minutes, Marcus's training camp was over and he was in the back of the team van, duffle bag in hand, headed to Denver International Airport with a one-way ticket home. He didn't know why.

Marcus didn't sleep on the five-hour flight, though he'd had an entire row to himself. He tried to watch the in-flight movie but was too distracted, playing and replaying what had gone wrong. He hadn't missed weight. He hadn't broken curfew. He hadn't missed a practice. He was undefeated and unscored upon for every scrimmage and match they'd held. Marcus stared blankly out the window, into the darkness, wondering why he was pulled away from the team. He knew it had to be his father, who complained about the cost of the camp. Marcus's anger intensified as the miles passed.

Logan airport was barren when he landed at 6:00 a.m. It was the middle of the week between winter holidays. His grandparents paced, waiting for him at the bottom of the escalator.

"Where's Dad?" Marcus said, looking for confrontation, frustrated at having to come home. He looked past his grandparents down the airport hallway.

Marcus's grandmother stepped forward and hugged him. Marcus didn't hug her back. He pulled back, confused. "He promised me I could go to the camp. He promised."

"Let's get home," Marcus's grandfather said softly as his wife released her embrace. Tom meant his home, not Marcus's.

"Where is everyone? Why are you picking me up?"

"Something happened at home," was all that his grandmother could say.

Marcus threw his duffle into the back seat and slammed the door. "I hate him," was all Marcus said.

Tom pulled over in the breakdown lane exiting the parking garage. The air was heavy and tense. Tom, his face etched with grief, turned toward his grandson seated in the back. Marcus, naïve to the depth of the devastation, looked out the window wanting nothing more than to see his mom and sister and get some sleep.

Joan, with trembling hands, reached back and gently placed a hand on her grandson's cheek, drawing his attention away from the cars passing by. Tom took a slow deep breath. "Marcus, there was a fire. A bad one."

Initially, the words washed over him like waves on a beach, with no effect. Instead his attention fixated on his grandparents. Their faces shook him. They'd always been his bedrock, a steadfast line of defense between Marcus's father and the rest of the family. That fortress crumbled before his eyes. The anguish on their faces alarmed him.

Marcus's voice cracked. "Where's Mom and Kelly?"

With tears welling up in her eyes, Joan struggled to find the words. "Your parents and Kelly . . . they were . . ." Her quivering voice trailed off.

Tom took over. "It was a terrible fire, Marcus," he said, his voice trembling. "They . . . they didn't make it." He wept, unable to hold back the grief.

Joan put her hands over her mouth, trying to hold back the sobs.

The shock and disbelief were suffocating. "No. That can't be true." He breathed the words in less than a whisper, his hands shaking violently.

"You don't have to worry about anything, honey. We are here," Joan said. Tears streamed down her and Tom's faces as the reality of their devastating loss sank in. Marcus unleashed a tortured scream and lashed out at the car window, cracking it in its frame.

As Tom accelerated from the breakdown lane into traffic, the gentle hum of the car's engine muffled the cries of grandparents and grandson, bound together by heartache. Top of Form

Marcus begged to go straight to his house from the airport. His grandparents insisted he go home with them first. They wanted him to eat and rest, promising they'd drive him later that afternoon.

From Logan airport, it was two hours north to his house in New Hampshire, but it would take almost three hours to get to his grandparents' house farther north on the lake, provided there was no snow or ice on the roads. The highways around the airport were clean, but as they drove north on Interstate 95 through Tewksbury and Methuen, across the state line to New Hampshire through Salem, the snowbanks grew.

Marcus spent a lot of time with his grandparents at their cabin, especially when school was out. It was comfortable and familiar to him. Tom and Joan Almeida's lake house had a relaxing aroma, a combination of wood fire, wool blankets, and chocolate chip cookies, with a hint of mothballs and Old Spice. In the upstairs guest room, Marcus shuffled across the floor, his mind rifling through memories. Some were good, like times on the lake with Kelly. Many were bad, like when his father was drunk and how he'd smack him and Kelly. His father's style wasn't always angry or violent, but it was always physical. It was his way of getting their attention. "Do your homework." Whap. "Clean up." Slap. "Passed a test?" Rap. He'd stopped giving his "love taps" to Marcus as soon as Marcus could choke him out. It wasn't as much of a power kick for his father, or as much fun, to bully somebody when they hit back harder.

Marcus slumped at the foot of the bed, blinds closed, in the gloom. His mind began to race with flashes of his family. His mother's laugh. Her unending attempts to bring peace and order at dinnertime. His sister smiling and laughing. Then his darker imagination triggered flashes that pushed all other memories aside.

Nobody talked during the drive from Ossipee Lake to his house near Madison, an hour south. The snowpack was normal for winter, but the roads where salted, clear, and dry. As their station wagon turned into the driveway, Marcus smelled the charred rubble before he could even see the burned husk of his home. It was an acrid and chemical odor with traces of melted plastic, burned foam insulation, and smoldering lumber. The snow around the home had melted and refrozen from the heat into crusts and iced puddles of yellows, browns, and blacks. They were toxic colors that matched the hue of the dimming winter sun setting behind low clouds.

The driveway had not been plowed and there were countless tire tracks cut through a foot of snow. There were branches snapped off the pine trees where large fire trucks hit them when pulling in, turning around, and leaving. It looked like a violent windstorm had blown through. Deep green pine needles were strewn everywhere. The piercing odor of pine sap intermingled with everything else. It was sickening and overpowering.

A fire investigation crew was packing up and readying to leave when Tom, Joan, and Marcus pulled in. The fire team stopped talking as his grandfather parked beside them and rolled down his window. None of the firemen noticed Marcus in the back seat surveying the remains. All that was left were two walls, a chimney, and a collapsed roof covering it all. Twenty feet from where the front entry had been a broken door was tossed into a snowbank, ripped from its hinges. The lawn looked ready for a yard sale. There was a refrigerator, a TV, scorched furniture, and mounds of curtains and rugs tossed in piles. Marcus looked at the bedroom dresser. *Was it mine or Kelly's?* he wondered. Some items looked perfectly fine and undamaged, but most of it was twisted, broken, melted, and destroyed.

"Hey, Chief, I'm Tom Almeida. They were my daughter and granddaughter." Tom spoke quietly and purposefully, trying his best to squelch is emotions. Tom motioned to the boy in the back seat. "That is my grandson, Marcus."

Tom didn't mention the other fatality. The chief wasn't surprised. Marcus's dad had a reputation in town.

"Are there any more details?" Tom asked.

"Not much more than you already know." The chief was a little uncomfortable sharing, especially seeing Marcus in the back seat, but he couldn't deny them a small bit of closure.

"We got the call at the firehouse at 7:00 p.m. The fire team was hear within twenty minutes. It took a little while to cut the ice on the pond and pump water up the hill."

Marcus's eyes never left the house.

"It ignited there." The chief pointed to where the living room had been. "The fire moved fast. It was a bad combination of heat and smoke. There was one smoke detector. It was pretty badly melted. It didn't have any batteries. I'm sorry, Tom." But he was looking at Marcus when he said it. "They passed quickly."

The chief left out some details, including the fact that the father's body was surrounded by empty vodka bottles and the mother and sister were found in their bedrooms. They tried to crawl out but never made it. They died alone and scared. It was every bit as bad as Marcus had imagined.

That instant, listening to the chief outline the senselessness of their deaths and imagining the helplessness his mother and sister experienced, tripped a fuse within Marcus. It was the precise moment where a young boy with a bright future started to spiral downward. It was the moment where he became unable to talk about his family or his sister by name. When he thought about her, his hair trigger for aggression emerged.

★ ★ ★

Joan and Tom Almeida finalized their adoption of Marcus when he turned fifteen. They were surprised it took five months because he'd lived with them since the fire, and they were his sole remaining relatives.

Marcus's adjustment to living with Tom and Joan was not easy. It was a new environment, with no friends, and a new routine. Ossipee Lake was larger than the pond where Marcus grew up. He always had fun with his sister when they visited Tom and Joan in the summer—waterskiing, swimming, exploring, just being kids. They didn't have a chance to do those things at his home, partly because the pond was much smaller, but mostly because their father made their lives miserable. Threats, insults, and fear were more common than the sounds of laughter and play in the Shea home.

Fortunately, Marcus had wrestling as an escape. The regiment of practices, weight cuts, dual meets, and travel tournaments were a good reason to spend little time at home with his father. When he wasn't sharpening for wrestling season, Marcus was a gym rat at a local Brazilian jujitsu (BJJ) studio. It was something Marcus and his grandfather had in common. Tom still worked out but had long retired from competition. Tom and Marcus enjoyed watching mixed martial arts tournaments and jujitsu when they were on TV. They practiced in Tom's home gym whenever Marcus visited. They were close and that closeness was all that kept Marcus grounded. Karl Shea hated jujitsu and despised Tom for the relationship he had with Marcus. The feeling was mutual.

✯ ✯ ✯

Karl was an asshole. In his prime, he was a backup Division II wrestler at Southern Oklahoma University. He never started for the Tornados, so he tried to relive his macho dreams through Marcus and had him on the wrestling mat as soon as he was out of diapers. As Marcus got older and better, Karl would scream from the bleachers, or when the coaches didn't see him, he'd sneak to the mat's edge and bark instructions. Inevitably the referee or another parent would complain, and Karl would be told to get back in the stands where his screams and howls were a loud, obnoxious, and a negative distraction.

Karl didn't like anything distracting Marcus from wrestling, especially anything that might make Marcus and Tom closer. He didn't understand the attraction of jujitsu. Folkstyle wrestling and Brazilian jujitsu are very different disciplines. Folkstyle wrestling emphasizes putting your opponent on their back and pinning them. BJJ was all about submissions and often those submissions came from a guard position, where the winner is on his back choking his opponent or manipulating joints. The idea of lying on your back, latching onto a leg or arm, and trying to make your opponent tap out was foreign to Karl. He took every opportunity to belittle and goad Marcus into quitting to focus solely on wrestling. Karl believed his son could be special. And he was. Marcus was a natural. But Tom won the argument. As Marcus moved into his early teens, he continued with BJJ under Tom's tutelage. And with that, Marcus became too strong, fast, and dangerous for Karl to manhandle or intimidate, but when drunk he often tried.

The clash between Karl and Marcus, the day before Marcus left for Colorado, was particularly heated. "You know why I'm going to camp," Marcus screamed. It was a statement, not a question. Karl didn't get the subtlety as he was four vodka tonics into his night.

"You're going because I'm paying the bill. And I can just as easily stop paying it."

"I'm going to get away from you," Marcus snapped, turning his back to his father.

"Get back here!" Karl barked, stumbling up from his recliner. He grabbed Marcus and tried to put him in a body lock. Marcus easily dodged Karl's grasp and hip tossed him to the floor, knocking his freshly poured cocktail off the end table onto the carpet. Karl withdrew, slurring his words and rubbing his shoulder from the fall, embarrassed at how easily he lost. Marcus didn't pursue him, fearing that Kelly would pay the price in his absence.

Unlike Marcus, Kelly couldn't run or fight back. She was two years younger than Marcus and wasn't big enough to stop Karl's abuse. Over the last year, Marcus watched her withdraw, becoming invisible, avoiding any attention, and hiding from her father. Before the fire she was withering and lonely. She never directly asked Marcus not to go to Colorado, but Marcus knew she was scared. He hugged her before he left for the airport, startled at how thin she was. Her wavy blond hair was shoved under a knit cap. Her deep brown eyes were shallow and empty. She was profoundly sad Marcus was leaving and afraid of being the only outlet for Karl's venom while Marcus was away for three weeks. That was the last memory Marcus had of Kelly: her wanting him to stay and protect her.

★ ★ ★

In his bedroom, Marcus lay on his back, staring at the ceiling, conjuring memories, and stoking horrific images. He repeated over and over, "I'm sorry. I'm so sorry," anger building. Marcus tried to reign it in, but he couldn't stop the chain reaction once it started. Loneliness to sadness. Sadness to guilt. Guilt to anger. Anger fueling even more vivid images. Kelly crawling on the floor, screaming for help, desperately trying to escape, and calling for him. Anger turned to rage, desperate for release. Explosive outbursts became common. Tom had replaced the door to Marcus's room three times already. Each time it had been shattered with kicks and punches.

Tom climbed the stairs when the quiet returned and the sounds of destruction ended.

"Hey, sport, looks like you need another door. Think I could get away with just tacking up a curtain? It's getting kind of expensive." Tom wasn't angry. He sat next to Marcus and mirrored his slouched posture, elbows on knees on the bed.

"I'm sorry." Marcus was back under control.

"How about we try something different," Tom offered. "Let's get you back on the mat."

There were several premier wrestling clubs within an hour of the lake. One had a particularly good reputation for preparing its members for successful high school careers, and Marcus was going to be a freshman in three months.

"They've got some open mat time tonight. Want to go?"

"Yeah. I'd like that."

Tom didn't want to push too hard or too soon, but Marcus needed a distraction. He needed something other than walls and doors to shatter. He'd been off the mat for six months.

"How far is it?"

"Thirty minutes if we leave right now." Tom knew this diversion was going to be a good thing.

For three nights a week for the rest of the summer and into the fall, Marcus could avoid small talk about being new to town. He would not be asked how he was feeling. No more, *I'm so sorry to hear about . . .* It would be two hours of drill after drill, working on stance, position, motion, level changes, lifts, arches, and cutbacks. It would be a summer of sweating, scrimmage after scrimmage, and match after match. It would take him right through the falling leaves, the first frost, the early snowfall, and into high school wrestling season. Wrestling became his oasis.

"It's only been a month and he's already making friends. It's good for him. Two of the other kids are going to be teammates at high school," Tom said to Joan as he grabbed the keys and headed to the car. She looked out the window. Marcus was already in the front seat.

"He's anxious to get there. That's a good sign," Joan said.

Tom noticed small changes in Marcus. He swore he'd even seen Marcus smiling on the ride home after the last practice. Three nights a week were great, but Tom wanted something he and Marcus could do together. He wanted something they could share. Open mat time at the jujitsu studio in town would be perfect. Tom introduced Marcus to a fourth night of grappling.

While Tom didn't have the experience to help Marcus become a better wrestler, he could give a more well-rounded understanding of ground fighting. "I'm game, but you are going to have to pull your old gi from the closet and roll on the mat with me."

"Let me check our insurance coverage and stock up on Aleve first." Tom laughed.

Tom's father arrived in the US from Sao Paulo, Brazil, in the late 1940s. Rafael Almeida was among the first practitioners of the Brazilian adaptation of the traditional Japanese martial art. Brazilian jujitsu is a relatively young form of combat sport, taking root in Brazil before World War II. By comparison, the Japanese have been practicing jujitsu for several centuries. The Brazilians placed a greater emphasis on ground fighting and grappling, while Japanese jujitsu placed more emphasis on stand-up techniques, strikes, and throws. Brazilians tended to focus more on sport and competition, while the Japanese emphasized it for exercise and self-defense.

Tom grew up in jujitsu and was an adequate teacher, but watching Marcus quickly surpass his own skill set, Tom sought more formal instruction for Marcus. He was already superb at the ground aspects of BJJ and could take larger and more experienced fighters to the mat with ease. Marcus's submission game was rapidly improving as well. He was quick and powerful, and able to apply a wide array of chokes, armbars, and painful holds manipulating ankles, elbows, and knees. But what caught the eye of his BJJ professor was his strikes. Even as a fifteen-year-old, his adult training partners needed proper headgear and padding whenever sparring with Marcus.

"We have to watch ourselves with him, Tom. He is vicious." The instructor chuckled. "Everything is delivered with maximum destructive intent. He tries to hurt you with every swing, like the best fighters do." The teacher was smiling.

Tom wanted no part of sparring with Marcus. "I'll roll with you, son, but it's been forty years since I got my brown belt. I'm not trading punches with you." Tom gave him a one-armed hug, happy Marcus didn't pull away.

"You are pretty old," Marcus quipped. "I'll go easy on you."

"Bring it, tough guy," Tom shot back. Grabbing Marcus's gi, he tried to spin him off balance but ended up on his back in an armbar.

★ ★ ★

"I hope he isn't pushing his anger down deeper." Joan was concerned. She'd noticed improvements once school started, but she still saw sparks of rage emerge when he was pushed, confronted, or made to think about his mother or Kelly.

"He's getting better. He's doing normal boy things with the other wrestlers. He's found friends and a healthy outlet," Tom replied.

"He's hiding his anger and it's building under a lot of pressure. A quick temper and unfamiliar surroundings are not a healthy mix." She was worried about the first day of wrestling season starting tomorrow.

"I've already spoken to his coach. Everybody is going to keep an eye on him," Tom assured her.

Marcus was an extraordinary student. He was creative, perceptive, curious, motivated, and driven. These traits also made him a good wrestler. But he wasn't good in groups. Scholastics is not a team sport. You competed and excelled alone. It was him versus the subject matter. He'd immerse himself in the material, practice, and game-plan, but he was lonely. He was getting straight As and was a year ahead of most of his peers in math and science.

When the season kicked off in November, Marcus walked into a championship wrestling room. "This team has won six consecutive state championships and is always among the top teams in the Northeast," his coach barked while walking along the circumference of the mat as the squad of high school wrestlers sat in the middle.

The coach knew he had another champion-caliber roster. The team was seasoned and skilled. Marcus was different, though. He was by far the most experienced and gifted wrestler the coaching staff had ever seen. The coach would do his best to motivate the entire team and get them ready for a grueling season, but he knew Marcus would have no difficulty earning a starting position.

He tried to set expectations. "Not everybody is going to wrestle each week. We have multiple potential starters in each weight class. So, many of you will be trading spots, wrestling up in weight classes, or wrestling off for a starting position each week. Be ready." The coach knew that a major conflict was inevitable. Marcus was going to take the spot from a senior who had been starting for the squad for three years and finished third in the state tournament last season.

For the first six matches of the year, Marcus and the senior split time on the mat. Marcus was undefeated and unscored upon in his three matches, and the senior was two and one. It was clear, from the first week of practice, that Marcus was the far superior athlete. As the senior realized his position was at stake, he became increasingly dirty and aggressive in practice.

The match hit the gasoline at a mid-season practice when the senior and Marcus lined up for a drill focused on balance and hand control. The senior broke protocol and applied a head lock and flipped Marcus at full speed. It caught Marcus by surprise. He regained his position on the mat and didn't say a word. The coach noticed the toss and yelled for them to reset and reengage. At the whistle, Marcus circled, dropped to a lower level, and launched a blast double, driving his opponent up and off the mat, over a stack of folded chairs, and into the cement wall at the back of the gymnasium. Marcus stood over him, not saying a word, but not backing away, and not letting him get back up.

"Fuck you, asshole. Try that again and I'll end you," the senior said as he rolled off the pile of chairs.

Marcus showed no reaction. No words. No threats. Nothing. Just the emotionless empty stare of a predator lining up its prey.

The senior tried to get a rise from Marcus. "How's Mom and Dad? I hear your sister is hot."

The coaches had fifty kids on the mats, and they weren't watching closely at first. Now all the coaches' attention was centered on the two of them. "OK, everybody, calm down and reset," Coach said, ready to step in if there was a beef. He blew the whistle. "Wrestle!"

The senior assumed Marcus would look for a blast double again and tried to beat him with a quick shot at a single leg. Marcus let him wrap his arms around his right leg. For the senior to work this hold into a takedown, he should have immediately moved his head to the outside of Marcus's right hip so he could turn Marcus and use his left arm to control Marcus's torso, driving him to the mat. But Marcus blocked his head from moving outside his hip, keeping it buried in his waist. His opponent's next big mistake was trying to step his right leg behind Marcus without having full control. With his head stuck and his right leg now trapped, Marcus reached his left arm through, locking the boy's left leg behind the knee and pulling it in.

It happened in a split second. Any wrestler who tells you they've been pinned in a spladle will do so hiding their shame. Nobody sees it coming until they are upside down, balls in the air, arms and legs wrenched apart and locked into place. It looks horrible, is excruciatingly painful, and is perhaps the most embarrassing way to lose a match because you are pretzeled uncomfortably with feet in the air, arms bound, and no hope of bridging, escaping, or reversing. Everybody in the wrestling room was watching the senior embarrassingly stuck and shrieking, "Let me go. Let me go!"

In practice, the rule is to release the hold when the pin is registered. But Marcus didn't release it. He squeezed and tightened his grip, arching his back, stretching his legs, pulling his shoulders, and straining his biceps against his opponent's weak resistance. Marcus was torturing him. In an official match, a pin takes one second of both shoulder blades being simultaneously on the mat. Marcus held him there for at least thirty seconds of agony. The coaches ran toward them screaming while the rest of the team pointed and laughed. The senior was in a blind frenzy, on the verge of passing out, unable to escape.

Before the coaches had to pull Marcus off, he let the senior go. Marcus sent an unmistakable message about who was better and who owned the varsity spot. Marcus whispered, "Never mention her again," as he loosened his hold.

The senior stood up and threw a wild punch, which Marcus easily ducked. The senior followed with an awkward front kick that Marcus easily caught and trapped under his left arm. Marcus stepped forward and punched him in the stomach, dropping the senior to the mat. Marcus held back with the punch. He could have broken the boy's ribs, but instead he just knocked the wind out of him with a precisely targeted blow. Marcus's temper had been sated. He unclipped his headgear and calmly left the gym.

That night the coach called Tom to let him know what had happened. "Don't worry, Tom. It happens. Two amped teenagers in a contact sport. Things can get heated." The coach didn't want his new prodigy to quit the team. "It gets fiery when the two kids are competing in the same weight class. In this case, the upperclassman is going to lose his spot to the new freshman in town."

"Do you want me to say anything to him?" Tom followed.

"No, I just wanted you to know. He's had a tough go. It will all be OK." The coach told Tom he'd keep an eye on things and was going to let it slide. Tom agreed to forget the incident. In his room, Marcus wasn't fixated on it. He'd won and it was over. But he also wouldn't forget it.

★ ★ ★

The regular season continued without any similar eruptions and a thirty-two-and-zero record for Marcus, the top ranked pound-for-pound wrestler in New Hampshire. Marcus was now gearing for the state tournament and New England championships. All his other teammates were done for the season, but Marcus had at least another three weeks to go. This meant his strict dietary requirements would continue.

Joan coaxed Marcus into joining her weekend sojourn to Stop & Shop. He'd had an earlier practice, and his weight was in the zone. His eating habits during wrestling season were spartan. Good protein, lots of vegetables, no bread, no pasta, no sugar.

A piece of fruit a day would be his reward if his weight were in check. Like all wrestlers, he hated to cut weight. Marcus preferred the suffering of a long slow weight drop and maintenance than the shock of dramatic cuts the day or two before each match.

Many of his teammates would starve themselves, dehydrate their bodies, sit in a sauna, or use a rubber suit, all in the hope of cutting five to seven pounds in the hours before the match. Laxatives were not an uncommon way to shed weight. Marcus saw a kid at nationals shit himself on the mat because he'd gotten the dosage and timing wrong. Marcus had a better way. He did it through portion control, high-quality, balanced foods, and a rigorous workout schedule. It took an immense amount of discipline for a fifteen-year-old.

"You are the one who has to eat it, and you know better than me what will keep you on target," Joan said matter-of-factly. Marcus suspected Joan was using his diet as an excuse to make him join her. He was OK with it. He knew he was difficult on his grandparents. He was trying to be better.

"OK, Nana. Keep me away from the bakery aisle, all right?" He rarely joked. It brought a smile to her face. She wanted to spend time with him. If it meant her spending it in the produce aisle and meat department, so be it.

The parking lot was fairly full when they pulled in. Marcus noticed the senior he scuffled with two months earlier was at the ice cream parlor next door to the grocery store. It was obvious the senior wasn't concerned about making weight. He didn't need to worry. Marcus took his spot, and he hadn't wrestled a live match in weeks. He was sitting with his girlfriend, halfway through an ice cream sundae that had more calories than Marcus would consume in a week. Marcus remembered her from his calculus class. She was a junior and Marcus was the only freshman in the class. She wore a wrestling letterman jacket to class one day and Marcus realized then she was dating the guy he regularly tossed around the gym.

Marcus tried not to stare at the couple as he pushed the cart past the window, but her body language was off. Something was wrong. She retreated into the corner of the booth, gaining distance from her boyfriend. The boy was devouring the bowl. She wasn't eating at all. He was talking, she was looking down, fidgeting with a paper straw.

Marcus walked over to where his grandmother was looking at the outside display of daffodils and pansies. "What do you think? Too early to get you to help me in the garden?"

Marcus ignored her, looking back at the couple in the window.

The first stop was the produce section. Kale, broccoli, spinach, and green beans were on the menu. Marcus's cart would have no carrots, no squash, and no bell peppers. He would not buy anything colorful, because color was an indicator of sugar. There would be no high-sugar foods and nothing high in starch. No potatoes, corn, or bananas. He knew starch breaks down to sugar in the digestive tract. Joan grabbed a package of boneless chicken breasts. Marcus would have loved steak, but his weight was right on the button, and he couldn't afford the fat content. There would be no hot dogs, no hamburger, and no cold cuts. They had too much salt, and salt made the body retain water, and water meant weight. Marcus wouldn't even walk toward the cheese section.

Marcus looked for his cheat foods. Blueberries, raspberries, and blackberries. He would grab small handfuls when he had earned it. Good practice? Won a match? Tap out his grandfather with an ankle lock? Then he'd grant himself a reward. The cart now had a week of food for grilled, steamed, baked, and stir-fried meals. Breakfast, lunch, and dinner would be like this through the state finals and into the New England championships.

Marcus had done his own research on diet and exercise. He read research papers on exercise physiology, diet, and weight cutting. He knew the impacts of fasting, dehydration, and diuretics. He knew about links between poor nutrition and poor weight-loss results. Doing it wrong could lead to depression, decreased cognitive performance, renal problems, and stunted growth. He was willing to suffer a little, but he wasn't willing to risk long-term problems. He knew the science of weight cutting better than his coaches. Marcus needed to maintain his weight and nourish his body.

He tossed Joan three heads of broccoli and gave the cart a furtive last look. "I think we are good, Nana."

"OK, let's go." She laughed at him as he took the long way around to avoid the aisle with bread, cookies, and chips.

Marcus let Joan push the cart to the parking lot. He peeled off to untie and retie his boot. In reality, Marcus was peering into the ice cream shop window to see if the couple was still there. A server was wiping the table, straightening the salt and pepper shakers, and refilling the napkin dispenser. They'd gone. Marcus headed to the station wagon to help his grandmother load the bags. As he turned, he spotted the couple standing and arguing a few cars down from his grandmother.

"Really? You're going to do this now? Right here in the parking lot?" the boy growled.

The girl didn't answer.

"Fine. Go fuck yourself." The senior wasn't concerned others could hear. He was preening and peacocking.

"If you don't think I can find a hotter girlfriend by Monday, you're high. You are such a needy bitch." He was now leaning into her. Her eyes widened with fear and were red from crying. She tried to regain her composure as she backed up away from him.

"I don't want to talk here," she said to him, embarrassed, looking around to see who might be listening.

"Give me my fucking jacket." He extended his arm toward her. She tried to slide it over her sweatshirt, and when she wasn't fast enough he yanked it off. She spun halfway around with the force, falling to her knees.

"Big man," Marcus said under his breath, slowly moving in their direction.

Marcus could only hear bits of the conversation. She said something about "taking time" and "cooling things off." Whatever was in the full conversation triggered the boyfriend to lunge forward aggressively into her, knocking her back against the trunk of his car. She looked afraid and for an escape. She tried to regain her footing but was upended when he gave her a two-handed push, bouncing her off the bumper and onto the ground. She fell hard and cried out.

"Let him go, Marcus. Let. Him. Go." Joan spoke to him softly but sternly.

It was her tone that caught Marcus off guard. What was she asking? Who was she talking about?

He looked up at his grandmother and then he looked down. He was on top of the boy. Marcus pinned the boy's face down on the tar, with a half nelson locked on his left arm and a chicken wing trapping the senior's right arm. The boy's forehead and left cheek were deeply scratched from the pavement and his nose was bleeding profusely. His left eye was swollen, changing colors, and starting to close.

Joan spoke calmly. "Marcus, get off and let him get up. Back away."

All Marcus could think to say was, "Sorry, Nanna." He remembered seeing the girlfriend falling backward and hitting her head. He remembered grabbing the boyfriend's shoulder and spinning him around. He didn't remember anything else.

The whole thing must have happened quickly because other than his grandmother, nobody else came to watch. The ex-girlfriend was now leaning against the car, her sweatshirt twisted and dirty and her scarf on the ground. She mouthed, "Thank you," to Marcus and walked away as Marcus let the boyfriend up.

Before anybody had the chance to come over to see what happened or call the police, the ex-boyfriend got into his car and slowly drove off, but not before he muttered, "It was her fault." He rolled down his window and yelled at her, "I should have broken up with you last summer anyway, bitch."

The boy didn't make eye contact with Marcus or Joan as his tires screeched in acceleration as he drove off.

"Marcus, do you remember what happened?" Joan was in front of him, holding his hands in hers.

He could see tears in her eyes. The sadness and concern were unmistakable. Marcus was still agitated and filled with adrenaline. He yanked his hands back. "Yeah, I remember. He hit her and threw her to the ground. I got angry."

She asked him again, "Marcus, do you remember what happened?"

It was so clear to him. "Yes, I remember. Jesus Christ, Nana. You saw it. He hit Kelly."

Everything froze around him.

He hadn't said her name aloud since the fire.

Suddenly Marcus had trouble standing. All strength left his body. His legs were uneven, and his arms were heavy. His head was light. He was groggy and nauseous. He looked around, confused.

Marcus fell into Joan's arms. It was guttural and anguished. He squeezed her. He couldn't catch his breath. The sobbing would not stop.

CHAPTER 10
Sharing Intimacies

"Marcus. What the hell was that? What did you do to them?" Beth was delicately contemplating a french fry, deciding whether it needed ketchup or not. Soggy fries get ketchup. Crunchy fries don't. This one was perfect, no ketchup necessary, and she popped it into her mouth.

The Starlight Diner was strikingly different from Marcus's original dinner plans at Bistecca. He was hoping for white linen tablecloths, a Chopin martini with three blue-cheese-stuffed olives, truffle and parmesan risotto, a cowboy veal chop cooked medium rare with a great bottle of wine. In front of him was a cheeseburger, medium rare with mushrooms and bacon, and a plate of fries to share with Beth.

The diner was clean and bright. The floor was a black-and-white checked pattern and the eight booths along the wall were upholstered in a red vinyl with silver glitter in them reflecting the fluorescent lights above. Everything was framed in brilliantly polished chrome. Strong coffee and bright lights were a perfect elixir for anybody wanting to stay awake or sober up, which happened here every night. The Starlight was open until 3:00 a.m.

The diner was on the corner, ground level, of the LAG building and was a popular stop for analysts needing take-home meals or seeking late-night refueling. It was 8:00 p.m. and there were four people in the diner besides Marcus and Beth. Two of them were working. Marcus and Beth sat at the corner of the counter on the opposite side of the room from the door so Marcus could see anybody entering. He was fairly certain the men from the bar would not be looking for them, but he was cautious for Beth's sake anyway.

Before Marcus could weave his answer to Beth's question, she put her hands on the counter on either side of her plate of fries and closed her eyes. Marcus watched her head subtly bob side to side and her lips purse and relax as if trying to recall the excitement from thirty minutes ago. Marcus could see she was searching for a mental replay of what happened.

Beth shook her head softly but negatively. "I was less than ten feet away from the whole thing and I can't picture what happened." Then she mumbled about the two women, the four men, the bartender, and other people in the crowd. She was trying to reconstruct the night and huffed, irritated, when she couldn't piece it all together. She was building a puzzle in the dark, discovering pieces were missing.

"OK. I get up and go to the bar to help Ellen and Kari. By the way, I found out their names when you went outside with those jerks."

"Ellen and Kari, yep." Marcus let her tell the story. He'd have less to say and would focus only on the bits he needed her to know.

"They are settling their check and leaving. I'm the tail end of the line heading away from the shit show, and the big guy reaches out and grabs my neck from behind." She looks at Marcus, making sure he's following along.

His mouth is full of food, but he is listening and nodding, signaling to go on.

"I wanted to kill him. And then you are guiding him out the front door."

Marcus bobbed his head, confirming her recollection as pretty accurate.

"The guy looks sick or hurt. Whatever. He isn't able to walk on his own. So, you get him outside, but instead of dropping him on the sidewalk, you drag him two blocks to the alley."

Marcus shrugged his shoulders and used a full mouth of cheeseburger as an excuse not to speak.

Beth's voice became incredulous. "What happened? How did he go from all handsy to legless? I'm confused."

Marcus swallowed. "Teddy. His name is Teddy." He took a french fry off her plate and dropped it in his mouth.

"OK, Teddy. You have Teddy's arm over your shoulder, and you are walking him out the door. Did his friends follow you right away?" Beth wasn't sure if she should reconstruct the story chronologically, or whether to follow each character.

"Forget that. How did Teddy go from grabbing me to wobbling out the door with you?" Beth decided to follow Teddy's timeline. It was her most significant curiosity, but she interrupted her own interrogation. "OK, OK. Start with this. Why didn't you drop him on the sidewalk and come back inside? Why not let his friends deal with it? Why take him away? And his buddy. He ran by me looking like he'd seen a murder. Where were the other two guys?" Beth started to pick up the tempo of her questions.

"Jesus Christ, Marcus, what did you do?" Her tone was more of a stunned laugh than anger. Her body language, with eyes wide, mouth open, balanced on the edge of the stool, leaning sharply toward him, screamed, "Tell me!"

"OK. That's a lot of questions." He took another fry, preparing to respond to at least part of her interrogation.

"Here is the rundown. You did the hard work. You made sure Ellen and Kari were safe. After that I just needed to get Teddy and his friends away from the three of you as quickly and quietly as I could."

Beth nodded. "And how did you do that?" she asked playfully.

"By making him unable to walk," he responded matter-of-factly.

"You made him unable to walk," she repeated in disbelief.

"I had to help him because he lost his balance after I hit him in the ribs."

She leaned back, studying his face. She'd seen Marcus for the first time yesterday and been formally introduced thirteen hours ago. She could not tell if he was holding back on purpose or casually omitting key facts, but he was not being cooperative. She tightened her lips, tilted her head, and gave him a highly skeptical glance, forcing Marcus to reveal more.

"He laid his hands on you. You weren't OK with that, and neither was I," Marcus added.

"And that made him unable to walk?"

"When you're hit in the right spot, yeah."

"Why take him and his friends two blocks from the bar? The situation was over. Just leave him outside." Her questioning was getting more narrowly focused.

"I didn't drop him on the sidewalk because it would have drawn a lot of attention from pedestrians, and his friends might have acted badly. I didn't want an argument or scuffle where you might be dragged in. So, I led them away." His answer provided only the barest details. It made sense, but it lacked the color and depth she wanted.

Beth shifted back on the stool and swiveled so she was squarely facing him. "All right. So, you lead them a few blocks away. Now you are in the alley with the guy who couldn't walk . . ." She was unable to hide her frustration in the nonanswers.

Marcus interjected, "Teddy," breaking the tension with a chuckle.

Beth laughed. "OK, Teddy. So, you lead them all a few blocks down the street and now you are in the alley with Teddy. There are four of them and you. Four against one. The next thing there is one of them running away and you come out looking fresh, like nothing happened. What happened to Teddy and his friends?" She touched on things he'd rather not share right now with somebody he met only a few hours earlier in the day.

"I tried to persuade them it was a bad idea to escalate this any further. Teddy was still catching his breath, so it was really only three against one. Two of them needed a bit more convincing. The guy who ran away thought it was a good idea to call it a day, so he left."

Beth didn't comment. Instead, she leaned in, extended her arms toward him, and opened her palms upward rather than say, *I want more.*

"I'm pretty comfortable defending myself," was all he offered.

Marcus hoped to change the subject. Based on previous relationships, he knew that most people don't react well to fight sports. He didn't want his relationship with Beth to begin with her looking at him funny. He'd shared all he was comfortable with for now. She was safe and that was his goal.

Marcus summed up their evening. "To recap: They were being jerks. You handled it perfectly with Ellen and Kari. Nobody is permanently injured, and I'm having a greasy burger and fries instead of a perfectly grilled veal chop." He took a big bite. The burger was cold, but it was still dripping juices onto his plate. He hoped a mouthful of food and his lies of omission were enough to close the day.

"Fine. Who's Kelly?"

He nearly choked when she said it. He still had visions of how his father used to grab Kelly's neck from behind and pull her down. Marcus hadn't talked about his sister with anybody but his grandparents since the fire. He still thought about her every day, but nightmares no longer jolted him from sleep with the horrific images. Instead, he imagined seeing her in crowds. When his eyes were closed, Marcus could still see her face and intensely brown eyes. In a certain light, her eyes were nearly black, but soulful, warm, and tender, unable to hide her sadness or pain. Until two days ago, Marcus had never seen anybody else with eyes like that. Not until Beth.

"She was my sister. I lost her and my parents when I was fourteen."

"I'm sorry." Beth immediately changed her tone. The interrogation suddenly ended. She swiveled her seat toward him and slid closer, inviting him to share.

Marcus started slowly. He tried to be as clinical as possible. She recognized his change. The man who was incredibly calm and confident at the bar was now diminished. His eyes cast down and his shoulders slumped forward. Beth could see his discomfort growing as his voice softened and became more raspy.

A moment ago, Marcus didn't want to tell her anything about fighting, but now he was cracking open the spigot to his whole family tale. He felt like he was fourteen years old again. He told Beth everything. Where he grew up. How his sister and mother died. What life was like for an orphan living with his grandparents in northern New Hampshire. His major in college. Where he went to grad school. How he met Rich. He told Beth the entire truth about everything in his background. Everything but the fighting; he didn't want her to be intimated.

Beth was stoic and patient and fully in the moment. For nearly an hour she never broke eye contact. She sensed his surprise at her reaction. As his story unfolded he gradually regained his composure, straightened his posture, and recovered his voice. The more intently she listened the more easily he shared. Beth never looked at her watch, never shifted her gaze toward the waitress restocking cleaned plates and cups, and never concocted a reason to leave. Her eyes never left his. They were sad and comforting eyes, like Kelly's, but different. Wiser. Stronger. Reassuring.

Beth reached for his hand. Her hold was soft and warm. Marcus's tale was poignant and heartbreaking. She would have sat there listening until closing time if he would keep talking. But his story concluded.

"And that's it." He paused. "The life story of Marcus Shea from birth to me finishing this last french fry at the Starlight." He ran it through the dollop of ketchup on her plate and put it in his mouth.

He was struck with a moment of clarity at what he'd shared, and he was overcome with a feeling of humiliation. "This was a bad idea. I'm sorry," he said, pulling his hands from hers. He turned his eyes toward the door.

"No. Please, no. You have nothing to be sorry about. It was beautiful. Don't be ashamed." She wanted to hold him. He noticed her blushing. He wanted to be held.

Beth stretched toward him, placed her hands on his shoulders, and said, "Well, Mr. Shea, we have something in common. I also lost my only sibling. It was four years ago."

CHAPTER 11
Elizabetta's Rise

They sat on a grassy mound shooting tin cans with a Smith & Wesson .22-caliber rifle. She wasn't interested in target practice, but she was infatuated with him. He was more like a brother than a cousin. Her real brother was much older, and he didn't spend any time with her. She was lonely. Elizabetta was seven, four years younger than he was.

"*Hace tanto calor. ¿No podemos volver y nadar en la piscina?*" (It's so hot. Can't we go back and swim in the pool?) Elizabetta asked, knowing Enrique wasn't interested in going home. Summer in Central Mexico is hot, dry, and dusty. The midday sun is unrelenting and suffocating. It broils the ground, evaporating all the moisture from the soil and plants. What is green and growing in early spring turns yellow and brown in August. The only green in sight was a lone cactus with its spiny arms reaching upward. Even the birds, snakes, and insects took refuge from the direct afternoon sun.

Elizabetta didn't whine, but she also wanted to swim. Enrique was teaching her to dive and to do the backstroke, and she almost beat him in a race last week. She didn't want to sit in a hot field and shoot cans.

"Beth, can we practice our English?" He said it perfectly. Listening to Enrique, you couldn't tell he was from Central Mexico. His short-cropped hair was dark brown, matching his eyes. He was tall and lean. Lengthy muscles. He looked like a military school recruit. His English was flawless, with little residue of a Spanish accent. He practiced a lot and welcomed having his cousin there to practice more.

Beth complied. "I'm hot. Can't we go swimming?" Her English was superb.

Enrique smiled. "How about a bet? If you hit more cans in a row than me, we can go back and swim." Enrique was already walking forward to prop the targets on the fence. Five on the right side of the post and five on the left side.

"If I win, we will go swimming?" She hesitated with the question because he had a habit of tricking her.

Enrique nodded.

"What do you get if you win?" she asked.

"If I win, we go on a hike to the river and back."

"I don't want to go on a hike." She sighed, rolling her eyes. But a bet is a bet. At least with this bet, she'd have a chance of going swimming.

"I'll go first." Enrique loaded the weapon. He knew he was not going home early today.

Enrique pulled the trigger in rapid succession, hitting the first four cans dead center, knocking them to the ground. On the fifth, he paused. When he pulled the trigger, the shot went a few centimeters high and right. He missed. On purpose.

"Your turn," he said, handing her the rifle. The ten-round magazine had five shots left.

Beth cherished Enrique's attention and his role as her surrogate older brother. She was smart, funny, and affectionate. She was also isolated and alone. Her mother and father struggled and fought and ignored her. Enrique filled the void and welcomed it as his role and responsibility.

Beth radiated when Enrique was with her. They did things kids do. They played and laughed, shared stories, and talked about school. They competed in everything. Running, swimming, horseback riding, board games, and, today, shooting. As her "older brother" he made her happy, gave her confidence, chased her demons, and made her feel safe. When she was visiting the hacienda, it was always Enrique's job to keep her busy and away from the adults. The looks she got and the pointed tone from her uncles let her know she wasn't really welcome there. It fell to Enrique to keep her out of the way.

Today, Enrique's father told her not to come back to the house until 3:00 p.m., when all his business would be complete. Afterward, she and Enrique could do whatever they wanted. As long as Beth was out of sight while they conducted business, Carlos would tolerate her.

"I can't beat you." Beth smiled, impressed by Enrique's aim. "You're much better than me." She puffed out her lower lip, tilted her head down, and gently kicked some stones with her left foot, looking for sympathy. She wanted to even the odds. Enrique knew she was bargaining.

"OK. Move a bit closer." Enrique took his heel and dragged a line in the dirt ten feet closer than where he had fired from. She was now ten yards from the targets.

"That's fair," she said in perfect English, thinking she tricked him into giving her an advantage.

He smiled and pointed at the targets. "It's your turn." He knelt behind and to her left. His left hand helped her find the right aiming position and his right hand was on her waist to make sure she had a proper stance.

"Perfect. Now spread your feet a little bit more for a solid base." She paid close attention.

"Now hold it like this. Yes. Put your hand right here."

She loved it when he took time to teach her.

"How does this feel?"

"Good." Beth nodded with the rifle properly shouldered.

"OK. Close your left eye and look through your right eye. Can you see the sight and the target?" He paused, making sure she was ready. "Here is the hard part. Now take long, slow deep breaths looking at the target. Be steady. You want to slowly squeeze the trigger. Don't pull it."

Enrique was the one who taught her to ride a bike and how to catch a baseball. He helped her with her schoolwork. He taught her ways to deal with boys bothering her at school. He was patient and never got frustrated or angry when she didn't get it right away.

Beth's first shot nicked the top of the can. It wobbled, tipped, and fell.

"Awesome. You got the first one. It's now four to one."

He got her set for the second shot.

"I can do it myself," she insisted.

This time she hit it in the center.

"Now it's four to two," she said proudly, head still, without taking her eye off the next target.

Enrique stepped back to let her do it. Her third shot was in the center again.

Beth was so excited. "It's four to three. Four to three!"

He loved her smile and how big her eyes got when she was having fun. Her body language changed when she had confidence. She stood taller. She held her head higher. Her shoulders were back.

She took the fourth shot, and it ripped right through the middle of the can. "Four to four." She was having fun now. "I'm going to win!" she said proudly.

As she focused on the fifth shot, Enrique leaned forward and whispered in her ear. "Did you know Maxie had puppies? Eight of them. Five boys and three girls. If you make this next shot, we can go to the barn and play with them after we go swimming."

Her pulse quickened. Her stance tightened. She snapped the trigger back and missed the fifth can by two feet.

"That was great. Four in a row!" Enrique smiled, wryly.

"Hey. You made me miss." She pouted but wasn't really mad.

"Did I?" He posed, pretending to be hurt by the accusation.

"What do we do now? We tied." Beth could guess his answer.

"Well, since we tied, we won't go on the hike. But we also can't go swimming until later."

She had an idea. "OK, how about this? Let's do more target practice and then see the puppies."

"Perfect." Enrique always had a way of getting what he wanted. He wanted to stay in the field shooting and now Beth happily agreed. Another hour and they could go back to the house. Father's guests would be gone, and they'd have the backyard, pool, and gardens to themselves.

Afternoons like this were what Beth remembered so vividly about her childhood. Her only fond memories of Mexico centered on Enrique. Beth's mother worked every day at the hacienda, leaving her father as her primary caregiver. Her father didn't have family and he avoided her mom's brothers as much as possible. Mom and Dad argued a lot. Beth's real brother joined the local police force and left home, deserting Beth. She felt the ache of being ignored by everyone. Everyone, except Enrique. She knew he was always there for her, even when he was playfully manipulating her.

When Enrique moved to the US, Beth was heartbroken. She was nine years old. Being a child of a wealthy family in Central Mexico was hard and lonely. Attending a Montessori school, having private tutors, and an omnipresent security staff stifled the peer connections she craved. She never understood why kids in her class didn't want to play, but she heard whispers about staying away from her. Beth's parents never let her invite classmates to their house, and Beth was never invited to their homes either. Beth sensed that her classmates' parents were afraid of her. Teachers always asked how her uncles were doing. They never asked about her mother and father. It was always about Carlos and Alejandro.

It would have been a dreadful existence for a child, if not for her cousin. Enrique was her anchor, and she was set adrift when he left to live with a family in Connecticut to attend boarding school. Beth remembered the shock and the endless nights of crying when he flew off.

Enrique promised her nothing would change and that they would talk a lot. But after a few months, his calls became less frequent to the point of never. Within a year, all she got was an occasional email or text from him. She ached for his voice. It was a terrible time for Beth. Nobody cared about where she was or what she was doing. Nobody paid attention to her. She was invisible. Her mother and father were divorcing, and nobody helped Beth understand or cope. Her mother was going to stay in Mexico while her father accepted a new job in Houston. It was decided, not by her, that she would move to the US with him. Nobody asked Beth what she wanted. Her mother tossed her aside, and her father simply packed her up and took her with him. There was no discussion.

She faced the move, the loss of connection to her home, the sting of her parents' divorce, and the abandonment from her mother alone, without her cousin.

★ ★ ★

Enrique lived in affluence in Fairfield County, Connecticut. Beth's reality was different. The odor in Houston, more than anything, was a constant reminder she wasn't home. The temperature, vegetation, and soil were similar to Mexico. But the smell was different and unpleasant. Scents of cedarwood and cinnamon were missing. If she closed her eyes, she could remember the smell of chilies cooking and fresh agave growing. Now she was buffeted by wafts of petroleum. There were ten major refineries processing more than 2.5 million barrels of crude oil a day within a few miles of her bedroom. She perpetually felt grease in her hair and on her skin. She missed the hills, low desert, and her cousin. She wanted it the way it used to be.

Beth's new school was sufficient. She was a strong student, though not a standout. She would not have dozens of colleges clamoring after her with promises of scholarships like Enrique. If she stayed on track, she'd get into a good university and have a chance to succeed, though she would never have a golden path like her cousin.

When her phone buzzed during class, her trigonometry teacher frowned. "Beth, you know the rules." He wouldn't confiscate the phone as punishment this time. "Airplane mode, now," he demanded.

She glimpsed the text message before she switched to silent mode: "CMB when class is over – E."

"Yes, sir." But Beth could barely contain her joy. Enrique rarely texted and never talked. She couldn't wait.

Beth often got extra consideration from the faculty. She was a solid A and B student with some very difficult classes. Her math and science teachers saw a spark. Confiscating her phone wasn't worth it. There was no need to add more drama to her life. As a talented, bilingual ninth grader who was still finding her way and just starting to make friends, it was important to her teachers to keep her engaged and enthusiastic about her studies. The teachers regularly pushed her, giving her assignments tenth- and eleventh-grade students were struggling with. Calculus, physics, and coding assignments were how she spent her free time.

When class broke, Beth could scarcely contain her joy. She ran through the hallway to her locker, grabbed her backpack, and hurried out the door. It was a ten-minute walk home, which she would stretch to over thirty minutes today talking to Enrique.

She was good at hiding her frustrations and sadness from her father. He was too busy to notice the subtle signs anyway. Her teachers had dozens of kids they needed to monitor, many of whom were in far tougher situations than Beth. They didn't see her suffering. Enrique hadn't spoken to her in months, but he recognized the sullen tone and deflections the moment she spoke about Houston.

"Hey, kiddo, how is it going?"

"I guess it's OK. I have a lot of homework and I made the track team. Papa is always busy." There was little enthusiasm in her voice.

"You don't sound very happy."

Beth could hide her emotions from everybody else, but not from Enrique. He knew it was his job, like it had been back home, to get her to refocus.

"Are you still working the statistics proof you texted me? The one your teacher gave you last month?" He was honestly curious, because as Beth described it via text, he wasn't sure he could demonstrate the theorem. He was a college freshman, and she was a ninth grader.

"Yeah, I solved it. The teacher game me another one. He said it's a problem he worked on when he was in college. I haven't started it yet."

She was apathetic about her school and wanted to talk about Enrique and his life. When he was evaluating his college scholarship opportunities, Beth texted him links to UT, Rice, and Baylor, hoping she could convince him to enroll in an engineering school in Texas closer to her. She could tell by his delayed text responses he was not interested in Texas.

"It's way different than high school. A lot more freedom, but a lot more responsibility. You are going to love it when you go to college." Enrique was careful to tell her what she needed to hear. He stressed how fun it was to work hard and succeed. Succeed in scholastics, succeed in athletics, succeed socially. He was selling her on the approach, process, and outcomes of hard work. It was the guidance her father did not provide.

"Let's set up some regular calls. Every other week. Just the two of us. I want to get you focused on college and what you need to do now to get ready."

"I'd like that." Beth didn't care what they talked about, as long as she could hear his voice.

Within minutes, Enrique pivoted the conversation, and with

it, her attitude. Beth was now focused on what she needed to do to be like him. By the time she got to her driveway she was convinced she could get straight As and go to any college she wanted. She believed, truly believed, in her abilities. Enrique got her back on track.

★ ★ ★

As Beth progressed to her sophomore and junior years of high school, her calls with Enrique became more regular and more impactful. Once she was on the path set by Enrique, Beth only needed small course corrections now and then, and Enrique provided them. He'd provide acknowledgement of her successes or a disappointing sigh to get her reengaged. A tap here and a push there. Congratulations and recognition or a kick in the ass, whichever was needed. All were small adjustments pointing her in a direction he wanted her to go. He gave her the right words of encouragement, and the right logic at the right time to help her make the right choices, or at least the choices he wanted her to make. Which classes to take. Which books to read. Which extracurricular activities to join. Which boys to date. He was her mentor and advisor through it all.

The call from Enrique at the end of her first month at graduate school caught her by surprise. They'd spoken the week before about her area of concentration and class load, and she wasn't expecting a follow-up discussion so quickly.

She could hear the seriousness and somberness in his voice. Something was wrong. Enrique wasn't his typical brash self. "I'm sorry, honey. Your brother was reported missing. My father didn't have any details. I wanted you to know."

He just dropped the news on her without any introduction or small talk.

"Missing? How long?" She hadn't seen or spoken to her brother, or her mother, in over six years. It was like she was getting unhappy news about a person she didn't really know. She empathized but wasn't sorrowful. She felt badly for her mother, now alone in Mexico, and for her father, losing his only son, but she didn't have a relationship with her brother, so she wasn't sure which reactions to have. It was strange knowing she should be sad, but she couldn't tap into any of those emotions without a connection to him or her mother.

"He hasn't been seen for over a week. His fellow officers are searching for him. Our people are in touch with the authorities."

Beth wondered who "our people" were. In fact, she found the whole conversation with Enrique odd. He was so clinical with specific details and timelines about where her brother went missing and how the search was progressing, but he showed little emotion at how the news might affect her, which made his next request curious.

"Please don't tell your father I told you. I don't want to come between you and your dad. If he calls you to share the news, I need you to pretend you heard it from him first." Beth didn't know it, but this was her first loyalty test. It was a way for Enrique to see if he could trust her discretion. Enrique would know if she tipped off her father or wasn't able to feign surprise. If Beth's father called her mother to question how Beth found out, Enrique's father and uncle would let Enrique know.

"Of course," she replied. "I'll play dumb."

Beth marveled at how quickly Enrique could switch lanes. His tone instantly brightened as he spent the next few minutes talking about his fledgling new business, and how he'd love her to work for him when she graduated. She marveled at how he could flip a switch like that. Melancholy to exuberant, instantly. She wished she could just turn off her emotions.

Two days later, her father called her to tell her about her brother. He didn't provide nearly as much detail as Enrique had shared. So, it was easy for Beth to pretend she was hearing it for the first time.

"Your brother was an officer in Buenaventura. You remember, it's about two hours northwest of Chihuahua."

She tried to remember the landscape, the sky, and the smells.

"He'd been working there for several years and just received a promotion. He was assigned to a task force cooperating with the military." It was all news Enrique had shared, but with a lot less detail. Enrique knew his rank, knew the name of his unit, and knew the specific military teams he was engaged with. He knew the types of equipment they used and how many men were searching for him.

Her father continued, "He vanished. It could have been an accident, or smugglers. Nobody knows."

Beth knew her mother would be devasted, but her father forbade her from calling Isabel in Mexico. "Your mother doesn't need you making her more upset. She's too busy helping your uncles." Her father paused. "I'm sorry, I didn't mean it that way. Let's just give her time."

"Fine. I won't call her."

With that, the conversation was over. Her father simply accepted the fact his only son was very likely dead.

When Beth moved from Houston to college in North Carolina and then graduate school in Virginia, her interactions with her father were put on a steady decline. After her brother was declared dead, a year after Enrique called her about it, she never had another reason to speak to her mother. And now she had no reason to speak with her father. Enrique was her only remaining family now and he continued to guide, direct, and advise her. Small corrections with each discussion. He helped her select her graduate school and her major in computer science, even helping to pay her tuition. Enrique provided the recommendation helping her to land her first job as a network security analyst at a financial services firm in Charlotte. Enrique promised he'd have a job for her when she was ready. She showed him time and again that she'd accept his guidance, act on his requests, and be worthy of his confidence.

★ ★ ★

It was a cool spring morning in Charlotte. The cityscape was framed in a tapestry of flowering trees and a thin fog, hovering before the warming sun. Enrique was in town for meetings with clients of his new company. He asked to meet Beth for coffee. It was a dark and out-of-the-way diner in a less desirable part of town, a place where there was little risk of being seen by somebody she knew, or he knew. It wasn't a social call. His dark gray suit, light blue shirt, and navy patterned tie befit his role and executive status. His hair was perfectly trimmed. He was clean shaven and chiseled. His demeanor mirrored his looks. He was serious. More serious than she'd ever seen him.

Before the coffee was poured he asked, "Do you want the job?" Enrique jumped right to the close.

"Of course I do!" Beth was hoping this day would come.

"Swear to me you will do as I say. If you do, you have the job. You will make more money than you could dream of. If you work for me, together we can change the world." Enrique remained solemn and serious.

"Of course." Her answer didn't require any thought. Of course she'd obey her cousin. She

owed him everything. She wanted to be with him.

"I'm serious, Beth. What I'm saying is nonnegotiable. I need your full loyalty." His sharp stare froze her. It was penetrating.

"I understand," she replied timidly. "You know I'm loyal to you. You are my family. My only family. I'll do whatever you say, Enrique."

"I'm not Enrique. My name is Rich Anderson. Never say the name Enrique Banderas again."

"Why?" Beth was bewildered.

"Your offer depends on this. I need your answer. Do you swear?" Rich was deadly serious. "I need to be able to trust you."

"Of course. You can trust me," Beth assured him.

"Swear to it." Rich's demeanor was grave and serious. "You can never tell anyone you are my cousin, and you can never use my old name, or I'll have to cut you out of my life. You'll have nobody."

It was the first time he'd ever threatened her. Beth trembled. "I swear."

"Great. It will take a few months to get everything set, but welcome aboard LAG."

CHAPTER 12
Temptations Aplenty

"I hate it here, Rich," Beth lamented. "When can I come to Boston and work for you like we discussed?"

"Just a little longer. I promise." Rich came off mute.

"These people have no clue. This whole bank could implode tomorrow, and they'd never see it coming. They have me chasing ATM skimmers and small-time identity thieves."

"Aren't those major problems?" Rich answered without giving her his undivided attention. He was copyediting a draft press release for LAG's Q1 earnings and not really listening.

Beth still struggled with his new identity, but in six months, she'd never broken her promise. "They are problems, but nobody here is concerned about more catastrophic threats like incursions, data breaches, ransomware, and denial of service. This bank has no protections or policies in place."

Beth impatiently awaited the day when Rich would give her a formal offer and she'd move to Boston to join LAG, but it was hard. The monotony and fruitlessness of her current job was unbearable. Her role, as director of security and network integrity for a regional bank in North Carolina, was unchallenging. She spent her time monitoring network activity for threats, conducting risk assessments, and configuring security tools.

Beth was superb at her job, but she saw bigger, insolvable challenges on the horizon. There were problems her management team simply wasn't prepared, or willing, to address. "These guys need help, Rich. Your LAG team is in here working with our CIO and CEO. You need to tell your analysts to grow a pair. They are sugarcoating their recommendations to our management team. They are not driving action. I'm trying to help their cause, but your analysts are pretty weak."

"Easy, Beth. These are the people you'll be working with when you join us. Don't burn bridges."

"I'm telling you, they aren't making a difference. You said you wanted LAG to change the world. These guys can't cut it." Beth paused for him to agree. Silence.

"Rogue states and bad actors are using new software and more powerful systems to attack US companies. Hackers are more brazen than ever. They are not only targeting customers and employees, they are also targeting suppliers and financiers, trying to corrupt their systems. Malware and ransomware are becoming common. My bosses are only bothered by stolen ATM cards and falsified loan requests. Honestly, if I have to chase down one more low-level mortgage scam I'm going to jump off the roof."

Beth warned her CIO, the bank president, and members of their board that they were vulnerable, but they would not listen. She passionately pleaded for them to increase security investments, to no avail. The executive team hired her because she was beautiful. They promoted her because she was smart. But the good-old-boy patronization, innuendo, and trivialization of her ideas was frustrating. Beth's strong opinions, sharp wit, and growing sarcasm clashed with the prejudices of the executive team. It was clear she didn't have the stature or visibility to drive change as an employee of the bank. She would do it all as an LAG analyst.

Beth saw firsthand the potential for LAG. Several analysts were in her offices regularly supporting her CIO's key initiatives. The bank's management team eagerly listened to and enacted the recommendations from LAG, but summarily dismissed or ignored those same recommendations when Beth made them.

Things had gotten marginally better for Beth after Rich met with the bank's operating committee and requested she be assigned as the key point of interaction between the bank and LAG. He told them that his analyst team spotted her expertise and that she'd be an ideal conduit between their organizations. Until this point, Beth toiled prettily in the background. With Rich's support and accolades, she gained visibility and stature in her role. But even with her elevated status, she believed the recommendations LAG was making to the bank were too watered down.

"C'mon, Rich. Get me out of here," Beth pleaded.

"Has it gotten better since I spoke to your boss?"

"Yes, but I can do so much more. I know more about this tech than your analysts do. I just don't have the cachet of being an LAG analyst. I want to make a difference. I can't do that here, from the inside."

"Soon. Be patient."

"Ugh." Beth was irritated. "You've been saying that for months."

"Cut your teeth at the bank a bit longer. I need my team to gain real-world expertise about how banks work with regulatory agencies to identify suspicious transactions, prevent money laundering, and identify fraud. We need that expertise."

"OK. I'm ready as soon as you need me," she said, disappointed.

Rich called Beth to check in from places like Rome, Barcelona, Mumbai, and Perth. Every time they spoke she became even more anxious to move to Boston. Rich would text her with links to business articles highlighting LAG's growth. He made sure she watched him on the nightly news when he testified before Congress on global technology trends and investments. It was odd for Beth to see his nameplate, *Rich Anderson, CEO, LAG*, alone at a long table, explaining to a Kentucky congressman about the emerging security risks facing US businesses from cyberattacks, data breaches, mobile computing, and social media.

The chance to be with her cousin, even if she couldn't reveal their relationship, was irresistible. The offer finally came from Rich on a Saturday in April, five days after the devastating Boston marathon bombing. Videos of the terror attack still played on nightly news broadcasts. Rich's offices were just beyond the finish line. She was surprised when Rich called her, not to tell her he was safe, but to tell her to pack up and move to Boston.

"Hey, Beth. It's time. The offer is in the mail."

"Is everybody OK? It looked horrible on TV."

"Everybody is fine. Business as usual." Rich impatiently dismissed her concern.

"We are about to reach another milestone and I need you here. I need somebody I can trust." He was tapping into her loyalty. "You'll love it here. The people, the opportunity to travel. The clients we are helping. We are making a difference."

"You don't need to push, Rich, I'm in," Beth interrupted.

Rich kept selling. "And the compensation. Wow. The salary is way above your current level. With the signing bonus, stock grants, and performance incentives you will crush it."

The offer letter arrived the next morning. She signed it first, then she read the details, objectives, and job description. She noted immediately that she would not be working directly for Rich. She nodded approvingly, knowing that would have been awkward. She wanted to prove she was worthy, without his help. Reporting to Marcus Shea was better than reporting directly to Rich.

★ ★ ★

From their first introduction in the conference room, Beth and Marcus found a cadence that worked. Their style was casual and comfortable. They were a team. They were connected. Their relationship made the late nights and a frenetic pace of building a business bearable. They could be fully focused on work while in the office, but when they were outside work, they flipped a switch. If a stranger saw them together outside the office, they'd recognize a couple falling in love. Smiling, laughing, warm glances, subtle touches punctuating their conversations. It was young and new, and Beth liked it. She was sure Marcus did too. She saw a change in him when they were alone. He was charming, sweet, and protective.

She liked when he pulled out her chair when they were at dinner and how he rushed forward to open doors. She welcomed it when he walked her home or shielded her from traffic or carried her groceries. Beth recognized what he was doing. He was her guardian. Marcus wasn't overbearing or intrusive, just protective. She had fun with it, dramatically overplaying the damsel in distress if he failed to open a cab door or check her apartment for ghosts.

Two years into their roles, and the Emerging Tech Team propelled LAG to surpass $1 billion in revenues. The foursome of Marcus, Beth, Jeff, and Deb dramatically outperformed every other group at LAG. All new tech markets fell into their domain. Artificial intelligence, machine learning, quantum computing, augmented reality, and security were their areas of specialty, but anything new and visionary cleared their desks first. Clients hungrily booked time with the Emerging Tech Team. On any day, dozens of vendors jockeyed to brief them on their latest offerings. Industry events wanted them as keynote speakers. Members of the business press sought them out for comments on the latest trends and tech. Marcus was on TV and in print nearly as much as Rich. But nurturing a relationship with Marcus, while working eighty hours a week, was a complicated juggling act.

LAG was still a young company, a city company, with lots of young people who worked brutally long hours and traveled together extensively. Staff socialized regularly and fraternized often as well. Professionalism was vital; however, there were no steadfast rules banning relationships among staff, even between a boss and a subordinate, provided good judgement and some discretion was employed. The HR team had more important things to focus on, like hiring and onboarding dozens of new analysts a quarter.

Nobody, including Rich, cared that Beth and Marcus were getting close. There were myriad examples of how it could work at LAG, the prime example being Jeff Knox and Deb Walters. They were married a year after they'd joined LAG. They proved it could work.

Beth celebrated her two-year anniversary at LAG, unceremoniously, with a thirteen-hour day to finish a ninety-hour workweek. It had been four years since Enrique confided his identity change to her. In the beginning it was hard calling him Rich, but it was now ingrained. There was no reflexive memory to call him anything else.

Beth was rewarded for her loyalty. Her most recent pay stub was in an envelope on her desk. Two years at LAG and she'd paid off all her student loans and all her credit cards, leased a sexy new BMW X6, and put over $30,000 into savings on top of a maxed 401(k).

But the workload was enormous. Beth felt it. Early mornings, late nights, long weeks, and working weekends were needed to keep up with client demands. There was no time to decompress or relax.

The Emerging Tech Team appreciated Marcus's collaborative style. He taught them their approach: agree on the priorities, collaborate on the approach, move forward together, and always look forward. The workloads were too high and client demands too important to allow distractions, indecision, or internal conflicts to sidetrack them. There wasn't time for debate or second-guessing once they started a project, so everybody needed to be on board at the start. It was comfortable for Marcus. It was how he'd approached wrestling. Now he had the team mimicking his style. Once a decision was made or a project delivered, there was no time to dissect it. They had to keep going. Beth knew that Marcus was there to protect his team from interference and distraction. That was the problem. The growing demands on their time was breaking the machinery.

✯ ✯ ✯

Beth felt the stresses everybody else did. What made it palatable was the time she spent with Marcus, inside the office and out. Late nights and weekends working together made it tolerable, but they were both so busy that time together, working or relaxing, was less frequent. She'd only been to his cabin in New Hampshire once since he'd bought it.

Beth expected to work late on Friday anyway when Rich put time on her calendar for a one-on-one meeting at 8:00 p.m. The invitation was clear, he wanted to meet with her alone, apart from Marcus and the team. Rich was always in the office roaming the halls, popping into meetings, and joining research discussions. His request didn't trigger any caution. As CEO, he often met with analysts and consultants to personally see how they were servicing clients.

Rich strode into her office with purpose. There would be no casual discussion or small talk. He closed the door and sat heavily in the chair opposite her desk. "I need your help." He added, "But nobody on the team can know," he paused, "at least for now."

Beth rocked forward perplexed, but before she could ask for clarity, Rich repeated, "Nobody can know. Not Marcus, not Deb, and especially not Jeff. Nobody in LAG."

The whole thing began so innocently. It was a plea. "I need your help."

"What can I do?"

Rich shared a vision of magnificent outcomes and incredible benefits. Faster growth, higher salaries, bigger bonuses, more recognition. Beth recognized the approach from when they were kids. Rich would paint a glorious picture of the destination but be short on the details of the journey. Only when you got halfway there did you realize it would be easier to plow forward than to double back.

Beth listened without interruption as Rich made one simple ask, "Can you get me draft copies of the research Jeff is writing?" Rich asked. "I want to see which vendors LAG is planning to endorse before we publish."

"I have access," Beth started, "but . . ."

"Perfect." Rich cut her off.

She continued, "Jeff is pretty protective of his work in progress."

"Can you or can't you help me?" he pressed.

"Is there an ethics or governance issue?" Beth was certain Jeff did nothing wrong but was unsure about LAG's policy about providing early access to draft research outside the authoring team. She leaned forward, elbows on the desk, encouraging Rich to provide more detail.

"I *am* the governance board. I'm the one who wrote all the rules and guidelines for compliance and client confidentiality. I'm just looking for some new ways to leverage our research." His exasperation was emphasized, making sure she knew he was mildly annoyed. Since they were kids, this was always how their debates would begin. She'd point out a perceived conflict or possible hypocrisy and he'd soothe her, assuring her everything was fine.

"Yeah, but . . ." She tried to reframe her question.

Rich talked over her objection. "Protection of our data and recommendations is important. Separation between the CIOs we consult for and the vendors who we advise needs to be absolute."

She was nodding. Yes. Yes.

"I'm looking to change a few things and looking for ways we can get more value from the research we already generate," he stressed, "while protecting that balance."

Beth did her best to hide her uncertainty behind a composed façade. "I guess it's OK." Beth capitulated with a slide backward in her chair and a slight slouch.

Rich recognized her retreat. "I just want to see the base research earlier, before it is accessible to clients." He made it easy and straightforward. "That way I can look for ways to better leverage the work you are doing and get other teams on board."

Beth's demeanor changed with mention of other teams. It sounded reasonable, but she offered one final hitch. "Why not ask Jeff directly for access yourself? You are the head of research. Why do this without him knowing?"

"I don't want Jeff to think I'm looking over his shoulder. He gets flaky. I don't want him to change anything he does because he thinks I'm standing over him."

Beth nodded, conceding that Jeff could be overly dramatic.

"It's not Jeff I'm worried about. It's the other teams. I want to use Jeff's work as a baseline."

Beth didn't understand what changes Rich planned, but it didn't sound like a big "ask." Rich was her boss and he seemed perfectly comfortable with the task he'd given her.

Rich had her cooperation, but he couldn't stop spinning his story. "LAG just surpassed $2 billion in revenue. Our growth is meteoric, but it would be even better if we found new ways to leverage our research. You guys are one small team among hundreds of analysts. I need to figure out how to make the other groups behave more like you. Seeing your research drafts early and comparing them to other teams is the first step."

He called it the first echelon.

Beth trusted him and absorbed it all. Rich let a smile emerge. He was at total ease, spinning his lie in real time.

"OK, so it's going to be a company-wide review, and you don't want everyone to start worrying about it until you've thought it through," Beth reframed his request.

"Yes. I want to use your approach to guide the other teams. Get me access to Jeff's reports for the next few months and I'll see how we can get other teams on board."

Beth relaxed. Rich knew if she discovered the truth, that he was not looking at any other teams and the Emerging Tech Team was his only target, she would have wavered. He still would have made her comply, but for now having her volunteer was better. He'd reward her efforts at spying soon enough and save harsher approaches in case she ever failed him.

"OK, what do you need first?" Beth was on board for this first step.

"Jeff is scheduled to author two major vendor ratings reports in the next few weeks. I believe one is on application security testing and another on data analytics. We will start there. I need to know what his early thinking is on the vendors, which ones will be included, and how he is going to rank them in the analysis."

She nodded. So, he pressed a bit more.

"I'm only interested in the vendors. Who is moving up and who we are moving down." He looked to see her reaction. Again, nothing. She was going to obey.

Beth knew how she could get access to Jeff's drafts without triggering any warning bells. "Our shared server has all his research on it. I'll copy the files and get them to you Monday morning."

"This is just between us." Rich's voice lowered. He stood and leaned toward her with both hands on her desk.

"Yes, it is just between us," Beth responded, a bit startled.

"No bullshit here. This is just between us. This whole thing blows up on you if this gets out." It wasn't anger, it was a warning.

★ ★ ★

Rich was anxious. The LAG business model struggled to reach scale and the Q3 earnings report fell flat among investors and fund managers. Shareholders were skeptical, looking for signs of increasing productivity from LAG analysts. It was Rich's outward plan to show LAG investors how it could happen, using the Emerging Tech Team as the model. It was a plan LAG shareholders and employees would see. He'd mesmerize them and obfuscate LAG performance as long as he could, pointing to the Emerging Tech Team as the model for others in his organization to follow. That was the plan for LAG that Rich wanted the world to see.

The real plan, the more secretive plan, the plan nobody but he and his partners would see, would focus on different goals and objectives from LAG. He called it Echelon 1. He'd mapped it out well before Beth and Marcus joined his team. This was the initial step, albeit a small one, on the path to building a new company and a new revenue model. LAG would continue to flow earnings to its shareholders, but this new venture served different masters and would generate far more cash. Cash that would never be captured in LAG's balance sheet.

Echelon 1 would demonstrate that his network of offshore corporate entities, sitting dormant since his meetings in Mexico three years ago, were ready for large-volume trades. All he needed was a prioritized list of IT vendors to invest in, and Beth would provide that list.

Rich needed to make sure no warnings were triggered, no SEC investigations were sparked, and no FBI agents came knocking when the stock manipulations started. If they did, he'd sacrifice Beth to the authorities as the source of inside information.

The Echelon 1 pilot would last several months. Huang's team in Hong Kong would make equities trades before Jeff's research became public and would benefit whether the firms thrived or died. With thousands of corporations worldwide awaiting LAG's advice on key tech markets, Rich's new company would take advantage of the markets made by LAG.

"Mr. Huang, the pilot phase for Echelon 1 is underway. I'll send your team the vendor list Monday. Are all the trading desks ready?" Rich beamed.

"We've been ready for months, Mr. Banderas. Oh, I'm sorry . . . Mr. Anderson." Huang was aggravated and didn't care what the boy wanted to be called. "Be faster, Mr. Anderson. I want to see results soon or Los Feroz will be my new trading partner in Mexico." He abruptly hung up.

Rich was the last person in the office after midnight and turned off the light in the lobby on his way out the door. He exhaled loudly with growing confidence he could deliver on the commitments he made in Mexico nearly three years ago.

CHAPTER 13
Step by Step

Agree, commit, move forward—the mantra of the Emerging Tech Team. Once they identified an approach and agreed to it, they would never reverse. They might adjust and realign, but they never went backward. Their workloads were too intense. Their client demands were too pressing. There wasn't time to pause, reflect, or retreat. Their deadlines were immovable and the demands from clients were unstoppable.

The only way to survive was to decide fast and engage, adapting if necessary, but not withdrawing. It was an approach Marcus and Rich perfected as wrestlers. Commit to the shot, adjust as necessary, but you never backed up. This mindset kept the Emerging Tech Team focused on the tasks to be completed and, as Rich intended, not what he was doing outside of LAG.

In the initial weeks, his pilot for Echelon 1, fed by Beth, was delivering impressive results but needed more investment targets. "Who's on the list this week?" Rich asked Beth during their regularly scheduled Friday-night meeting.

Exhausted, she sat down and yawned, handing him copies of Jeff's upcoming research and her own analysis of prioritized vendors on a thumb drive.

"Tired?" Rich observed.

"Handling my analyst responsibilities and working for you on this secret project is a lot. I'm drowning." Beth was exasperated. Rich demanded more and more from Beth to keep Hong Kong busy.

It started with Beth accessing Jeff's files and providing copies. It morphed into her preparing prioritization lists and stack ranks of vendors likely to grow, or regress, based on LAG's research. Now he needed to goad past her physical breaking point. He needed her to provide specific vendor and buyer company names. Which vendors will grow, which will decline, which buyers will accelerate, and which will fall based on LAG's research. Beth responded to the growing responsibilities with no questions or concerns. Overworked, tired, and on deadline for countless deliverables, she just plowed forward. She simply wanted to check the box. Deliver it and move to the next task.

Rich marveled at how easy it had been to move Beth down the path, step by step, cranking up his expectations and demands bit by bit. She knew which buying organizations would flourish by embracing LAG's recommendations and which vendors would profit most. Based on Jeff's research, she knew which vendors were declining and which were on the brink of failure. She knew which buyers were embracing LAG's recommendations and would materially improve their earnings per share and which were in trouble. She never knew where her recommendations went after she gave them to Rich, and she did all of this on top of her growing workload at LAG. There was always more to be done. She didn't have time to look back and see how far off course she had sailed. All that was important to Rich was that Hong Kong had all this information weeks in advance of LAG's clients and was poised to profit wildly.

Rich witnessed early signs of Beth's burnout with bouts of irritability, small disagreements bubbling into heated arguments, and cracks forming in her relationships, especially with Jeff and Deb. It was exactly what he wanted. He needed her weakened and frayed.

He needed the entire team under stress and pressure. It would make them perfectly ripe to make some bad decisions, and he'd use Beth as his way of showing them there would be significant rewards for compliance. He just needed to push her a bit more, nudge her closer to the brink.

※ ※ ※

Rich's plan worked. The method to identify investment targets worked. The trading desks worked. The flow of monies between various LLCs and from country to country to evade regulatory investigations worked. Now the pilot needed to scale, requiring the entire Emerging Tech Team be brought on board.

Recruiting them would be delicate and dangerous, but he already had Beth in line, and he would use her to enlist the rest.

Rich welcomed Beth to his new apartment overlooking the harbor. "It's been a year since our little project began. You recommended 104 growth vendors to me. Any guesses how well their stocks performed in the past year?" Rich sat back in his chair, head tilted up, looking out the window as jets landed and took off from Logan airport in the distance. He was so incredibly pleased that he was unable to suppress his smile.

"I'd say a 20 percent increase." Beth wondered where this was headed.

"Try 53 percent. Their stock prices grew an average of 53 percent in twelve months." Rich had spoken to his partners earlier in the morning to report his progress. He'd taken $300 million of their initial investment and spun back $160 million in capital gains on these plays alone. He was beaming.

"And those vendors where we predicted problems? The ones we diminished or dropped from LAG research. You identified thirty-seven of them. Any guesses on how much they fell?"

"OK, I'll play. 15 percent." She didn't understand the game.

"Not even close. Their capitalizations fell an average of 40 percent." Rich struggled to restrain is delight. There was no benefit in

Beth knowing the size and significance of the stakes he was placing based on her recommendations, but a 40 percent return on a $125 million investment on short sales pleased his partners.

"And the CIO organizations we'd identified as most benefitting from our recommendations? How do you think they did?"

"C'mon, Rich, I have no idea. A 5 percent increase in their stock price?"

"Nope. It was 28 percent. A pretty good bump." Rich only leveraged $75 million in purchases here, anticipating it would be the lowest area of return. "Twenty-eight percent! The big venture guys would kill for that annual return," he blurted.

Not every recommendation he'd made was a home run. A few moved modestly up or down resulting in unremarkable returns. But the winners outnumbered the losers by a mammoth ratio, and the returns from the big winners were eye-popping. Altogether, Rich delivered nearly $230 million in returns in the first year. That was $115 million in clean cash to the cartel and $115 million to Huang.

Beth was vaguely aware of how much money LAG clients made and saved based on the Emerging Tech Team's recommendations, but she was curious why Rich was much more focused on how much money others—investors, VC firms, and Wall Street analysts—were making than how well LAG was performing.

"What is the priority here? LAG clients or the Street?" Beth asked.

Rich wasn't ready to share that the investment company in Hong Kong was now his primary focus and that LAG would have to muddle forward on its own. His new venture was owned by an LLC based in the US, which was in turn owned by a pool of corporations and LLCs in Asia, the Caribbean, and Latin America. The Banderas cartel and the PRC were equal owners of it all and nobody could trace it. Money would flow in irregular amounts and at random times. Funds moved in, out, and around these entities and to accounts in Belize and the Cayman Islands, working their way back to Hong Kong where the stock purchases were made. Huang's team would purchase shares in dollars, pesos, yuan, and Bitcoin. It masked everything Rich was doing from US authorities. All Rich had to do was give Hong Kong the buy and sell recommendations and the network would rotate, spin, whirr, and do the rest.

The trading desk established by Huang was associated with a private equity bank. Hong Kong was the perfect location with its proximity to China, its low tax rates, and its international appeal. Huang's Chinese partners controlled the bank, and Hong Kong's banking privacy ordinances enabled his partners to avoid the scrutiny of US regulators.

If all went according to plan, within three years he'd sell the assets of LAG, take a portion of the analysts with him, and convert his investment company into a full-throated venture and tech investing firm, generating unimaginable returns to his partners. At least that was the plan. But to get there, he'd need Marcus, Jeff, and Deb on board. Beth alone would not be enough, though it was fun watching how far he could push her.

It was time to recruit the others, and Beth opened the door. "Rich, I can't keep up this pace. Something has to give. I can't do both jobs much longer." Beth looked tired. Rich knew it was difficult for her to keep her work secret from Marcus and even more so from Jeff. But it was another loyalty test, and she passed. The work, the demands of the two companies, and the secrecy was getting too heavy to bear. Beth's dark brown eyes were masked by darkening rings. Her wavy blond hair was rumpled and frazzled. She had lost weight, and with it some of her curviness. She looked worn.

Beth was exasperated, knowing she was going well beyond reasonable expectations working one hundred hours a week, while keeping her team in the dark. She hadn't slept in her own apartment for three nights in a row in months. She hadn't spent time at Marcus's place in weeks. She hadn't had a weekend off to relax since winter, and now the trees on the common where budding.

"I know you're exhausted. You've done everything I've asked. I promise, it will get better, soon." Rich was amused by how wobbly she was, on the precipice of breaking, and he was surprised it took her this long to say something. He was prepared to make concessions regarding her compensation a few months ago but waited and watched for signs she was going to snap. He'd kept increasing the pressure and her workload, looking for cracks. The rest of the team was tired, but Beth was on the verge of collapse, as he had hoped. He'd need them all burned out, frustrated, and exhausted to get on board with the other phases of his plan, and she was first in line. Tired people make bad decisions. Rich counted on it.

"Here are the five vendors from Jeff's latest research I'd invest in, if it were my money." She sat heavily in the chair across from him and stretched.

Rich commented, "Man, you look rough."

"I need a break."

"I wish I'd known. You should have come to me. I know you've been nonstop for the last year on our project." He wanted to see how she'd react to a plain-old attaboy, a job well done. She cracked a tired smile.

Rich passed her an envelope. "This is for you."

It contained a bank check, made out to her, for $250,000.

At first, she mistakenly thought it said $25,000. Then she noticed where the comma was.

"Holy shit." She focused on the amount. It was a big check. She looked closer. "Cayman National Bank?" she said, confused.

"It's for all the work you've done and for the work you are going to do." She heard the first part of the sentence but didn't listen to the last. She wondered why it was on CNB paper and not from LAG's account.

Rich ignored her question about the bank for the moment. "This part of the pilot project is over. I think we are ready to get

Deb, Jeff, and Marcus on board."

"How do we do that?" Beth was relieved knowing she wouldn't have to keep up the charade any longer.

"Well, let's *not* start by telling them you've been spying on Jeff's work and feeding it to me for the past year," he said with a wry smile.

"That's fine with me." Beth didn't want Rich's pet project blowing back on her with the rest of the team.

"Why don't you let the team know you raised workload, travel, and compensation concerns with me and tell them I've listened and have something for each of them," he said, pointing to the check. "Tell them I'm planning on joining your team meeting to bring them all up to speed."

"OK." She was waiting for the *but*.

"Tell them there are big bonuses in play. But don't tell them how much. I want to be there for the surprise."

"And how do you explain the bank check?" It still didn't make sense to her.

"I'll cover that too," he assured her. "There is an opportunity for these checks to be a regular thing."

"I know the team will appreciate this, Rich. We've got a team meeting first thing in the morning. I'll text them tonight that you will be joining us." All Beth heard from the last few minutes was, *There is going to be more compensation.* It was enough for now.

"OK, I'll swing by the meeting a little before 7:00 a.m." He ushered her to his private elevator and sent her home. He had an important call to make.

CHAPTER 14
Expanding the Machinery

Rich sat on his roof-deck smoking a Cuban Cohiba Behike, trying and failing to blow smoke rings. "Our pilot has been successful. We are ready to go with a full commitment to Echelon 1."

His conference call with his partners went far smoother than his recent investors meeting for LAG, where fund managers and investors pressed him on how he was going to keep LAG growing. His report for his father, uncle, and Huang was much more eye-popping than LAG would ever experience.

"We generated over $200 million in capital gains during the test run."

"Did you say $200 million?" Alejandro stuttered over the phone line.

"It's all clean money, ready for you in our bank accounts in the Caymans," Rich followed. "I'm bringing the rest of my team on board for the full launch of Echelon 1. We will double our trade volume within six months."

His son's bravado made Carlos proud. "Very impressive."

"With the additional cash you've committed and our expansion into Echelon 2 next year, we will reach $5 billion in total assets in three years." Rich was well ahead of his original plan. The payouts were stunning.

He knew Huang was anxious for Echelon 3, but for now, everybody was happy with the returns from the first phase. This meant, for now, that Huang would keep the chemicals flowing and other cartels at bay so the Banderas cartel could more safely manage its narcotics trade.

"I'm happy to hear your cousin is doing as you require. Will the rest of your team present any problems?" Carlos pressed.

"Elizabetta did exactly what I needed. The others will too. Tomorrow I'm offering them a tremendous opportunity; their cooperation will be no issue."

"And Mr. Shea? You are sure he will play along?" Huang asked.

"You'd be surprised how much he relies on our little Elizabetta." Rich chortled. "They have a special relationship."

"Is that so?" Alejandro laughed.

"With the pilot, I asked Beth to prove herself and she did. Now I am asking her to use her influence on the rest of the team to bring them on board," Rich said confidently.

"You've done well. We will keep the funds coming from our end and make sure our traders can handle the volume you'll be sending our way. But I want to see movement toward Echelon 3 soon," Huang interjected.

The festive mood and celebration ended with his criticism.

Huang repeated, "Soon," as he hung up the phone.

Rich had only six hours to sleep and still have time to rehearse his sales pitch one more time.

★ ★ ★

The LAG offices were usually empty until 7:30 a.m. when the administrators and analysts would begin to flow in from Boylston Street. It was common for employees to get an early start because they often had to support European clients who were six hours ahead. The parking garage under LAG's offices was always full by 8:00 a.m., which was another motivator to get there early. Parking was scarce in this part of Boston during a workday. Even those employees arriving via the commuter rail at Copley Station were at their desks before 8:00 a.m. The offices were still empty when Marcus, Jeff, and Deb walked into the conference room for their 6:30 a.m. meeting.

The team looked beaten. Marcus had flown in late the night before from client meetings in Dallas. He'd missed three days at the gym and needed to blow off steam, knowing it was unlikely. His workload was too intense to train regularly, and it was frustrating.

Jeff had been working on critical research reports and reviewing IT contracts for clients until 3 a.m. Deb was on client inquiry calls with Asia until an hour ago. At least Marcus had had a chance to shower and change. Jeff and Deb looked like they were in the same clothes they'd worn yesterday.

Unlike the others, Beth looked magnificent. She slept well last night. Deb couldn't tell if Beth was dressed for work or to head to the club. Her hair was perfect. Her makeup, subtle and flawless. She wore a tight-fitting navy-blue dress and a white silk blouse, all accentuated by her high-heel black pumps. She was gorgeous.

"God, you look great." Marcus said it out loud. He was tired and didn't catch himself.

She gave him a look, and mouthed, "Thank you."

"Are you meeting with clients today?" Deb questioned. Jeff hadn't noticed Beth's attire until Deb's comments. "Impossibly high heels." Deb pointed to them and playfully nodded.

"Nope. I have three conference calls this morning with new clients. At noon I'm going to meet a real estate broker and then to pick out my new car." It was the perfect segue.

Marcus snapped to attention. "A car?" Even though his apartment was within walking distance, he'd been thinking about a new SUV but couldn't justify it.

"Yeah, I was thinking about a Mercedes S-Class. There is a dealer in Newton." She said it so matter-of-factly they all paused and stared at her.

"I was going to lease it, but if I can get a reasonable deal, I may pay cash."

"Must be nice. Will you be summering on Nantucket with the Wellingtons this year as well?" Jeff snarked.

"I thought that might wake you guys up." She grinned. "I actually am getting a new car and looking at a bigger apartment in my building. I got a bonus check last night from Rich. He'll be here in a few minutes to give you yours."

"What bonuses?" Jeff asked.

"We've been killing our numbers, and he knows how hard we are working. He is going to give us all a bonus and talk about a new opportunity for our team." She knew Rich needed them all on board.

Like a shot of caffeine, Jeff and Deb perked up immediately. They'd been saving for a house for a year and had found one in the suburbs of Boston but could not afford the 20 percent down payment. They wondered if their bonuses would be enough for a start. Marcus wondered why Rich had given the bonus to Beth first, without letting him know. He'd be lying if he didn't also think about the Range Rover Sport, featured on MotorTrend TV last month. He was convinced $130,000 was too much money for a car he'd barely drive.

Rich selected his $5,000 Armani suit for this meeting. Classic gray with an almost imperceptible pinstripe, pressed white shirt, and a tie with spring colors. All tailored perfectly. The fabric draped smoothly and elegantly, emphasizing his physique without being restrictive or tight. It was the perfect costume for delivering his message. The edge of a black-on-black Tag Heuer Monaco watch edged out from his starched shirt cuff.

For Rich, arriving to their meeting at 7:00 a.m. meant he would have about thirty minutes with Marcus's team before spying eyes from other analyst teams would be problematic. He looked across the hallway and through the floor-to-ceiling glass wall into the small conference room off the lobby. Other than Beth, they looked like they had been through the wars.

Rich had slept well last night, a full and deep sleep like when the pressure was off. With his plan moving into place, the stress from his partners was diminishing. "Good morning, everyone." He entered the room smiling. He caught a small whiff. At least one of them could have used a shower. The malodor definitely was not Beth. *Exhausted and frustrated people can make rash decisions*, he thought. *Perfect.*

"I'm sure Beth filled you in on the bonuses I've committed to you all." He paused, trying to judge how far Beth had gotten in her introduction.

"We learned bonuses were in play, but didn't have details," Jeff said in a way to make sure Rich would fill in the blanks.

"OK. Last night I met with Beth at my place to talk about a new project I was working on. I'm looking at productivity measures for our analysts." He wasn't directly answering Jeff's question, namely, *How much?* Rich wanted them to feel more drama.

"When Marcus joined the firm, and we created the Emerging Tech Team, I told him I wanted to create something new. Something with a new approach. I wanted a fast attack team of the best, smartest, and most prolific analysts in the world." He rapidly inflated their egos.

"You delivered. No matter how I measure your performance you smash all our benchmarks. You publish more research. Your market forecasts are more accurate. You engage more clients. You do more advisory sessions. Your bill rates are higher than any other team. LAG makes more money from this team than any other." Rich's strategy was to talk fast and toss out lots of compliments. His goal was to get them agreeing to fact after fact and provide details they couldn't argue. He'd make them agreeable before making them agree.

Rich had been honing this skill since he was a boy. He'd start with a barrage of irrefutable facts and then weave a theory of causality across all the data points and arrive at a glorious conclusion everybody wanted, sprinkled with unattractive alternatives if they didn't comply. He'd convinced teachers to change his grades when he was failing, coerced beautiful coeds to break up with their boyfriends when he wanted to date them, influenced his father to send him to the US, and compelled investors to provide early funding to LAG when he was an untested entrepreneur fresh from MIT. The Emerging Tech Team would bend to his will, and they'd think it was their idea.

"The Emerging Tech service generates more revenue for this firm than any other. Altogether, Marcus, we can attribute over $120 million in sales to your team. You are the best by a long shot."

They were fixated on Rich. They all sensed their performance levels were better than other teams, but the gap between them and the other analyst teams was surprising. It explained why they were perpetually slammed with work and exhausted.

Rich continued. "The problem is scalability. You're killing yourselves. You are writing, advising, and traveling. You are entertaining clients. You are headlining industry events. You are providing insights on news shows. You are working with the business press." They knew what their job responsibilities were but were pleased Rich recognized them too.

"You guys are celebrities. Corporate leaders hang on your words. Your opinions drive billions of dollars in investment and make billions of dollars in income for investors, shareholders, and executives." They all nodded. Rich knew he had them.

"Other people make billions of dollars based on your recommendations." Rich framed the facts and outcomes clearly, succinctly. "Others get rich on your hard work." Rich let that hang in the air a moment.

The team sat silent, waiting for Rich to continue with the story.

"I understand your workload. Ninety hours a week with no time off. No weekends to unwind. Your calendars are maxed out." Rich had them nodding rhythmically, recognizing that he understood their frustration. "It isn't fair," he added for emphasis.

"You do all this work, and other people make billions of dollars based on your recommendations. Vendors get rich selling their products. CIOs get rich following your advice. And Wall Street uses your research to make investments." Their heads bobbed in agreement. Gut punch: "Everybody profits, but you."

Rich paused, readying them for a vision of what their days would be like if they didn't accept his change.

"LAG's model works great for them, not so great for you. You only make more when we deliver more, and you guys are at your limit. Within LAG, I can't pay you more. Our business model isn't built that way. It can't reach the scale needed to compensate you properly." Slam.

Rich ripped the figurative wrapping paper off to reveal an empty box. There was no reward. He could see them sink and slouch, each thinking some version of *It isn't right*.

"There has to be something we can do," Jeff said with a tone of desperation. "I can't generate more." It played right into Rich's script.

"I know, Jeff. Your hard work is benefiting others. People are getting rich, and you are getting exhausted." Rich wanted them to bristle at the unfairness and injustice of their plight.

"LAG's brand and business model prohibits you from trading in the stocks of the firms LAG covers. But it doesn't stop investors, venture funds, banks, and brokerages from taking our insights and making trades. It isn't fair. Especially when low-level investment analysts are making ten times what you do, using your research as their guide."

With that, Rich detonated their hopes of more compensation and a better quality of life within the current LAG business model. In that instant, all four of them knew how they were working now and that what they got paid could never come into balance. The LAG model was restrictive.

Marcus, Jeff, and Deb sat heavily in their seats, weighed down with the reality of their plight. The realization that nothing would change deflated them. Rich could see their postures hunch. Deb put her head in her hands. Jeff sat back in stark realization that nothing would change. Each of them had been too busy and overworked to really think about the operational economics of LAG until now. Their visions of the future darkened. Rich forced them to see the unfairness. There was an ecosystem of IT buyers, IT vendors, investors, financial analysts, and venture executives raking in massive profits on the work the Emerging Tech Team was doing, and it made them angry. *Perfect*, thought Rich. *Now to be their savior.*

"There is an opportunity, however." He paused, disrupting the pity they felt for themselves. He'd bring them back from the edge of despair. Rich ignited a beacon of hope.

"Last night I gave Beth a bonus. It was a thank-you for the hard work she'd been doing. I have an envelope for each of you as well." He handed them each a bright white envelope. They opened them and he could see it on their faces. It was the single largest check any one of them had ever received.

"There is one string attached to this bonus, and I need your word. This is confidential. You cannot discuss this bonus with anybody else, especially your peers in LAG." Rich looked each one of them in the eye to confirm. It was a small ask and it was pretty easy to agree to a small thing when holding a check for a quarter of a million dollars in your hand. It was a small first step. Soon there'd be another, then another. Rich would get them to where they'd need to be.

Beth was not thinking about how she got here. The first step for her was a year ago and she'd long buried any concerns over LAG's rules or ethics. What she was thinking about was, *Here it comes. He is going to have to explain the bank check.* She was curious how they'd react.

Rich addressed it straightforwardly. "You'll notice your bonus is on a bank check, not from LAG. These bonuses are from me, personally." He paused and watched each of them. His gaze lingered on each one of them, one after the other, making sure they knew he was the source of their newfound wealth. For now, he wanted them to celebrate him and applaud him. For now, he wanted to be linked to the joy they felt. Later, if ever needed, he'd have leverage. At any point he could reverse this and be linked to their anxiety or fear.

His father's advice echoed, *Surround yourself with people you can trust, rule, and intimidate. Reward them when you can. Show no mercy if they are disloyal to you.*

"I've launched a new venture not tied to LAG. I've started a new venture capital firm." It stopped them. Siphoning off resources from a publicly traded company to equip a new venture separate from LAG sounded like a conflict. But nobody said anything, partly because they wanted to hear the full story, partly because they were exhausted and not thinking clearly, and partly because they all held a small fortune in their hands.

Rich anticipated their concern. "I'm working with a small group of investors, bankers, and lawyers on a new business. The story of your work, your effort, your sacrifice is one example of how those doing the heavy lifting are not those sharing in the rewards. But that is not the only unjust reality of the tech industry." He'd practiced this part of the speech until it was perfect. He was now a preacher.

Where is this going? Marcus wondered. He placed the check face down and crossed his arms.

"In addition to the financial spoils often going to those who don't do the work, the opportunity to even participate in the market is limited to those in the richest parts of the world." Rich was building toward a crescendo none of them anticipated.

"The same investors, bankers, and venture fund leaders who reap the benefits of the work you do are stiff-arming struggling entrepreneurs and investors in parts of Asia, Eastern Europe,

Africa, the Middle East, and Latin America. They are denying these brave innovators access to capital."

Nobody was prepared to argue against that fact.

"US-based tech firms get 70 percent of all venture funding. Asia and Europe get 14 percent each. That leaves about 2 percent for everybody else. The current investment model is starving innovation in the rest of the world to death." Rich's face was somber. He slammed the table. "We should be ashamed."

All the Emerging Tech Team's clients, IT executives, IT vendors, and investors were in the US, Western Europe, or a select few rich nations in Asia. The way Rich spun it, it did sound patently unjust.

Rich made it clear and simple. He made the finish line starkly obvious. "My new company will invest in firms tracked by LAG. We will use our profits to provide investment capital and advice to entrepreneurs in markets that have been shut out of global finance opportunities, simply because they were born in the wrong country." Rich painted a picture of a social justice investment firm. The Emerging Tech Team believed Rich was smiling at the heartwarming altruism of his story. They were wrong.

"We will make investments, raise capital, and fund innovation in areas US venture funds avoid. We will bring fairness and level the playing field as best we can." Rich was smiling because it was total bullshit and they bought it. They agreed with the inequity and bigotry of who was able to play in the market. They bought the story about who was profiting and how LAG's current model could not work. They believed Rich empathized with their stress and low pay. And most importantly, every member of the team kept the cash.

"It's inspiring," Deb offered.

"I'd never thought of our role that way," Jeff added.

He made sure to goose it even further. "And this bonus is only the beginning. They will get bigger, and you'll see them every quarter."

Jeff and Deb did the math immediately. Combined they'd get $500,000 a quarter "Forget the western suburbs. We are looking for a house in Dover or Weston," Jeff whispered to Deb with a childish grin.

Marcus studied the body language of his team. They were in. Though he was cautious, his trust in Rich overrode his concerns. "I guess we're all on board, Rich," he said, making it unanimous.

Rich looked at his watch. In less than thirty minutes, he had closed the deal. The LAG Emerging Tech Team was moved into full launch mode for Echelon 1. His broad outline about how they would use LAG research and their expertise as a blueprint for investment strategies was enough for now. The team was able to justify taking the first steps, and that was all Rich needed. More importantly, he left room for them to dream about how they'd spend their newfound wealth.

It was all about small steps. They committed to Echelon 1 for him. Echelon 2 would take some convincing, though they'd be too well paid and in too deep to stop. By the time Rich introduced Echelon 3, the team would be overwhelmed, overworked, and incapable of making sound decisions. Rich was confident that by that time, they'd be on autopilot, doing whatever he wanted, without fear of consequences. They'd be financially bound to him. And if any of them refused or pushed back, he'd tighten his grip and replace rewards with something far less pleasant.

★ ★ ★

In the five months since they got their bonuses and started supplementing their work at LAG with support of Rich's new project, the Emerging Tech Team selected three hundred targets for investment—more than twice what Beth had done on her own the prior year. Marcus's team identified IT vendors who were about to rise, those destined to fall, and user organizations that were either going to prosper or crash based on their use of the technologies recommended by LAG's analysts. With the additional capital infusion from the cartel and China, the team in Hong Kong grew Rich's capital base to nearly $2 billion, providing both the Banderas cartel and Huang with an immense flow of clean cash.

Of the investments identified, the Emerging Tech Team was particularly good at spotting imminent losers. Nearly half the firms they'd identified for Rich, which he in turn sent to Hong Kong, were "shorts." Namely, they were betting against these firms because LAG's research discovered they were very likely to crash.

In a short sell, an investor "borrows" the stock from a broker and sells it on the open market at the current market price. The gamble is that the stock price would fall and that they could buy it back later at a lower price, return the borrowed shares to the broker, and pocket the difference as profit. Traditional venture capital firms don't participate in short selling. They focus on early-stage or high-growth companies aiming to generate significant returns on their investments over the long term. Rich didn't hamstring his team. They followed their own rules.

There were two categories of shorts the Emerging Tech Team identified. The first were IT vendors whose massive product investments and rollout strategies were doomed to failure due to poor engineering, poor planning, or weak competitive positioning. Many established tech vendors were missing new market opportunities and were getting demoted in LAG research. All were short candidates. It was not uncommon for these firms to spend tens of millions of dollars on the development and launch of new products only to crater because they misunderstood the competitive marketplace. When they failed, they failed spectacularly, causing share prices to plummet. Jeff's research and consulting projects from Marcus, Beth, and Deb identified dozens of vendors that would fall.

The second short selling group were IT buyers in large industries whose technology spend was so erratic and so misguided their management teams would soon founder, causing their stocks to plummet. LAG analysts often had access to confidential buyer strategies and budget challenges that were telltale signs of major problems. When a client came to Marcus's team and said, "We need to take 50 percent out of our IT spend," they knew the problems were deep and the firm was likely to announce cuts to staff and other budget items in advance of major negative earnings news. This gave Rich inside information on which Global 500 firms were girding for major losses and which would see significant declines in stock valuations well in advance.

Both types of short sales were ideal for the aggressive trading strategy Rich had established and were routinely identified by Marcus's team as part of their normal duties at LAG. That was the beauty of Rich's plan. It didn't require the Emerging Tech Team to produce anything more than they were already delivering as part of their roles at LAG. All it required was for the team to ignore areas of confidentiality and discretion, two key tenets for LAG, but not for their new roles.

The contradiction between how LAG operated and how Rich's new endeavor behaved was not at all a concern for Rich, but it was stirring suspicions in Marcus. He began logging the recommendations his team made and tracking stock movements. The success rates for their picks were remarkable, but what caught his eye was the trade volumes coinciding with his team's recommendations. The average shares traded daily, in the firms the Emerging Tech Team brought forward, spiked like clockwork within a day or two of giving them to Rich. It was a curiosity, not because anything his team was doing was overtly illegal, but more because if Rich's efforts were responsible for even a small portion of the increased volume, it meant moving hundreds of millions of dollars in tech stocks. Curious.

CHAPTER 15
Tightening the Grip

"Gentleman, Echelon 1 has been an astounding success." Rich beamed, striding across his roof-deck, a glass of very expensive bourbon in hand. "Tonight we embark on Echelon 2." He raised his glass and toasted himself as the others listened via conference call.

"The numbers are as expected based on your initial test with Ms. Rivera." Huang offered less enthusiasm than Rich anticipated. It was 8:00 a.m. in Hong Kong. Rich could hear the traders already in action in the background.

"Mr. Shea is delivering all you need?" Alejandro questioned.

"The entire team is working perfectly," responded Rich. "The rewards are working. They're accustomed to their new lifestyles."

"Watch them, Mr. Anderson," Huang interjected.

"We meet tonight. I have another incentive planned, one that will be too good for them to refuse," Rich offered.

"Mr. Huang, thank you for organizing the latest shipments." Carlos had other business to discuss. "Demand is growing among the other cartels." Carlos wanted to reinforce the other part of their bargain.

Huang cut him off. "We will honor the arrangement as long as there is continued progress with your son's venture. Keep things moving. You are all getting what you want from me. Get me what I want." Huang hung up.

Rich wondered if Huang enjoyed amplifying his anxiety with threats to his father's business.

★ ★ ★

The Emerging Tech Team met with Rich twice a month, typically late on Thursdays, after their work at LAG had wrapped for the day. Rich's condominium in Boston's Seaport district was the working headquarters for his new endeavor, Perseid Research Capital. Rich preferred nights to mornings. It meant the team would have the day's client and vendor interactions fresh in their memories, which helped him identify new investment opportunities for the Hong Kong trading desk, thirteen hours ahead of Boston and just opening for business. Late-night meetings would also mean the team would be tired. Tired people often agree to questionable ideas for no reason other than to finish the discussion and get home. Late-night meetings were also an excuse for the team to have a couple laughs and a few drinks, ending in the same result.

The Emerging Tech Team still generated all the research, fulfilled all the inquiries, and engaged all the clients LAG expected of them, but now they did it with an eye toward how they could monetize those efforts to make money for Perseid. They were tired and overworked.

Echelon 1 began as a small effort, barely over the ethical line: "What firms should we bet on because they will appear strong in the research we are about to publish?" It soon became: "Which vendors should we bet against because our research will show they perform poorly?" Rich then asked the team, "What new firms can we introduce so they get a measurable bump in share price?" And then, "Which vendors can we drop from our research so they see faster declines?" Each new task, even small ones, moved the team further and further from their core beliefs. Their thumbs on the scale were getting heavier. Their paths had strayed further and further from their start. Step by step.

When the team delivered on these questions and tasks without objection, Rich made their focus a bit darker. "Which vendors would most benefit if we raised them in our ratings a bit faster?" And then, "Which vendors would be most negatively impacted by an even harsher evaluation?" Rich was preparing them for Echelon 2. He was preparing them to manipulate markets.

Hundreds of millions of dollars in returns flowed through a network of LLCs, banks, and brokerage accounts across the globe, all headed for bank accounts in tax havens in Costa Rica, the Caribbean, the Cayman Islands, Singapore, and ultimately Hong Kong. Rich's design laundered it all.

The appetite from Hong Kong for more trade volume was growing. To attain the returns Perseid promised, Rich needed bigger deals, not simply more deals. Rich needed the scale Echelon 2 promised. His team would need a push.

When Rich didn't think that alcohol alone would be enough to make the team sufficiently pliable and agreeable, a few chemical adjustments would be introduced. If Rich believed a meeting might be particularly contentious, like the one tonight, he'd slip a touch of Dr. Feelgood into their drinks. Echelon 2 would certainly trigger questions and concerns from the team. A hint of Ecstasy dissolved into the wine would do the trick. Enough to take the edge off.

Rich crushed the capsules and poured the powder into two bottles of wine aiming for a perfect mix of drowsiness and wooziness, with a pinch of euphoria. He peeled the corners off the labels of those two bottles to make them identifiable. He didn't want to risk drinking from them.

The team arrived at Rich's together. They walked from LAG's offices rather than drive. It was a warm and beautiful fall night and they rarely had free time together. Jeff and Deb were obviously paired and enjoyed seeing Marcus and Beth together, no longer hiding the affections that everybody else had witnessed for months. Beth smiled and leaned into Marcus as they walked. The four of them laughed, caught up, and thoroughly enjoyed the twenty-five-minute walk from Boylston Street to Boston's Seaport neighborhood.

The doors of Rich's private elevator opened adjacent to his kitchen and dining room. The view was stunning. To the left, Rich's living room looked across Fan Pier and Fort Point Channel into Boston's financial district. To the right, a massive, orange full moon hung over Logan airport, glimmering on the calm water at low tide.

Rich's apartment took the entire top floor of his building. Adjacent to the dining area was a large media room with a massive drop-down screen. It spanned the length of the wall. Four large recliners were backed with a custom-built bar, stocked with the best vodkas, bourbons, and tequilas. Down the hallway, his home gym was magnificent. It had over one thousand pounds of free weights, kettlebells, a treadmill, an elliptical, a stationary bike, and a rowing machine. Battle ropes and a heavy bag hung from the ceiling. Rich rarely used any of it. The flooring was an NCAA-regulation wrestling mat, with the Ohio State logo in the center. Beth could see the envy on Marcus's face.

The rumble of a jet reverberated in the distance. The glass wall separating the dining room from the penthouse deck was accordioned open, making for a spectacular visual twelve stories above Boston Harbor.

The drifting aroma of the ginger and soy sauces mingling with the beef and fish were intense and delicious. "Soba?" Jeff excitedly asked, looking at the menu the delivery driver left on the kitchen counter.

"Nothing but the absolute best. Three Michelin stars." Rich replied with a large smile. "The finest Wagyu beef outside of Tokyo."

Deb was a connoisseur of Japanese cuisine. Of the team, she'd spent the most time in Asia. "Matsutake mushrooms, Suppon, otoro, Yubari melon." She walked parallel to the table pointing out each course to her colleagues. "What, no fugu?" she joked.

"No, they weren't willing to send their best sushi chef. Besides, I'm not a fan of puffer fish, or dying." Rich laughed.

The dining table looked magnificent, decorated for fall with brown, green, cranberry, and orange. The scent of the candles was masked by the aroma of the meal.

"I guess this isn't going to be one of our regular planning sessions," Deb marveled.

"Not tonight, Deb. Tonight is special." Rich's grin widened.

"Penfolds Grange Hermitage?" Jeff's voice cracked in disbelief when he saw six bottles opened and breathing at the center of the table. Jeff was a bit of a sommelier, but until recently he had not had the wherewithal to stock his wine cabinet with anything more expensive than Silver Oak. He bought it by the case now so he could keep the price under $100 a bottle. Penfolds' $38,000-per-bottle price tag was not an option. He could barely wait for a glass.

Sitting atop each place setting was a bright white linen envelope. The setting, the meal, and the wine was perfect; now it was time for Rich to ask them all for more.

The call-to-action Rich would present to them, and more importantly the method to get there, was risky. As far as the team had strayed from its LAG origins, Echelon 2 for Perseid would stretch the boundaries of their moral comfort. Rich remembered the advice his father shared, but before he resorted to threats and fear, he'd try something different. He'd make them impulsive. He'd distort their perceptions of reality.

Rich sensed a problem in the way they bunched in his kitchen. The team was nervous. Acting like a herd. Or better, a flock. Clustered to avoid any one of them being picked off by a predator. He was working them hard recently and rarely gave them time to assemble as a group. It was by design. He could deal with them individually. Convincing a group was more difficult. Tonight he had just the remedy.

"Before you sit, let me pour a toast," Rich said with a synthetic smile of gratitude on his face. Jeff could barely contain his excitement as his glass was poured. "Here's to your first five months at Perseid. We smashed last quarter's performance. Our capital gains topped 60 percent."

"Here. Here." Everybody took a big gulp. Jeff was disappointed in his first taste. It started full-bodied and rich, with layers of blackberry and plum and hints of oak and vanilla, but ended with a bit of unappealing bitterness. Rich's glass didn't have any bitterness because he poured his from a different bottle.

Marcus studied Rich, keying into the over-embellished smile and highly animated movements. Large fast strides, unable to stand still in one place. Exaggerated emotions. Fist bumps and high-fiving Jeff as he passed. The others were more interested in finishing their first glass of wine than observing how Rich performed in front of them. Marcus found it odd that Rich's first toast would be for the venture firm he was managing clandestinely instead of celebrating the continued successes, growth, and profitability of LAG. For Rich, it was a purposeful omission. He wanted them focused on a bigger prize.

Rich circled the dining table. Drawing them in. The timing of this meeting, the setting, the meal—Marcus knew something was coming. Beth, Jeff, and Deb, on their second glasses of wine, appeared more fascinated with the spoils of their efforts spread across the dining room table than where this was headed. Rich noticed Marcus breaking from the flock, but before Marcus could derail his flow, Rich motioned them toward their seats and the bright white envelopes, each with a name on it in calligraphy, centered on the Wedgwood china. "Here is your Q3 bonus check from Perseid."

It had been a nonstop barrage of long days and little sleep since they got their first bonus checks five months ago. The burden of successfully delivering on the demands of LAG and Perseid simultaneously was taking a toll. So, they could all be forgiven for their bewildered looks when they saw two commas in the number.

Each of them was holding a $1 million check from the Bank of Belize. The room went still and silent in disbelief. They stared, numbly, at the piece of paper in their hands. Marcus recognized the source bank for this check was different from their May bonus.

Jeff broke the silence. "Holy shit."

"Yeah. Holy shit. You deserve it." Rich grinned, still holding his glass, beckoning them to take another gulp.

Rich needed to be careful in the next few minutes. The sum of money at stake was substantial, enough to raise suspicions among the team. Rich couldn't afford any hint that he was in fact buying their cooperation. Even with a bump of ecstasy swirled into the $38,000 bottle of wine, any member of this team might balk. Rich waited to let the rush take hold. He watched as they all acted identically, elbows on the table, holding their checks delicately at the corners by their left and right hands, as if the checks were written on spun glass and could shatter at any movement.

The astonishment slowly washed away, and smiles grew on two of them. Jeff and Deb were giddy. Each of them took a big gulp of wine. With Jeff and Deb committed, Rich knew he could secure Beth. Rich succeeded in isolating Marcus from the flock. Marcus would have no choice but to reunite with them and accept their new mission.

Marcus watched it quickly unfold: Jeff and Deb, grinning, holding $2 million between them. Beth staring at her check, nodding. Marcus was alone and uneasy while rest of his team was marveling at their fortune and acknowledging Rich as their benefactor. But another deep swallow of wine and holding his check for $1 million made Marcus's concerns less vivid. Apprehension faded as Marcus felt his feet, hands, and face warm. The appetizing aroma of the food grew in intensity. The bright colors of the room started to glow.

CHAPTER 16
Spiraling from Safety

Rich had let them study their million-dollar windfalls long enough. It was late, the Emerging Tech Team was sufficiently inebriated, and an ample amount of ecstasy saturated their bloodstreams. It was time to pitch Echelon 2.

"Thank you. You've accomplished everything I'd hoped." Rich knew he needed to get to the point quickly before they were too intoxicated to respond or before the weight of the money and the downside of the ecstasy triggered paranoia and mistrust.

Rich watched Marcus place his check on the table and shift his stance in the chair, rubbing and blinking heavily, trying to clear his vision. Rich was the boss and Marcus's friend, and Marcus was a loyal subordinate, but Rich knew he was walking a fine line and Marcus would interrupt. Rich cut him off. "Our strategy is working. We've made aggressive investments in a number of the businesses you've researched. Those long-term plays are paying off." Rich's plan was to begin with the most psychologically positive news. "Your 'buy' recommendations are beating average market returns by two to three times."

The new millionaires listened intently.

"In some cases, you identified weaker players in the market, and we took short positions against them." Rich wanted to soften this. "We are not a vulture fund, but we will take advantage of the downside trends you identify."

"So, we are making money off a company's failures," Jeff confirmed, still looking at his check.

"We aren't the only ones who short stocks, but right now we are outperforming the market there too." Rich made it sound so clinical. Even routine. "They all do it."

There was no pushback from the team.

"Even more important is how we are investing in emerging markets, enabling new companies to bring products to market. We all want to change the world. We are doing it." It was time for Rich to appeal to their altruism.

"How are we doing that?" Deb asked.

"In the last few weeks we have taken subordinated ownership positions in dozens of small and visionary tech firms in Asia, Latin America, the Middle East, and Africa. These are promising young companies who, in normal capital markets, would rarely be given enough oxygen to survive." He was troweling on a thick veneer of shit talk with an honest smile. Everybody believed him.

Rich handed them a small PowerPoint deck and started flipping pages. "Let me tell you a story about TechWave, a start-up based in Lagos, Nigeria."

"Nigeria?" Beth said with surprise. "You are investing in Nigeria?"

Rich ignored her skepticism. "A talented team of young entrepreneurs lacked the resources to develop their product."

The Emerging Tech Team had listened to hundreds of vendor briefings, but they'd never heard their boss give one. He was magnificent. Rich's posture and his controlled movements exuded confidence and expertise. It was like a choreographed dance. He was captivating as he walked around the room spinning his story and referring to the slides in front of them. His tone was well paced. It was exciting and enthusiastic, but hushed, forcing them to lean in to hear. He had command of all the technology, market, and societal realities that made TechWave a superb investment opportunity for Perseid.

"Their vision was just a dream. In a world where Silicon Valley ruled, it was a vision that would never turn into reality. They couldn't fund their emergence. Nobody was going to put any money into a third-world start-up. TechWave had a spark, but it was rapidly extinguishing. They were a dying dream."

The reality of small firms failing to survive was not surprising to anybody in the room. They'd seen it every day as LAG analysts. Great ideas lacking proper funding failed all the time.

"What makes them so special?" Deb asked.

Rich continued, "Their first product, a mobile app, helps farmers in rural areas better manage their crops and increase their yields by tracking water usage, fertilizer consumption, weather patterns, and local commodity prices. It has incredible potential not just in Africa but in Asia and Latin America too. It's a $10 billion market. We provided them with $5 million in seed funding to ensure they've got the resources necessary for testing, packaging, and distribution."

Jeff and Deb smiled, impressed with the market opportunity for TechWave and proud that in some way they played a part. Beth, perched on the edge of her seat, tilted toward Rich, fixated less on the story he was weaving and more on the excitement and sincerity in his voice. Rich was convinced that whatever concerns Marcus had moments ago were falling away because he was reading deep into the slide deck, nodding with approval.

Rich held up the slide deck, waving it in front of team. "This is the good we can do. This is why I created Perseid. Firms like TechWave are outside the geographic play of traditional venture firms and rarely attain the size or growth needed to qualify for conventional funding from Silicon Valley. We were there for them early and now they are thriving. Our equity stake in them will drive massive returns for us. They win and we win." Rich grinned.

The heads of every member of the Emerging Tech Team bobbed in appreciation. Rich put down the slide deck. He had them. They all believed the narrative. The slide deck took him twenty minutes to create earlier that day, and all marketing numbers and pro forma financials were pure fiction. The pretty pictures were clipped from the Web. The team was giddy and in full support of a total lie. There was no Nigerian company. Rich wasn't going to toss any of the cartel's money into a third-world country, no matter how much societal good it would generate. There was one firm, based in China, poised to do incredible things with LAG's help, and it was Perseid's only play outside of the US.

The myth of TechWave was used to coerce the Emerging Tech Team. Rich wanted the glow. He wanted the Emerging Tech Team to envision Perseid as a white knight helping young, hungry entrepreneurs in developing countries level a playing field tipped hopelessly against them because they were born in the wrong place on a big planet. Rich wanted the team to feel noble about Perseid, so they'd ignore what he was about to instruct them to do next.

"We are doing good. Good for these firms, good for these emerging economies, good for our investors, and good for us." Rich smiled as he sat back down.

"To keep this pace we need to think about two things. The first is, no distractions. You now have money, a lot of money. You've bought new apartments. You've bought new cars. You've bought toys and trinkets. Until we have our business model working to its full potential, we can't draw attention to ourselves. Your colleagues in LAG don't know about Perseid, and neither do LAG's competitors. It must stay that way." His voice raised and he repeated, "It has to stay that way." He paused for effect.

"Why hide?" Marcus asked, skeptical.

"We need more time to establish our position and we have to be careful not to raise unwanted curiosity. So be smart. No big toys." Rich spoke to them like a parent handing the keys of the family wagon over to a newly licensed driver.

Rich wasn't terribly worried about LAG employees or shareholders asking questions. He was worried about drawing the attention of FinCEN, the Financial Crimes Enforcement Network, a bureau of the US Department of Treasury, who would then involve the SEC and FBI. FinCEN requires financial institutions, including banks and money service businesses, to report transactions involving large amounts of cash or other suspicious activities to help prevent money laundering, terrorist financing, and other financial crimes. Perseid was doing all three.

"I've got a package for each of you. It outlines the accountants, investment experts, and banks you *will* work with to manage your funds. These are the same people who we are working with at Perseid. They are the people who manage my assets. They know how to safely and securely put your money to work, in a tax advantaged way, without drawing unwanted attention." Marcus didn't sense any pushback from his first point. Objective number one: check.

"The second thing is what I call Echelon 2, and it requires a new approach from all of us, which makes the first item, your discretion, so vital." Rich's tone lowered to a baritone. He was not growling or gravelly, but suddenly lowering his tone and volume made it a bit menacing. It was something that all four of them had experienced before. It was how Rich communicated seriousness. They traded glances across the table.

As Rich had explained to his father and uncle, if Perseid remained in its current state, Echelon 1, they would have wealth beyond the wealthy. Within five years, Perseid would have a venture fund with billions in assets. For the most part, it would all be legitimate. But legitimacy was not what his father and uncle needed and not what Huang demanded. The future of Perseid started today with a bold step forward. Rich's team needed to forget about how far they'd already moved for Echelon 1 and focus on the incremental steps required for Echelon 2.

Marcus, Beth, Jeff, and Deb still basked in the heroic feelings from TechWave. They were loose, cloudy, and floating from the fortified wine. Rich needed them to trust him, believe in his vision, and swallow his bullshit. He needed them to go with him willingly on a new path.

"Perseid is unique. Our vision and mission is exceptional. We are doing good things, honorable things. But venture funds of our size are commonplace. Our size is well below the big guys like Horizon Ventures, Apex, and Empyrean." The David versus Goliath story was always a popular trope.

"We are growing faster, but we need several more years of progress to be a true global player. Time is not on our side. Our window of opportunity is now. If we don't expand our focus and grow even more rapidly, we will flame out. It will all be over. No more help to companies like TechWave. No more bonuses." As Rich said it, he walked behind Jeff and tapped his finger on the check Jeff held.

"The problem with Perseid is the same challenge we face at LAG. Scalability. To get to the next level we need to expand our output substantially." Rich could see their faces change. They were high, but not oblivious. The tension in the room grew immediately. There was anxiety in their faces, especially Jeff's. Eyes widened, traces of sweat building, fidgeting, tenseness in the jaw.

"The last time you said this, you told us there was no plan to increase head count." Jeff was already at his maximum capacity working on both LAG and Perseid projects. This sounded dire. "I can't do more." Jeff slumped in his chair.

For Rich, having them dwell on the possibility of their compensation falling was exactly what he wanted. Each of them were thinking, *What will happen to my lifestyle if massive bonus checks stop coming?* Rich let their concern hang in the room like a mist.

"Jeff, all I'm saying is we need to accelerate. We need to increase returns for our investors. Perseid needs to make more money so we can each make more money." It was a nonanswer, but the team trusted him to have a solution. With that, they were ready for Rich to lay out Echelon 2 in detail.

"The only way to do this is with bigger and more profitable deals. I'm not asking for the quantity of deals to increase, but instead for the deals we select to be more lucrative."

Rich knew it would soothe Jeff but raise flags with the other three, so he focused on Jeff first. "Jeff, I'm not asking you to generate any more research than what you already have planned."

Rich made sure the other three could see the relief on Jeff's face before he proceeded. "And, you guys, I'm not asking you to do any more meetings, projects, or client engagements." The four of them relaxed a bit. Stiffened shoulders dropped. Rigid postures sagged slightly.

"How will that work?" Marcus questioned suspiciously.

"We can keep the bonuses coming if we make the work you are already doing for LAG more significant to Perseid. We need to drive bigger swings in the recommendations we make." Rich casually raised the biggest ethical restriction they'd faced so far with Perseid and tossed it aside as if it were irrelevant. Rich did it by camouflaging behind the promises of, "the bonuses will continue," and, "there will be no increase in work volume."

"How do we make the financial outcomes bigger? We can identify firms who are going to grow and those who will decline, but how do we make them grow or decline more?" Deb asked.

Rich answered slowly, with a calm, matter-of-fact tone. "LAG inquiry engagements are our greatest asset." They all knew that. It was where the analysts personalized and customized LAG research for specific clients. Rather than give clients all the same data and all the same recommendations, LAG analysts would customize them based on the specific circumstances each client faced. Access to analysts via inquiry sessions are why CIOs and IT vendors bought LAG services. CIOs learned what to buy, when to buy, how much to pay, and how to deploy. Vendors learned what to build, how to sell, and how to price their solutions. It was all customized to each client based on their size, industry, geography, and investment priorities.

"LAG does not monetize inquiries. Through Perseid, we will."

"Where is this headed?" Marcus asked. "What will we do differently to help Perseid?"

"Are all the picks you are making for Perseid on the top of your recommended lists during LAG inquiries?" Rich asked.

"How about this? Are the firms you said we should short actively diminished in your inquiries? Are you specifically telling LAG clients to avoid them?"

They all knew the answer. It was: *Sometimes*. Even though the Emerging Tech Team worked for both LAG and Perseid, there wasn't perfect alignment between LAG research and Perseid investments. The Emerging Tech Team wasn't leveraging LAG to its fullest extent to drive Perseid valuations.

"Right now, our work for LAG is often couched in *maybe*s and *on the other hand*s."

"You are losing me. Explain it to me like I'm a five-year-old," Deb chimed.

"Starting tomorrow, we are going make sure all the vendors who are in the Perseid portfolio, all those vendors you have staked your research reputations on, are prominently featured in LAG inquiry sessions. You are going to introduce these vendors, by name, into all your discussions. This will eliminate LAG's disconnect with Perseid."

And with that, Rich obliterated the line. The shackles constraining LAG analysts were removed, enabling Perseid to operate freely, unbound by LAG's ethical principles. As Perseid employees they were going to amplify vendors covered by LAG.

"What does it mean for how we are working right now?" Beth asked, worried about her already suffocating workload, not the ethical and moral conflict.

"I want to be clear. I am not saying we tell our clients to buy this product or buy that product, but instead to say, 'Hey, this vendor should be on your radar, or this one should be removed from consideration.'" Rich made it innocent and straightforward.

Facing no pushback, Rich continued, "Once the Perseid portfolio of vendors are more aggressively covered in your inquiries, other analyst teams at LAG will inevitably surface them in their work as well."

It was a lurch toward market manipulation that the team accepted as logical and even honorable. "It becomes a virtuous cycle. You identify firms for Perseid. We then reinforce those firms in your LAG inquiry sessions. I'll make sure other LAG analysts follow your lead. They will endorse the vendors for coverage if they are growing or eliminate them from research if they are declining. It will all be consistent with your Perseid recommendations." Rich described the illegality of market manipulation and pump and dump in the sweetest and most nonthreatening terms, and his team nodded approval. He was telling the team to elevate or decimate vendors in LAG research based on investment decisions Perseid was making, and nobody scoffed or objected.

"Back to your original question, Deb, we don't need to double the number of investment targets to hit our goals, we just need to double the size of our positions and returns from these companies. Echelon 2 does that." Rich's tempo quickened. He talked faster and planted all the signals for easy positive feedback. A nod. A quiet *yes*. Relaxed postures. Subtle smiles. They agreed to walk the path Rich paved. And he was filling their glasses with more wine.

"It's work you are already doing. It's a process you already embrace and are familiar with. It will be no more work than what you do now. And it will be consistent across all of LAG." And now the kicker.

"And it would mean quarterly bonus checks, like tonight's, will be a regular thing. Bank on it." They heard that part loud and clear. All they had to do was augment the process they were already committed to.

"That isn't a problem for me." Jeff beamed as he looked again at the check in front of him.

The rhythm of the discussion, the late night, the food, and the wine worked on Deb and Beth, who were already teetering in Rich's direction. Marcus was exhausted and outnumbered.

"Great. We start tomorrow," Rich concluded.

They called two Ubers, one taking Jeff and Deb to their apartment in Southie and the other taking Marcus and Beth to his apartment in Back Bay. It was nearly 1:00 a.m. Their headaches and hangovers had already started. Marcus could hear his pulse through his eardrums. Pressure was building behind his eyes through his forehead. He was incredibly dehydrated. Marcus and Beth fell asleep, in their clothes, with the lights still on.

It was a shallow sleep for Marcus with Beth under his arm. She was warm, soft, and beautiful. But he couldn't quiet his mind. Every attempt to surrender to sleep was met with anxiety and apprehension. Marcus was sinking.

CHAPTER 17
Crossing the Threshold

It was a hurriedly planned trip and most of it would be spent in the air aboard Rich's leased G700. Flying private made transoceanic flights tolerable. The jet could cruise faster and higher than any commercial airliner. Rich, Marcus, and Beth would arrive in Macau more quickly and more rested than if they flew commercial first class.

"Come on, Beth, be more specific about their competitors and which buyers they should target." Rich was unusually agitated. He insisted they meticulously role-play and practice. "We need to show Sinotech how we can help. This is a huge opportunity for us."

"Who's 'us,' Rich?" Marcus asked. "Us as in LAG or us as in Perseid?"

Rich shot him a fiery glance and Marcus retreated.

"Why are you so concerned? You are great in these meetings." Marcus was confused about his role and was surprised Rich was agitated. They'd met with dozens of vendors for Perseid, but Rich acted unusually anxious about this one. It was out of character. "Don't worry. Beth has got this," Marcus reassured Rich.

"Let's go over it again." Rich wasn't easily calmed.

"Am I playing the role as a LAG analyst or as a consultant to Perseid?" Marcus pressed Rich.

Rich described the trip to Marcus and Beth as a meeting where LAG analysts would join the Perseid CEO. Marcus didn't know exactly what the client expected, but Rich was pacing up and down the jet aisle, flipping madly through his notes, unable to mask his concern. The question reverberated as Marcus listened to Rich practice his pitch for the tenth time.

"What do you want me to do here?"

Rich was immersed in his talk track and didn't pay attention to the question.

"Do they expect LAG analysts to be there? Or are we Perseid analysts?" Marcus asked again.

"We are all on one team, Marcus," Rich snapped as a nonanswer. "Sinotech is meeting with us to gauge our expertise and to share theirs."

Sinotech, a Hong Kong–based software firm, was a start-up specializing in security and cryptography. According to their marketing materials, and they were only drafts, Sinotech had developed a quantum security algorithm that would prepare enterprises and IT vendors for a world where everybody's data and privacy were at risk.

Beth stepped in between them to deescalate the growing tension. "Within the next five years, all sorts of bad actors, rogue nations, industrial spies, and terrorists will have enough compute power to crack the most robust security platforms."

Her tactic worked. They sat back in their seats and reoriented their focus from each other back to her.

"Not a single computer connected to a network will be safe. From your aunt's Gmail account to passcodes for the military, it is all at risk. Passwords, encryption keys, security fobs, firewalls, and intrusion detection systems will be obsolete."

"All because of quantum computing?" Rich asked.

"Quantum tech will change the world. Its capabilities will grow tenfold in the next five years. All the big players are investing like crazy—Microsoft, IBM, Amazon, and Google." Beth had their attention. "It isn't just the growth in raw power that makes quantum computers so special. It's what they can do that current computers cannot."

"Like what?" Rich asked, crossing his legs and relaxing.

"Within a few years their capabilities will be revolutionary." Beth was to be their quantum security expert in the meeting. Before LAG, she oversaw all the security initiatives at the bank. Even then, she knew they were hopelessly outmatched. "Once quantum computers become mainstream, current security approaches will be obsolete."

"OK, I'm listening. Why?" Rich poured a vodka.

"Everything we do today with traditional computers uses circuits. They are basic electrical switches. Two distinct states: off or on. We imagine this as zeros and ones." She walked back and forth in the aisle, popping peanuts into her mouth. "When combined into massive strings, these binary bits are used to build instructions telling the computer what to do and how to store data. Your email system, your banking application, and even the pictures on your iPhone are generated, managed, and stored using binary technology."

Rich's and Marcus's eyes followed as she strolled the cabin.

"Rather than the classical binary approach of today's computers, quantum computers work by tracking the location and rotation of electrons. Quantum computing uses ones and zeroes, as well as any quantum superposition of those two. So the options are now a zero or a one or both simultaneously."

"Interesting." It was a weaker affirmation than Marcus intended.

"And instead of a linear string of zeroes and ones, quantum computers can entangle multiple bits, enabling complex calculations traditional computers cannot solve."

Both Marcus and Rich responded to her tale with blank stares. They weren't getting it. She laughed.

"OK. Let me start this way." She would dumb it down a bit. "Physics is key here. Instead of looking at data sequentially, item by item, quantum computers have the ability to view, measure, and calculate it all simultaneously. They are exponentially faster and more powerful than traditional computers. Today, traditional computers, no matter how large, face limits when confronted with massive data sources or an immense number of variables and potential outcomes. Quantum computers don't have that limitation." She was met with more blank stares. "You know the old joke about the three blind men and the elephant?"

Rich looked at Marcus, confused, and said, "Do you?" Marcus had no idea.

Beth smiled. "One blind man touches the elephant's leg and proclaims the object to be a tree. The second touches the trunk and announces it to be a fire hose. The third touches the elephant's side and says it's a wall. Well, those are like today's computers. They only see a small part of the whole picture. Quantum sees it all instantly from all angles, inside and out. It sees the whole elephant every time and recognizes it instantly."

Beth gave them a real-world example. "Think about why your nightly weather report can be so wrong and have so much variability. Classical computer systems have hit their limits. There are too many variables, too much data, and too many potential outcomes. Jet streams, humidity, pressure fronts, Earth's rotation, sun intensity, cloud cover, temperature gradients, ocean currents. The computers we use today can't model all that data. They don't have the capacity or speed. By the time a traditional computer solves the algorithm and has an accurate forecast the answer is already visible in the real world. Traditional computer models are incredibly limited. The storm they predicted dissipates or takes another track. The stock market rally they expected crashes instead; the strains of flu they planned for didn't occur, which means scientists created the wrong vaccines."

Marcus knew enough about quantum computing to bore guests at a cocktail party. He liked her tutorial. She had tried to share the basics of quantum computers with him last night at her apartment, but it was while she was in the shower, and he was brushing his teeth and was totally distracted looking at her curves reflected in the mirror as she arched forward shaving her legs.

"Hello, Marcus! Are you with us here? This is important." Rich condescendingly snapped his fingers.

Beth continued, "Traditional computers are too slow and too limited. Quantum computers will do incredibly wonderful things. They will make amazing improvements in medicine, climate modeling, and materials science." She sat down opposite them and lowered her voice. "Now what if quantum computing was used for something not so good?"

Rich began scanning his notes again, losing focus. He looked up.

"What if, instead of identifying new drugs to combat a virulent new disease from the dizzying array of proteins and compounds, or instead of making air travel safer by modeling passenger volume, location, weather, maintenance, and availability—what if terrorists used one of these quantum computers to decrypt usernames, passwords, and account numbers from a major US bank and routed all their automatic payments to quantum-encrypted accounts overseas using cryptocurrency?" Marcus tilted his head. He hadn't thought about quantum computing that way.

"What if somebody locked weapons systems on a battlefield? How about if all the cars on the highway signaled to accelerate to one hundred miles per hour, or if someone turned off the power grid and North America went dark?" She talked about it with a sense of wonder, without getting wound around the axle of the sheer terror of what she described.

"A properly aimed quantum attack could propel the world into a preindustrial state." She could see they were skeptical. Rich and Marcus were by no means neophytes to tech security, but they were a bit incredulous.

"It sounds a bit sci-fi at this point, doesn't it, Beth?" Rich tried to pop her balloon.

"Hey, this isn't like social media companies or data firms screwing around with voter identities to influence an election. What if a rogue adversary could break into every election station, database, and tabulation machine, invisibly changing just enough votes to produce a different winner? A few hundred here and a few hundred there. No password, firewall, or security system could stop them. They'd leave no trace. Without better security, all of these will happen within fifteen years."

Marcus and Rich were silent.

"If Sinotech is for real, we have a defense against quantum incursions. We are the first research firm to meet with them. We have a major advantage. LAG would have insights nobody can match." She said *LAG* and not *Perseid*. Beth caught her mistake too late and could see the grimace on Rich's face.

"Sinotech promises the first quantum-based security protocol that surrounds existing systems and protects them. They can put a quantum shield around everything."

Marcus loved the way she wove her narrative.

"Governmental security agencies like the DOD, NSA, and CIA are all scrambling to prepare for quantum, but they aren't saying anything publicly because they don't want to scare people." She popped the rest of her bag of airplane peanuts in her mouth.

"Why not go public with their concerns?" asked Marcus.

"Tell people their iPhones are going to be hacked and they get annoyed. Tell them the username for their email has been stolen and they get frustrated. People get irritated when their Facebook accounts are corrupted." They followed her logic.

"So, what do you tell them? That their banks will be raided and their accounts emptied? Or that there will be no electricity? Or that all the nuclear codes will be hijacked? You'd be telling them there is nothing our government can do about it. There would be global panic." She crumpled the empty bag and playfully tossed it at Marcus.

"Without something like Sinotech, there is no defending force on the horizon. There are no white knights to defend the kingdom. No other firm has even announced a statement of direction for this kind of security yet, not to mention an actual working prototype of a solution. Sinotech is very interesting to me," she concluded.

Beth sat back, stretched, and gave them both a smile. She loved it when she was the smartest one in the room. Marcus loved it too, but it didn't address his immediate concern.

"With this discomforting news," Marcus asked again, "am I here on behalf of Perseid or LAG? How will we play this out?"

Rich murmured, "One team, Marcus," and went back to rehearsing his presentation.

The pilot's voice disrupted the tension. "We will be landing in ten minutes."

Nobody spoke during the twenty-minute drive from the private terminal at Macau International Airport to the hotel. The activity outside their windows was frenetic. Streets were jammed with cabs, tuktuks ferried tourists to the casinos, sidewalks bustled with workers ending their day, and tourists headed to dinner and entertainment. There was movement everywhere. Colorful neon signs and massive LCD billboards illuminated the avenues and alleys. Faint scents of street food wafted through the window of their limousine. The road traveled alongside the waterfront, where the expanse of the South China Sea shimmered under the last rays of the waning sun. Top of Form

Bottom of Form

★ ★ ★

The team barely had time to grab a drink at the bar when Rich's phone buzzed. Their guests had arrived. The Sinotech executive team met with Rich, Marcus, and Beth in a large suite on the fiftieth floor of the Mandarin Oriental, Macau. The sun had set a little over an hour ago. The lights of the ornate Macau casino to their left and the eleven-hundred-foot Macau Tower to their right were spellbinding from the conference room. Traffic flowed chaotically in the streets below, but the Sinotech team presided above it all.

※ ※ ※

Marcus wasn't the subject matter expert on quantum security, Beth was. Marcus wasn't the senior executive from Perseid, Rich was. Marcus was uncomfortable with the ambiguity of the role he'd play. His comfort level sunk further when the Sinotech executives entered the room. The four men were dressed in nearly identical charcoal-gray suits, white button-down shirts, black shoes, and black belts. Only their selections of neckties easily distinguished them. Mr. Blue Tie was the boss, taking the seat at the head of the conference table. Misters Pink, Red, and Maroon Ties were subservient, sitting after he selected his chair, nodding in agreement when Blue Tie spoke, and speaking only when acknowledged by Mr. Blue Tie.

Mr. Blue Tie didn't engage in pleasantries. There was no small talk, nor any attempt at pre-meeting introductions. He was all business and all Sinotech, without any concern about how Perseid and LAG worked together, or the process for engaging analysts. More concerning for Marcus, Mr. Blue Tie didn't share any details of his firm and never asked Beth, the expert in the market, for feedback, opinion, or inputs.

Marcus turned away from the Sinotech executives in an effort to camouflage and suppress a deep yawn, wondering if jet lag made him overly suspicious or if some cultural nuance was at play. He felt exposed and frustrated with Rich at how this meeting was dropped on him, with no time to conduct due diligence on Sinotech's offerings, principals, or background. Marcus was unprepared, unbalanced, and off guard. Marcus always managed his environment, and a loss of control was disconcerting.

Mr. Blue Tie limited his interactions to Rich, acknowledging Beth and Marcus but not engaging them directly. Furthermore,

Sinotech wasn't here seeking advice from LAG analysts; they were demanding commitments. It wasn't collaborative. It was confrontational, almost adversarial. "The timing is critical, Mr. Anderson. We need your help before our market launch in two months." They assumed LAG would deliver. Marcus was dumbfounded because Rich was not pushing back. He was uncharacteristically subservient, especially to Mr. Blue Tie.

According to the brief overview Rich had given Marcus and Beth on the flight, Sinotech had secured $20 million in seed capital from Perseid earlier that year and they were now weeks away from having a commercially viable product. As Beth noted, they were the only quantum security game in town. Even so, these executives should be imploring LAG for insights, not demanding coverage. They should be aligning their market launch strategy with LAG's research calendar. They should be asking for support in positioning and messaging. They should be listening more and talking less. And they certainly should not insinuate LAG owed them any level of attention. But Rich didn't correct them or reset any of their expectations.

As a start-up firm, operating with seed funding, Sinotech had zero revenues. Most early-stage companies are extremely careful with their cash; $20 million from Perseid was not a lot of money for a firm that had to pay developers, lease office space, purchase computers, install infrastructure, and pay for R & D. Yet Sinotech somehow found enough cash to purchase a $500,000 service contract with LAG. It was a crazy amount for a firm with no revenues. When Marcus raised it on the flight to Macau, he was the only one curious as to why. Now he knew.

The Sinotech team spent ninety minutes outlining their expectations for coverage in LAG research and walking Rich through the basics of quantum technology, in far less detail than Beth had done at fifty thousand feet. Marcus perched forward on his seat, looking for an opportunity to interject and engage Mr. Blue Tie directly. He cleared his throat in a way to politely interrupt the monologue. Rich shot him a furious glance and rocked his head side to side, signaling Marcus, "No. Not now."

Marcus sat back, deflated and angry. After a recap on market drivers that even Marcus easily understood, the Sinotech team stopped. Marcus was sure Beth would have a lot of probing questions, but she remained silent. Beth had seen Rich's reaction when Marcus tried to interrupt.

In perfect English, Mr. Blue Tie asked, "Mr. Anderson, we've paid your firm a lot of money. When can we expect to see a return on our investment? When will we be featured in your reports to your clients?" There was no mistaking the demand; he clearly meant LAG clients.

Marcus leaned forward, putting his elbows on the table, prepared to set proper expectations, but Rich quickly interrupted, motioning to his colleagues. "We will publish research within weeks as a foundation for our work in quantum security, Mr. Huang. You will be showcased in that effort."

Marcus couldn't speak, stunned at Rich's assurance and its blatant violation of LAG's corporate ethics. Sinotech expected positive coverage for their LAG investment. Huang made it clear that Sinotech paid LAG, and LAG would do their bidding. This was pay-for-play in its most basic form. To make matters worse, the line between LAG and Perseid was now shattered. Rich committed that LAG would produce research and make recommendations that would directly benefit a company within Perseid's portfolio. The violation stunned Marcus into a rigid silence. Mouth open, arms crossed in a defensive position, a subtle nod in disbelief, the nonverbal cues from Marcus were obvious.

Rich smiled and stood. He didn't need to say anything to Marcus. He got the message. Rich's proclamation was all the Sinotech executives wanted to hear. They rose, shook hands, and left abruptly, Huang asking Rich to join them for a private discussion in the hallway.

Marcus, left sitting alone with Beth, was bewildered. Beth's body language and demeanor wasn't as sour and frustrated as Marcus's.

"What the fuck was that all about? Did you hear that?" Marcus was infuriated.

"I thought it was a good meeting. I didn't really need to be here, but it was a good meeting," she replied.

"Twenty-six hours of flying for a two-hour meeting? Neither of us needed to be here to watch Rich sell our integrity."

"C'mon. That's a bit harsh."

"It's true, and I don't want any part of it." Marcus was fuming.

"We've got a long flight home to discuss this," Beth said calmly.

Rich rejoined his colleagues, looking like a man who just received a stay of execution. He wasn't happy, just anxious to leave. Rich took a big deep breath, exhaled loudly, and forced a smile, but he didn't offer any details from his sidebar conversation with the Sinotech team. "We need to get back in Boston. We aren't staying the night."

※ ※ ※

Huang was there as an interested investor in Perseid as much as the primary point of contact between the Chinese government and Sinotech. The hallway conversation with Rich, albeit short, was sharply pointed.

"It's nice to see you, Mr. Anderson." Huang snarked at having to use Enrique's stage name.

"Mr. Huang, good to see you again." Rich spoke to him regularly but had not seen him in person since their meeting at his father's hacienda in Mexico five years ago. His attendance caught Rich by surprise. The surprise was intentional. Echelon 3 was taking too much time.

"I'm here to see how well my two top investments are working together. I wanted to see firsthand how you leverage LAG in our work for Perseid." Huang was intrigued by the scheme Rich shared at their first meeting, leveraging LAG to manipulate equities and funneling returns through Perseid. China's multibillion-dollar share of the capital gains was not sufficient, however.

"It is time, Mr. Banderas. I told you this months ago. Move forward now or Perseid loses its Hong Kong privileges and I look for other distribution partners in Mexico." It was a jarring threat that startled Rich.

"We need to have our software installed into US business and governmental systems before the next election. It is time for you to do what you've promised to do, Mr. Anderson. Echelon 3 needs to launch now." Huang's stare punctuated his demand.

Rich bristled. He didn't like being lectured to.

Recognizing signs of the boy's insolence, Huang continued, "Your father and uncle have annoyed rival cartels in Mexico. They need my help. Am I clear?" Huang was as good at sending a message as Rich's father and uncle.

Huang was confident Rich would deliver. He had no choice. But he was curious about the others on the team—another reason why he'd taken the ferry forty miles from Hong Kong to Macau. The woman was very attractive and mildly helpful. But Huang was concerned about Marcus. Like Rich, Huang easily spotted the fidgeting, negative facial expressions and signals Marcus radiated.

"Keep an eye on Mr. Shea. I've seen his type before. You cannot let him become a problem."

Rich nodded.

"I've spoken to your uncle. At my request, he is sending people to watch everybody on Mr. Shea's team."

★ ★ ★

As they sat at the conference table in the aft of the G700 preparing for takeoff, Marcus couldn't hold back anymore. "Jesus Christ, Rich. According to Beth's research, Sinotech isn't even on the radar screen of any of our analysts, or any governmental agency for that matter. Now we are going to advocate for them in our research?"

Rich's tilted his head gave him an apathetic stare. "It was my call, Marcus."

"Beth? Will global companies bet their systems and security on an unknown start-up?" Marcus wanted her to be on his side. She didn't reply, desperate to stay out of the middle of an argument that was building in volume and intensity. Beth shuffled in her seat, shifting her eyes from Marcus to Rich and back, caught between them and not wanting to add fuel to the conflict.

"I said it was my call, Marcus." Rich expected that to be the end of discussion.

"Beth, you said hostile foreign governments were the top security concern. Doesn't this fit that description? How does it make sense for LAG clients?"

"Hong Kong isn't the same thing as mainland China," Beth interjected weakly. It derailed Marcus for a moment.

Marcus closed his eyes, took a breath, and sat back heavily. "What are we doing?" His tone softened. It was a rhetorical question. It was a comment from somebody losing the debate.

Rich shut out Marcus's concerns and closed his eyes, replaying the hallway conversation with Mr. Huang. His plan was to strengthen his grip over the Emerging Tech Team by dangling even greater incentives. Huang and his uncle were devising a darker approach.

CHAPTER 18
Irresistible and Irreversible

Dark circles surrounded Rich's glazed and reddened eyes. Dark whiskers grew in patches on his chin and jawline. He was exhausted from two days without sleep, but there was no time. He scheduled an immediate team meeting the moment their plane from Macau touched down. Marcus's dour mood and objections about pay-for-play needed to be squelched. The only way to do that would be to rally the rest of the Emerging Tech Team in unanimity against Marcus's position.

The October sky was vivid, cold, and blue. The morning sun was harsh and overwhelming for the three travelers suffering from jet lag. Jeff and Deb were weary from their workload, but not nearly as foggy as Rich, Marcus, and Beth when they gathered in Rich's apartment.

"This is an immense opportunity." Rich's tone was excited but forced. The caffeine wasn't enough.

"Which opportunity?" Marcus interrupted grumpily. "For Sinotech? For LAG's clients? Or for Perseid's balance sheet?" Marcus paused between each choice, watching the irritation on Rich's face grow. Marcus was certain the team's reaction would be suspicious toward Rich's plan, which he'd called Echelon 3 and previewed to him and Beth during the plane ride.

Rich paused, his jaw tightening, struggling not to let the team see his frustration. "That's the beauty of our opportunity with Sinotech. It can be an incredible opportunity for all of it."

Rich provided a quick, highly edited recap of the Sinotech meeting, the market opportunities Beth identified, and the prospects it presented to the group, all without any mention of pay-for-play or without stating which opportunity was his true priority. After thirteen hours on the plane, Marcus was certain this was a Perseid play above all else.

"Can we really do all three?" It was a plea to his team, not a question to Rich. Marcus was conflicted. Rich was his boss and his best friend, and nothing ran more counter to Marcus's internal programming than disobedience and disloyalty. He struggled, wondering if Echelon 3 was really that much more problematic than everything else they did in Echelons 1 and 2.

Rich's face, flushed with frustration, stiffened with annoyance escalating toward anger.

Marcus tried to lower the pressure. "The global IT market will be desperate for a solution like Sinotech. There is potential with them that we should assess, but I'm concerned because we don't have all the details about their approach." Marcus wondered if his tone would ease Rich's irritation.

"Sinotech will be the first billion-dollar equity play for Perseid. It's going to happen," Rich said, accepting Marcus's semi-withdrawal.

"What does everyone else think?" Marcus looked at the rest of the team, begging for their feedback.

Jeff was always fairly malleable, but Marcus figured Deb would push back at Rich's plan and join in his dissent. She didn't have time. Rich laid an incentive on the table that ended the debate. It caught Marcus off guard and brought a stunned silenced to the room. Before anybody could interject, and before Rich said a word about how they'd bring Echelon 3 into being, he handed them stock certificates. "Each of you has been issued fifty thousand pre-IPO shares of Sinotech."

The Emerging Tech Team turned their attention away from the debate between Marcus and Rich and looked at the piece of paper with confusion, unsure what it meant. Rich took advantage of their silence and painted a glorious picture. "Conservatively, Sinotech's opening price in six months will be $100 to $150 per share. With Perseid's 49 percent ownership in Sinotech, this will be our first multibillion-dollar investment."

The team didn't do the math for Perseid. Instead Rich could see them calculating their own take. Holding the certificate by its corner in his left hand, Jeff lifted it above his head. "This is a $7.5 million bonus for each of us?" Rich said, looking for confirmation from Rich.

"Yes, $7.5 million." Rich repeated it for Jeff, but looked at Marcus with a nod confirming he won the debate.

Jeff put it back on the table and raked his hands through his grayed hair, unable to contain his smile.

"Money makes all the ugly go away," Marcus quietly huffed, confirming he was the only one with a creeping suspicion. Agree, commit, move forward. Marcus was trapped by his own approach.

With the team's apprehension appropriately softened, Rich laid it all out in front of them. "In Echelon 1 we used our research as an early indicator for which clients and vendors were prime targets for investment. It was a massive success, and we will continue to employ those tactics."

Rich buttressed what was coming by showing them what they'd already done and that nothing bad had happened. They had already abandoned their roles as independent analysts and were taking a financial stake in the client firms they advised and the vendors they analyzed, and nobody got hurt.

"Echelon 2 ensured Perseid investments were prominently featured in all LAG research reports. Each of you drove buyer interest in those vendors. The cycle built on itself with other LAG teams. Our velocity accelerated." Marcus noticed that Rich didn't add the obvious. Namely, that Perseid profited massively. It sounded innocent enough, and none of them wanted to rethink how they got here. Everybody but Marcus was nodding acceptance and approval.

"Sinotech is our pilot for Echelon 3." Without any resistance or defiance, Rich laid out the plan where there were no rules, no lines of demarcation, and nothing stopping them from engaging however they wanted to generate returns for Perseid. LAG was a tool to manipulate, inflate, or derail vendors, and Perseid used it all to its advantage. Now there was only one direction to go, forward. There was so much money, and Marcus was the only one bothered by the steps they'd taken to get to Echelon 3.

Rich had their silent attention. "All we need to do is start injecting Sinotech into the client meetings you take every day. As you talk to CIOs who are investigating new security solutions, mention that Sinotech should be on their list and let LAG's research do the rest." Rich looked around the room. Nobody was bristling. "We all believe that new security solutions are needed, and we all believe Sinotech has a viable solution." The Emerging Tech Team nodded their commitment. Marcus wasn't a part of the *we all believe*, but it didn't matter to Rich.

"Easy enough," Jeff punctuated Rich's narrative, still giddy about the $7.5 million payout.

"Jeff, as you work with your LAG peers on other teams, get them to mention Sinotech as an up-and-coming player to their clients. I want Sinotech discussed in a hundred of one-on-one client sessions by the end of next week." The plan was so easy. This was the first domino to fall, starting a chain reaction.

"That's a breeze between the four of us," Deb said, with a smile directed toward Jeff.

Rich kept pace. "Within the month all LAG analysts will be buzzing, asking, 'Who is Sinotech?' The entire firm will be amplifying your recommendations." This was going to be too easy. The Emerging Tech Team listened in support, eyes fixed on Rich, without disruption. Domino two falls.

Rich continued. "Your LAG colleagues will readily jump on board with Sinotech because this team endorsed them. As chief of research, I'll select Jeff and Beth to author the research reports on Sinotech and the dangerous market risks they solve." Rich didn't pause for feedback. The Emerging Tech Team offered no challenge. It was like Rich was reciting directions for a recipe. Simplicity. Step by step. Domino three falls.

"With our new research in the market, LAG will be the only advisory firm to have a compelling point of view on Sinotech. We will prepare an alert for all our clients, raising the specter of catastrophic security failures in the next year and pointing to our research as a road map for preempting the crisis."

The team was absorbed in Rich's plan. Even Marcus had uncrossed his arms and removed the scowl from his face.

"Nobody in our government is preparing businesses for the risk. It's our duty to raise the issue. This is our chance to save the world." Rich's pride was manufactured. "We only need to shine a bright spotlight on the looming global security threat. LAG's reports will show Sinotech is the clear leader and needs to be strongly considered." Domino four falls.

Rich confidently circled the room, building pace and motion as the team's verbal affirmations grew.

"Now we set up briefings with all our vendor clients. Hardware, software, services, all of them. We start grinding them on their security protocols and standards. We warn them they are in jeopardy. We reinforce they would bear legal and financial liability if they don't embed new quantum security protocols into their systems. We provide them with Sinotech as an example. We tell them our research is going to review which vendors are prepared for the looming threat and which aren't. We have both the carrot and stick. Sinotech can save them. If the vendors don't heed our warnings, LAG will wipe them out." Rich's tempo was verging on frantic and frenetic. "This is a global emergency." Domino five falls.

All their eyes were on him, mesmerized with the logic and simplicity of the plan. Even in his skeptical state, Marcus was caught up in the story.

"Our next task is to broaden visibility and publicity. With a growing number of client meetings centered on Sinotech, LAG's published research, the buzz among our analysts, and skyrocketing interest among vendors to partner with Sinotech, we blitz the press. They love stories of impending doom. We write articles on the coming security nightmare. We comment via opinion pieces. We appear on nightly news and cable programs. We solidify our brand as experts in this space and we bring Sinotech right along with us." Every word from Rich imbued conviction and purpose wrapped in a confident smile. Domino six falls.

"This sounds a lot like the Y2K furor analysts ignited twenty years ago," Jeff mumbled half-heartedly, still stroking the stock certificate.

"And what happened there, Jeff? That crisis was averted, and a lot of people got rich. So, yes, this is similar in a way," Rich added, not at all looking for Jeff's endorsement.

Rich continued, "Finally, we have all we need to move from recommending clients to consider, including Sinotech on their evaluation list, to advocating for Sinotech as the single best alternative. All the data supports it. Every analyst, research report, vendor rating, stack rank, news story, and peer review points in the same direction. Sinotech is a critical, nonnegotiable cornerstone of business infrastructure. Our CIOs need to buy it, and each piece of hardware and software they deploy must support it." The final domino crashes down.

Rich marveled at his plan. In Echelons 1 and 2, he'd nudged the team with baby steps, nosing them over the line of what was ethical and blurring the demarcation between LAG and Perseid, between right and wrong. They took modest step after modest step. The final steps into Echelon 3 were bold, big, and not subtle. And only Marcus felt any apprehension. He knew there was no way this could all be done without much greater effort and output from his team, especially Jeff. It would be a crushing burden, but for now it was hidden behind a whopping paycheck and a beautiful story, and the rest of the team didn't care.

★ ★ ★

Less than two months later, in early December, LAG published a five-part series on the looming security and cryptography crisis and produced a lightly vetted list of vendors who LAG recognized as capable to help the world's largest and most complex businesses prepare for the coming security onslaught. Only one of them was in the "must buy" category: Sinotech.

All the major trade publications reported on LAG's research. A national news anchor interviewed Rich about the pending computer security disaster. The story pushed global warming out of the headlines for a full news cycle. The national press loved stories of approaching catastrophe. Press requests to interview members of the Emerging Tech Team skyrocketed. Rich noticed Marcus wasn't as eager as Deb and Beth to participate.

Based on LAG's strong-arm tactics, vendors were tripping over each other to secure partnership and distribution contracts leveraging Sinotech's capabilities in their solutions. These vendors immediately started to embed links and interfaces from Sinotech into their products in anticipation of lucrative integration deals. The panic among vendors, not to be left behind, was unmistakable. In the rush to be on the list of certified Sinotech partners, none of the vendors noticed the few lines of computer code embedded deep in the background of Sinotech's source code, designed to sit dormant until triggered.

With a skyrocketing revenue stream and a massive backlog of business to be booked, the Sinotech IPO out of Hong Kong was fast-tracked. Perseid owned 49 percent of a firm valued at over $10 billion. The four Emerging Tech Team analysts from LAG, moonlighting for Perseid, each had over $7 million in Sinotech shares, sitting in secret brokerage accounts in Belize.

Nobody on the Emerging Tech Team considered reevaluating, questioning, or slowing down, except Marcus.

CHAPTER 19
Shattering Trust

The workload to support Sinotech, buoyed by a steady stream of new IPO candidates from Perseid over the next eleven months as part of Echelon 3, was as suffocating as Marcus feared and as smothering as Rich hoped. The workload overwhelmed the Emerging Tech Team, and they became increasingly robotic and repetitive in their efforts. Perfectly compliant for Rich.

Marcus could not keep up. He was running in sand. Sinking and watching his team sink alongside him. He was especially concerned about Jeff, who was an increasingly weakening link in the chain, twisting, straining, and misshapen under stress. With growing suspicions about what Perseid was doing, and the rising tide of work Rich demanded of his team, Marcus monitored everybody on his team. All were tired, but Jeff was breaking from the stress.

Rich told them all he wanted was "bigger deals, not more." It sounded fine, but in practice it wasn't the truth. Marcus, Deb, and Beth had to keep the Perseid investment portfolio fed and identify new IPO candidates for Echelon 3. Jeff had to generate and author all the research the team needed to make it happen. It was nothing but more, more, more and deadline after deadline. It was all about completing tasks and projects and getting things off the to-do list. Rich was giving them a lot more to do, not less, especially Jeff.

Rich wanted them buried in an avalanche of work demands so there was no time to think ethics, or propriety or legality. He couldn't risk anybody worrying about stock manipulation, insider trading, pump and dump, or pay-for-play.

But Marcus, heading the entire process, looked at the team's deliverables and interactions in their entirety every day. In seeing the whole picture, Marcus struggled with the brazen disregard for LAG company policy. The team was way beyond Sinotech now. A dozen new vendors were in the Perseid pipeline for IPOs, all getting "the Sinotech treatment." For Marcus, vague unease evolved into suspicion and paranoia.

He watched as, on Rich's orders, Jeff introduced unvetted and unproven vendors into LAG research to elevate their stock prices. Rich pushed an exhausted Jeff to raise ratings or cut rankings of vendors, so they appeared more positively or negatively based on Perseid's investment goals. Other LAG analysts would recommend or blackball vendors because of the Emerging Tech Team's research. Perseid, of course, would either buy or short the stocks depending on how Rich placed his thumb on the scale.

The growing demands on the team pushed them to the precipice of breaking, just as Rich planned. It made everybody compliant. Rich didn't need to intimidate or bully the team, just overwhelm them with work. They would mindlessly "check the box" to keep things moving. They'd never look back. They'd finish the to-do list and move to the next task. Rich left them with no time to ask questions. Their sole focus was on delivery. To make sure they kept conforming, Rich would pay them off with bonus checks and stock grants. Fatigue, positive reinforcement, and money was his plan.

Rich had the team operating with "highway hypnosis." It was a trancelike state in which the driver was completely focused on the road and unaware of time or surroundings. It could lead to decreased reaction time and an increased chance of making mistakes or even falling asleep at the wheel. But in many cases, a driver could go long distances in a sort of daze, accelerating, steering, and braking but without noticing anything around them. Often, the driver would arrive at their destination with no recollection of what they passed along the way or how much time it took. They awoke on arrival.

Often something small could break the hypnosis. A car horn, a deer running across the road, a song on the radio. When it happened, the person may experience an acute sense of clarity and alertness, like being snapped awake from a deep sleep. All senses became hypersensitive and sharp.

The team had been operating in a trance for months, working on incredibly complex projects for Rich, but unaware of what was happening around them. Little sleep. Poor diet. Different hotels every night. No exercise. No fresh air, or sunlight, for that matter.

The television in his office, tuned to CNN, shattered Marcus's hypnosis. The image on the screen was tied to what he was doing. Or did it remind him of what he was doing? The young reporter stretched his microphone through the small throng following the senator as he walked the passageway connecting the Capitol Hill visitor center to the Senate wing of the Capitol building. "Senator Haverstock, have you found evidence of espionage?"

It was a wide, brightly lit corridor with marble walls, terrazzo floors, and a central skylight. The gaggle of reporters walked past the bronze statue of women's rights activist Susan B. Anthony. Senator Scott Haverstock loved the visual of him on TV hurrying to an unspecified meeting on behalf of the country.

"Right now it is an ongoing investigation. It is very worrisome. I'm working with committee members, including those on the other side of the aisle, to get to the bottom of the situation." He paused so the cameras could get a clear picture of his good side.

He continued, "I've been briefed on reports of state-sponsored hacking groups targeting US software companies to steal sensitive customer information and trade secrets. New strains of malware, spyware, and malicious code are emerging. Hearings are warranted. I'm headed to talk with the majority leader right now." Haverstock had no idea what any of that technobabble meant, but he looked good saying it.

Marcus had been in the office for eighteen hours straight reading Jeff's research, conducting conference calls with clients and prospects, and practicing for a major industry association speech. The research draft he was in the midst of editing focused on security firewalls and prominently featured Sinotech. Marcus hadn't really thought much about them in the months following their IPO; he'd been busy with all the new IPO candidates in Perseid's pipeline. Marcus was well versed in the structural weaknesses of corporate computing platforms rogue entities might exploit. Social engineering tactics like phishing and password attacks captured a lot of news coverage recently because the typical audience for the evening news could easily understand how they might be vulnerable. But approaches like rogue code injection, cross-site scripting, cloud security breaches, or back doors were more in line with what Jeff was investigating and now Marcus was reading.

It was the television Q and A with the senator that lifted Marcus's fog. He murmured, "Why was Rich so anxious to get Sinotech mentioned in all the security-related client meetings and embedded in the research after Macau?" The fog burned off. Marcus was awake. The answer had been there all along but buried under a $7.5 million bribe. Marcus's weekly 7:00 a.m. team meeting was scheduled in fifteen minutes. He'd raise his concerns to the whole team out of sight of Rich.

★ ★ ★

"You are blowing this out of proportion, Marcus. Why can't we just move to the next project? I've got three more vendor profiles to complete next week and two market landscapes. The pipeline of IPOs isn't getting smaller." Jeff was tired and looked to Beth and Deb for consensus.

"I've got three meetings with board members from our largest vendor clients and an industry keynote coming up," Beth added, in support of Jeff. She did not want to revisit the decision they made a year ago. She had immediate client deliverables due.

"I need research too. I'm in London all next week for a consulting project," Deb added, wondering why this was even open for debate.

"Marcus, you raised concerns a year ago and we got over it. Why now?" Beth added. She saw how agitated Marcus was and wanted to soothe him, feeling guilty that the team was unanimously at odds with his position. She'd spent so little time with him lately. She missed him.

Jeff sighed loudly. "Rich has been crawling up my ass to get more security notes published since Sinotech went public. I finished two within a few weeks of your trip to Macau and another one just before they registered their IPO six months later. Now he is asking for more. He's asking me to hype the cryptography market. He's got a list of reports he wants me to author and the conclusions he wants me to draw. He wants LAG's seal of approval on it all." Jeff uttered, "I don't have time to dissect what we did last year. Rich is becoming brutal."

They listened to Marcus's concerns but hoped he was just venting frustrations. They all had work to do, and they needed Jeff to regroup and finish the reports scheduled, not recast reports that had been finished months ago.

Marcus knew he was not getting through. "I was thinking like you. Like all of you." His emotions bled through. "We've always had the same mindset. Get it done, check the box, and move on. But the press announcements of investigations into foreign government tampering with US vendor code got me thinking. Rich is asking us to change research and create new reports specifically to benefit Perseid clients. A light went off."

"Have you said anything to Rich?" Beth hoped he hadn't.

"Of course not. I wanted to speak with you guys first."

"He will lose his fucking mind if we miss upcoming deadlines," Jeff added.

Marcus recognized the constriction they were in. "I know you guys are tired and the workload is crushing. Maybe I'm wrong. But I'm not making this stuff up about the Senate investigation."

"I've been mentoring a new analyst at LAG. He has a brother in the Justice Department. Maybe he could ask him to sniff around the SEC or FBI and see if Sinotech is on their radar?" Jeff offered, with concern rising.

"Jesus. How will Rich react to that?" Deb questioned.

Beth shrunk back in her chair, pulse quickening, trying not panic. She knew how Rich would react. "God, we can't do this."

"Rich would explode if he knew," Jeff added. "He reams me out daily if I'm even a few minutes late on a project. I've never seen him with such a short fuse."

The mention of potential investigations, even quiet ones, startled the rest of the team. It became their moment of clarity. Their highway hypnosis lifted.

"What have we been doing for the last two years?" Deb asked. Each step, each breach had been so small. But now, Marcus ripped off their blindfolds and turned on the lights. He forced them to see the distance they had traveled. Looking back to their original starting point, the day they all met in the conference room during the onboarding session, seemed beyond their view, behind them, and past the horizon. They'd gotten comfortable bending one rule, then another, and then trusting Rich about the necessity to do things differently. Rich controlled everything they did as LAG employees, as contributors to Perseid, and in the gray areas in between. Now the gray areas were sharpening, becoming more stark and well defined.

Marcus could see the team coming to a new consensus. They'd crossed the line long ago. Not as one big step, but inch by inch.

Confidentiality breaches led to research biases led to client coercion, which fed insider trading schemes and finally stock manipulation. All of it would be hard to prove. But being an accomplice to potential espionage was another matter. It was the specter Marcus raised now.

Marcus imagined the worst-case scenarios. Prison, extortion, and physical danger. "We need to keep this to ourselves until we figure it out. Nobody talks to Rich about this, and nobody makes any calls to the FBI until we know what we are dealing with."

The entire team was hyperaware and sharply conscious.

"For now, everybody just keep doing what you've been doing. We don't know the extent of what we've already done or if LAG, Perseid, or Sinotech are being watched," Marcus reinforced. Everybody agreed.

Nobody on the Emerging Tech Team knew there were others already monitoring them. One of the observers, sitting at a dining room table with his back toward the jets landing at Logan airport across the harbor, watched and listened to the video feed from security cameras he'd installed in all the conference rooms in LAG's Boylston Street offices. Rich angrily reached back and slammed the sliding doors closed so he could hear their conversation more clearly.

The other watcher had been following members of the team learning their work patterns for months following the meeting in Macau. This man followed them as they arrived in their offices in the morning and spied on their homes at night while they slept, just as Alejandro had instructed.

CHAPTER 20
Pressure and Collapse

The breakdown was inevitable. Continuing to work, as if everything were normal, was possible for Marcus, Beth, and Deb. They had the distraction of traveling nearly full time and being shielded from Rich.

But not Jeff. His panic intensified. There was no moderation in the workload Rich demanded, and the pressures of constant inspection and furious criticisms were suffocating. In the weeks that passed since Marcus opened their eyes, nothing changed for Jeff. Deb and Beth were overwhelmed with their responsibilities. Marcus was thousands of miles away fulfilling LAG duties. Rich had them all so busy, they didn't have time to interfere with his plans. Nobody on the Emerging Tech Team was any closer to solving the conflicts between LAG and Perseid today than when Marcus raised it: "How do we unwind the Emerging Tech Team from Perseid? How do we stay out of jail?"

The problem was particularly acute for Jeff because he was left alone in the office with Rich every day. And every day, Rich angrily insisted on more and more output while simultaneously inspecting every word and recommendation included in Jeff's reports. There was nobody to help him. The work grew and grew. His sense of vulnerability, loneliness, and fear was devastating. Jeff had nobody.

Deb traveled six days a week. Jeff believed he had become invisible to the one person he trusted above all others. Marcus and Beth only engaged him via email and text when they wanted something. None of them saw how Rich kept increasing the pressure on Jeff, stepping on him and grinding him down bit by bit and day by day.

Jeff slept alone, ate alone, lived alone, and worked alone. He and Deb moved into their new Brookline home, but moving boxes, filled from their apartment in Southie, overflowed their spare bedroom and garage. He and Deb hadn't painted a single room or hung a picture. They hadn't bought any houseplants or purchased any new rugs or drapes. There were no decorations on the shelves. They hadn't taken any trips to HomeGoods for odds and ends. Jeff didn't have a lawn mower, rake, or snow shovel. The furniture shoved into the rooms by the movers was the same they'd used in their apartment, which meant three of the four bedrooms were empty.

There was nothing about this house that gave Jeff the comfort of a home and there was nobody there to watch his mental state and physical health decline. Every waking moment was work. Rich ensured there was no time for anything else. Jeff stopped caring for himself. He only ate food from a take-out bag. His bathroom towels never needed laundering because he rarely showered. He was unshaven, sallow, and losing weight. His hair, severely thinning and fully grayed, was matted and unwashed. His clothes were baggy, ill-fitting, and grimy. He looked homeless, not like a man with a massive Tudor-style home on a golf course and $20 million deposited in offshore accounts on the other side of the globe. Jeff paused on his way out the door. "It's been six months. We've been here for six months." He headed into Boston well before sunrise.

Jeff wilted under unrelenting pressures from Rich. He went to work every day because he had an obligation to his team. Rich kept applying the whip. Jeff was the critical link between LAG and Perseid. The cycle that delivered massive returns for Perseid began with Jeff. If his research output wavered, it would delay Rich's timeline and trigger violent eruptions and physical threats.

It was a quiet, cold, and gray Sunday morning. Boston in late fall. Jeff had to finish one project and catch up on two more. Rich demanded his final drafts by 3:00 p.m. that day. Jeff begged for more time and was denied. Rich needed the research completed and his entire analyst corps to start promoting the vendors Jeff selected. They'd be placed on LAG's recommended-for-purchase list. It was the last step before Rich would crank up the process to get their IPOs pumped. Rich made it clear that Jeff was the only thing holding back the Perseid portfolio, the only barrier to the team receiving several million dollars in new stock grants each.

Jeff could not bear the weight. His research wasn't done. It wasn't ready to publish. He asked for two more weeks to finish it, and Rich responded with immediate threats. At first Rich said he'd yank his and Deb's bonuses and then said any delays could put Perseid in the crosshairs of lawyers and the SEC. Rich promised Jeff that he'd take the fall if Perseid were investigated and cited at least half a dozen securities violations he and Deb had breached. "You'll both go to prison."

Jeff knew there was no end in sight. He'd finish one analysis for Rich, as CEO of LAG, and then be ordered to frame two new vendor ratings reports as a way to keep the pipeline full for Rich, as CEO of Perseid. Jeff sat at his desk, back to the door, looking out the window onto Boylston Street with the Fairmont Copley Plaza hotel diagonally across the street. He lowered his head into the palms of his hands knowing there was no way he'd finish the assignment today. He was going to miss Rich's schedule and Rich would be furious. It was six thirty in the morning, on the last day of a hundred-hour work week, and Jeff broke.

The last time he cried, even a little, was when he put the ring on Deb's hand during a small ecumenical service in Woodstock,

Vermont, six years ago. Before that, he might have been six or seven years old. Falling off a bike. His childhood dog getting hit by a car. His grandmother dying. He couldn't remember why he cried then. Now his sobs built, grew, and intensified, and it shattered him. The hopelessness was unbearable, and he wept in isolation. No amount in a bank account in the Caymans or Belize would provide the comfort, calm, and rest he needed. The guilt and pain he felt letting his team down would not go away. Not being strong for Deb shamed him. Everybody relied on him, and he was going to fail.

Jeff suffered alone, but still, Deb sensed it. She wasn't always with him, but she knew. He'd degenerated quickly in the past weeks, and she felt his anguish. She hadn't been able to get him to talk about it on the phone, but she could see it. And when she walked in quietly behind him as he sat weeping, she knew exactly what he was thinking and what he was feeling. He was alone and drowning. He needed rescue.

Deb's red-eye flight from San Jose landed early and she stopped at the office to drop off expense reports. She wanted to surprise Jeff at home. She hadn't expected him to be in the office. He looked terrible. She'd seen it coming and hoped it would get better. She hoped Marcus would magically find a way for them all to get back on the right side of their ethical dilemma. She hoped Rich would recognize Jeff's pain and take his foot off the accelerator. She hoped his workload would diminish. None of that happened.

Now she understood, as Jeff was critically aware, it would not get better. Rich believed the massive bonus checks, sprinkled with founder's shares of Perseid's pre-IPO investments, would be the permanent cure. Rich believed money was the elixir to heal all their wounds and rejuvenate their souls. Jeff was evidence that Rich was wrong. Rich pushed too far.

Deb placed her hands on Jeff's shoulders, bent, and hugged him around the neck. She was startled at how boney his neck and back were. He was terribly thin. "It's OK. We are going to be OK."

Jeff broke down. Deep anguished cries, originating in his gut and rising through his throat, escaped. Tears streamed, tracing glistening paths down his cheeks to the corners of his mouth. His eyes were bloodshot. Jeff was a little embarrassed when he got teary on the altar in front of Deb and her parents in the chapel. He wasn't embarrassed now. He wanted it all to stop. He didn't know a way out. Deb held him as he unloaded it all. The hopelessness was heavy and smothering and more than he could bare. But for the first time in a long time, Jeff felt the burden was something that they could share.

"Let's finish these last few reports together today and then make a plan. A real plan to get out. Let's be done within six months." She needed him to listen and believe. She was no longer concerned with potential ethical conflicts or the questionable legality of their work. She was only interested in saving her husband and escaping.

She rotated him in his chair and looked at him eye to eye as he sat there. Deb was shocked at what she saw. The man she loved was hunched before her, eyes cast down, shoulders caved forward. He looked older and frail. Deb put her hand to his unshaven chin and raised it. His sunken eyes followed upward slowly. "We will do whatever we need to do to get out."

He took a deep breath and put his arms out to hold her. He believed her and he took a deep breath. The tears stopped.

"We need two things. Secrecy and money. We already have the escape route." Jeff nurtured an ember of a plan. It burned hotter now that Deb was there with him. It was their way out.

Deb helped Jeff to his feet, and they headed to the office kitchen. Their movement triggered the security camera to turn on. At his desk overlooking the harbor, Rich's monitor showed them holding hands as they walked down the hallway.

☆ ☆ ☆

"That's sweet. Now get back to work," Rich barked at the screen. He'd just finished a call with his investors minutes earlier and had been spying on Jeff since. The financial projections he shared made his father and uncle happy. China was less enamored by the money, instead wanting more technology partnerships and licensing relationships for Sinotech. They wanted their code inside those systems. Rich promised to get Huang a priority list of fifty new vendor candidates by the end of the week. He'd put Jeff on it tomorrow after he delivered what was promised today.

There had always been a security system at LAG, but Rich upgraded it recently with several high-definition cameras and microphones throughout the offices and conference rooms. His security team provided him closed-feed access via the cloud. At the same time, his IT department gave him the ability to monitor his team's emails and internet search activity. Nobody from Marcus's team met, emailed, searched, or texted without him seeing it.

Rich knew Marcus's team was sharing problematic emails and texts. Rich was looking for signs of disloyalty. Whiffs appeared. The team's search patterns were concerning, looking for information on Sinotech. The team sought information on other Perseid IPO candidates too. The man his uncle hired to trail the team also saw potential problems. It didn't require more aggressive intervention yet, but it was enough to mention to his father.

His advice, "Remember the night in the desert."

Rich fumed as he watched and listened to Jeff and Deb make coffee and scheme.

✯ ✯ ✯

"I think about it a lot when I'm not sleeping. About how we get away," Jeff started.

Deb hadn't thought about it at all until a few minutes ago.

"We need enough cash to live on. Forever. Then we need to get off everybody's radar. We need a way we can't be found. Not by Rich and not by any governmental agencies."

"What about Marcus and Beth?" she asked.

"We can't tell them," Jeff responded coldly. "If we let them know, the chances increase Rich will find out. He's already threatened me. Once we run, all the bank accounts and funds we have through Perseid will be frozen. We will lose it all if we aren't careful."

"OK. If we can't take all the Perseid money, how do we get enough to escape?" She paused, waiting for more details.

"If we try to pull all our money without moving it carefully, it will trigger financial regulators. Our best shot is to aggressively invest the cash we control," Jeff replied.

"The money from our LAG bonuses." Deb nodded, understanding Jeff's strategy. "It's not managed by Perseid. But is it enough?"

"No. That's why we are going trade on Perseid's positions. When Rich uses LAG to find new investment opportunities for Perseid, we make sure we are there first with our own money. We will get an even bigger jump than Perseid will."

"So, we are going to use our own money and play along with the stocks Perseid is buying," Deb repeated.

"Yes, and maybe we even hold back a few LAG recommendations from Rich and buy them on our own." Jeff smiled.

"That's going to make us some enemies," Deb countered.

"True, but by the time Rich finds out we will be gone."

"And that's why we can't breathe a word of this to Marcus and Beth?" Deb affirmed with a question.

"In addition to our LAG bonuses we also have the house. If we sell it, it will give us another $1 million to invest. Do you remember Chris Maxwell?" Jeff asked.

"He's the analyst you worked with to expand LAG's coverage of Sinotech," Deb replied.

"I'm pretty sure he's doing some trading on the side," Jeff added.

"OK, so what about him?"

"He gave me an idea of how to get the rest of the money we need. I asked Chris to do some digging on our friends at Sinotech to see if he could spot anything suspicious. Smart kid. He found reasons for concern. He's going to keep digging for me. I think we can use these concerns to tank them. That will be our play. We will take a major short position in Sinotech on our way out the door." Jeff smiled broadly at the notion.

"You fucking son of a bitch." Rich could hear them clearly via the hidden microphone in the kitchen. "You disloyal motherfucker." Rich seethed from his apartment overlooking the harbor and airport.

"I don't know. How do we do that if there isn't a clear problem?" Deb asked.

"That's the thing. It doesn't need to be proven. All LAG has to do is whisper to its clients 'we have concerns' about Sinotech. A short news flash from me to all our clients would trigger LAG analysts to stop promoting Sinotech. CIOs would stop buying and cancel open orders. They'd stop paying their bills to Sinotech. Vendors would stop partnering with them. We could send the note to SEC regulators and the FBI to take a look for good measure. Their stock would plummet." He paused to make sure she was hearing what he was saying. "We'd take a major short position in them and then crater them. It would give us all the money we'd need to disappear."

Rich angrily paced in his dining room listening as Jeff calmly outlined how to kill Sinotech. "Those motherfucking assholes. Fucking disloyal fucks." He launched his coffee cup against the wall, shattering it.

"I've already written the news flash. All I need to do is press send and it will go to all LAG's clients," Jeff continued. "But before it happens, we need to get ready. Once I send this their stock will plummet and all hell will break loose. We'll make millions and disappear in the chaos."

Deb kissed him on the head. "OK, we have a plan."

Rich stood back from his laptop and watched them on camera leave the kitchen. "Get back to work, you ungrateful son of a bitch, and finish the research you owe me." He grinned. It was a sinister grin. There was still time. It would take weeks for them to accumulate all the money they needed to run, and before they escaped, he'd take care of them. For now, he needed Jeff and Deb to keep working. There were too many deals, too close to the finish line, that he could not take Jeff and Deb off the board. But Chris Maxwell was another issue.

"Such a shame." Rich sneered as he dialed. "Another victim of gun violence in Boston."

The man at the end of the line picked up without saying his name.

"Hey. Meet me at my place. I have a job for you." Rich was emotionless in his orders.

"When do you need me?" the man replied.

"Soon. This will need to be done soon."

"Got it." Stevie hung up. He hoped to go to Florida for a few days of fun. He'd been following the Emerging Tech Team nonstop for a couple of months and knew their routines. He wanted to get some sun to break up the winter routine, but a job is a job.

★ ★ ★

Two days later, the Boston Globe published a story, deep in Metro section, about the death of Christopher H. Maxwell, a junior analyst at LAG. He was a West Point graduate who served in army intelligence in Afghanistan. He was shot in the head Thursday night as he left a bar near Faneuil Hall. The police had no suspects.

He was twenty-nine years old.

CHAPTER 21
Treason Unveiled

Christmas passed. Jeff and Deb didn't celebrate the holiday and barely took notice of the work crews already removing the lights and decorations adorning the shops, walkways, and buildings on Boylston Street. They barely remembered Christmas Day and definitely couldn't remember what had happened Thanksgiving, Labor Day, the Fourth of July, or Memorial Day. It all smeared together. The temperature changed, the sunlight dimmed, days shortened, but the demands from Rich only grew.

The pressure to perform, while plotting their escape, made them restless. However, knowing they were inching closer to their goal made it tolerable. Rich was more distant toward them lately. He looked over their shoulders less and less. His threats were less frequent. Jeff didn't know why, and he didn't care. Maintaining a regular routine, they believed, concealed their plans from Rich.

Their Brookline home sold within thirty minutes of the first private showing. It was the easiest $200,000 the broker ever made and nearly a $2 million windfall for Jeff and Deb. The gains from the house were tax free and were routed through a couple of financial pitstops before landing in one of their tax havens. They now had nearly $10 million in their Caribbean accounts, and they could see the finish line. All they needed was a bit more time to make more money, and to stay off Rich's radar. Investing in the same firms Perseid was targeting paid large rapid dividends.

Their plan had worked flawlessly so far. Deb had opened LLCs in the Bahamas, Grenada, and Nevis. Small amounts of money flowed between them, and she began pulling funds from the Perseid's accounts in the Caymans, Belize, and Hong Kong. Initially she transferred funds from one Perseid bank to another. Then she bounced them back and forth between Rich's banks and the accounts she opened. With random amounts and timing, it was easy to siphon funds and park the money in offshore accounts outside of Perseid's view. It was called smurfing.

While they played their roles and kept Rich satisfied, their money grew, and they readied their escape at a marina in Quincy.

★ ★ ★

It was a day more springlike than winter, ten months ago, when Jeff and Deb attended the boat show at the Boston Convention Center and bought a gift for themselves. A big one. Their assignments had already reached unbearable levels and Rich was ramping up his inspection and his expectations of Jeff's work. Deb convinced Jeff to splurge. It was an impulse buy, and a major one. They bought an Oyster 565 with their combined bonus money from LAG. They paid cash. It was sleek and well-appointed and the most expensive thing they'd ever bought.

"Are you sure? This is a pretty audacious splurge." Jeff wanted it so bad. "Plus, it will cost another $600,000 in upgrades for gear, sails, and electronics." At $2.8 million, it was more lavish than their house on the golf course. Before they renovated it in preparation to sell, of course.

When he was in his teens, Jeff summered on his parents' Catalina 30 sailboat. In college, Deb had crewed several trips, ferrying sailboats to and from the Florida Keys. But nothing that either of them had ever sailed matched this beauty. While it was much larger than what they'd captained before it was much easier to sail. It was built for transoceanic travel with the saftest and sturdiest hull design in the industry. Its sails were Kevlar-reinforced carbon fiber and were hydraulically raised and trimmed. There would be no hoisting the mainsail or struggling in high winds with the genoa or spinnaker. A single person could skipper this boat for long periods of time, and two seasoned sailors would have no problem at all. And if winds subsided its twin diesel Cummins engines were powerful, rugged, and made the *Dividend* spectacularly easy to maneuver.

The cabin, or as Deb called it, "her work-from-home address," was spacious and versatile. They'd been sleeping and working aboard the boat for weeks as they prepared their home in Brookline for sale. They'd eaten turkey sandwiches she'd prepared in the galley for Thanksgiving. They had a small tree decorated for Christmas. They popped champagne on New Year's. It was now their permanent home and soon would be their escape module from Perseid.

They were still moving boxes out from Brookline, while the new owner prepared to close with the bank. This made the marina in Quincy Jeff and Deb's new address, at least for the next few weeks. Soon their address would be somewhere on an anchor line, floating in eighty-degree water with blue skies and white sand.

The main sleeping quarters had a king-size bed, an in-room head, shower, desk, seating area, and a high-definition TV. It had a diesel generator for electricity but was rarely needed because their solar panel array and bank of lithium-ion batteries provided plenty of juice to run everything they needed. The galley was small compared to their Brookline kitchen, but it had granite counters, twin propane burners, a full oven, a large refrigerator with freezer, wine refrigerator, and table with seating for six. Jeff had already stocked the wine rack. Eight bottles of Silver Oak and one bottle of Penfolds Grange Hermitage.

"Fuck Rich," he snarled as he tucked it away. All in, including the wine, they'd be about $3.5 million into their forever home and have the means, privacy, and mobility to live there for the rest of their lives.

★ ★ ★

The commute from the boat in Quincy to LAG's offices was easier than from their Brookline home. Jeff and Deb, each in their own cars, pulled into the LAG garage with Rich driving in right behind them. "The good thing about being this early is we get spots close to the elevator." Jeff looked at the bright side as he locked his car door.

Deb rolled her eyes as she grabbed her backpack from the trunk of her brand-new fire-engine-red Porsche Macan. His was exactly like hers, but pearl white, with matte black trim and hubs. Rich parked alongside them. His headlights were still on. Every day was a long day. They all arrived before the sun rose. They all ended long after the sun set.

Jeff held the elevator for Rich, which was a mistake. Rich chewed on them all the way up. "Jesus, guys. Somebody is going to notice. Fuck sakes." He was annoyed they had purchased their new cars, driving around for everybody to see.

Thank God it's a short elevator ride, Jeff thought.

"The wrong people are going to notice. What did you pay, $200,000?" Rich scolded.

"Yeah, about that," Jeff said looking down, feeling guilty. It was closer to $300,000, but he didn't correct Rich.

They knew Rich was right. But this was a calculated purchase. They wanted Rich to see their new cars in case he noticed anything about them moving money around. It was part of their cover. By the time anybody got suspicious they'd be gone.

"Don't buy another goddamn thing without my approval. Understood?" Rich's glare amplified his edict. He was far more irritated than Jeff and Deb anticipated.

Jeff sheepishly nodded false agreement with Rich. "Sorry. It was a gift to each other for the holidays."

"Nothing else. Am I clear?" Rich dismissed Jeff's explanation. "Terrible news about Chris," Rich said sadly, changing the subject as Rich left the elevator.

"So horrible. We didn't see you at the wake," said Deb.

"I was busy." Rich headed to his office.

Walking to their offices in the other direction from Rich, Jeff leaned into Deb and whispered, "If he's this irritated now, just wait until we disappear." Jeff let a sneaky smile emerge because he had a copy of the file he'd prepared for the FBI in his briefcase, right there under the nose of Rich. Their last moment at LAG and Perseid would be punctuated by an ominous flash report sent to all LAG clients and the file arriving at the Boston field office of the FBI with all the Perseid documentation needed to shut down the operation and put Rich in jail.

Jeff amassed evidence of insider trading, misleading statements to investors, falsified financial documents, and had typed out and signed a lengthy whistleblower statement with names, dates, and research irregularities linking LAG to Perseid. He threw in evidence of misappropriation of LAG's corporate assets and resources on behalf of Perseid for good measure. All of it was going to the authorities to blow up Perseid and mask their escape.

Jeff and Deb were haunted by their inability to confide in Marcus and Beth. They were victims too. Marcus and Beth were shackled to the same scheme and facing the same threats. The cruel reality was that there was no way for all four of them to escape simultaneously. Rather than warning them, Jeff and Deb evaded them. Communications became less personal and less frequent. Email was used instead of meetings. Text messages instead of phone calls.

In the package for the FBI, Jeff did his best to exonerate Marcus and Beth. He detailed Rich's coercion and how he threatened all of them. He praised Marcus for his leadership and reinforced how he raised concerns and tried to stop Rich on numerous occasions. Jeff wanted Rich to face the consequences and to shield Marcus and Beth.

"I hate to admit it, but Rich is right. We do need to be careful," Deb said. "It's probably better if we are more discrete from now on. We can't draw attention. We are too close to our freedom." All the pieces were sliding into place. They'd be ready for the last big play within a few weeks, and they'd be in turquoise water shortly thereafter, weather permitting.

Jeff and Deb kissed. "By the end of March we are gone. Ten weeks."

Rich was still steaming when he flipped the lights on in his office. He'd spied on Jeff and Deb more and more closely over the last few weeks, looking for signs they were ready to run. He didn't know their entire plan, but he knew he would need to replace the carrots with sticks. "Better yet, bullets," he muttered.

Perseid's returns were flattening and IPOs in the pipeline were dwindling. Rich's investors were asking uncomfortable questions about Marcus and the team. The call he'd had with his father, uncle, and Hong Kong before he left for the office this morning spiked Rich's concern. Huang's bankers flagged a series of movements within and across Jeff's and Deb's accounts recently. Neither Marcus nor Beth had similar trades or transactions but there was no proof Marcus and Beth weren't conspiring with them.

He switched on his computer and connected to the video bridge. He'd find out either way, very soon.

CHAPTER 22
The Setup

Rich slouched back in his chair, looking out to Boylston Street. He stretched his arms side to side and then extended them, reaching above his head, trying to get blood flowing. His top two LAG analysts were attending a conference on Web 3.0 in Rome. In truth, Marcus and Beth were there on behalf of Perseid, meeting with thirty start-up CEOs and prioritizing which ones would get pumped via LAG and funded via Perseid in Hong Kong. After their success with Sinotech and a few other firms, Rich needed more IPOs in the pipeline. There were several promising candidates at the conference for Perseid to consider. Three were from China.

Marcus and Beth didn't know how Rich closely monitored their travel patterns, looking for anomalies that might indicate a problem. He noticed over the last few trips they'd gone from turning in receipts for rooms at the same hotel, to turning in receipts for adjacent or adjoining rooms, to turning in receipts for a single room they were sharing. Rich didn't care. In fact, he'd hoped their relationship would progress this way when he'd hired them five years ago. It gave him more control and leverage.

But now, knowing that Jeff and Deb were planning to run, Rich was suspicious of the entire team, and he needed to know if Marcus and Beth were part of the conspiracy. The only way to do that was to pivot from rewards to something far less pleasant.

Rich's bank of fifty-inch monitors was on and his earbuds were in for the video call. "What have you got for me?" Rich didn't try to hide his annoyance. He was all business.

Marcus tried for humor. "The pope says hi."

Rich didn't smile. "Tell me about the conference." He was uninterested in small talk.

"Great event. Well worth the time, but it will be good to get home and spend a few days in my own bed." Marcus's tousled hair, unshaven stubble, and darkening circles under his eyes underscored his exhaustion. Beth didn't add anything to the conversation; clearly fatigued, she only yawned.

"How many deals do you think could come from the meetings?" Rich pressed.

"A dozen firms should be covered in our next market landscape report. One or two could be featured in the blockchain and AI vendor profiles Jeff is writing." Marcus knew Rich wasn't asking about business for LAG, but Marcus wanted to test Rich's reaction since LAG was technically paying his expenses for hotels and meals during the trip.

"I don't give a shit about that. Which vendors will make our other project a lot of money?" Rich was unusually aggravated.

Marcus complied. "OK, boss. Nine of the firms need seed capital. Four of those are worth the risk. Five are dogs. We found another three firms who could use mezzanine support. Two of those are strong bets. The other is pre-IPO but a total shit show. With new boards and better financial structures, the good ones could be billion-dollar players in a couple of years. Also, I spotted one or two short sale opportunities."

"How about the Chinese-based firms? Are they good candidates for Perseid?" Rich was buckling under the pressure from Huang to prioritize some of his other pet projects.

"I think they could be. They seemed much more open to working collaboratively with us than Sinotech had been. But I'm still wary of the whole geopolitical angle."

"So it sounds like ten good opportunities," Rich summed, adding the Chinese firms to that total, ignoring Marcus's unease.

"That will keep the lights on for a few more months," said Beth with another yawn.

"Send me a full write-up on each of them," Rich instructed.

"I'll get them to you before we land in Boston," Marcus offered.

Marcus's and Beth's travels, on behalf of LAG, but truly in support of Perseid, was nonstop. They visited magnificent places. Today it was Rome, but they'd been in Monaco, Perth, Goa, Barcelona, St. Andrews, and Buenos Aires in the last four weeks. The company jet was at their disposal, as was a limitless expense account. But business travel, no matter how exotic, was exhausting. They were worn and wanted to sleep in their own beds, or each other's beds.

"About that. I need you to hang in Rome for a couple of days and get some rest." Rich would twist this in a way they'd do what he wanted, even though they'd hate the idea at first.

"I've booked you the most expensive suite in the city for three nights. The plane has been ordered to the ground by me. You cannot take off until Saturday afternoon. I want you to have two solid days of rest. Enjoy the city."

Both Marcus and Beth knew by the way Rich was selling his request there was a *but* coming.

"On your way home Monday I need you to stop in Mexico City for a meeting." Rich didn't offer it as an option. It was an order.

"What the hell is in Mexico? There aren't any tech players there," Marcus pleaded.

"No tech players, but a key banker. He's in Mexico City and he has a couple hundred million dollars he is thinking about adding to our capital structure."

Rich didn't have to say whose capital structure. Marcus knew it wasn't for LAG.

Beth perked up. She had never been to Mexico City and hadn't been home to Mexico since she was twelve. She wondered if she might have time to travel north to see her mother. She doubted Rich had that visit in his plan.

"As long as I can get a day or two of sleep first, I'm up for Mexico," Beth cheerily chimed in. At this point, Marcus's opinion didn't matter. He'd been overruled. In this case he would happily comply because it meant a weekend, alone and not working, with Beth.

"All right. Looks like we're going to Mexico," Marcus conceded.

Rich disconnected from the call.

★ ★ ★

The lobby of the Aurelian Palace Hotel in Rome looked like a Renaissance castle. Leaded windows allowed for an airy feel. The fresco on the ceiling gave the sense of daytime at all hours. A row of crystal chandeliers mimicked candlelight. The marble floors looked like they came off the Spanish Steps. It was stunning. Anybody who had the money and needed to stay in Rome would spend whatever it took to stay at the Aurelian Palace.

Rich booked the Royal Suite for them. It was a huge room by Rome's hotel standards at twelve hundred square feet. It fetched 2,400 euros per night. Room service would be another 1,000 euros a day, especially since neither Marcus nor Beth intended on leaving the room before heading back to the airport. There would be no tour of the Colosseum and its iconic and grand amphitheater. They wouldn't stand in line at the Vatican waiting to see the Sistine Chapel adorned or Michelangelo's masterpieces. They wouldn't toss a coin in the Trevi Fountain and make a wish, admiring its grand baroque sculptures.

They'd sleep and eat and rest and laugh and totally decompress. They'd use every drop of hot water the rain shower head could produce and sink into the massive, jetted bath where they would eat breakfast and finish a couple bottles of ridiculously expensive champagne. The last time they spent time together, for anything like a vacation, was over a year ago, before leaf-peeping season at Marcus's cabin on the lake. The both agreed it had been too long.

"This is perfect," Marcus said as he sunk backward in the tub, totally submersing his body in the warm soapy water.

Beth splashed him in the eyes when he reemerged.

"Can we talk about our future?" Marcus tried to get serious.

"Why, Mr. Shea, what are you asking?" She laughed, enjoying his growing blush.

"No, not that. At least not that yet." His smile faded. "I'm talking about how long we stay at LAG and Perseid."

"At least long enough to finish my crepes and caffe latte." She tried to redirect the conversation.

"You know this can't last forever. At some point Perseid is going to flame out or Rich is going to pressure us to do something illegal if we haven't already. We need a plan."

"We can't leave." She said it like a prisoner, shaking her head in the negative. "I can't leave."

CHAPTER 23
Condemned and Pardoned

While Marcus and Beth were having an early Sunday breakfast in Rome, forty-five hundred miles away a man, too large to be stealthy, was trying to be quiet as he rooted through the construction dumpster at 302 Bentham Lane in Brookline. It was 3:00 a.m. It was an older Tudor-style home undergoing significant renovations. Stevie wasn't worried the homeowners would catch him. They didn't sleep there anymore.

He'd followed the husband from LAG to the house a day earlier and watched him exit the house with a box full of books and pictures. The husband took the box to a storage locker in Dorchester and continued south on the expressway to the parking lot at the Quincy yacht club. They were sleeping on a sailboat.

Stevie poked at the scrap wood and general construction waste. He found copies of the renovation blueprints and receipts for windows and doors, totaling over $100,000. By the looks of the cabinets and broken granite countertops in the dumpster, it looked like a total gut job.

Stevie slipped in through a slider the construction crew had left unlocked. His boss, the one in Mexico, not the kid in Boston, wanted him to look for evidence about how much of a problem Jeff and Deb were going to be.

Walls were missing. Floors had been ripped up. There was plastic over the windows. There were no kitchen cabinets and no functioning bathrooms. He went to the basement level. It was a walkout. He wondered what golf hole they were close to. It was a moonless night and too dark to see the course. He'd watched matches from the first tee on the final day of the Ryder Cup in 1999. He could remember being sprayed with Bud Light when Justin Leonard sunk a forty-five-foot birdie putt on seventeen to close out José María Olazábal to win.

The media room had eight massive leather recliners, four on the floor and four more on a riser directly behind them. There were twelve speakers recessed in the ceiling and walls. The NEC TV was over one hundred inches across. *Would be nice to see the Bruins play on that.* Stevie wondered if the leather recliners were wide enough for him. There were a handful of pictures still on the credenza. Four of them where shots of the couple on vacation. Stevie laughed at the lone picture of the sailboat. "*Dividend*. Fucking civilians. Trying to hide a $3 million boat but leaving pictures of it in a house you already sold. Idiots."

He called the big boss in Mexico first to report in, then he called his boss's son in Boston. "You have a problem. A big problem."

"What kind of problem, Steven?" Rich asked, knowing he hated to be called Steven.

"The married couple is paying for a massive renovation project on the house. They aren't living here anymore. They've moved out." Stevie was matter of fact.

"What do you mean they've moved?" Rich's voice cracked with a bit of panic.

"They sold it. I looked at the county records today. The house is in escrow. They made $2 million profit on it."

There was silence on the other side of the line.

Before Rich could digest that news, Stevie smacked him again. "And they have a boat."

"Who cares? Let them putt around Boston Harbor," replied Rich.

"It's not a Boston Whaler. I looked it up on the internet. It's a sixty-foot sailboat with all the bells and whistles." Stevie struggled to get Rich to understand.

"So what?" Rich tried to hide his furor at Jeff and Deb spending so much money after his warnings.

"You are not listening to me. It cost nearly $3 million." Now Stevie had Rich's attention.

"What?"

"You heard me. I said $3 million. They could live on it anywhere in the world. Sail right out of the yacht club and you'd never find them."

Rich started screaming obscenities into the phone.

"Hey, don't raise your voice at me. I was asked to find out, and I found out. Now I'm telling you. You have a problem. If they have enough money, they could run anytime." Stevie waited for a response.

The line was quiet.

Rich replied, "Let me think."

"There is nothing to think about. I'm going to handle it," Stevie replied.

"What do you mean, you'll handle it?" Rich asked meekly.

"Don't ask. It's not your call," Stevie replied with authority. "Orders from Mexico."

"What about Marcus and Beth?" Rich asked.

"They're not your concern." Stevie hung up.

★ ★ ★

The Monday-morning flight from Rome to Mexico City on the G700 would log six thousand miles but only take nine hours at fifty-one thousand feet. They'd land at 10:00 a.m., two hours ahead of their meeting. The time zone changes meant the entire flight would be on the cusp of the sunrise chasing them across the Atlantic. Marcus would get no sleep. Instead, he wrote the Rome trip report and emailed it to Rich's personal account as they crossed over Tampa headed to the Gulf of Mexico.

Marcus struggled with fatigue, unable to calm his mind. The conflict amplified as he pressed "send" on the communiqué to Rich. LAG paid their expenses, but this work was performed for Perseid, and all the investment targets were emailed to a private email account not associated with either. It felt wrong.

Turbulence over the gulf jostled Beth awake. "Morning." She stretched, leaned forward, and gave Marcus a kiss on the cheek. "What do you want to do when we get back home?"

"Build an exit plan." He looked at her intently. "I know you don't want to talk about it."

"Can't we take time and just enjoy Mexico first?" Beth said, avoiding the discussion.

Marcus pressed, "Have you noticed changes in the team lately?"

"Yeah. Jeff is hurting," Beth responded.

"It's more than that. Both Jeff and Deb have gone quiet. They are missing deadlines and meetings. They don't talk to us anymore. I barely get text messages," Marcus added.

"They are just tired and overworked," Beth countered.

Marcus took another angle. "Rich has become unbearable. No amount of work is good enough. He's angry and cutting too many corners. Perseid is going to have $5 billion in holdings and he's asking us to do things." His voice trailed off. He paused and looked out the window. "I don't know. He's asking us to do things that make me nervous. Things that make me worry about our security." He turned his head and brought his eyes back to hers. "I'm worried for us. I don't know if we are safe, if you are safe."

Beth tried not to react, but her autonomic response was unmistakable as she held back the truth. Her cheeks flushed slightly, her pupils dilated, and she cast her eyes down, trying to avoid Marcus's glance.

"You see it. I know you do," he said softly, reaching across to raise her chin and see her eyes.

Tears slowly welled. She did see it.

Marcus continued, "I promised Jeff and Deb that I'd find a way to walk us back from this mess, and I've failed."

"It's not your fault, Marcus. It's Perseid. It's . . ." She stopped before she said the other name. "Rich."

"I've cut back on giving Jeff anything more to do, but Rich won't lighten up. He is going to crush Jeff if things don't change." Marcus's strength had always been his ability to take ownership and command of his environment. On the wrestling mat or jujitsu tatami Marcus found a way to focus, persevere, and overcome. He felt helpless now. It was too big. There was too much to do. The pressure was unending.

"I'm going to call a friend of mine from grad school for a legal consult. I want to know what kind of trouble we are in."

Beth's emotions changed from sadness to abject fear. Fear of her cousin.

"Wait to get back home. We can talk about this." Beth wanted to buy time.

"The way Rich has Perseid tied to LAG, I can't see a way to separate us. He has us manipulating stocks with insider information. I don't even know what trouble we are in for working with Sinotech or some of the other companies Perseid has invested in." Marcus felt confined. He felt ashamed. Marcus was failing Beth and failing Jeff and Deb. It was his responsibility to shield them from jeopardy even if it meant him going to the authorities. He'd fight for Beth, Jeff, and Deb at all costs.

Beth listened to his faltering voice and saw his clenched fists. She recognized the crushing pressure on Marcus as he shouldered the weight of everything happening between LAG and Perseid. She wiped her nose and dried a tear. "You're not going to face it alone."

"We need to get out," Marcus said gravely.

She held his hand and nodded. She knew he was right, but the *how* was elusive.

The pilot came on. "Landing in ten minutes."

✯ ✯ ✯

The private terminal at Benito Juárez International Airport had well-appointed club facilities, giving Marcus a chance to shower, shave, and share breakfast with Beth before their noon meeting with the banker in Mexico City.

Traffic from the airport to the headquarters of Banco Nacional was heavy on late Monday morning. Ozone and sulfur were still thick in the air, especially as they got closer to the city center.

Beth stared out the window. Nothing felt familiar. Nothing reminded her of her childhood home in the Mexican desert. She was born in a more arid region. Mexico City was vast and crowded and much greener. The low hills of her home were more monochrome and undefined. Mexico City was magnificent. The architecture, history, and culture blended seamlessly. It was the most populous city and the most populous metropolitan area in the Western Hemisphere. It was bigger than New York City and two thousand feet higher than Denver. Beth immediately noticed difficulty in breathing.

"It's a beautiful city," Marcus commented. He'd been to Rome several times. He wished Rich had booked them a suite here instead. They passed stunning gardens and plazas. They whizzed past Alameda Central park with its beautiful fountains, lush green spaces, and shaded benches. The city's history went back seven hundred years. It was a mixture of modern buildings, ancient ruins, historic sites, and museums. Marcus would have liked some free time to explore the city, but he was too tired, and they were leaving for home as soon as the meeting ended.

Marcus was thankful for the time with Beth, even if Rich manipulated them on this trip. He knew Rich was playing him, but he was still grateful that Rich brought him and Beth together in the first place. Rich's fingerprints were all over this. It was no coincidence they were on the same team, starting the same day, and now working so closely together. Marcus was worried about the path Perseid had taken and his team's involvement. He knew Rich was controlling them all. But when it came to Beth, Marcus didn't mind being controlled. As long as Beth was with him, he had hope.

They arrived at the bank just before noon. The security guard let them in without question or identification. After a casual two-hour meeting, where they spent more time talking about the history of Mexico City and key tourist destinations than about Perseid's business model or vision, the chief of investment strategies for the bank stood, shook their hands, and said, "Thank you." He promised he'd contact Rich to get instructions on where to wire the funds.

"How does it feel to be unnecessary?" Marcus said to Beth as they exited the elevator into the bank's lobby.

"What do you mean?"

"Rich used us as window dressing on a deal that was already closed. We didn't need to be here," Marcus declared.

Marcus was tired and he wanted to get back to Boston, to his apartment, and sleep off the jet lag with Beth. He didn't want to glad-hand a banker in Mexico, even if it meant a couple of hundred million in new capital for Perseid.

The city center was animated on a vibrant Monday afternoon. Pedestrians and tourists enjoyed the bright, but smog-obstructed, sun. Marcus and Beth exited the bank lobby onto a large square with cafes and restaurants surrounding the plaza. The rattle and scrapes of pushcarts on the cobblestones echoed off the buildings. Vendors sold everything from food and drink to tourist trinkets and T-shirts. Their driver told them he'd meet them around the corner when the meeting was done. It was time to go back to Boston.

Beth was distracted, thinking about her childhood home, while Marcus people watched. They strolled arm in arm toward their pickup point. Neither of them saw the windowless blue van parked ahead of them. It looked like any of the dozens of construction vehicles Marcus saw each time he walked to work in Boston.

As they passed in front of the open sliding door, four men rushed them from the side and tackled them into the van. Marcus went from tired and relaxed to fight mode instantly. He hit the inside wall of the van, rolled to his left, and put a man in a triangle choke. Another was already unconscious from a flying knee to his head. Marcus was furious but focused. He'd tear these guys apart. As he pivoted to strike, a third man, with a big smile, extended his arm.

In rough and broken English he said, "That's enough, Mr. Shea." He held a Beretta to Beth's head. Marcus stopped fighting, knelt slowly, and placed his hands behind his head. Zip tied, gagged, and blindfolded, they were driven north.

CHAPTER 24
Sentenced and Sanctioned

Dividend was on a slip at Marina Bay, twenty minutes south from LAG's Boylston Street offices. It was comfortable living aboard. The marina was quiet in winter. Jeff and Deb had converted the galley kitchen into a workspace with multiple monitors, two servers, and secure Wi-Fi. All the pleasures of home in four hundred square feet of living space. They felt protected and invisible. They felt safe. They were not.

It wasn't Jeff and Deb's conspicuous consumption that raised a flag, it was money movement. The Hong Kong team watching Perseid's employees didn't know about the boat. Jeff and Deb bought it with bonuses from LAG, so there was no way for China to uncover that. But they did identify cyclical money flows as Deb converted portions of their Sinotech holdings to cash and began moving funds in and out of their accounts. It was the number of transactions, not the amounts.

Deb's method to transfer, shield, and clean money was well planned, for an amateur. It would have escaped the view of Perseid if they'd stuck to liquidating stocks and cash deposited in banks in the Caymans, Belize, Monaco, and Luxembourg. But it was the bank in Hong Kong that exposed them, Huang's bank. They ran regular analyses of all accounts tied to Sinotech. Deb's sell order for one hundred thousand shares of Sinotech raised attention. When cash was transferred out later in the week, Huang connected the dots fairly easily. He called Carlos Banderas and shared the details. Carlos asked Stevie to take care of the situation, regardless of what his son wanted. Carlos wanted his son to coordinate it with Stevie, but there was no question who was in charge, and it was not Rich.

Boston was seasonably cold, with the ice sculptures remaining from the First Night ceremonies slowly melting into unrecognizable spires, spikes, and misshapen mounds. Jeff and Deb drove to the office Monday morning separately. Rich's demands were unpredictable, and neither of them wanted the other to have to wait if a new project was identified.

Following Rich's harsh reaction to their his-and-hers Porsche Macans, Jeff and Deb stopped all new spending. Today, Jeff opted to park at the Copley lot, across the street from LAG, and walk the two blocks to the office, hoping to avoid any further confrontation with Rich. Changing his parking routine didn't confuse Stevie, who followed Jeff into the garage, parked and walked to the exit. Jeff slinked across the street, trying to avoid Rich's prying eyes. "Some fucking James Bond–level spy craft right there." Stevie laughed.

Stevie exited the garage a few minutes later in his stolen car. He'd jacked the tan Toyota Camry earlier that morning from the off-site long-term airport parking lot. Stevie planned to take his time, meander south along the expressway, and get lunch. There would be plenty of opportunity for a meal, a nap, and to read the paper. He wasn't sure what time either one of them would reach the dock or who would get there first, but it didn't matter. His plan worked either way.

Stevie had been to Harbor Bay years before, but in the summer. It was a real meat market. Young professionals with lots of money partying late into the night. Music, bars, and lots of recreational drugs. Today it was cold and gray. It was Stevie and a couple of locals having lunch at the Wheelhouse, a local dive adjacent to the marina that served good bar food.

Stevie ordered a cheeseburger and fries. He never drank before a job. He wanted a cold beer, but he was a professional. No alcohol and very little water when working. He once had had a few cups of coffee before a job in Providence and needed to pee the whole time. He didn't have the prostate of a thirty-year-old anymore. Better to be a bit dehydrated than to miss his mark while taking a piss behind a tree in the parking lot.

Stevie dragged lunch on for as long as he could, but he didn't want to draw attention. Nobody took notice when he got up and paid in cash. Stevie was an enormous man but worked to be as invisible and unrecognizable as possible. That meant not chatting it up with anybody while he ate and not giving the waitress anything more than a standard tip, nothing that would stand out.

He went back to his car and read the paper, listening to gulls squabbling for scraps of trash. The Pats beat the Vikings, missing Gronkowski and Edelman. Jayson Tatum and Kyrie Irving continued to lead the Celtics in scoring. His eyes grew heavy on a full stomach.

As he napped, the tide fell from high to low under the waning afternoon sun. In four months, this would be a perfect spot to sit outside in the warm sun to wait. Nobody would notice him alone on a bench overlooking the jetty enjoying the day. Today, nobody would notice him because he tucked his car in the back corner of the lot behind a dumpster. Once darkness came, at 4:54 p.m., the marina was deserted. The Wheelhouse was closed for dinner.

Day turned to dusk and dusk into dark. Stevie grew restless and took a walk around the perimeter of the parking lot to stretch his legs. He found a plastic deck chair next to the restaurant and carried it behind the dumpster. He sat waiting, breathing the crisp air, sharpening his senses, getting ready. His phone buzzed just before 9:00 p.m. with a text. "He's leaving the office now."

Stevie was ready. He hid out of sight as the white Porsche Macan pulled in, spraying gravel and skidding to a stop. "It's the husband. Figures." Stevie laughed. "It didn't take long for him to learn to drive like an Masshole." Stevie was from Providence, RI.

Out popped Jeff with a goofy smile on his face. He loved his new toy. So much so, he parked under a light as far away as he could from where other cars might park. Jeff took his obligatory walk around his car, making sure nobody in the garage dinged his doors. Stevie crept up to Jeff while he was checking out the brake dust on his new twenty-one-inch rims. The grinding gravel of footsteps behind him sounded heavy, but Jeff had no reason to be concerned. Lots of people are impressed with the Macan and want a closer look. There weren't many GTS editions in Brookline, let alone Quincy. And the marina was a safe place. So, when Stevie smashed him in the head with the butt of his pistol, Jeff wasn't ready. He didn't have time for fear or panic. It was a sharp blinding pain with an electric flash of light. Then it was dark and quiet.

Jeff regained consciousness as they passed the gas tanks on the Southeast Expressway headed north to the city. He was belted into the passenger seat of his Macan with his hands duct taped behind his back.

"Don't worry, Jeff. I'm only here to rob you. I don't want any trouble. If you do as I say, and don't cause any issues, you and your lovely wife will be driven to the suburbs and set free," Stevie recited.

Jeff had never been hit before. He'd never seen any real violence in his life. He'd never even been in a violent screaming match. Jeff was terrified and he'd do whatever he was asked.

Stevie needed Jeff and Deb to tell him everything he wanted to know, tell him if they had any files or records, and tell him what their plan was. He needed to know how Marcus and Beth were involved. If Jeff and Deb cooperated, it would be over quickly.

"I need you to call Deb and tell her to meet you at the corner of Tremont and Lagrange. Tell her to walk over and that you have a surprise for her. Don't try to warn her or I'll hurt you. I'll hurt you both." Stevie explained the steps pointedly, slowly, and with no emotion. He reinforced his demand with a sharp backhand to Jeff's face.

"You understand me? If you can do that, you both will be free in time to watch Jimmy Kimmel on your boat."

He knows about the boat. Jeff's eyes opened wider with fear.

Deb was immersed in writing her latest research analysis on cloud applications and AI adoption when Jeff called. He sounded like his allergies were acting up. Stuffy and wheezing. She was on a roll with this research note. It had been several weeks since she authored a report on her own, and this one was flowing quickly and elegantly. She didn't want to stop. But the last time Jeff called her with a surprise he showed up with pictures of the new Jet Ski they'd haul on their sailboat for added fun in the summer. "I'll be right down."

Deb didn't process the fact that he'd asked her to walk five blocks instead of parking right in front of the building. It was approaching 10:00 p.m. and Boylston Street was cold and traffic-free on a Monday night. When she rounded the block, Jeff was sitting in the passenger side of his car. It didn't register. Deb walked to his window and tapped. She gasped at the blood dripping from his right temple, out from his ear, and oozing down his cheek. His hands were bound in behind him.

"Jeff!" she screamed. "What . . ."

"Step into the driver's seat, Deb." The voice came out of the dark behind her. Before she could run, a huge man appeared from the shadow with a gun leveled at her head.

"Step into the driver's seat, Deb. Everything will be OK."

She was frozen in fear, paralyzed.

Stevie guided her behind the car and then forward, ushering her to the front door. "Get in the driver's seat, now." He didn't raise his voice. Stevie's orders were short and precise. Her body was shutting down, so the tasks Stevie conveyed needed to be very specific. "Get into the driver's seat and shut the door."

She climbed in and sat, reflexively putting on the seat belt after closing the door. Stevie lumbered into the back seat. It was a tight squeeze and Stevie had to sit slouched at an angle with his right leg up on the seat next to him.

"Good. Now please start driving. Take the Truman Parkway headed toward Blue Hills." He reached forward, past her head, and adjusted the rearview mirror so she could see him in the back seat with the Glock pointed at the back of Jeff's head.

Stevie's breath smelled like onions and ketchup when he leaned in. "Go slow, Deb."

Her driving was stiff and cautious. Stevie provided regular feedback and simple steps for her to follow. Stevie learned early in his career that when you want people to function in times of high stress, the key was a calm tone and straightforward instructions. She was in shock.

"Turn right here. Speed up. Bear left. Slow down." He was able to guide her with no explicit threats other than the gun pointed at Jeff. She made no irrational moves and never tried to bring attention to them. She stopped smoothly on yellow traffic lights. She accelerated responsibly on green lights. She slowly passed a squad car involved in a routine traffic stop. She believed what he told her. "Provide the information I need, and this will just be a robbery. I'll let you go once we are done. I will be violent if I have to. It's up to you. Just do what I say, and it will be all right."

They pulled into the parking lot for the Blue Hill Observatory a few minutes after 10:00 p.m. It was dark and cold, and the lot was empty. He told her to back into the woods at the deepest and farthest point away from the entrance. The Porsche settled into the woods amidst a cluster of small pine trees.

"Turn off the car and turn off the lights, Deb." She obliged. "Give me the keys." She handed them over.

Stevie pulled a lighter from his pocket. They'd talk in the dull glow of his burning cigarette for now.

There is a theory in interrogations that if you start with an immediate, heavy, fact-based question first, you will catch the suspect off guard, and they will break faster. Stevie agreed with the theory.

"When you transferred your shares of Sinotech from the bank in Hong Kong, what were you planning?" Stevie's question landed hard.

Jeff was concussed, having trouble processing the question. "Sinotech? What do you want? Why are you doing this?" Jeff was disoriented.

Deb was whimpering softly.

"Jeff. Shut the fuck up. Deb, I asked you. What was your plan with Sinotech? What were you going to do with the money?"

"I don't understand," she replied.

Stevie viciously cracked Jeff in the back of his head with the barrel of the gun, snapping Jeff forward violently. Only the seat belt kept Jeff's head from rebounding off the dashboard. Jeff shrieked. He was now bleeding from both his right and left ears. Stevie only needed one of them to talk and Jeff's concussion made him useless. But he was effective as an example of what would happen if Deb didn't provide clear answers.

"Deb. Turn your fucking head and look at me.
She bawled.

"I said turn your *fucking* head and look at me."

Deb rotated her head but did not look at Stevie. She kept her eyes down, trying to avoid his focus.

"Good. Concentrate. What was your plan with Sinotech?"

She spoke slowly. "We sold some shares from Hong Kong and then transferred more to an offshore bank in Panama as a tax haven."

"OK. That's a start. What are you planning to do with the stock?"

"We liquidated all of it. All our shares in Sinotech. We took the cash."

"What else is in your bank accounts?"

"We took another $5 million from shares in other companies and from our bonuses."

"How much money have you pulled from Perseid and LAG," Stevie pressed.

Deb had no idea how this man could know so much about her and Jeff.

"About $12 million so far," she replied.

"What else, Deb. Was there anything else you were going to do with Sinotech?"

Jeff was bleeding badly and barely conscious. She would tell this man everything.

"We were planning to take those funds and buy put options on Sinotech in a couple of weeks. That's when . . ." She was about to explain finance to the lumbering man in the back seat.

"I know what short selling is, Deb. Don't be a cunt. Why would you take put options out on a stock you just sold for a huge profit?"

"Because the stock is going to get obliterated when Jeff's new research report is published." Her eyes, full of guilt, finally looked at Stevie, knowing her prediction was a certainty.

"Deb, darling. That is what we call stock manipulation. It's a crime, you know." Stevie was having fun.

"Are you going to arrest us?"

Stevie was entertained.

"I might. I just might arrest you, Deb." Stevie needed her to keep talking. He needed to figure out how bad this already bad situation was.

"Tell me, what was Jeff going to write?"

She was having trouble understanding why this guy was holding them hostage over a stock transaction that had not happened yet and would impact a company eight thousand miles away. Stevie could see he was losing her.

"Why, Deb? What is Jeff writing?" He rapped the barrel of the Glock on top of Jeff's head.

She watched her husband wince with every tap. "He was going to raise concerns about China's possible infiltration of Sinotech's business and that Sinotech is now embedded in hundreds of US companies. He was going to say the SEC and FBI were beginning an investigation. He was going to say there was a critical risk for any LAG clients that have deployed Sinotech. He was going to recommend our clients immediately stop implementations and remove the code wherever it existed."

"And what would that do to Sinotech, Deb?"

"A billion dollars in income would dry up. Lawsuits would be launched. The US government and security agencies would investigate. The FTC and SEC would get involved. The FBI would launch investigations."

Stevie knew what that would mean, but Deb made it plainly clear. "LAG is the world's most influential tech advisory firm. It would end Sinotech."

"And what would it do for you, Deb? What would you get from it?" Stevie pressed.

"We were going to have a massive short position in Sinotech. We'd get rich."

"And then, Deb? What then?" Tap, tap, tap on Jeff's head.

"We were going to send evidence to the SEC and FBI to implicate Rich and Perseid. Then we'd disappear."

Stevie digested their whole plan.

Deb was in full confession mode, hoping he'd go easy on her. "We have bank accounts all over. We'd have enough money to live, and we'd be gone." Deb was sobbing violently at her confession.

"And who else would go with you, Deb? What about Marcus and Beth? Are they in on this?"

She was sobbing. "No. Nobody knew what we were doing. I created all the LLCs and Jeff opened the bank accounts. We wanted to tell Marcus and Beth, but they are too close to Rich. We would never have gotten away. They might have stopped us or told Rich. We couldn't tell them. They don't know anything."

Stevie nodded. She was incredibly scared and emotional. Incapable of lying to him. "What then? What were you and Jeff going to do?"

"Jeff and I were going to take off on our boat alone. One day we simply would not show up. We'd be gone. A couple of weeks from now the Emerging Tech Team will be invited to meet at Rich's condominium for our regular meeting, and we won't be there. No trace. No word. Gone."

As she said it aloud to a stranger it sounded like a terrible plan. A mistake. And now he knew it all. He knew their entire plan.

"You can have the money. Take it. Please let us go." She started to beg.

"I won't take your money, Deb. You've given me what I need."

Stevie had to make sure all the details she gave were consistent, especially about the other two. If what she said was accurate, Stevie could stop the whole thing from unraveling right here, right now. But if the other two were involved, the entire program would need to be uprooted. That would cost the cartel billions of dollars and its only source of clean cash.

Stevie opened his door and walked across to the passenger side. "Jeff, time to get out of the car." Hands bound, Jeff could not unclip his belt. Stevie had to open the door for him. "Come on, let's go." He pulled Jeff from his seat and dropped him on the ground. Jeff was dizzy, bleeding, and in no shape for a fight. It was cold and dark, and he was shivering, partly from the chill and partly from his state of shock. Stevie dragged Jeff by his bound hands a few yards deeper into the woods.

"OK, Deb, get out of the car and come here."

She complied without any resistance or need for assistance. She wanted to live. She wanted to save Jeff. She would cooperate.

"I'm going to leave you both here safe and sound. Tell me the whole story again from beginning to end. Sit right here and walk me through every detail."

She repeated the story, exactly like she had before. Selling the stocks, transferring funds to new banks, writing the research to tank Sinotech, doing it all alone, with no help from Marcus or Beth.

"OK, it makes sense. Thank you." Stevie smiled at her, turned, and shot Jeff in the head.

Deb looked up at Stevie in horror in time to see the muzzle flash a foot from her face.

Stevie climbed into the driver's seat and slowly exited the lot. Unlike the asshole in the woods behind him there would be no spinning tires or spitting gravel. He would drive in the middle lane of Route 95 North at sixty miles per hour for fifteen miles and exit at Route 9 heading into Wellesley. He'd leave the Macan in plain view in a public lot there. It was another expensive car in a rich town. Nobody would even look at it for days.

As Stevie merged onto the highway, he made the first call.

"Sir. It's done. Your problem was more immediate than we expected, but I caught it in time. Your son will have some cleaning up to do, but the Sinotech situation is safe."

"And what about the two people we are hosting here tonight?" Carlos wanted to know how deep the problem was.

"I talked at length with Jeff and Deb. This genius plan was theirs alone. Rich didn't know anything about it. Neither did the two you have in Mexico."

"Thank you, Stephen. Stay in Boston. There will be additional work." Carlos was certain of it.

"OK, I'll stay local. I'm going to take a drive to New Hampshire tomorrow to scope out the cabin."

"Good. I have somebody heading to Boston shortly that will help you."

"Yes, sir."

"His name is Javier. He will text you his travel itinerary."

"I'll meet him at the airport when he arrives."

CHAPTER 25
Separated and Forsaken

Marcus brushed against Beth as they bounced in the back of the van. The cloth hood over his head blocked any light and his hands were tightly bound with zip ties. But he felt her as she jostled back and forth.

Two men were talking softly and laughing.

"¿Cómo está tu cabeza?" (How is your head?)

"Él era más fuerte de lo que esperaba. Me ahogó." (He was stronger than I expected. He choked me out.)

Marcus knew Beth could understand what they were saying, but he wasn't going to risk talking. They were armed and Beth was vulnerable. He had to wait for his chance. He had to shield her.

"No te preocupes, no le diré al jefe si tú no le dices que me noqueó." (Don't worry, I won't tell the boss if you don't tell him he knocked me out.) They laughed.

Abductions were a serious problem in Mexico City. Marcus was convinced this had to be a kidnapping. They must want money. Marcus and Beth were not politically valuable, so they must want a ransom. Marcus would wait. He would not put Beth at risk. He needed to know their terms.

The van pulled over after a long drive on highways and paved roads. Then they waited in silence for an even longer time. A deep growl and rumble of another vehicle pulled up alongside them and they were thrown into the back of a large pickup truck for another hour of off-road travel. It was rough terrain, but the truck had little difficulty. Nobody talked. The only sound was the aggressive rumble of the engine and occasional scratches, snaps, and scrapes as the vehicle drove through what Marcus assumed was dry brush.

When the pickup stopped it was quiet. It was tranquil. There were no sounds of traffic. There were no mechanical sounds at all. The air was cool and dry. There was no odor of smog or haze. The air was clear and sweet with hints of smoke, like sweet burning wood. Beth was helped off the tailgate first. She was quiet. Marcus knew she was terrified, and he wanted so desperately to talk to her and kill every one of them. He was scared too, but his fear was turning into rage. When his feet hit the ground, he stood on coarse sand and stones.

In perfect English, a man said, "Welcome to Mexico, Mr. Shea and Ms. Rivera."

Would kidnappers know their names? Marcus struggled to understand.

There was movement to his left. They were taking Beth away and she was fighting them. She was screaming in Spanish.

"*Déjame ir. Para. Marcus. No. No.*" (Let me go. Stop. Marcus. No. No.)

Marcus's hands were bound, and his head covered, but he instinctually tried to move in the direction of her voice.

"Leave her alone," he growled.

The butt end of a rifle caught him below the sternum. Unable to see the strike before impact, it compressed his diaphragm, temporarily paralyzing the muscles, making him unable to breathe or speak. It was a common occurrence when he was fighting, but in those cases, he knew the punch or kick was coming and could brace. Here, he took the full force and fell to his knees. By the time he regained his breath there was no sound of Beth. The high-pitched whine of an ATV sped away in the distance, confirming she was gone. It was totally silent again. They were separated.

Marcus had no idea what was happening, who these men were, or what they wanted. The worst scenarios flared in his mind. None of them involved him being killed. They all were about what was happening to Beth. What those men were doing to Beth. Touching her. Groping her. Hurting her. Hope was draining from him and taking with it his strength.

Two men, one under each of Marcus's arms, dragged him several paces and dropped him. Marcus thought he slid down a ravine or a bank of a dried riverbed. He leaned forward, but the wall of rocks, dirt, and sand was higher than his shoulders. He could only take one step back. There was a similar wall behind him. Left and right, more walls. He hadn't been thrown down an embankment; he was in a hole. Two men laughed as piles of dirt and rock were shoveled onto him. Within a minute he was buried to his knees, and unable to step up. Then he was buried to his waste, pinned in place, arms bound behind his back. He was screaming as the dirt piled higher and higher. Chest, shoulders, neck. *They are going to bury me alive.* Marcus twisted and shifted violently, trying to escape, but he was cemented in place. All he could think about was Beth, deep in the desert with a group of men, being raped and buried.

He was wild with rage. Screaming, spitting, trying desperately to move, twist. Anything to get free so he could rip these men apart. Anything to save Beth.

The shoveling stopped. His neck and head remained above ground. A man silently approached and lifted his hood. The man, with a ghoulish grin, crouched in front of him with a bottle in one hand and a pistol in the other. It looked like an Old West–style six-shooter.

"Mr. Shea. Welcome to Jiminez. I hope your trip was pleasant."

"What do you want?" Marcus was enraged.

"I don't want to waste your time. What can you tell me about your colleagues Jeff and Deb?"

Marcus didn't understand the question. He tightly squinted his eyes and turned his head to the side. The spotlights from the truck were brilliant and blinding. His rib cage was compressed by the sand and rock. His lungs burned as he inhaled dust.

"Answer my question," said the man, gently slapping Marcus on the cheek.

"What the fuck are you talking about?" Marcus snarled.

The gunshot was immediate. The crack was sharp and intense. The bullet ricocheted a few feet behind him. Marcus's ears were ringing.

"Your two colleagues in Boston. Are they working with your FBI and your SEC?"

"No. We work for a technology company. We don't do work for the FBI. You have the wrong people. Why did you kidnap us?" None of this made sense. This must be a mistake.

"Mr. Shea. This is no kidnapping. We want information. We know about your work at LAG, Mr. Shea. LAG is not important to me. What I want to know is about your work at Perseid and if you or your team are working with US authorities."

Marcus seethed at thoughts of Beth being interrogated and didn't speak.

A firm backhand to his face brought Marcus to attention. "Mr. Shea. Marcus. Why are your colleagues transferring their money out of our banks and selling stock in companies where we have invested? What are they planning?"

This wasn't a mistake. Marcus had no idea what Jeff and Deb were doing, but this guy with a gun to Marcus's head and a malevolent smile knew awfully specific things about their business.

"The reason you and Ms. Rivera are alive is because we have not seen any suspicious activity in your accounts."

"Where is Beth?" Marcus shouted.

"She is being cared for. If you want to keep her alive, you'll answer my questions."

"Beth and I haven't withdrawn any money from the banks. We aren't working for any US authorities. Rich Anderson controls all of this."

"Apparently Richard Anderson hasn't been cautious enough. Jeff and Deb were planning to withdraw all their cash and disappear on their boat."

"Disappear? What boat?"

"Yes. Disappear. Vanish. Jeff and Deb were planning to leave Perseid, you, and Beth and sail away."

"I don't understand. Jeff and Deb are part of my team."

"Mr. Shea, on their way out they were going to significantly damage one of Perseid's biggest investments and provide evidence of Perseid's wrongdoing to the FBI and SEC."

Marcus struggled with the story he was being told. None of it made sense. Could they have planned this and not said anything? "Jeff and Deb wouldn't just leave us." Marcus's voice trailed off. It was a weak reply.

"Have you seen the research Jeff was planning to send to all of LAG's clients regarding the dangers of working with Sinotech?"

This psychopath knew every detail of their business. Everything he was saying was true. Marcus started to believe that Jeff and Deb were getting ready to run.

"I haven't seen anything from Jeff in weeks. Rich oversees it all."

"Well, he didn't see this. Jeff's report would have caused us harm," said the man waiving the pistol in front of Marcus. "He also was preparing to send the FBI a file on Perseid that would have done major damage. You wouldn't know where that file is, would you? Maybe you have a copy on your computer at your cabin?"

"I don't know anything about a file." Marcus was stunned. They knew everything about him.

"Thank goodness we stopped it all." He was waving the Ruger back and forth in Marcus's face as he said, "Thank. Goodness. We. Stopped. It. All." One flip on each word.

The grin. Marcus could not stop focusing on his pursed lips and thin, ghoulish smile. He'd seen a smile similar to that before. Where?

"Jeff and Deb are no longer a problem. You, my friend, better not be a problem either."

The man placed his hood back on Marcus and walked away, leaving him buried in the desert. Marcus was pinned, convinced he was going to be shot or left for dead. Violent visions of Beth flashed. Her torture. Her pain. Flashes and grotesque images. An hour passed.

The sound of a cell phone buzzing in the distance alarmed Marcus. It was followed by a short conversation in Spanish. Marcus didn't understand the exchange, but it sounded like an argument.

The man with the gun and the grin walked up to Marcus and lifted his hood. "You are valuable to our partners, Mr. Shea. You are important. But you are not irreplaceable. If we find out you are working with your government or you are looking to damage any of Perseid's investments, you will be taken care of. If you try to run you will be killed. You will be shot and buried in the desert, burned in your apartment, or drowned in the lake at your cabin. We can find you anywhere you go."

The grin grew. It was tight, thin-lipped, and sharply angled, showing his sharp yellow teeth. *Where have I seen that smile?* The thought was a brief flash for Marcus.

Two men came out of the dark with shovels to excavate Marcus. His shoulders freed. His chest next. Dirt, rocks, and gravel removed from his waist. They grabbed his arms and pulled him upward and out of the hole, laying him on the ground.

His hands were still restrained but they added another zip tie for good measure. The hood was placed over his head again. Marcus was tossed into the back of the pickup and driven for an hour. The truck pulled over and the whir of cars speeding by on smooth pavement told him he was out of the desert and next to a highway. With the Hummer parked roadside, he was told, in broken English, to wait. His ribs ached. The bed of the truck was uncomfortable. It was a cold night in mid-January in the Mexican desert. He had not slept since Rome, nearly thirty-six hours ago.

Two men sat silently guarding him. Marcus was defeated. He'd lost hope when Beth was taken, and he had no hope now. She was gone. He was alive, but it didn't matter. He was of value to the men who took him. Marcus didn't care. His body craved sleep, but he couldn't get the images of what was happening to Beth out of his mind. Two hours went by, waiting in the back of the pickup.

Eventually he began to sense warmth. He could not see the sun, but he felt it. A vehicle drove up and parked behind the pickup truck. Marcus was transferred into a van. He presumed it was the same one used to take them hostage.

"*Ahora no parece ser un tipo duro, ¿verdad?*" (He doesn't look tough now, does he?)

There was laughter.

Ninety minutes later they cut the binds on his hands, took off the hood, and unceremoniously pushed Marcus out of the van door as it slowly rolled forward. He was dumped in front of the chain-link fence surrounding the private aircraft terminal of Benito Juárez International Airport in Mexico City.

Beth was there waiting for him.

Marcus couldn't speak. It took all his energy to rise and stand. He'd envisioned the worst, most violent, vile, and wicked things possible happening to Beth. And here she was. He held her and wept in joy for her safety.

She looked at him. Marcus was beaten, bloody, and covered in dust from the desert. His wrists were cut and bleeding from the zip ties. His face was hollow, filthy, and matted with dirt. His eyes were bloodshot and sunken. The stubble from his beard was muddied. He had scrapes on his arms and ankles and abrasions on his cheeks and neck. He was a mess. But he was alive, as they told her he would be, if she cooperated.

✯ ✯ ✯

From the back of the pickup truck eight hours ago, they took Beth via all-terrain vehicle to a large hacienda. They gently cut her bonds and let her remove her hood. She was in the courtyard at the back of the building. It was well-lit with a beautifully manicured lawn, a large garden with hundreds of flowers, and a massive in-ground pool. It was dark so she could not see the barn and horses to her right or the guest house to her left. But she knew they were there. She knew because she'd been there hundreds of times as a young girl. This hacienda belonged to her uncles. It was where her mother worked.

She was led inside to an office. She'd never been in this part of the house as a child. Her uncles always asked her cousin to take her outside to the stable, to the fields, or to the pool. She was never allowed to roam freely inside, especially if her uncles had guests.

"Elizabetta. I am sorry for having to do this." It was Carlos. He was much older than she remembered, but she immediately recognized him.

"Where is Marcus?" It came out more shrill and with more rage than she intended.

She retreated. "Please, Uncle. Don't hurt him. I beg you," she cried. She so desperately wanted to be angry. To scream at her uncle. To strike him. But all she could do was plead for Marcus's life.

"He will be fine if he tells Alejandro the truth. And you can help him if you tell me the truth as well."

Unlike the interrogation Marcus underwent, this one had no threats, no physical violence, and no gunshots. There was a Ruger, unholstered, on Carlos's desk but he never pointed it at her. Instead, he went item by item looking for confirmation and clarification. "What do you do as part of Perseid? What was Marcus's role? What duties did Jeff and Deb perform?" It was much like small talk with a family member over dinner. "How is your job?

What do you do? Who do you work with? Do you like what you do?"

When she relaxed, Carlos posed questions about Jeff and Deb that got more specific. He asked about their house in Brookline, their new cars, and their boat. Beth didn't know how, but Carlos knew a lot about everybody on her team.

He recognized her slow-growing realization and confirmed it. "We've been watching you for some time." Carlos knew details about where they traveled, the restaurants they frequented, and the hours they worked. He knew she and Marcus were together.

Beth's eyes wandered and lost focus as her mind raced with distractions, desperately grasping for an explanation and clarity. Carlos recentered her.

"They were spending a lot of money, Elizabetta. If I could see it, the authorities would see it too. It was sloppy. A big mistake. It puts us all in jeopardy."

"What do you mean, 'us'?" she asked.

"The Banderas cartel is a 50 percent shareholder in Perseid. We now have several billion dollars invested with the firm. Your recommendations have helped us launder a fortune from the US authorities. You belong to us."

Beth was stunned, trying to process what she was hearing. She knew her uncles were wealthy businessmen, but she was twelve years old when she left Mexico. Her father was always wary of her uncles, but she never questioned why. Now she knew. This is why her father would never talk about her uncles or their business. Her father was protecting her.

Carlos saw her wheels turning. "Where do you think Enrique got the money to launch this business? The Banderas cartel and our partners in China funded him years ago. We are now generating more cash from our investments in Perseid than we are from our traditional ventures. The drug business isn't what it used to be." He laughed and shook his head side to side.

Beth stared at her uncle in disbelief.

"We've been watching you and Marcus. You haven't been suspiciously transferring money or buying lavish things, now, have you?"

She was still processing what was happening and answered his question reflexively, "No."

"Have you been working with your friends Jeff and Deb on any of their schemes to move money, sell shares of Perseid's clients, and open new accounts?"

"No."

"How about research? Were you aware Jeff was planning on exposing Sinotech as a security risk to LAG's clients?"

"What? What research?" She jolted back to the present. "What was Jeff doing?"

"Jeffrey, with the help of Deb, was going to take all their money and short hundreds of thousands of shares of Sinotech. He was going to publish a research report accusing Sinotech of being a front company of the Chinese government. Of course, he is correct, but it is beside the point. He was going to send your FBI and SEC all sorts of information to destroy Perseid."

"This doesn't make sense. I work with both of them. When was this going to happen?"

"They were close. Within days or weeks. They were trying to get rich from their disloyalty."

"I don't believe you."

"It's true. They were going to abandon you. Vanish from Perseid and blow it up on the way out. But we found out and stopped them." Carlos's voice changed when he said, "stopped them." It had a soulless finality to it.

"What did you do?"

"They won't be causing any more problems," he said, his eyes boring straight through her.

"You can thank them for saving you and Marcus, though. Alejandro was going to shoot Marcus in the head, but before he did, I got a call letting me know you both are still loyal to the family. Jeff and

Deb saved your lives. Your cousin called me as well, explaining how important you both are to his business," Carlos added. "I had to convince Alejandro to let Marcus go. He was not happy about it." Carlos pursed his lips and shook his head side to side. "Not happy at all."

"You kidnapped us to see if we were disloyal to Enrique?" Beth was still piecing it together.

"Alejandro arranged for you both to come to Mexico to see if at least part of Enrique's Perseid project could be salvaged. The banker did a favor for me. He's been loyal to the cartel for years," Carlos offered. "And the good news is, *yes*. You and Marcus will remain on the team."

Carlos was congratulating her as if saying, *No harm. All is OK. Back to what you were doing.*

Beth couldn't reply. She was shocked at the story and stunned at how close they'd come to dying in the desert.

"You don't have a boat or plane or something you will use to try and escape, do you, niece?" He laughed.

"No."

"Before you go. I want to impress on you a few things. Under no circumstance will you tell Mr. Shea about our relationship. He is not to know anything about the cartel or our relationship with the Chinese. He can't know that you and Enrique are related. Rich is your boss. He is an American. Enrique Banderas is dead. He is resurrected as Richard Anderson."

It was the same demand Rich made when he hired her, phrased almost exactly the same way.

A warning flashed for Beth: *Rich knew all along.*

"You know what will happen if you try to harm this family or any of our businesses. We will do unspeakable things to Marcus if you violate our trust."

Beth stiffened, staring at her uncle.

"I want you to close your eyes and imagine him beaten to death in the desert, or on the streets of Boston, or dead in his house in New Hampshire. We will kill him if you say anything."

Beth didn't have the will or power to raise her head to meet his eyes. She sat stiff and straight in her chair, nodding her understanding.

"In a moment, I am going to allow you to see your mother. She has been asking to see you for years. I have never let her go. If I ever suspect you are working against us, I will have Alejandro bring her into the desert and shoot her in the face. Like I did to your brother eight years ago."

Beth's head snapped up. She looked up at him, mouth open, tears welling, in shock.

"Am I clear, Elizabetta?"

No answer.

"Do you understand?"

"Yes," she murmured in obedience.

He made a gun with his index finger and thumb and said, "Click."

Beth was defeated. She was cornered. There was no escape without getting her mother and Marcus executed.

"Now go to the bathroom down the hallway and splash cold water on your face. Freshen up. When you return here your mother will be here waiting. She will see you off. It's a long drive to the airport. You will be reunited with Mr. Shea there."

CHAPTER 26
Surrounded and Suffocating

The private terminal for charter flights at Benito Juárez International Airport in Mexico City had a staffed kitchen and bar, a comfortable lounge, and a large locker room with shower. Its floor-to-ceiling windows looked out onto the airstrip. They provided a full view of the taxiway but blocked out all the engine noise of the jets taking off.

Marcus spent thirty minutes under the hot water. For many people following a near-death experience, a feeling of peacefulness or lightness is common. The release of endorphins under acute stress causes changes in brain chemistry and can alter consciousness. The sense of time can slow, and cognitive clarity can sharpen.

Marcus was incredibly focused, but he was not peaceful. He was enraged. More furious for the anguish of envisioning Beth being hurt than for the physical trauma he experienced. He needed to get out of Mexico. Marcus needed clarity. He needed a plan. He needed to take action. Marcus needed to be in control.

Those men knew everything about him and his team. They knew about LAG and Perseid. They knew about their jobs and responsibilities. They knew where they lived. They knew about their bank accounts, what they bought, where they ate, what they drove, and when they worked.

"They're watching us," he said to nobody in the shower. But Marcus could not fit the pieces together. He was missing something. He was still rattled.

Marcus knew he wanted to kill those men. Not figuratively. He wanted them to die in his hands. He needed their cries and blood and breaking bones to replace the scenes of Beth he'd imagined. He wanted them dead, but he didn't know who "they" were. It was confounding and confusing, but he was sure Rich would have information Marcus needed. He'd call from the plane once it was airborne. It would be another hour to get the fuel and flight plan and then they would be out of Mexico.

Marcus was clean but his clothes were filthy and torn. He did what he could to shake out the dust and dirt, but it was ground deeply into his pants and shirt. He washed his socks and underwear in the sink and laid them across the air dryer. His shoes were destroyed. He would get his luggage from the plane when he boarded and at least put on clean pants and a pullover. He remembered the thugs took his wallet and phone. "Fuck. They have the keys to my apartment and my car." Panic overtook him again.
Bottom of Form

Beth slept in the lounge, curled in one of the leather couches. When she and Marcus were reunited at the gate, she told him she was fine but all she could do was sob and hold him. Now, as she slept, Marcus looked more closely. There didn't appear to be any bruises or cuts. She was unhurt. Clearly, she wasn't dropped in a hole and buried. But her tears, hyperventilated breathing, and choking sobs confirmed something awful happened. She woke and he asked her about it, and she forced a smile. "I'm OK." She wasn't ready to talk, and he would not force her to. She'd had enough. They both had.

The pilot looked at them, one looking tired and one battered and bruised, without reaction. He didn't ask any questions. He was paid well by Rich and was getting a lot of stock from Perseid. His job was to ferry executives across the globe and not to get involved in their business. He wasn't going to stick his nose into anything. They looked rough, really rough, but his job was to fly them home, and the jet was ready to depart. He shut the door and finished the checklist with the copilot. "Wheels up shortly, then five hours to Logan," he said over the intercom.

They were airborne in five minutes and headed to cruising altitude. Marcus wanted to call Rich right away. His thoughts were erratic and unstructured. Why did Rich send them to Mexico? Why did they need to see the banker? Did Rich know they were followed? How was Sinotech involved? How did these men know so much about Perseid? What happened to Jeff and Deb? Marcus wanted to scream.

"Wait." It's all she said. "Wait." Beth was calm and soothing, but strong. "I want to process it all," she said.

Marcus didn't want to wait. It was a function of time and distance. Hours had passed and he felt safer now. He knew she was safe. They were moving farther away from their shared terror and distancing themselves from Mexico. A switch in his brain flipped from being a victim to wanting revenge. He wanted to act. He wanted Rich to assure him he was not involved and that he didn't know anything about their abduction. Marcus needed to hear it directly.

But Beth was somber. "Don't call him. We don't know what is happening. We don't know who those people are or what they want." She was composed in her lie.

"We don't know if Rich is even aware of what happened or if he is involved," she started to inject uncertainty into Marcus's thoughts.

"If he is involved, you are going to tip him off that we know. If he isn't involved, you may be putting him in danger. I'm asking you to wait." Beth's recommendation was calm and measured.

"Something happened to Jeff and Deb. They were going to kill me." Marcus was frenzied and furious, but Beth's tone and reasoning made sense. At least it sounded like she was making sense. Marcus preferred action to hesitation, but he didn't know what action or where to apply it. Beth made sense. Marcus desperately wanted a plan.

"Get a couple of hours of sleep. You look exhausted. Let's get you into clean clothes and get to Boston. We will talk this through. You can't talk to Rich until we know more." Beth needed time to create a plan too, a plan to keep Marcus safe.

He wanted to argue with her, but he was tired. The leather seat was warm, and the vodka was kicking in. Just a quick nap. He'd discuss it again after a few minutes of rest.

Four hours and fifty-five minutes later they were wheels down at Logan. Marcus slept the entire time. His nightmarish visions of being separated from Beth were replaced in his subconscious with calm, knowing she was safe and with him.

The Uber driver dropped Beth off at her apartment first. He kept looking at Marcus in the rearview mirror thinking he must have had one hell of a good night to look so bad. "Mexico will do that to you." He laughed as Marcus exited a few minutes later.

Marcus had a spare key hidden in a box in the community storage closet under the stairs. He grabbed it and headed to his apartment. He was going to call a locksmith to change it out first thing tomorrow. There was a package addressed to Marcus Shea leaning against his door. No address, no postage. A plain, white, sealed box. It had been delivered, not mailed. He grabbed it, went inside, and laid it on his counter.

Marcus still felt dirty. Even after showering in the airport, sitting for five hours in the plane made him grimy. He needed a run. He needed to block out everything that had happened. Maybe he'd swing by the gym. Anything to clear his head.

He looked at the package. "What is this?" He took a steak knife and cut through the clear packing tape.

The document was spiral bound. About an inch thick. Clear acetate cover. The title page read, "This is What a US Criminal Complaint Against Marcus Shea Would Look Like." Inside were pages and pages of highlighted copies of US statutes, laws, and SEC regulations. There were clippings from the SEC website on equities fraud, stock manipulation, insider trading, and embezzlement. There were several pages on federal sentencing guidelines. There were clippings of news stories featuring Bernie Madoff, Jordan Belfort, Sam Waksal, Raj Rajaratnam, and Ivan Boesky—the Murderers' Row of financial fraudsters.

The final page in the binder had a mock-up of a front-page newspaper story. Whoever prepared the package was pretty good at using Adobe. It was made to look like an advanced copy of the *Boston Globe*. "NH Man to Serve 40 Years for Fraud." The fake news story described everything the Emerging Tech Team had done at LAG and for Perseid. It had names, dates, payouts, and a list of all the firms they'd covered. Whoever wrote the story portrayed Marcus as the leader of the entire operation, the mastermind of an investment crime syndicate. In the middle of the page, where a newspaper would typically place a photograph, they had stapled a headshot of Marcus. It was a copy of the picture LAG used on his employee badge. The same one that was in the wallet they'd taken from Marcus in Mexico.

He sat at the counter and flipped through the binder over and over. Not reading it, but instead slowly thumbing through the pages trying to piece together everything but arriving at no answers. He slid the box to his right and a folded piece of paper jostled out. It was a page torn from this morning's *Boston Globe*. The headline said, "Couple Found Dead in Canton."

It was the story of Jeff and Deb. It described how Jeff was beaten and bound. Both were shot in the head. Police were still looking for their car and asking for the public's help.

"Oh my God," Marcus gasped. "They murdered them. They murdered them because of Perseid."

Marcus closed his eyes and tried to structure his thinking. *Rich ordered us to stay in Rome. Did he orchestrate all of this?*

He wandered across his kitchen, thinking.

The meeting in Mexico was not necessary. Was it a setup? Marcus could not, would not, believe his friend was involved.

The men in the van knew exactly when and where to capture us. Was the banker involved? Were we being followed the entire time?

Marcus placed piece after piece.

The men were well trained. Military. It wasn't a kidnapping.

Fragments were falling into place, forming clearer and larger elements.

The asshole in the desert said Jeff and Deb were taken care of. It means they have contacts in Boston. We are home, but we aren't safe.

He shuddered when thoughts of Beth were recounted.

They took Beth someplace else. She was not hurt, but she was scared. They asked her the same questions as me. Why did they separate us?

Marcus could not fill in the gaps.

They knew exactly where to drop me off and knew she would be there waiting for me. She knew I was coming. But I didn't know she would be there. What isn't she telling me?

The clues weren't enough, and he slammed the table, frustrated.

She wanted no part of me calling Rich. She is afraid.

He replayed their warnings over and over. The Mexicans threatened to kill him if he cooperated with the authorities. They showed him they could get to him and Beth at will. They knew about his apartment and his cabin. They murdered Jeff and Deb.

The puzzle ended with the binder on his kitchen table. *Whoever put this together is threatening blackmail or to lock me away. They have all the evidence in one neat package.*

Sitting in his kitchen he felt like he was back in Jiminez, buried. Without knowing Rich's involvement, he couldn't move forward.

The Mexicans were watching them in Boston. He couldn't move back. The FBI and SEC were going to investigate. He couldn't move left or right.

Marcus was surrounded.

CHAPTER 27
Implicated and Cornered

"What package?" Beth heard Marcus's strength devolve into vulnerability.

"It's all here." Marcus's voice cracked, still coughing from the dust. "It's one hundred pages thick. It has all the SEC regulations I breached and copies of all the laws and statutes I've supposedly violated. It lays out the clients I engaged for Perseid and builds a case for stock manipulation for each one." Marcus waited for Beth to comment. She was silent. "Every fucking one of them, Beth!" It was the first time he'd ever raised his voice at her.

Beth couldn't tell him anything without her promise to her uncle and cousin unraveling.

"Who could get all this information?" Marcus asked.

Beth knew. Rich was the only one with access to it all. She didn't know if Rich prepared it or if her uncles coerced him to do it. Marcus was too close to Rich and just too angry and scared to see it.

"Jesus Christ, it has twenty pages on money laundering and lists of where and when transactions were made to hide money from the IRS, SEC, and FBI."

"Did we launder money for the Mexicans?" He was getting louder, not giving Beth a chance to reply.

"And what about Sinotech? They knew about that too. What do the Chinese have to do with this?" He was exasperated. Beth heard a thunderous crash.

"Marcus?"

"Fuck. I just smashed a chair against the wall."

"I don't know what Sinotech has to do with it all. We'll find out." Her promise was brittle and hollow.

"Whoever put this package together makes me out to be the ringleader. It says I'll get forty years in jail, Beth. It even has pictures of the prisons where I could be sent."

Beth tried calming him. "I'm going to see Rich. I will find out what's going on." She sounded angry. She wasn't, she was frightened. She knew more than Marcus but could not tell him. She had to protect him.

"Beth, did you see the *Globe* today?" Marcus had the torn page flattened in front of him. "Jeff and Deb were murdered. They kidnapped Deb from right in front of our offices. Her laptop and purse were still at her desk. They were shot and left in the woods. Jeff was bound and beaten. They were fucking murdered." Marcus's anger boiled over.

"No," Beth gasped. She'd focused so heavily on protecting Marcus, she hadn't thought about what her uncle told her about her friends.

"Marcus, I'm afraid. They know everything about us. They knew everything about Jeff and Deb." Beth closed her eyes, trying to remember the last time she saw Jeff and Deb together. She wouldn't let anything happen to Marcus.

Her mind jumped frantically from one threat to another. She replayed the threats Carlos made. From one unwinnable scenario to a worse one. From victim to victim. Enrique kept her anchored. His call to his father saved them. She trusted Enrique. She loved him. There is no way she could imagine him putting them in danger. He'd protected her since she was a child. She was sure he'd help her now. He'd fix this. He'd save her and Marcus from her uncles, but only if she kept Marcus oblivious.

"I have to talk to Rich," Marcus announced.

"Promise me, Marcus. Let me talk to him first." She kept hearing the click her uncle made when he formed his hand into a gun and pointed it at her. He would kill Marcus if he found out about Enrique. He would take her mother to the desert and shoot her. Her mother sacrificed and saved Beth and her father twenty years ago. Her mother agreed to stay in Mexico in exchange for allowing Beth to escape to a new start in the US. Now, Beth needed Enrique to save them all. She needed answers from him, and she would do whatever he asked. She needed to work with Enrique to build a story Marcus would believe. It was the only way to keep them all safe.

"All right, you talk to him first. Call me as soon as you are done. We need a plan." Marcus thought about how to protect Beth, and all she wanted to do was to protect him.

"I'll call you as soon as we are done. Go for a run. Go fight somebody at the gym. Get out of your apartment. Clear your head."

★ ★ ★

The LAG offices were closed in remembrance of Jeff and Deb. Beth was certain her cousin would be at his condominium in Seaport. It was a twenty-minute walk from her place to Enrique's and it was almost 7:00 p.m. The streets were dark, and it was frigid. It was unusually cold for mid-January in Boston. Families were skating on Frog Pond. She had her heavy coat on, Uggs on her feet, a scarf wrapped around her face, and a hat pulled low on her head. She was so layered and bundled that even if Marcus walked by, he would not recognize her.

The walk would give her a chance to play out the scenario with Enrique in her head. She needed to organize her story. What did he know? Had he spoken to his father and uncle? Was he as frightened as she was? What would they all do next? Did Enrique have a plan? How could they keep his identity from Marcus? What story could she tell Marcus to keep him safe? She wanted a way out. She'd beg her cousin to protect Marcus.

Beth attempted to put the times, places, and emotions of her ordeal into order. It was twelve hours of terror, but the order in which the scenes played out mattered. She needed to get the details straight so Enrique could understand and help. She also wanted to know what happened in Boston. What did Jeff and Deb do? How were their plans discovered? What are the police saying?

Since she had been small, Beth was terrible at reading Enrique. It always gave him the advantage. He knew exactly what she wanted, and she never knew what he was angling for. She was convinced she was ready this time. She'd be focused on every detail, every word, and every movement he made. She buzzed her way up to his unit. She'd been there dozens of times, but she was more nervous now than she had ever been with him. She paced back and forth in the elevator for the ten-story ride.

Beth ran from the elevator into his arms. She needed his embrace. She cried harder in his arms than when she was reunited with Marcus. In Mexico she was still numb and in shock. Marcus was broken and beaten. She needed to be strong for him. Now, with Enrique, she had hours to internalize everything that had happened. She was able to see the danger and threat in its entirety and it terrified her. She saw Marcus's exposure and vulnerability. Enrique would protect her. All of the sadness, grief, fear, confusion, disorientation, and anger poured out. She wanted to jump right into what had happened. She wanted to be clinical about it. But instead, she became too heavy to stand as Enrique held her, crying.

"It will all be OK," he assured.

✯ ✯ ✯

Enrique was prepared for her visit and was surprised Marcus wasn't there too. It made it so much easier she was there alone, and even more simple she was in the emotional state she was. He gave her a glass of water to calm her. He needed to slow her. He needed her to look to him for support like she had always done. He wanted her as vulnerable as possible. She would be more easily influenced, more impressionable, more pliable. But he didn't have all day. He needed her to get to the point, because he had a call with China at 9:00 p.m.

"Tell me what happened from the moment you left Rome."

The chronological outline she had in her head was demolished. She jumped from scene to scene in random order, hoping he'd listen. Her plan to observe him and to gauge his reaction was falling apart. She let it all fly. Marcus made her feel safe when they were reunited in Mexico. But Enrique could make her feel safe about everything. Her mother. Marcus. Their future. She wanted her cousin to help her find a way for Marcus and her to be protected and free.

Enrique knew the whole story, and frankly his father and uncle told it to him in a much more logical and progressive timeline than she did. Even knowing what had happened, Enrique had trouble following her. But what he did understand, from her jumbled narrative, was she wanted him to fix it. The good news was she had clearly understood his father's threats, and she would not defy his demands. Beth would comply. She knew what the punishment would be. She knew her mother and Marcus would die. The message was received. His father was very good at this.

Enrique was certain Beth would do whatever he wanted. What he needed to ensure now was that Marcus would continue to play along. If not, Enrique didn't need either of them. But now, they had work to do. Perseid work. It was critical their investment portfolio continued to expand and their new IPO projects get completed on time or his partners in China would be irate. They needed to infiltrate hundreds of more companies.

Enrique peered over her shoulder to the wall clock behind her. This was taking too much time. He tired listening to Beth's rambling, incoherent recall and interrupted. "Beth. Our uncle called me once you'd been released. It was all his plan." He would deflect, lie, and spin a story to make her trust him and make her believe he could protect her.

"Alejandro had a man in Boston spying on everything we did. He was the one who killed Jeff and Deb."

Beth listened, looking for signs or signals he was lying. Enrique's eyes didn't tear. His voice didn't tremble. He didn't lower his eyes in search of meaning or to recollect a memory of them. He wasn't enraged at the senselessness of their murders and wasn't infuriated by the treatment she and Marcus received in Mexico. His veneer was cracking.

Enrique continued. "They were planning to run. They had opened their own offshore accounts and sold all their Perseid stock. They were going to leave on their boat, but on their way out they were going to provide the SEC and FBI with enough information to put us all in jail. They were going to implicate all of us."

She heard the change in her cousin's tone. He was both dismissive and impatient. Angrier at what Jeff and Deb had done than their murder. She felt uneven and unstable and sat down.

"I tried to work with them. I tried to convince them to leave our team another way. They lied to me. Our uncle's agent here uncovered their whole plan. Alejandro ordered their death. I didn't know it. Neither did my father. It was Alejandro who was tracking your plane from Rome. He knew when you had landed, and he had you followed the moment you touched down."

Beth listened and watched him, hiding her emotions at the cracks and discrepancies in his story.

"The moment I asked you and Marcus to fly to Mexico City my uncle put his plan in place. It was a terrible set of coincidences. Jeff and Deb were getting ready to blow up everything and you two were headed to Mexico. Alejandro saw it as a fortuitous situation and put his plan into motion. He used cartel members to abduct you both." Enrique's story was tight. It was his delivery that triggered suspicion. There was no fear, no sense of betrayal regarding his uncle, no remorse, and no anger at what had happened to Beth and Marcus or how close to execution they'd been. It was orchestrated and staged. His impatience showed through as his charisma was laced with false charm. His empathy was hollow, and his concern was manipulative.

"Beth, I think our uncle had the banker call me to offer funds for Perseid as a diversion. I think it was a setup all along. I'm sorry, Beth. He played me to get to you and Marcus." Enrique wandered across the room. "I'd never let anything happen to you. You are family. Marcus is my best friend."

His story had myriad connections to what actually happened. Beth wanted to believe him. Enrique needed her quick acceptance. He had work to do. Enrique stopped roaming and stiffened, caught off guard by her next question.

"What about the package Marcus got? I didn't get one. You didn't get one. Who sent it? It had to come from somebody who had access to both LAG and Perseid."

Enrique didn't have a clean, simple answer. "It had to come from Jeff. I'll bet he planned this all along. The package may have been a warning to Marcus about the trouble he..." Enrique paused, "well, all of us, would be facing if our business was exposed." Enrique caught his slip, but not fast enough. It wasn't Marcus that was the cause of their trouble; Enrique was. It wouldn't be Marcus alone facing the consequences; they'd all face them.

Enrique saw Beth's expression change subtly. There was a brief flicker of disbelief. More rapid eye blinks. A mouth briefly agape. A quick intake of breath.

"Jeff was upset at Marcus." Enrique's explanation was piercing and untrue and his smile could not hide it. Instead of backtracking and clarifying, Enrique doubled down on the lie.

"Jeff was burned out. He was exhausted. His work was suffering. So was his health. His relationship with Deb was faltering." Enrique studied Beth's face for agreement. There was no affirmation. No nodded approval. No confirmation. Instead she had a furrowed forehead and an almost imperceptible frown.

Enrique wandered the room, spinning the yarn, trying to win her back. "I should have known it was coming. I've known Jeff longer than any of you. Even longer than Deb. He could not take the pressure I put on him. This whole thing, all of it, happened because Jeff lost it. And it's my fault." Enrique lowered his head. Enrique tried embedding enough facts and logic into the lie to short-circuit Beth's concerns. For the first time, he couldn't read her. *Does she believe me?*

Enrique kept explaining, becoming more animated and enthusiastic. "I've spoken to my father. He will reign in my uncle. We will have no more problems. This ugliness is over. As long as we continue to deliver for Perseid, and as long as you keep the promises you made to my father, we will all be safe." Enrique gave her a reassuring smile in hopes this would be the end of their conversation. He had to prepare for his call with Huang.

"We had a horrific few days. It will take time for us to heal. But Beth, it will be OK. You are safe and Marcus is safe."

Enrique's vanity and conceit blinded him. His impatience to get this problem over and behind him made him careless. He couldn't resist one more "ask," believing his control over her was incontrovertible. "Let's meet in a few days. We need to recruit new analysts into the Perseid team. I want you and Marcus to select candidates for me to interview. We need to rebuild. We have work to do."

Enrique pulled her up from her seat and hugged her.

Beth flinched. She pulled away, seeking distance. Her cousin felt it.

★ ★ ★

With that simple decree, *We need to rebuild*, Beth saw through him, fully, in a stark frigid light. Enrique lost her forever. It was the coldest statement he could make. Unfeeling. Uncaring. Emotionless. Sociopathic. For the first time, he was a stranger to Beth. Calculating and detached. She watched him confidently and defiantly swagger across the room with no fear, no panic, and no remorse. *Everything is fine. Now, get back to work*, is what she heard.

Beth playacted with a yawn, a deep stretch, and a smile. It was an excuse to leave without suspicion, not knowing he wanted her to leave anyway. She needed to talk to Marcus, to warn him. She and Marcus were safe as long as Enrique thought they were playing along.

"I'll talk to you in a couple of days." He smiled as the elevator door closed and then descended.

On the sidewalk, Beth was disoriented and terrified. She drew on all her strength to avoid panic, walking briskly toward Marcus's apartment, but she was ready to break, with tears forming and her breathing verging on hyperventilation. Beth's eyes were open. The veil lifted. She could see.

Walking toward Enrique's place, she had built one set of talking points. Walking in the other direction now she grappled with a different, even more difficult conversation. She had to tell Marcus what he needed to know to remain safe, but nothing that would put him in danger.

She was bundled against the cold, head down, mouthing her anticipated conversation and his anticipated replies and questions. She didn't see the two men converging on her.

"Hello, Elizabetta. Welcome home."

CHAPTER 28
Ambushed and Silenced

Beth was trapped, on a dark street, alone, with no witnesses. Whatever minimal sense of safety Enrique gave her was now shattered.

She tried to run, but the heavier man prevented her exit. She tried to knee him, but he blocked it and bellied her into the doorway of an empty and out-of-business coffee shop. There was no traffic, no pedestrians, and no streetlights. It was a few minutes after 9:00 p.m. on the edge of Boston's financial district and there was nobody to help.

The larger man had her pinned and was smiling. The other man, a Hispanic male, said, "You were just with Mr. Banderas. All is well?"

Beth didn't reply.

"Did you produce a plausible story to keep Mr. Shea in line?"

They knew. She had left Enrique's condominium fifteen minutes ago, and they already knew everything.

Flashes came to her. She had been followed. Enrique's building was being watched. They were listening in on all their conversations. It was none of those. It all came back to her cousin. He would not provide safety. There was no safe place.

She writhed and shifted trying to get away. She brushed against the large man's stomach and crotch. He smiled wider and touched her face with his plump fingers. She felt violated. Beth turned her head away, sick with panic. Stevie welcomed her reaction. She was getting the message.

"*Por favor, mire estas fotos, señora Ramírez.*" (Please look at these pictures, Ms. Ramirez.) The Hispanic man stepped forward and showed her his phone, scrolling slowly through pictures of her mother and uncle eating dinner. Isabel looked blankly at the camera without emotion. "These pictures were taken an hour ago," he said. Her mother was a hostage. She was in danger.

"I saw your mother a few weeks ago myself. Lovely woman. Your uncle would prefer not to have to take her to the desert and bury her in a hole next to your brother." Beth's eyes were on fire. She wanted to kill this man.

He flipped to the last picture. It was a picture of the Hatch Shell, an outdoor amphitheater along Boston's Charles River. It was after dusk. The sun had set. There were small snowbanks on the sidewalk. Sitting on a park bench adjacent to the sidewalk under a streetlight was the fat man who had her pinned in the doorway. And behind him, illuminated in the flash, was Marcus jogging. The Hispanic man used his thumb and forefinger to expand and enlarge the picture so there would be no doubt.

"This picture was taken less than forty minutes ago, Ms. Ramirez."

Beth had trouble concentrating as the large man rubbed his fat gut against her, rocking and sliding back and forth.

The other man snarled, "*Podemos encontrarte donde quiera que vayas, señora Ramirez. Nunca estarás a salvo.*" (We can find you wherever you go, Ms. Ramirez. You will never be safe.)

The fat one pulled a Glock from his pocket, holding it in his right hand. He rapped it against her skull and said, "We are watching you both."

As quickly as they had cornered her, they evaporated into the darkness. Beth stood alone in the doorway, shivering and crying. It was cold, but her tremors were more emotional than environmental. This would never end. They had no way out. Enrique could not, or more likely would not, protect her or Marcus. It didn't make sense. Alejandro couldn't oversee all of this. Enrique was involved. He knew everything.

It was nine-tenths of a mile from Enrique's doorway to Marcus's apartment and she was nearly halfway there when the men stopped her. She walked and ran the remainder of the way, seeking the most well-lit streets and areas with other late-night pedestrians. Beth wanted people around her. She wanted witnesses for cover and protection. She traversed the last hundred yards in a full sprint, holding back tears. She needed to get inside. She needed Marcus.

★ ★ ★

Marcus nurtured a plan. Pieces were missing, but it was a start. He knew where he would have the advantage of the surroundings. He knew as long as he stayed here, he could not spot adversaries in a crowd. He knew he needed to flush them out, like hunting pheasants with his grandfather. He knew they were being watched. Several times tonight he felt it. There was a young couple walking near the Common. A woman with the telescoping lens near the Harvard campus. There was a group of men at the T station, and a guy on the bench at the Esplanade. Everybody was a suspect. He didn't know who he could trust, other than Beth.

Marcus needed to lure out the real threats and end them. He'd find a way for him and Beth to drop out of sight. They had enough money to escape, but not to hide forever. For now, getting away from Boston, LAG, and Perseid would have to be enough.

Marcus reclined on his couch staring at the ceiling when a sharp knock disrupted his meditation. He looked through the spy hole. It was Beth.

"Marcus," was all he could make out when he opened the door. The rest of the sounds were drowned by dread and sobbing. She was cold, pale, and unable to communicate. She rushed at him, flinging both arms around his neck, pushing him back into his apartment. She was shaking.

He unwrapped her arms and stepped back. "What happened? Are you hurt?" He looked at her face, arms, and neck. "Are you all right?" She wasn't. Whatever it was, she only wanted to be held.

Beth's plan was falling apart. The fiction Enrique spewed was unbelievable. She had no plausible story to keep Marcus safe. Saving her mother and protecting Marcus were her only priorities. She had to convince Marcus that Rich wasn't fully involved in what happened to them, though she knew it wasn't true. She needed to buy time.

Marcus had trouble following her fiction. It sounded like Rich was aware of what happened in Mexico but was not directly responsible. The story she was spinning didn't make sense between the cries and labored breathing. She oscillated between deep sobs and long tortured pauses.

Beth struggled to tell him everything he needed know, but not enough to get him killed. She told him how Rich wanted them back at work immediately and wanted them to recruit new analysts for Perseid. She burst into tears. "Marcus, there is no way out."

"What do you mean?"

"Marcus, they're here. They're in Boston. Two of them. They know everything. I could not get away." She could only form simple and direct sentences describing the assault. The images of the men and the fear she felt swept over her. It was like Mexico.

She recounted the attack in vivid and enraging detail. It was all Marcus could do not to run out the doorway and hunt them. He wanted to break them apart and make them suffer. Break bones, burst organs, and choke the life from them. When he and Beth landed earlier that day he vowed to keep her safe, and within hours of arriving home she was ambushed. He did not keep his promise. Marcus was losing control, again.

"Tell me what they looked like," he raged.

She couldn't get the image of the fat man out her mind. She'd never forget his large gut and the sharp stench of garlic on his breath. She felt his hands touching her face. The raspy laugh when he rubbed against her. She remembered him. But the other man, he was harder to recall. He spoke to her in Spanish. He was the one who knew everything about them.

She did her best to describe how they were dressed, how tall they were, anything she could recall. "They told me they were here to send me a message."

He cut her off. "I saw them earlier. They were taking pictures near the river."

As she looked up at him, Marcus noticed a small patch of dried blood mixed in her blond hair. The taps with the pistol were harder than she remembered.

"We can't wait anymore. It's my turn." Marcus's plan was hardening.

"How can we do that? They are watching us. You know what they will do if we fight back."

"If we don't fight back, we will never get free. I can't live the rest of my life waiting for them to decide we aren't valuable anymore or for the FBI to kick in my door. I want us to send a message."

"What are you going to do? We can't go to Rich. He is more interested in getting Perseid back to work than protecting us," she whimpered.

"The first thing I need to do is get them away from here. To get them away from you."

Beth focused and leaned in.

"I need to speak with the men who followed you. Get them to fill in some blanks." Marcus didn't tell her what those blanks were or how he would get them to talk. It was his turn to demonstrate violence. The idea of brutality calmed him, for the first time in over three days.

"No, you can't. It's too dangerous." She looked at him.

Marcus's jaw was clenched and his posture stiff. To Beth, he looked like he did the night he dismantled Teddy and his friends at the bar. Her story successfully steered Marcus away from her cousin, but she knew she was not going to win the argument about how he'd handle the two men stalking them. She'd help Marcus if it meant she could keep him alive.

"I need to get them away from Boston and get them to tell me what I need." Marcus withheld the details of this part of the plan. She'd worry. His adrenaline was peaking, and his thoughts were racing. Jeff's plan gave him a few ideas, but it wasn't enough. Jeff and Deb left too many pieces on the board, thinking they could simply walk away. Marcus would not make that mistake; he would destroy everything, and he'd start with the two men from tonight and then work his way to the end, making whatever adjustments, shifts, and changes were necessary.

Beth knew she could not stop him.

"We need a plan for what we do when this is over. I need you to handle that." Marcus wanted her to focus on something other than what he was planning. "Don't touch any of your accounts. Do some research on where we'd go and how much money we'd need." Marcus needed her to be distracted, thinking of the future, while he took care of the more brutal and short-term responsibilities.

"I'll walk you home. When you get there, pack an escape bag. Take what you can easily carry. Think of it like camping. Clothes, comfortable shoes, toiletries."

"OK." Beth didn't argue.

"Transfer money into your local bank. Less than $10,000 from each source as it doesn't have to be reported to the Feds. Give me your account number. I'll do the same."

Beth nodded.

"Figure out how much money we'd need for a year or two on the run. Assume they are watching everything we do and tracking every purchase we make."

She was on board so far.

"I need you to be ready to run. Check into the Fairmont Copley. Wait until there is a woman at the check-in desk. Tell her you are hiding from your boyfriend. Tell her he's abusive. Tell her you want to pay in cash so he can't find you. Get a room facing Boylston Street so you can see the LAG offices. I need you to be able to see who goes in and out of the building. Maybe we can do a little spying ourselves."

It was good for him to be in charge again and not reacting. Marcus would make things happen from now on. Beth was calmer because he became calmer. He became more confident because she was more confident. They worked perfectly together.

By the time Marcus and Beth arrived at her apartment they had their plan. Now they needed a way to get the two men to follow Marcus north, away from Boston. It was the first step in his equation, and he hadn't solved it. To get this whole thing in motion, he needed the two men to leave Boston and pursue him. Beth listened to him outline and then dismiss several ploys. They were all too cute. "I could convince them I'm going to the SEC, or somehow have them overhear me planning to run, or threaten to implicate Rich." Nothing was convincing. Marcus was frustrated.

"Goddamn it," he barked.

"If I can't get them away from Boston this won't work. It is too dangerous to do it here." Marcus paced back and forth across her living room.

She shattered his stream of consciousness. "Marcus. I can do it."

He abruptly stopped.

"I can make sure they follow you." She wasn't eager to explain, and she hoped he would not press her on it.

"How?" Doubt evidenced in his tone. Marcus didn't want her involved in this part of the plan.

"Do you trust me?" She held his hands and bore into his eyes.

"I can't have you in danger. I won't put you in danger."

"Do you trust me?"

"With my life, but . . ."

She stopped him. "No *but*. I'll be safe. I'm going to drop breadcrumbs. They will follow you. You will become too threatening for them to ignore." She had a plan, but she didn't want to share it with him. She needed his faith. She could not tell him how without revealing things that would get her mother, and Marcus, killed.

He gawked at her, marveling in her transformation. Two hours ago, she was shaking, crying and without hope. Now she was the strong one.

"Trust me. Go home and rest. Get some sleep. I'm going to make a call in the morning." She had a plan.

Marcus followed her lead.

"Tomorrow morning, get in your car and drive. I'll call you at exactly 11:00 a.m. and confirm. When I call you, you'd better be working on whatever you need, because they'll be coming."

"I love you." It wasn't the first time he'd said it to her, but it was the first time it was teeming with such incredible vulnerability and emotion.

"I know." She wasn't going to discuss her plan anymore.

Marcus leaned forward and rested his forehead against hers and reached down to hold her hands, interlocking their fingers. He closed his eyes, trying to enshrine this memory. He had to win. He had to end this. She had to be safe. Everybody that hurt her had to pay.

It was after midnight when he left her apartment. He ran back to his place as careful as possible to make sure he wasn't followed and wasn't observed. He couldn't be sure, but he didn't see any fat men in his path. No obvious threats.

He opened his bedroom closet and took out his hunting boots and packed his winter gear. He ate a frozen pizza and had exactly one beer. He needed to sleep. When he wrestled, he had trouble sleeping the night before big matches if his mat plan wasn't thorough. Lack of preparation and planning worried him. On this night he slept solidly for five hours. It was a lot compared to a typical work night. It was a sound sleep.

Marcus was on the highway before 9:00 a.m. On a good day, a day without New Hampshire ski traffic, it was a four-hour and twenty-minute trip door to door from Beacon Hill to his cabin. He'd stop wherever he was at 11:00 a.m. sharp and wait for her call.

Marcus pulled over alongside the highway, fifty miles south of Conway, when his cell rang. "They are coming for you and your hard drives."

"There is nothing on them about Perseid."

"I know. But I needed something to make them act. I love you. Please finish this and come get me. I'm at the hotel on the fourteenth floor looking at the garage. Rich just pulled into the office."

Closer to the lake, the snowbanks were high, but the pavement was cleared and dry. He backed halfway down his three-hundred-yard driveway. The four-wheel drive had little trouble navigating the twenty inches of fresh powder. He'd forgotten to renew his plowing contract. *I won't need it next year anyway.* He shrugged.

The fact that he left clear tire tracks in the snow wouldn't matter. Nobody would notice them or his footprints by the time the investigation was done. Marcus tapped the keypad raising the garage door, then closed it and bolted it behind him. They wouldn't come in that way. He grabbed the five-gallon can of gas for the snowblower and the stack of newspapers inside. The thermometer was set for fifty-eight degrees to keep the pipes from freezing. He turned the heat up to seventy degrees. There was no need to sit there and wait in an empty and cold house; it would be a few hours before they'd arrive. There was a list of things to prepare.

He piled the newspapers on the table, made sure the Wi-Fi was working, tested the speakers, and arranged the wireless video cameras in key areas.

Marcus ate a protein bar, drank some water, and warmed up in his office. He spent thirty minutes on the speed bag and ten minutes hammering the heavy bag. He game-planned and visualized. It was just another fight where he was controlling the action.

Marcus repeated his timeline. *They don't know the roads well and they won't risk speeding, so it is at least a four-hour trip. They will be here at about 4:00 p.m. Then they'll take their time working their way to the house from the road. It's at least four hundred yards in deep snow. The sun will be low, and it will be cold. Really cold. Perfect.*

As a last step, Marcus unlocked the kitchen door and opened the dead bolt. He went upstairs to the second-floor bedroom to wait. It had the best view into the backyard.

Welcome to the cabin, assholes. I can't tell you how happy I am that you are here.

CHAPTER 29
Justified Cruelty

Javier leveled his pistol on target as he skimmed the cabin wall, remaining hidden in the shadows. He edged his sight line out of the darkness just far enough forward to see Stephen seated on the floor across the room with Marcus shielded behind. Javier could barely hear the music now with the volume so low.

From this angle, a bullet would have to go through several layers of Stevie's fat, bone, muscle, and cartilage before it struck its target. Marcus kept his left arm tight around the big man's neck. It wasn't used to keep Stevie incapacitated, but instead to keep Stevie balanced with his back up against Marcus's chest. Stevie had stopped breathing a minute ago.

Javier scanned the room from the edge of the threshold. There was no clear exit and no effective cover if Marcus decided to run. Javier weighed the option of trying to shoot Marcus where he sat but hesitated. It wasn't a clean shot, and he didn't want to shoot Stephen if he didn't have to. "I told you to be careful, Stephen." Javier said it loud enough for Stevie to hear. Javier looked for a reaction. Nothing. On the other side of the room, neither man moved.

Javier's eyes shifted slightly left, trying to see Marcus through Stevie. "What do you think is your next step, Mr. Shea?" Javier continued to use the doorway as partial cover. "There is no way out." He was hoping to goad Marcus into making a mistake, into moving, so he could get a clear shot. It didn't work. No reply. No movement.

He tried another tactic. "Do you think Elizabetta is going to walk away freely, without taking responsibility for the mess you've both caused?" Still no movement. Dusk was looming and there were faint streaks of illumination from the dimming sunset glistening through the window behind Marcus and Stevie. It was becoming more difficult for Javier to see them in the half-light twenty feet away.

"You've provoked some very important people, Mr. Shea. You'd be lucky if it were the FBI hunting you. But no. Now you've got powerful men that want you dead." Javier continued to provoke him. No change in position.

"You know what Stephen did to your colleagues. That is your fate. And now it's her fate too. Maybe it will be even worse for her." Still no movement. Javier continued to provoke. "In fact, I can say with certainty, her fate will be worse." Javier's voice sparked Marcus's rage, but not movement.

"She is a very beautiful woman." *Stephen will have fun with her.*

Marcus knew Javier was grinning. He wanted to break him apart. But Marcus wasn't moving. He knew Javier was angling for a better shot. Marcus was angry, but in control, for now. He needed to keep Javier talking.

"I came here to get what you wanted." Marcus finally spoke as he slid a bit lower and to the left of Stevie, putting as much flesh between him and Javier as possible.

"I came here to get the hard drives and to trade them for our lives. We want it to end. To be free again."

Javier listened but stayed still, everything but the barrel of the gun remaining out of sight, hidden in the gloom on the other side of the doorway.

"We wanted to get out, but you idiots had to show up." Now it was Marcus's turn to try and provoke Javier through the doorway.

"I don't even know what is happening or why this fat slob and a dumb Mexican are in my house." Marcus was hoping the combination of Javier believing he was in a superior position and Marcus making him angry would change the terms of this standoff and lure Javier into the room. But Javier was cautious.

Marcus did, in fact, know what was happening. He didn't have all the details, but he knew why Javier was standing in his great room. Beth sent him as she'd promised. Marcus didn't know how she did it, and at that moment he didn't care. Right now he needed Javier to be talkative and sloppy. He needed Javier to make a mistake. He needed Javier to be visible and vulnerable.

"We produced billions for your boss, and I don't even know who he is or why he wants us dead. Can you at least give me that?" Marcus prodded.

Javier offered nothing.

"There has to be a way to come to an arrangement," Marcus feigned. He knew there was no way to fix this. But he wasn't getting the answers he needed from Javier this way. Neither man was moving.

Javier grinned confidently in the growing darkness. "We know you came to get the hard drives for the FBI, Mr. Shea. Now I have them." Javier's smile gently faded, and his voice deepened. "All you have is a hostage and no way to escape." Javier was puzzled why Stephen wasn't struggling or fighting back. "You have nothing." Javier's pitch raised and his eyes narrowed in that moment, wondering if Marcus really had nothing.

"You put my jefe at risk. He wants you eliminated. You now, and Elizabetta as soon as I finish with you. I may let Stephen take a bit of time with her. He has grown fond of her." From the hallway, Javier did not see any panicked movement. No reaction from Marcus or Stephen at all.

Javier kept his Beretta on target looking for a way to kill Marcus but not hit his large partner. The whole time his eyes were searching the area, clinically working through a checklist. What position is he in? Does he have a weapon? What is the best line of fire? Where are the paths to escape? He had Marcus cornered in the fading light.

Javier felt uncomfortably warm as his pulse quickened. His arms and legs were tingling with increased blood flow as an autonomic response to preparing for a fight, but something was wrong. Marcus was too calm. Javier craned his neck and scanned the room. *"What am I missing?"*

Javier slid back a half step into the darkness and closed his eyes, trying to replay events. After Marcus subdued Stephen, he didn't run. Maybe Marcus didn't have time, or he froze and panicked. He wanted something. Maybe he stayed for the hard drives. Maybe he was a foolish businessman who thought he could negotiate his way out of this. Maybe he was braver than Javier gave him credit for.

To Javier, it did not sound like Marcus was begging for his freedom and his life. His voice didn't waver. His tone didn't quiver. He didn't plead for his life or hers. He had millions of dollars in offshore accounts, but he hadn't offered a bribe. He wasn't negotiating. He was waiting. He was delaying. *But for what?* The questions nagged Javier.

Aggravated and losing daylight, Javier had no reason to continue the conversation. He needed to kill Marcus and head home to where it was hot this time of year. Javier was curious about Stephen, however, and impressed he could be overpowered by a man little more than half Stephen's size and weight. It was scratching at his brain. Something wasn't right.

The most important question, one Javier had yet to ask, pierced the darkness. *Was Stephen breathing?* Javier should be able to see movement or hear gasps from the overweight man sitting on the floor twenty feet away. It was hard to see in the shadows, but he was certain Stevie wasn't moving. He wasn't struggling. All this time, Javier focused solely on the man he came to kill. And all this time, while Marcus maintained the choke hold with his left arm, Marcus's right arm was hidden by Stephen's hunched shoulder and large belly.

In the final rays of the failing winter light, Javier noticed a puddle of water in front of Steven spreading toward the doorway. Javier huffed and gave him a pathetic and condescending glance. The snow had melted from his pant cuffs and shoes.

But something wasn't right. Javier squinted, fixated on the floor. What is that smell? Ammonia? Bleach? Javier eyes widened and his body tensed at the shock of the answer. He knew what the odor was. It was urine. Stephen was leaking. The pool of piss was radiating outward. He was dead.

What initially was mild admiration for Marcus turned to astonishment as Javier looked at Stephen's body. It was his third underestimation in less than fifteen minutes. This man hadn't subdued Stephen, he killed him. Killed him with his bare hands. For the first time, Javier broke his pattern. In shock, Javier moved abruptly, taking two steps forward in a rage. Javier was now fully in the room with his Beretta M9 pointed straight through Stephen's body, at Marcus, ready to fire.

The release from Stephen's bladder was warm. It soaked through Marcus's pants as he sat hidden. In the few moments it took Javier to realize Stephen was dead, Marcus had reached his right hand behind his back and pulled out the nine-millimeter Glock Stevie had dropped. As Javier was distracted with what happened to Stephen, he didn't notice Marcus smoothly push the weapon to his right and aim it through the gap between Stevie's inside right elbow and a roll of fat along Stevie's hip. Marcus shot Javier in the left thigh, right shoulder, and stomach.

Javier's gun was no longer pointed at Marcus.

Bullets can do horrifically unpredictable things when they enter the human body. If they strike muscles and organs, they might rip straight through, leaving a small hole in the front and a gaping crater in the back. If they hit large bony areas, they can ricochet internally, causing catastrophic damage to soft tissues. For Javier it was a terribly unfortunate day.

The initial bullet shattered his femur and angled immediately upward, piercing his liver. The second shot bore straight through his collarbone and shattered his scapula. From there the bullet proceeded down and left, puncturing his lung and lodging above his heart, causing a spasm to jerk the gun out of his hand, landing eight feet to his left. In that instant, Marcus was enraged Javier had threatened Beth. The gut shot, unneeded, was for good measure. The stench of gunpowder, blood, and urine hanging in the room was unmistakable.

It was a few minutes before 5:00 p.m. and the sun had dipped below the tree line. Javier was bleeding out in the slowly consuming darkness. Javier was accustomed to death. He was a soldier and an enforcer for the cartel. But now his heart was pounding with fear, knowing this time he was going to die. Seated, he wobbled backward toward the door, stiffening with anger. He was furious he wasn't told what he needed to know to kill Marcus and seething that Enrique had not prepared him.

Javier had surprising respect for Marcus. He was in control the whole time. And now Javier was curious, wondering what was next. Marcus wanted something, which is why he didn't kill them when they first approached. Javier didn't care about loyalty to the cartel now. All the years of him demonstrating unwavering allegiance to Carlos and Alejandro were over. He believed his Enrique set him up.

Stevie's body rolled backward and to the left when Marcus loosened his hold and stood up. Marcus was even smaller than Javier expected but more muscular. Five feet, ten inches, and eighty kilos. A fighter's build. Marcus's eyes were blank, emotionless. They were the eyes of a man who had committed violence before.

"I have a few questions for you." Marcus said it without inflection or anger as he slid Javier's gun away from him. It was a measured statement, not disturbed by the brutality or blood. Marcus was in control, glancing first at the puddle he had been sitting in, and then turning toward Javier and the streaks of blood he was leaving on the floor as he shimmied backward on his ass toward the doorway.

Javier didn't owe his boss anything anymore. He'd tell Marcus everything he wanted to know before he died. He'd talk. At this point, *¿Por qué no?* (Why not?)

The music was soft. Set at background level. It was an unfamiliar song to Javier. Drums, eerie synthesizer, electric guitar, and vocals. Not the style of music Javier would listen to. He sat on the pine floor with his back against the doorjamb, looking at the bloody smear on the floor in front of him. Sliding backwards to where he was now was exhausting. At least he could rest against the wall while they talked.

Marcus watched without interruption, giving Javier time to get comfortable.

Javier liked the room. Change the animals on the walls and add terra-cotta tiles to the floor and it would work well in Mexico.

Marcus spoke first. "I have a few questions. But first, tell me your name."

"I am Javier Diaz. Believe it not, I was sent here to kill you." Javier stressed the *I* and *you*. Neither man laughed. Both got the joke. "The Banderas cartel sent me after your trip to Mexico."

Marcus cut him off. "I only asked for your name," he said, satisfied Javier was going to tell him what he needed to know. Marcus was going to be clinical in this interrogation. Judging from the amount of blood on the floor, he'd have less than fifteen minutes to fill in the gaps.

"When were you told to kill me?"

"This morning. My jefe called. You met Alejandro Banderas in Jiminez. He and his brother, Carlos, control the cartel." Javier had trouble speaking. Fluid was pooling in his chest cavity and filling his lungs. As he talked, small bubbles of saliva and blood escaped from the corners of his mouth. Congealed fluid and mucus seeped down his chin. His pain spiked with any movement.

"I hired the men in the van that picked you up outside the bank. We were planning to kill you both in the desert that night." Javier shrugged his shoulders and attempted a smile. He motioned to the corpse in the corner. "Stephen called that night to inform us you were not working to take down Perseid."

Marcus remembered the phone call in desert.

"He confirmed you and Elizabetta were not conspiring with the other two. I recommended that Alejandro kill you anyway, but after Enrique demanded you be released, my men brought you back to the airport." Javier shrugged.

Marcus remained quiet, maintaining eye contact, prompting Javier to continue.

"Ultimately, it was determined you were too important to Perseid."

Marcus studied Javier as he bled on his floor. He was older. Lean. Close-cropped hair. Clean shaven. Prototypical military. He was very good at hiding his pain, but the twisting scowl on his face showed the discomfort was clearly winning.

"I've worked for the Banderas cartel for more than a decade. Soon I'd run the cartel in Mexico, leaving the international finance business for Enrique in Boston."

Marcus, sitting on the corner of the coffee table, adjusted his posture, tilted his head to the side, and glanced downward, as if he'd heard something he didn't know. Javier recognized his confusion. For the first time today, Javier knew something Marcus didn't. He'd toy with Marcus a bit.

"Enrique has always seen me as a threat. Perhaps this is why he withheld critical intelligence about you. He is clearing me from the field. He sees me as a rival. He sent me here to kill you, but maybe he wanted you to kill me." Javier's paranoid sense of betrayal grew.

Marcus shifted back from the edge of the coffee table and placed his hands on his knees, refocusing his eyes on Javier. "Who is Enrique?"

Javier wanted Marcus to twist a bit more. "At first, I was instructed to leave you alone. Only to watch you once you returned to Boston from Mexico. I knew about the discussions Elizabetta had with Enrique." Javier coughed a heavy, bronchial cough. Thick and pasty. Wincing with the spasms.

Marcus reacted to the mention of that name again. "Who is Enrique?"

Javier skirted the question. "This morning, I was told about the argument you and she had. You were going to run and leave her behind. She told us you were going to destroy Perseid and hurt our Chinese partners. I knew once you got back to the US from Mexico you might run. She confirmed it."

"So, that's why you followed me. Beth told you I was running away and going to work with the authorities to destroy Perseid." Javier nodded immediately, but it wasn't a question from Marcus; it was a statement. Marcus was proud of her. Beth pushed the right buttons. They bought it.

"Who is Enrique?" Marcus repeated.

"You had to be eliminated. My colleague there," nodding toward Stevie's body, "and I tried to scare Elizabetta, but it was a mistake. We should have taken care of you instead." Javier threw a disgusted look toward Stevie.

"Who is Enrique?" Marcus leaned toward Javier. His demand more abrupt.

"Enrique ordered us to follow your friends and then to follow you. Originally he wanted your life spared. Now he knows you need to die. Perseid can start again with new experts."

"So, Enrique had Jeff and Deb killed and Enrique ordered you to kill me." It was spoken as a slow statement of facts.

"No and yes. It was Carlos and Alejandro's decision to kill your colleagues. The brothers make all decisions like this as a team. But it was their son Enrique's decision to kill you. In my opinion, they all waited too long." Javier kept talking. He enjoyed the tortured look on Marcus's face as he still missed pieces of the puzzle.

"Javier, who is Enrique?" Marcus demanded.

"After our discussion this morning, Enrique wanted you killed first. Stephen and I knew eventually Elizabetta would need to die too." Javier took a deep breath and coughed. "I wanted to shoot you as you were jogging yesterday. We had you all scoped out." He took another breath but struggled to get air. "After we killed you we would kill Elizabetta and bring her body back home for a desert burial. The Banderas brothers thought it a fitting end to a traitor in the family."

"A traitor in the family?" Marcus's words fell off to almost a whisper. Marcus looked up as if he misheard.

"We'd kill Elizabetta and then bury her in the desert, next to her mother and brother." Javier's voice weakened. The gurgling deepened in his throat and sputum flowed out in surges as he tried to clear his esophagus with shallow coughs. His face contorted with each breath.

"How are Perseid and LAG connected to the cartel and the Chinese?"

It was difficult and painful for Javier to laugh, but he did. Loudly and intensely. It cleared a surprising amount of blood and mucus from his lungs. "Is this a serious question?"

"Yes. It is a serious question," Marcus replied coldly.

"Connected? Enrique is the connection. Enrique Banderas is the son of Carlos. Nephew of Alejandro. They control the Banderas cartel." He waited to see if Marcus understood. He grinned a bloody grin. "Enrique Banderas is your boss. You call him Rich Anderson." Javier provided the final missing piece.

It was as if gravity tripled. Marcus wanted to rise but didn't have the strength to stand. He shook his head and slumped. He wanted to believe Rich was a target or a hapless victim. Marcus stared numbly at the dying man. Javier's teeth smeared with blood under his broad smile.

"*¡Por el amor de Cristo!*" (Jesus Christ!) Javier could see Marcus having trouble processing. "Don't you understand? Enrique is the cousin of your Elizabetta. He is heir to the Banderas cartel. The cartel killed her brother in the desert eight years ago." Javier's laugh sprayed blood onto the floor. "Enrique used Perseid to launder billions of dollars for the Banderas cartel." Two shallow coughs regurgitated another mouthful of blood and mucus. He was too weak to spit it out. It oozed from his mouth and down his neck.

Marcus was unable to speak.

"What got you in so much trouble is you and your team threatened to interfere with the Chinese. We work with Chinese spies who are infiltrating all those American companies you recommended for Sinotech." Javier paused.

Marcus was too unbalanced to stand. He wobbled, struggling to remain seated without sliding to the floor. He extended his legs outward and bent at the waist as he settled back on the coffee table to gain his equilibrium. It was disorienting. It was too much.

Javier enjoyed toying with Marcus. "We need the Chinese to be happy, so they keep providing us what we need for our drug business. They are the only thing keeping the Los Feroz cartel from attacking us. We'd lose the war to them. Enrique Banderas wasn't going to let it happen to his father's empire."

Marcus stared in disbelief. "How are the Chinese involved?"

"We help the Chinese with their technology spying, and they provide us with all the materials we need to manufacture drugs. They keep the other cartels in check. They protect us. The cartel and the Chinese funded everything you did at Perseid. All your work and all the money benefitted them."

Marcus stared in disbelief.

"Did you know you are a spy, Mr. Shea?" Javier rasped, managing a smirk. His lungs were too full of fluid to laugh.

"There is no Rich Anderson." Marcus said it out loud. His anger intensified as he struggled to decipher a barrage of memories in an instant. He'd known Rich for over ten years. He'd seen his home in Connecticut. He'd met his father, and he was no Mexican drug dealer. They'd competed against each other in college. They were teammates on the US developmental team. They worked together. Rich introduced him to Beth. Rich blessed their relationship and was happy for them. They were friends. There was no Rich Anderson. It was all a lie.

"Fuck." Marcus said it through tightly clenched teeth. His eyes sliced through the man bleeding on the floor as though Marcus was focused on an object miles away. "Fuck!" Marcus barked.

Javier answered all the questions as he'd promised. Marcus refocused on the man suffering and bleeding to death a few feet away. Javier hated Enrique almost as much as he did. Marcus stepped forward and shot Javier in the head, ending his agony.

Murder scene investigations report 50 percent of people who experience a fast and violent death defecate. As the heart stops and messages from the brain end, muscles relax, and the sphincter controlling the bowels releases. It's unpleasant to be around. The great room was now an open sewer. Marcus was surprised at the mess. Stevie was slouched over in a puddle of his own piss. Javier was on his back fifteen feet away, lying across the doorway with four gunshot wounds and shit filling his pants.

The reek of gunpowder, blood, feces, and urine mixed into a noxious combination. But Marcus was not going to be there long. Stevie was dead. Javier was dead. He'd learned what he needed. Enrique was the next target, and he'd answer a few new questions before he stopped breathing.

Marcus cleaned off the gun and placed it in front of Stevie. He needed the hard drives. They were only good for one thing: proximity, as bait. The hard drives would get him close to Enrique.

But now Marcus needed time. A little over an hour for a clean exit. Javier made the first step easy. He'd already removed the hard drives. They were sitting on the floor of the hallway. Marcus picked them up, took them outside, and put them on the railing of the back deck.

He went back inside and grabbed all wireless cameras he had placed throughout the house. He didn't want any chance for recorded evidence to survive. He put them in the middle of the kitchen floor on top of a stack of unread *New York Times* Sunday editions. Marcus poured the contents of the five-gallon gas can in the kitchen, dining room, hallway, and into the great room. He tossed a match down the hallway and dropped another on the gas-soaked newspapers on the kitchen floor. He waited on the porch for a few moments, watching the blaze grow.

Fire is a serious threat for any home. Ironically, log homes are often safer than traditional structures in the case of fire. They are very dense buildings. Their frames, walls, floors, and ceilings are much thicker and more resilient to heat than traditional stick-built homes. They can endure higher temperatures, and it takes much longer for them to burn through. The problem with log homes is once they are engulfed, they burn much hotter and longer. Marcus had ripped the smoke alarms from the ceilings and turned off the water to the home. This fire would grow without any signals, sirens, or sprinklers interfering.

Marcus needed to stay long enough to make sure the inside of the cabin was fully engulfed before he left. He didn't have any emotional connection to this home, and there was no remorse as he watched through the windows as the flames climbed higher toward the ceiling. As the heat became more intense, he backed away from the deck, into the backyard, pulling back farther and farther from the building. The heat melted the snow around the cabin, masking all the footprints. From fifty yards away, standing in the snow next to his car in the driveway, the heat was unbearable and the hissing and popping of pine logs was deafening. Explosion after explosion echoed as moisture within the broiling logs shattered walls, floors, and ceilings like sticks of dynamite detonating. The air was heavy with the clouds of charred wood and burning plastic. He was thankful he couldn't smell Stevie or Javier broiling.

He'd taken their wallets and phones. Javier had an airline receipt in his jacket pocket. Stephen had a billfold with $375. Marcus took it all. He could not risk the authorities identifying either of them quickly. The heat, flames, and heavy smoke would destroy fingerprints and DNA, so there would be a lot of guessing taking place with an investigation. There would be speculation that one of the bodies was his. It would be even better if the investigators believed the two had killed each other. They'd find a charred and melted gun near Stevie.

Marcus's SUV was ready to go in the driveway. Firetrucks and ambulances would disturb the whole area as they pulled in and jockeyed for position. After a dozen or so vehicles pulled in and out of the driveway, investigators would be lucky to determine another vehicle had even been there. They'd find the stolen sedan Stephen had driven with Javier first. There would be no sign of Marcus.

The fiery glow grew behind him. It cast a shadow of his SUV through the darkness as he pulled away from his cabin for the last time. He didn't look back. No last check in the rearview mirror was necessary. The cabin was fully engulfed. As Marcus turned onto the roadway, he pulled out Javier's phone. It had biometric security and was unusable. He stopped and placed it on the ground next to the stolen car as he passed. Stevie's phone was an older Nokia model with no security code or locking feature. Marcus used it to call the fire department.

"I'd like to report a fire. Yeah. A big one. One of the cabins on the lake. I think I saw bodies inside." *Click.*

Marcus remembered it took the volunteer fire team twenty minutes to get to his childhood home when it caught fire and another ten minutes for them to get water from the pond onto the flames. It would be at least thirty minutes for them to arrive at his cabin once they were called. There wasn't a hydrant within miles, so they'd have to cut through twenty inches of ice to pump water to the blaze. Before they put the first drops of water on the flames, Marcus would be over the mountain on Route 16 headed toward 95 then south to Boston.

He kept it under sixty miles per hour the entire way, unwavering in the middle lane, drawing no attention. Marcus pulled into the rest stop in Seabrook, New Hampshire, about two hours into his drive home. There, he made a second call from Stevie's phone.

"WNHR Channel 9 News. How can I help you?" The front desk operator was about to get a tip on a major breaking news story.

"Hey. Yeah, my name is Kevin. I'm calling from Umbagog Lake. I thought you might want to know about a massive fire here. It was arson. They found several bodies inside a big cabin. They'd been shot. The police say it may be a gang murder. Lots of drugs and guns were found. There may have been children in the house. It was a sex thing. Police and fire are all over the place. I think I saw the FBI." Marcus used all the buzzwords needed to ensure this would not stay a local New Hampshire story for long.

He hung up. WNHR would feed footage and analysis at 11:00 p.m. to all their ABC affiliates. No doubt, WCBH in Boston would run with the salacious story.

From the rest area, Marcus used Stephen's phone to send Enrique a text. "It's done. Watch the late news." Next, he texted him a picture of the hard drives. Enrique would be happy right until the moment when Marcus choked the life out of him.

The next call he made was from his iPhone. "Beth, I'm OK. Stay hidden. I'm coming to you. They won't bother us again." She cried at the calm sound of his voice. She'd paid cash twelve hours ago for two nights at the Fairmont Copley Plaza under a fake name. Her room on the fourteenth floor had a view of the front door of the LAG offices as well as the side entrance to the parking garage, as Marcus had asked. She'd watched Rich leave thirty minutes ago, headed home.

Her hotel door was locked and bolted the whole time. She sat in the corner, hidden behind the couch, in the dark with her cell phone. She wasn't sure which would come first, a call from Marcus or a knock at the door from the men trying to kill them.

"Oh God, Marcus." She couldn't form any other words. He knew what she felt. He'd felt the same way when he learned she was still alive in Mexico. But right now, he needed to know if what they had was real.

"When I get there, you are going to tell me about Enrique and your family."

Her secret had been discovered. "I'll tell you everything."

CHAPTER 30
Re-Earned Trust

Marcus called her as he rode the elevator from the lobby to the fourteenth floor. From the moment he called, she waited at the door, shaking and sobbing, staring out the peephole. She had to see him. Part of her would only believe he was safe when he was standing there in front of her.

He knocked quietly and she pulled him into the room. Her hug was suffocating. She hung her full body weight from his neck, trembling. If it were any other time, he'd have held her tightly and kissed her. He wanted to so badly, but he couldn't. He wasn't ready. Marcus needed to know how much of the truth she was holding back. Did she love him, or was she using him for protection? Was she playing a game? What did she know about the cartel and the Chinese?

"He is your fucking cousin?" It was a blunt accusation shrouded in distrust and anger. "How could you not tell me?" Marcus said through gritted teeth.

He put his hands on her shoulders and forced her away. Beth tried to tighten her hold, but Marcus extended his left elbow and forearm as a barrier, driving her backward. Separated from him,

Marcus could see her weaken and diminish. She sat back on the corner of the bed, inconsolable. She wasn't acting. At least this part of it was real.

"I wanted to tell you," she replied solemnly, staring at the carpeting beneath his feet. "I wanted to tell you everything. I couldn't."

"Beth, all of this is because of him. LAG, Perseid, Sinotech, Mexico. Jeff and Deb were murdered because of him."

It was all true. Everything Marcus said was caused by her cousin and his family. Her family. Tears surged down her cheeks and flowed off her chin in drips to the floor.

"Your cousin was a lie. Jeff and Deb were murdered. People tried to kill me, and if I don't die, I'm going to prison. You weren't mentioned in any of the evidence. Only I was."

"He manipulated me too." Beth said it softly, regretfully. "He's been doing it to me since I was a little girl. Enrique's good at it. I only saw how evil he can be when we got back from Mexico." Beth's anger swelled. Her rage was not aimed at Marcus. The person she was closest to and trusted longest betrayed her. Now the man she loved had lost faith in her.

When Marcus called her from New Hampshire she had about an hour to prepare an explanation. But there was no answer, no justification, and now Marcus looked down at her with anger and suspicion. She knew her mother's life was at risk, but there was no way to escape this this. She began to talk, quietly, like a small child.

"I wanted to tell you, but it got harder the longer we were together."

Marcus stood, back to the door, as far from her as he could get.

"In the beginning, I didn't say anything because he ordered me not to. He wanted everybody to believe he was Rich Anderson. He didn't want anybody to know he was from Mexico. He said he wanted to create something honest and new on his own. He made me swear to keep his identity secret. He threatened to abandon me. I was alone."

Beth looked up, hoping for a sign of support or sympathy. Marcus stood motionless and emotionless, with his hands in his pockets, looking down at her.

Beth continued, "When you started the team, I didn't say anything because I didn't want anybody to think I was hired because of him. I was his cousin. He used me to reinforce his lie, and I wanted to prove I deserved the role. It was important I made my own way."

Marcus started to pace the room, judging every word she said and looking for any indication she was holding back. His stride broadened. His back hunched faintly, neck cocked forward, his shoulders curved slightly, subconsciously in a stance prepared to fight. He looked like a predator circling prey. Purposeful steps, side to side and around, but eyes never leaving his target. Was she being honest?

"He changed toward me when Perseid launched. It was different. I thought it was the pressure he was under to keep LAG growing while he launched the company. He was frustrated and threatening."

Beth's face tightened and strained. Her jaw tensed, remembering Enrique's menacing ultimatums.

"One minute he'd tell me how great I was doing and the next he'd tell me I'm putting the team in jeopardy and that I'll be responsible if anybody finds out about Perseid."

Marcus kept his distance. His anger slowly dissipated as she added detail after detail.

"I tried to talk to him about legal and ethical issues, and he blew up. I raised the issues before you, Jeff, and Deb were ever involved. He told me if I didn't keep helping him, we'd all be exposed. He told me I'd go to prison."

That news changed Marcus's posture. His circling slowed. His stance slackened.

Beth remained on the edge of the bed, sitting on her hands, tears continuing to well up and spilling over.

"When we were all working for Perseid, things got better for a while. I was numb to what was happening and making so much money. All along, I knew I was the reason you, Jeff, and Deb got pulled into Perseid. I had doubts, but he scared me. I was in trouble."

Marcus approached her slowly, closing the distance.

"In Rome I wanted to tell you everything. I wanted to run away with you. I wanted to take whatever we had and disappear. Jeff and Deb must have felt the same way. We were all coming to the same conclusion at the same time. Something was wrong. Enrique must have sensed it or uncovered it, but I never considered Mexico a threat."

Marcus started to believe.

"When they separated us, my uncle brought me to my mother. I hadn't seen her in twenty years. Carlos told me he'd kill her if you or I ever put Perseid at risk. He said he'd take my mother into the desert and shoot her in the head if you ever found out Rich Anderson was Enrique Banderas."

She unloaded her whole history. Marcus moved closer and sat next to her.

Beth turned and looked at him, eyes red and swollen. "Marcus, they killed my brother." That admission broke her. She sobbed uncontrollably, recalling the discussion when Enrique told her he was missing and feeling guilt now for not grieving for her brother then.

Gently, slowly, unconsciously throughout her tale, Marcus edged closer and closer to her. Their shoulders touch imperceptibly.

"Enrique acted like he was my brother, but his father killed my real brother. There never was a Rich Anderson, he was always Enrique Banderas, the heir to the Banderas cartel."

She ached to be held.

"My uncle told me if I ever crossed them, he'd kill you. I love you. I had to protect you."

It pierced his heart. *I had to protect you.*

"Who was the man in Connecticut who raised Enrique?" Marcus pieced it together, but elements were still vague and missing.

"Ralph Anderson was camouflage, hiding a monster," she responded.

She spent an hour telling Marcus everything about her past and everything she knew about Enrique. She held nothing back, filling in all the blanks. She gave him all the names, places, and dates she'd remembered. She recounted what happened to her in Mexico when she was separated from him. She shared what her mother told her about her uncles and the cartel before Beth was driven to the airport. She told Marcus about Enrique moving to the US and how Carlos was able to hide him. She confided in Marcus how she got to the US with her father to escape the cartel, how her mother saved her life, and how she mistakenly resented her mother and father for it.

At times she talked lovingly about her cousin, but mostly there was a deep sense of betrayal about how he guided and manipulated her since she was in grade school. Enrique was always watching. Only now did she know he was cultivating her. Every move she made was manipulated by Enrique.

"He was there, moving the chess pieces of my life at every step." As she confessed everything to Marcus, she felt like she was telling somebody else's story. The tale took place in Mexico, Houston, and Boston. A story of love and murder, sacrifice and false illusions, trust and betrayal. Only now, with the full picture spread out in front of her, did Beth see how Enrique had engineered everything. The agony was raw, an exposed nerve.

Marcus listened to it all. Her grief, anger, and pain were real. It was like a physical blow. It sent shock waves through her. She'd trusted Enrique more than anyone, until she met Marcus. She no longer had Enrique. She couldn't lose Marcus.

Beth raised her head, looking at him. "Yesterday, I asked you to trust me. I knew I could get those men to follow you to the cabin." She wanted him to know she would risk it all for him.

"How did you do it?" It was the one remaining thing Marcus didn't know.

"I went to Enrique's apartment. I told him you were scared and you weren't listening. I told him I tried to convince you to play along but you said you weren't going to prison for him. I told him we fought and that you were going to the cabin to get all your files and the hard drives, and you were going to turn them into the FBI and testify in exchange for immunity and protection."

A wry smile broke through Marcus's intense veneer, impressed at her bold betrayal.

"It was the first time I've ever seen Enrique panic. He left the room and made a call. He told me he never found the package Jeff had created and it freaked him out thinking you had it. Ten minutes later those two men showed up. They asked me to tell them your plan again and I repeated every word of that lie to them. They left in a hurry. I called you as soon as I was outside."

"Why did you risk it? They might have killed you. Why go there?" Marcus asked.

"I wanted to see his eyes as I betrayed him. I wanted to remember the look of trust he had in me as I lied right to his face." Beth smirked. It was the first time she'd smiled since Rome.

Her last confession made Marcus smile too. It was the first time she'd manipulated Enrique, and it was perfect.

"Marcus, the night in Mexico, somebody called to tell them to let us go and take us back to the airport. It was Enrique. He told Carlos and Alejandro we were too valuable to kill. The fat man told them we weren't involved with Jeff and Deb, but Enrique was the one who told them to set us free."

"Yes, but he did it because he wanted to use us. He needed us. It wasn't because he was my friend or your cousin. He is a sociopath," Marcus added.

"One more thing. The package left on your door when we got back from Mexico. Jeff didn't create it."

"Who did?" Marcus asked.

"Enrique. He got the basics from Ralph Anderson, but Enrique put it all together."

Marcus had met Ralph ten years ago. "I believed he was Rich's father. Who is he really?"

"Enrique said Ralph is a lawyer for the cartel. He said Ralph provided advice in laundering money and establishing shell companies. He was the one who arranged all the Perseid LLCs and offshore accounts. He helped maneuver around US laws to help the cartel avoid detection. He created all the paperwork to transform Enrique into Rich."

"I remember him as a quiet Connecticut gentleman," Marcus offered.

"Marcus, as I was leaving his apartment, Enrique told me you'd never have to worry about spending a minute in jail. He said you'd never go to trial. He assured me you'd be dead, shot in the head and your body burned. He said I'd end up dead and dropped in the desert for the scorpions and crows to eat, next to my mother, if I crossed him. He told me that, and I still lied right to his face." She was laugh-crying and managed a little smirk. She was proud.

It was all in the open now and Marcus believed her. He wanted desperately to finish this and protect her. But killing Enrique alone wouldn't end it. The cartel and the Chinese were problems. Saving Beth's mother was a problem. Avoiding the FBI was a problem. But before anything else, he'd deal with Enrique.

"Marcus, please, please, please. Let's go. We have a head start. We can disappear."

"Enrique had Jeff and Deb killed. He tried to kill me. He's threatened to kill you and your mother. I'm not running."

CHAPTER 31
Retaliation and Payback

The sound of the TV echoed in Enrique's apartment. "Good evening. This is Scott Matthews with breaking news. A massive house fire in New Hampshire is drawing the attention of local, state, and federal authorities. You can see from News Copter 5 footage that local firefighters are on the scene and the flames are not yet under control. According to a news source, two badly burned bodies have been recovered from the scene so far. Narcotics and human sex trafficking are suspected. More details as soon as they are in."

Enrique was confused where they'd get the idea it was drug related, but regardless, Stevie had done his job. It sounded like Javier was in the rubble, which was OK with him. Javier was getting too close to Enrique's business, and he didn't like that Javier was constantly reporting back to his father and uncle. Enrique was now in charge.

He took the last gulp of wine from his glass as his phone buzzed. It was another picture of the hard drives. The text said, "On my way up." Enrique was thrilled. Stevie was back from New Hampshire. He'd show his father and uncle he could handle problems without their help.

"Perfect timing," Enrique muttered. He'd get them both a glass of wine to celebrate and toast Marcus's and Javier's demise.

"They wanted me to send a message. Message sent. Now it's time to rebuild. Perseid 2.0." Enrique said it aloud, alone in his kitchen, as a way to reset his mind and to start preparing. He'd have to negotiate with the Chinese for more time, but they'd agree once he outlined the roster of companies he'd deliver with a new team. Reaching into the wine refrigerator, Enrique had his back to the elevator as it opened. "Welcome back, Stevie, let me get you a glass of the good stuff."

With a glass in each hand, he turned right into a stomach punch from Marcus. He didn't know which surprised him more, the immediate inability to breathe or the fact a dead man was now standing over him in his kitchen.

"You son of a bitch. You fucking asshole. All of this was you," Marcus raged.

Marcus reached back and threw all his weight into a left cross. The punch struck Enrique in the jaw as he tried to stand, spinning him 180 degrees on his knees and knocking him across the tile floor into the refrigerator. Marcus was enraged, barely in control. This man was his friend, past tense. This stranger tried to kill him and threatened to kill Beth.

Marcus dragged Enrique, dazed and bloodied, across the hallway into the gym. "You are going to tell me everything, but only after I demolish you."

Marcus needed to be cautious. He'd wrestled Enrique four times in college and lost three of them. Enrique was fast and tremendous on his feet. He'd only allowed five takedowns his senior season when he'd won a national championship at Ohio State. One of those takedowns was to Marcus, who took silver in the tournament. But Enrique was most effective when there were rules, referees, coaches, and spectators. It was going to be different now. Marcus was going to kill Enrique, and he wouldn't use wrestling to do it. There was no referee there to stop it.

Marcus propped Enrique in the corner where he could barely stand. Enrique's jaw was broken, but Marcus was certain he could still talk if properly motivated.

Marcus dropped his heavy coat outside the ring and took off his sweatshirt. He kicked off his boots and took off his socks. Better for traction.

Enrique slowly regained his bearings. He knew immediately what Marcus was doing. He obliged and took off his shoes, stripped to his T-shirt, and stretched his arms, neck, and back. He was heavier and softer than Marcus. He didn't work out. He wasn't in fighting shape.

Marcus approached and Enrique attempted to drop a level and take a shot. He was out of practice but still good. He grabbed Marcus's leg and drove him back, smashing into a treadmill. Marcus underhooked his right arm and hip tossed him violently against the wall.

If Marcus adhered to wrestling rules, he might lose for the fourth time. But as Enrique regained his posture and launched a shot for another single-leg hold, Marcus caught him with a knee to the forehead, snapping him back and nearly knocking him unconscious.

"This isn't going to be a wrestling match, asshole. I'm going to kill you." It was Brazilian jujitsu versus a wrestler.

Collegiate wrestling and jujitsu are similar in many ways. Both have a flow to them. Both are contested by opponents of similar size and weight. Both have a strong foundation of grappling. It meant both had shots, locks, escapes, and reversals. Marcus was an all-American wrestler. Enrique was better.

But when it came to this fight, the wrestler would be at a major disadvantage. Wrestlers don't strike and Marcus had very heavy hands. Enrique was already rocked and shell-shocked from the punches and the knee strike. His muscle memory, that of a wrester, would kick in and he'd revert to the rules he was familiar with. He'd look to put Marcus on his back, to control him and pin him.

Sure, he'd also throw in a punch, knee, or kick for good measure, but those weren't his best skills. He was an amateur. Marcus was a world-class striker. Marcus got hit harder in sparring practice every time he went to the gym than Enrique could do to him here.

Marcus preferred to fight on the ground anyway. He'd look to get top position for ground and pound, or fight from his back and break Enrique's bones, dislocate joints, tear cartilage, rip ligaments, and choke him out. Enrique would revert to what he knew, and Marcus would show him a style of fighting he'd never seen before. Marcus planned to inflict unthinkable pain. And when the agony was at its greatest and Enrique was ready to black out, Marcus would get all the information he needed.

Enrique shook his head and blinked his eyes heavily, clearing his vision and regaining his equilibrium. He'd had minor concussions before. This one was severe. His arms and legs were not quick to respond. He was cloudy. He needed to slow Marcus.

"OK, so it's not going to be St. Louis in 2015." Enrique was referring to the NCAA tournament when he beat Marcus four to three in overtime.

"No, it's not," Marcus snarled.

"You sure you want to do this? You can't beat me. I know it, and you know it." Enrique was winded and angling for a shot.

Marcus watched Enrique rotate right, looking to grab a leg. Marcus let it happen. Enrique spun, grabbed both of Marcus's legs, and took him down hard. But Marcus did something unexpected. He rolled onto his back. In wrestling, nobody does that. Ever. You will always put your belly button to the mat and look to defend arm, head, or leg holds trying to rotate into a pinning position. Instead, Marcus pulled guard on his back, inviting Enrique to mount.

Marcus's tactics were foreign to Enrique. As Marcus settled on his back, he bent his knees and pulled them toward his chest. Enrique was trying to pull his way up and mount Marcus, thinking he'd rain blows from above. Marcus used his knees and feet to push Enrique's hips backward and away. Instead of punching or dropping elbows, Enrique used all his energy trying to balance and move forward. When Enrique was sufficiently tired and off balance, Marcus let him slide up, but instead of trying to roll out and away, Marcus interlocked his fingers behind Enrique's head and pulled it into his chest while Marcus kept his back on the floor. Off balance, Enrique was yanked forward, unable to post up his arms. A couple of sharp and well-placed elbows from the bottom opened up a major cut on Enrique's scalp.

Enrique tried to pull back from the elbows, but Marcus swung his knees open like the wings of a butterfly, rocking Enrique's body side to side so Marcus could secure his torso in a body lock with his legs. It looked like a figure-four, and Marcus contracted his quads and hamstrings, ferociously squeezing the air out of Enrique's lungs.

Nothing Enrique tried got him any closer to striking Marcus. Marcus arched his back, compressing his legs even tighter around Enrique's floating ribs, fracturing them on both sides. The stabbing pain across Enrique's back was blinding. With Enrique squeezed and scrambling to pull away, Marcus struck him hard in the jaw with a punch from the bottom position. Several of Enrique's teeth fell to the mat covered in mucus, spit, and blood.

Enrique was out of his element. He could not outstrike Marcus from a standing position, and he could not evade the elbows and fists from top position. His jaw was broken, his ribs were cracked, he couldn't take a full breath. Blood streamed from the gash on his scalp.

Enrique's only play was to press back down to avoid another punch in an attempt to reduce the crushing pressure of the leg lock on his waist and ribs. As he did, Marcus used his closed guard to pull Enrique into a triangle choke. Using his hands, he pulled Enrique's head down and used his right arm to underhook Enrique's left arm. In an instant he took his right leg and pivoted it up and behind Enrique's head and then raised his left leg up and over Enrique's shoulder, locking his right foot behind his left knee. Enrique's neck was jerked into Marcus's chest. His right arm was trapped, and his left arm was slung behind Marcus's right leg. Enrique couldn't rise up and he couldn't punch. All Marcus had to do was to keep pulling Enrique's head down and tighten the leg lock crushing Enrique's windpipe and pinching the carotid artery in his neck. Enrique struggled, attempting to role away, but he was trapped. In less than fifteen seconds, Enrique was unconscious. Marcus held the position for another ten seconds, just to make sure, and to make it hurt.

In a BJJ match, the competitor in this vulnerable position would either tap out, and be saved by the referee, or would pass out, and the referee would stop the match and revive him. There were no referees here. Enrique went to sleep. Beaten, broken, and bloodied.

Enrique regained consciousness in the gym, seated in one of his dining room chairs. His ankles were tightly wired in place to the legs of the chair with twisted coat hangers. His arms and hands were bound, crossed in front of him, pulled to his chest, and tied tightly using electrical cords. Enrique's own belt was tightly looped around his neck, choking him, and his sock was rammed in his mouth, making breathing difficult. The blood had stopped flowing from his scalp, but his ribs and jaw throbbed painfully with each heartbeat. Sitting in the center of the mat in his own gym, Enrique was unable to move, cry out, scream, or escape.

"What do you think about all that soundproofing now? Your contractor did a great job," Marcus said flatly, seated on the weight bench across the room.

Banderas stared at him, still trying to clear his head and understand what was happening.

"This is how I felt in the desert. Except tonight, nobody is going to call to save you. Your only savior is me. You are going to talk."

Marcus rose and stepped forward. He slapped him in the face, for no other reason than to make sure he had Enrique's full attention. Marcus removed the sock.

"Why me? Why did you bring me into this?" Marcus was barely under control.

"I needed you. You were the most important piece of my puzzle," Enrique replied through a badly swollen smile.

"Why? LAG hired hundreds of people. You could have found lots of analysts to do what I did." Marcus was incredulous.

"No, Marcus. You had everything I needed. Only you. You were smarter than any other analyst at LAG, except me. But as I sit here, I confess, you may be smarter," Enrique replied. His tone conveyed submissiveness, but his icy stare and growing smile belied his defiance.

"Not a good enough answer." Marcus slapped him in the face again.

Enrique recoiled from the blow. "You were a wrestler. A fighter. You don't know how to quit. To you, getting to the goal was more important than how you got there. You would focus so much on accomplishing the tasks I set out, you'd lose sight of how you were doing it. I needed that drive. I harnessed you."

Enrique saw Marcus was boiling and prodded him.

"You were also a perfect match for Beth. She'd push you and you'd push her. Though, I have to admit, I never thought you'd get sexual with her so quickly. It was a big win for both of us. Yeah, team!" Enrique grinned. The man in the desert had the same smile.

"When did you start recruiting me, manipulating me?"

"Long before our first wrestling match in 2005. I did my research on you. It was no easy feat, Marcus. You didn't have much of a social media presence. Nothing on Facebook, Instagram, or Myspace."

Marcus paced slowly back and forth in front of Enrique, never taking his eyes off the stranger.

"I read about your success in high school. I investigated where you came from. And boom. I found the article about your father burning your house and killing your mother and sister. Even through that, you excelled. You maintained an impressive wrestling record and got fantastic grades. You intrigued me."

"Bullshit. You didn't know me then."

"No, it's true. When I was at Ohio State, I had Ralph hire an investigator to look into your background. You had anger issues, my friend."

Enrique goaded Marcus. He rolled his head and tried to spit on the floor. It was thick and bloody and clung to his mouth and cheek like jelly.

"What does any of it matter? I had a tough childhood. So what?" Marcus said, incredulously.

"Oh no, Marcus. It is the most important part of what makes you you."

"You're full of shit." Marcus could not tell if Enrique was serious or playing him.

"Maybe I am full of shit. But I did groom you. For five years I worked on you. You were unrefined, like a gem. I polished and prepared you," Enrique said proudly.

Marcus's head spun. He paced, encircling Enrique.

"As an orphaned, angry, but gifted boy, you were exactly what I needed. Did you know my American father went to Penn State? He leaned on their dean of admissions on your behalf."

Marcus turned in disbelief.

"You weren't the only one I'd recruited. Jeff was another. Others never made it to LAG for one reason or another. Some made it but were disloyal and had to be eliminated. Chris Maxwell should have kept his head down and mouth shut," Enrique said with annoyance.

"But you and I were drawn together. You kept being pulled toward me and me toward you."

He paused and smiled at Marcus. "We made a good team."

Marcus listened to the story of his life, and all his accomplishments played out like he had no free choice or will.

"You fulfilled your role perfectly, Marcus. And now you've utterly fucked it up."

"You killed my father's favorite lieutenant. I thank you for killing him, but my father will be pissed. And you killed Stevie. I liked him. Bad form there, Marcus."

Enrique manipulated Marcus's history and blurred fact and fiction. Marcus struggled to keep up.

"Nice touch burning them, though. It will slow the investigation, but now you've put LAG's entire business in jeopardy. Worse, you've put Perseid at risk."

"Yes, I did."

"The cartel will not just let it go. Our partners in China are going to pull funding if we can't get them the deal flow and infiltration targets they need. We have work to do. You have work to do."

"That's not going to happen," Marcus insisted. He had almost all he needed from Enrique. There was one more line of questioning.

"I bet Ralph knows a lot about your father's business and Perseid, doesn't he?"

That disrupted Enrique's smug superiority. He wondered where this was headed. "Of course. He has been in my father's employ for over thirty years. He had no children, so when my father asked him to look out for me and to raise me in Connecticut, he could not say no.

Marcus nodded, thinking, *Continue* . . .

"But he is getting old. We don't ask much of him anymore. When needed, he knows he is bound to us, but he is slow and less useful now. I had to send Stephen to his house last week to pick up a package and send a reminder to him."

Marcus pressed, "He probably wants a relaxing retirement. Never having to look over his shoulder for the cartel or having to risk prosecution for helping you."

"We all want a quiet life at some point. His will be quiet when he's dead." Enrique tired of this discussion. "None of this matters, Marcus. You have a choice. You can fix this all now. Let me go. Work with me to rebuild Perseid and be my full partner. If we play it smart, we can break away from my father and uncle. We can even ween ourselves off Chinese investments. There is a lot of money to make together."

Marcus could not believe Enrique still thought he was in charge.

"Or you could run for the rest of your life. Never safe. Hiding in a hole with my slut cousin, afraid of every shadow behind you." Enrique's jaw was broken. Blood was crusted in his scalp and dried on his cheek. The bruising on his face was blossoming. But he still found a way to smile that awful family smile.

"Perhaps you want to tell Beth her mother was violated by father's security team and dragged to the desert? Shot in the head?" That smile again.

"If that is your plan, Marcus, to blow it all up, you'd better tell her soon, because it won't be long before my father's men kill you and Beth. My sweet Elizabetta. You won't be there to help her. You will be dead." Smile.

Marcus stopped pacing and glared.

"If you kill me, Marcus, they will never stop. There is nowhere on this earth you can go. Your money will be gone, your home is unsafe, you will be unable to travel. You will be found, and they will end you and they will end her, most gruesomely."

Like so many times before, Enrique took it too far.

Marcus walked toward him. Defiantly. Without rage or fury. He was in control.

"You are losing your touch, Enrique. I thought you studied me. I thought you knew me. I don't care how you threaten me, but you know what happens when you threaten people I love. You've made your last mistake."

Now it was Marcus's turn. He ridiculed Enrique, taunting him. "I'm going to rip apart your family. I'm going to kill your father and your uncle. I'm going to obliterate the cartel. I'm going to burn Perseid to the ground. And you can't stop it."

Marcus knew Enrique was correct. The cartel would never let them escape. Marcus could not negotiate for their freedom. But Enrique had given him the last bit of information he needed, and now Enrique had no remaining bargaining chips or value. He'd threatened the one thing Marcus cherished above all. It was a fatal mistake.

The last sound Enrique made was a grotesque crack, like a broken celery stalk, and a muffled groan ending in a guttural exhale. Marcus locked a front guillotine choke and lifted Enrique, still bound to the chair. He violently yanked Enrique forward and down like snapping a fresh sheet on a bed. Marcus broke Enrique's neck. The coroner would label it as a "judicial hanging fracture." As the name describes, it is most typically seen when a body is dropped with such force during a hanging that it breaks the second and third cervical vertebrae located at the base of the skull. The weight of the body jerks the noose tight, separating the bones in the neck. It is a quick, but particularly grisly, way to die.

Enrique's arms and legs were bound to the hand-carved, oak dining room chair. It was flipped forward, so his face should be planted on the mat. But instead, he was face up, his neck wrenched impossibly skyward, with a sharp angle sideways. His eyes bulged red with broken capillaries. It was monstrous.

Marcus pulled out Stevie's phone and sent one last text to the number Stevie had logged for Javier's phone. "Took care of Enrique. He won't bother you anymore."

On his way out, Marcus dropped Stevie's phone, billfold, and cash on the floor.

Would the authorities link the two bodies in New Hampshire with the phones and wallets in Seaport? Maybe. Would they think it was chaotic cartel vengeance hit? Who knows? They would find fingerprints from Stevie and Javier in Enrique's apartment. They'd find the car and phone in New Hampshire with the new text message. This would be a strange and messy case for investigators.

Marcus had some ideas for how to help the authorities along. He'd fill in a few of the blanks for them and put them on the right path.

The first step was to get help in Connecticut from Ralph Anderson, whether he'd volunteer it or not.

CHAPTER 32
End Game

"What do you think he'll do?" Beth had doubts Marcus's plan would work.

"What I want him to do and what he agrees to do may not be the same thing. I'll have to convince him our interests are aligned." Marcus trusted it was a good plan, but trying to explain it to Beth again made him less certain. It sounded better in his head than out loud.

"I could always threaten him, but I'd rather not. He's got to be in his late seventies." It had been a decade since Marcus had seen Ralph Anderson. Rich invited him to Connecticut to work out and meet his "father" during the offseason when Rich graduated OSU and Marcus headed to his senior year at Penn State.

"I always wondered how his son could have been such a talent and the father knew nothing, not a thing, about wrestling," said Marcus. "He never even once went to see Enrique wrestle at Ohio State. He won a fucking national title, and his 'father' wasn't there." Now Marcus knew why.

"He helped Enrique all those years. Why would he risk helping us now? Why turn on the cartel?" Beth struggled with the idea.

"I'm betting he wants out. I'm betting he doesn't want the risk and doesn't want the danger. I can show him how to remove the danger of the cartel and prevent them from ever coming back into his life."

"OK, but aren't you asking him to trade one devil for another?" Marcus's plan required them to negotiate with some very dangerous people.

"In a way. But he won't be bound to the new devil. Neither will we. And neither will your mother. It's the only way we get out."

She wanted to believe Marcus could save her and her mother. She didn't have any alternative. She trusted him with all their lives.

They pulled over next to the driveway of the address he'd visited long ago. "If he gets weird and won't help, or if he threatens to turn us into your uncles, we are going to run fast and hide."

Beth wanted to escape, but her mother's captivity made it impossible.

"The cartel, the Chinese, and the FBI will all be chasing us. If anything goes sideways, we have to disappear with the money we have and keep running. If that happens, we will try to pay a ransom for your mother. We will buy her freedom."

Marcus dialed his phone. "Mr. Anderson? Hey, this is Marcus Shea. Yes, it has been a while. I think it was the summer of 2006 after Rich graduated."

The call was pleasant so far. No indication of a problem.

"Rich? Aw, he's doing well. Yeah, I know. He doesn't socialize much. I barely ever see him. But things are good."

Ralph Anderson was actively looking for small talk. Whether he was genuinely interested in Rich's well-being or not didn't matter. He was eager for interaction and personal contact.

"I was headed to Manhattan for meetings and was driving through Darien. Traffic on 95 is a mess. Can I swing by while it blows over? I'd love to catch up and fill you in on everything. I'm five minutes out. We can talk until rush hour passes."

Standing inside the threshold to his home, Ralph Anderson looked more elderly than Marcus had expected. He was slower and hunched over. Ralph appeared more fragile and looked much older than his age. Though he moved carefully, he still had a quick wit, and his mind was sharp.

"Marcus. So great to see you again. And who is this?"

"This is Beth. She works with Rich and me."

"Please, come in. Get out of the cold. Can I get you coffee?"

"We'd love that," Beth said with a reassuring smile.

Good so far, Marcus thought. *At least there won't be a fight on his front porch.*

It was a large house. Much larger than a man in his seventies living alone would need. There were several pictures of him and his wife on the table and shelves inside the door. Pictures of them on the beach, on a cruise, and in Europe. *No pictures of them in Mexico*, Marcus noted.

The couple looked happy. Interestingly, there were no pictures of Rich anywhere. No pictures of him on vacation with them. No pictures of him winning medals. No high school or college graduation pictures. No wrestling pictures.

Mrs. Anderson passed away while Rich was a junior at OSU, thirteen years ago. Marcus offered to travel back to Connecticut with him but was told it would be a small private ceremony. He learned the following year, quite accidentally, that Rich never went home for the funeral. It was another clue Marcus had missed.

Nothing Marcus saw within the first ten feet of the front door made him think there was anything normal in Ralph's relationship with Rich. Enrique Banderas was not considered part of the Anderson family.

They moved inside. The house looked like an aging bachelor pad. Newspapers neatly stacked in the kitchen and copies of *Sports Illustrated* scattered all over. The Sunday *New York Times* sports section was open on the coffee table. He'd been reading the week-old box scores when Marcus called. The house was old, cold, and lonely. It was dry, dusty, and smelled of stale coffee and cologne. It was a home where every day was exactly the same as the day before. It was a time bubble, which is why Ralph was happy for the diversion and a chance to talk to guests.

They moved to the living room. More pictures. None of Rich. Marcus put his briefcase on the floor. For half an hour Marcus kept the conversation light. They talked about the Rangers and the Giants and why New York sports were always better than Boston. He was passionate about his Yankees and said he was patiently waiting for spring training to start. "The Yankees head to Tampa in four weeks. Aaron Judge is a monster. They are a shoo-in for the AL East. Your Red Sox don't have a chance." He laughed.

"Betts and Bogaerts are going to be hot this year," Marcus continued the banter.

He watched closely to see if Ralph would tip his hand. Would he have a tell? Would his actions indicate concern or panic? Did he have any idea why Marcus and Beth were there? There was nothing so far.

Marcus pivoted to the purpose of his visit. "Rich is doing great things in Boston. He's so modest. I'll bet he doesn't tell you how well he is doing."

"I rarely hear from him. He asked me for a favor a few weeks ago, but it was the first time in months we'd spoken." The truth was, Ralph hadn't spoken to his "son" in much longer.

"That's too bad. A lot is happening."

"So, Marcus, what do you do with Rich?"

"I run one of his research teams. We focus on new and emerging tech. Beth and I help large companies evaluate, purchase, and deploy these technologies."

"Rich really respects you. He said you and he would take over the world." Ralph didn't say it like a proud or gloating father. He said it flat and monotone, as if he had no vested interest in Rich's success.

"We also did work for Perseid." Marcus dropped a grenade into the middle of a genial conversation. Ralph's demeanor changed immediately. He stiffened and sat up. "Was this the document you prepared for him?" Marcus pulled out the inch-thick binder Enrique left at his door when they'd returned from Mexico.

"Marcus, what do you want?" Ralph transformed immediately. He wasn't a slow old man wanting to talk sports rivalries anymore. He was the sharp attorney who'd secretly been the US counsel for the Banderas cartel for the past four decades.

"Ralph, Beth is Enrique's cousin. Her mother is the sister of Carlos and Alejandro."

"I hadn't spoken to Enrique in two years until he called before Christmas. He demanded I prepare an overview of the laws, statutes, and penalties for the activities I helped Perseid perpetrate."

Marcus and Beth sat unmoving, enthralled by the details Ralph shared.

"After I arranged all the corporate structures, offshore accounts, and bank connections for the launch of Perseid three years ago, Rich told me I wasn't needed anymore."

Marcus softly nodded in empathy.

"Every night I go to bed expecting one of Alejandro's enforcers to come here and kill me. I still wake up with nightmares of that fat man standing over my bed with a gun. They don't leave loose ends."

Ralph's voice, weathered by time and experience, trembled slightly. "And then Enrique asks me to build that damn file," he said, pointing his finger. "I wondered if it was one of his sick games. I wondered if he had me outline the penalties I'd face if things went bad."

Ralph studied the way Marcus held the binder, like it was toxic and contaminated.

"But that wasn't it, was it? The package he wanted; it was for you." It made sense to Ralph now. "He was sending *you* the message, Marcus." Ralph shook his head and looked up, realizing they were in the same situation.

Marcus replied, "He had it delivered to me after he had us both abducted in Mexico. His uncles threatened to kill us. They did kill Beth's brother. They murdered two members of my team in Boston last week."

Ralph turned to Beth. "Your mother is Isabel Rivera."

"Yes," Beth said, surprised Ralph would know her mother.

"I met her twenty years ago. It was awful the way your uncles treated her. They spoke to her like she was their servant, not their family. She was never part of anything her brothers did."

"They are holding her as a hostage," Beth said.

"Sounds right." Ralph didn't need details or convincing.

"They had their hands around my neck for over thirty years. I thought I was out, until Rich called. All these years and I still sleep with a gun next to my bed. They want total loyalty, and they'll kill you if they even think you are going to betray them."

Ralph was warning them.

"Whatever you are planning, Marcus, I can't help you. I'm too old and too tired to fight."

"You don't have to fight, Ralph. Enrique won't be calling you again, and the two guys who the cartel was using in Boston won't be paying you a visit either." Marcus had his attention. "I took care of them."

Ralph studied Marcus's face.

"There is a way we can end it all. All I need is information and an introduction. It won't implicate you. If I'm successful, you will never have to worry about the Banderas cartel again. They will never show up here. You can sleep at night."

Ralph wanted to live a few more years without fear. Marcus had already eliminated three major threats to him. Ralph conceded, "Maybe this could work."

The next hour was spent mapping the Banderas cartel, its business, its leaders, and their underlings. Carlos and Alejandro both held the title of capo. Boss. Because leadership was split between them, there were fewer lieutenants. Marcus had already shot their top enforcer in the head and killed their hired bruiser in the US. Their heir apparent was dead.

The Chinese contacts were known to Ralph. Their chief worked out of Hong Kong but had offices in New York City as well. The Chinese were more pragmatic and less prone to messy outbursts than the Mexicans. Marcus's plan would disrupt them, but also give them a new partner and a way to save part of their investment. Marcus's only goal was to end the Banderas cartel.

Ralph was impressed with Marcus's plot.

The last thing Marcus needed was the most critical. "Would I be correct to believe the other cartels also use attorneys in the US, much like the Banderas cartel used you?"

"Of course."

"Would you have 'professional' relationships with any of these lawyers?"

"I do. Often when there is an opportunity to work together, the negotiation begins among the lawyers. We frame out the agreement, shares, and payments. We create a contract, so to speak. It isn't legally enforceable, but the promise of violence is enough to motivate each side deliver on their word."

It made sense to Marcus.

"In other cases, when there is conflict, we may meet to see if there is a way to avoid prolonged unprofitable actions, like a gang war."

"Perfect. Can you connect me with the lawyer for the Los Feroz cartel? I'd like to share an idea with them."

CHAPTER 33
Enemy of My Enemy

Cabo San Lucas, Mexico, is spectacular in February. At the southernmost tip of the Baja Peninsula, it is a popular tourist destination with beautiful beaches, crystal-blue water, and a warm climate that changes only a few degrees from summer to winter. It may be the most perfect weather on the planet.

Its marina has restaurants, bars, and shops and is the ideal harbor to find day trips for sport fishing, sailing, and scuba diving. It was the port of entry for Marcus and Beth. They'd bought their way onto a crew taking the mega yacht eleven hundred miles south along the coast from San Diego. The captain was making a delivery anyway, and taking two sturdy deckhands who handed him $10,000 in cash made it an easy call.

Their story, newlyweds seeking an adventure while they were in between jobs, fit. They were chasing the sun and looking for relaxation, adventure, and culture. It was their cover. In truth, they needed to be invisible. No passport triggers, no credit cards, and nothing to tell the FBI or the Banderas cartel where they were headed.

For anybody escaping the cold of the north or the heat of Central Mexico, it was an ideal destination. It was also the part of

Mexico where the cartels grant each other space and freedom. Esteban Cordozo recommended it to Marcus because he could be seen in public by rival cartel members and not risk his safety. He could walk the streets, eat at the restaurants, go to the clubs, or lounge on the beach in total security. It was Switzerland, south of the border. Today he'd have breakfast on the pier under a totally cloudless sky. He was just like any another tourist.

Mexican cartels often have complex relationships with one another. Their interactions can range from cooperation and teamwork to intense competition and hostility. Ralph confirmed it was not uncommon for cartels to form alliances with one another to increase business.

In these situations, they often shared resources and information. This is where the Banderas cartel had changed. They now had billions of dollars in new revenues, and they were not as reliant on traditional cartel income streams. They didn't negotiate well and didn't share information. The Banderas cartel was getting arrogant, and it annoyed the Los Feroz cartel. Banderas was smaller and controlled less territory, but their stranglehold over the Chinese supply chain for drugs, and their funding from Perseid, enabled them to be dismissive and not cooperate in good faith. Yes, the Los Feroz cartel knew about Perseid. But they did not know how to replicate it, and it pissed them off. The Banderas brothers were becoming a nuisance. As their visibility, influence, and profits grew they were becoming more inflexible, more uncompromising, and more intransigent. They were a growing threat.

When Los Feroz' attorney in New York told them a solution to the Banderas problem might be in play, Esteban agreed to meet Marcus and Beth. It was timely. Four days ago, he'd left a gathering with his bosses who were increasingly frustrated with the Banderas clan. They were debating next steps. They could agree to pay more for the Chinese chemicals they needed, or they could go to war and take what they needed. Neither was a good scenario. If Esteban could bring a better solution to them, he'd make his bosses happy.

They met at a dockside coffee bar at 9:45 a.m. Esteban looked like a vacationer in his flowery shirt, shorts, and sandals. Marcus and Beth played their roles as tired deckhands perfectly. They blended in with the tourists, marina staff, and anglers heading out for daily charters.

There was no introduction or pleasantries. Esteban sat and Marcus dropped a file folder in front of him.

"This is the start. It is the business plan and the earnings report for Perseid. This is the business venture funded by the Banderas cartel in partnership with the Chinese."

"I already know the Banderas brothers are expanding their business. What interest is it to me?"

"In this folder is all the information on what they've done, how they've done it, and how much they've earned. It also contains all the banks, accounts, and brokers they deal with. In total this is a picture of their entire business—$10 billion in assets under management." It got Esteban's attention. Los Feroz knew Perseid was generating a lot of cash, but they had no idea it was that much.

"Their business will generate several billion in assets this year. They will spin out a little under $4 billion in free cash next year and it will go higher, if not checked." Marcus paused.

Esteban was actively flipping through the pages.

"How will you compete with this?" Marcus wanted to know if Los Feroz was concerned.

Esteban looked at the financial report. "Their structure is quite unique. Perseid gives them clean access to US dollars. Billions of dollars." It was more threatening than his leaders had fathomed. It could change the balance of power. "Major wars are coming," he said, sitting back heavily in his chair.

Marcus probed. "How long until their new sources of money are used to finance broader attacks on your business? They will become too big for you to control or push around. When will their resources force you to report to them?" Marcus didn't want to make him angry, but he did want Esteban to be uncomfortable. Marcus succeeded.

"Mr. Shea, you are almost as arrogant as the Banderas brothers." Esteban laughed. He especially hated Alejandro. His ego was intolerable.

"OK. What is your point?" Esteban closed his eyes and leaned forward.

"Insider trading and stock manipulation is just one part of Perseid. It is also used as a front to help the Chinese infiltrate US businesses. They are engaged in industrial and political espionage." Esteban slowly opened his eyes and looked nonplussed.

"Why do I care about China's spying efforts?" he said, shrugging and shaking his head.

"It presents two problems for you. First, it cements the Banderas relationship with the Chinese. If Perseid continues to provide access to US companies, China will continue to award the Banderas cartel with monopoly access to their pharmaceutical business. Your access to the chemicals and precursors will be at the whim of Carlos and Alejandro Banderas, and there is nothing you can do about it. The Banderas cartel becomes irreplaceable to the Chinese." Marcus let it hang for a minute. He could see Esteban bristle.

"Second, when the US government learns of the Chinese espionage, and they will find out, they will fight back hard against all those involved. All the cartels will take collateral damage because of the Banderas brothers. Access to financing, banking, tax havens, and offshore accounts will dry up. All banking or investment streams tied back to Mexico will be deemed poisonous and forbidden. The Banderas cartel is going to crash, and when it does, their mistakes with Perseid will rain down on everybody, including Los Feroz."

Los Feroz were boxed in by a smaller rival. Los Feroz was larger but had been outmaneuvered by Banderas. There was no reason for Banderas to negotiate more favorable terms. For Los Feroz, instigating a gang war was the only strategy, but it would risk access to the Chinese suppliers. There was no clear win.

"What can you do about it, Mr. Shea?" Esteban asked skeptically.

"I can tear it all down. I can turn off their source of revenues from Perseid. And I can break their connection and make them too poisonous for the Chinese. I can serve up the Banderas cartel to the US government, and while they are dismantling Perseid across the globe, you will have a chance to replace them as the preferred partner in Mexico for the Chinese."

Esteban looked at him in disbelief. "What specifically are you offering to do, Mr. Shea?"

"To obliterate their entire business with one stroke of my keyboard." Marcus sat back.

"We have been watching Carlos and Alejandro. You are right, they have become rich and overconfident. We have been preparing for war. But you say you could solve this faster and in a more devastating way?"

"I can," Marcus confirmed.

"Even if this is true, we would still need to remove their leadership. We cannot allow them to rebuild. It would be bloody."

"We agree." Marcus was negotiating now. "Wouldn't it be easier for you if they lost all their money, had their businesses exposed, and they lost their favor with the Chinese?"

"And for your participation, what would you ask of us, Mr. Shea?"

"Two things. First, Carlos and Alejandro need to die. They cannot escape. Their lieutenants and enforcers too. Their entire organization needs to be eliminated. Second, I am asking you to protect and rescue Isabel Rivera. She is their sister and is innocent in this. We need you to intercept her and smuggle her over the border."

"And what about the two of you? What will you do?"

"We will disappear. We are forever off the radar."

"Would you like to run a Perseid operation for us? It would be a shame to let this business opportunity pass by." Esteban suspected the answer, but there was no harm asking.

"Thank you, but no. We are done. You will never have to worry about anybody rebuilding Perseid. When I burn it to the ground, nobody will ever recreate anything like it. You can do as you wish with the files I give you, but no, once we do this, we are finished. You can establish your own relationship with the Chinese."

Esteban placed both hands on the file folder he'd been given, leaned forward, and nodded agreement.

"The moment we see Isabel is safe, I will incinerate their business. Their relationship with the Chinese will be demolished. They won't know what happened. In the turmoil, you can eliminate the Banderas cartel."

Esteban knew this was the best alternative to his problem. It would be much easier to isolate and kill the Banderas leadership amidst the chaos of their crumbling empire. He'd welcome the chance to kill Carlos and Alejandro himself. "Very well, Mr. Shea. I will pass your proposal upward. Keep close to your phone, Ms. Rivera."

CHAPTER 34
Fire and Rebirth

Parrot Cay is a secluded resort on a private island adjacent to Isla San José, five miles off the west coast of Cabos San Lucas. The boat captain recommended the resort to the artificial newlyweds. He arranged for a local fishing boat to take them there secretly, bypassing customs.

The resort was famous for sugar-white beaches, brilliant blue water, and wellness programs. The sand was so clean and so bright, sunglasses were needed to walk the blinding surf line. The rooms were luxurious with teak and bamboo furniture. The door from their villa opened to a private plunge pool that ran over an infinity edge onto the horizon of the Pacific Ocean. It was perfect, though Beth wished they weren't just pretending to be married.

"It's not as nice as Rome, but still, not bad," Marcus deadpanned, dipping his toes in the warm pool water. "Wi-Fi is good," he said. She rolled her eyes, but knew it was important.

Their unit was separated from the other structures, which gave them the privacy they needed. They would have breakfast in their villa, walk the beach, and sit by their pool waiting. They waited every day for two weeks since their meeting on the pier in Cabo San Lucas. It was almost March, and nothing had happened yet.

It was taking too long. Marcus regrettably and reluctantly planned for them to go on the run. They had stashed away their LAG bonuses in a bank in Antigua. Nearly $1 million. It would have to be enough to last a long time.

There were other monies in Perseid accounts tied to them, but regardless of what happened, those would be forfeited.

"It's all dirty. It's blood money. We can't take any of it." Marcus was firm and Beth agreed. They would only keep what they needed from the LAG bonuses. It was gray money, not totally dirty.

Marcus sat on the bed, trying to decide which non-extradition countries they could go to, how long their money would last, and how they would generate enough money to survive if needed. His current research centered around the Maldives, the Marshall Islands, Vietnam, and Vanuatu. He was starting with countries with large English-speaking populations as well as those with no extradition laws specifically targeting financial crimes committed in the US. They'd be fugitives from the US, unable to return home, always looking over their shoulders for cartel killers.

Searching Boston websites, Marcus learned the authorities in New Hampshire had identified one of the bodies and were unsure if the second was Marcus. So far, the threat of US agencies was at bay. However, a neighbor of Marcus's from Boston left a phone message asking why the FBI was searching his home in Back Bay. Whether it was due to the fire or to Perseid, Marcus was unsure. Sooner or later, he was certain his face would appear on a "Most Wanted" sign.

Marcus prepared himself to tell Beth to begin packing. He'd confess to her his plan failed. He would tell her they'd have to leave the resort within the next few days, or he'd risk extradition. He'd find a way to bargain for her mother's life. It might give Beth comfort, but it was empty hope.

Beth's phone pinged with a WhatsApp message. She cried softly at first, and then began shaking uncontrollably.

Marcus both anticipated and dreaded this. He planned what he would say if his scheme failed and her uncles followed through on their plan. There was nothing he could say. He hugged her. "I'm so sorry. It's my fault. Beth . . ."

She turned and looked at him, tears flowing but smiling. "She's safe. She's in Texas with my father. They got her out yesterday."

Within ten minutes Marcus had two packages sent via FedEx from his account in Boston. Ahead of their arrival, the agencies would receive a detailed email outlining what was coming. The SEC and FBI were getting a far more accurate version of the package Enrique had dropped off at Marcus's house four weeks ago. It provided all the accounts, all the trades, and all the companies LAG and Perseid had manipulated. It had all the Sinotech technical specifications, and the types of rogue software code authorities should scan for. It also had a complete list of all the US tech vendors in which China had invested, those where they had established technology integration agreements, and where those licenses were installed among LAG clients. It had copies of Rich's calendar and all the meetings he had blocked off coinciding with meetings with Chinese authorities.

The package laid bare precisely where the rot was within LAG's business model and everything Perseid had done to manipulate securities and launder cash for the Banderas cartel and the Chinese government. It also had a copy of the Banderas organization chart Ralph drew for them.

The package did not acquit Marcus or Beth of their wrongdoing, but it gave the FBI and SEC context. It gave them the big fish, the ones who controlled all the assets, its leader, Enrique Banderas, aka Rich Anderson, and his ties to the two Mexican drug lords. It gave the FBI and SEC all they needed to shutter Perseid, recoup the illegal gains from foreign accounts, eradicate all the rogue code and systems from Sinotech, and a way to ensure it could never happen again.

Marcus also fired off a blast email to LAG clients with a research note warning of Sinotech security risks, as good measure.

Three days later, Marcus and Beth looked online to see if there was any news from Mexico. It took only one Google search: "Gang War Claims Leadership of Banderas Cartel." It had grainy pictures of Carlos and Alejandro with the word *KILLED* stamped in red diagonally across their faces.

The timing was perfect. The intersection of finding the bodies in New Hampshire, Rich's body in Seaport, and the cartel war killing the rest of the Banderas leadership played into a plausible story. They were all killed as part of a turf war that had spread from the deserts of Mexico to the neighborhoods of Boston to the lakes of New Hampshire. All the people identified were tied to the Banderas cartel. All the key players were dead.

The FBI had everything they needed to abruptly and forcibly close Perseid. They had billions of dollars in assets to recover and tens of thousands of lines of code to inspect to determine how much damage the Chinese government had done. It was a strategic victory, in a nice, neat package provided by Marcus.

Ralph Anderson provided Marcus with further good news. The Chinese were unlikely to be a threat. With the Banderas infrastructure obliterated, he'd met with a Chinese contact in New York and provided cover for the whole mess. He'd learned that the Chinese threw around a lot of money, and Perseid was only one of the shiny objects attracting their attention. Enrique panicked and struggled to scale to China's needs. With Enrique dead and cartel wars raging, China preferred to step back. Being discovered by the US was a nuisance for Huang, but not an expected or uncommon occurrence in covert intelligence gathering. For technical infiltration, they'd go back to low-tech approaches like copying products, stealing copyrights, infringing on trademarks, and funding labs at US colleges and universities. It was a slower process, but a tried-and-true approach. Perseid was a new tactic that didn't work. New isn't always better. There was no reason to track down Marcus or Beth.

☆ ☆ ☆

Beth pleaded with Marcus to declare victory and run, but he couldn't. She carried a Mexican passport as well as a US passport. She could travel at will. She wasn't on anybody's radar. He needed to know, after all he had provided to the US authorities, would a relentless field agent chase down every remaining lead and discover Marcus's involvement? Was he going to have to hide in Vanuatu for the rest of his life with Beth, or would they be free?

The online version of the *Boston Globe* had a long article tying together the LAG and Perseid storylines. It had pictures of Jeff and Deb and a sidebar on Chris Maxwell. It had an expose on the double life of Enrique Banderas/Rich Anderson with pictures from his days at OSU. It had tie-ins to the cartel murders in Mexico. It had pictures of the rubble in New Hampshire and purported the bodies found were those of an American and a Mexican national. The story did not mention Marcus or Beth. But it did mention a field agent from the FBI's Boston office who was assigned to lead the case, Special Agent Michael Colson.

The challenge was that Marcus needed to contact Colson without being traced. It required technical expertise and access to specialized tools, all of which Marcus had. With no high-traffic public-access points on this lush Pacific island, Marcus used a virtual private network and a disposable email service. This would make it difficult for the FBI to trace his online activity, identify his IP address, or find his location.

>Your Confidential Source
><Cartel&China@BurneMail.com>
>
>To: Colson.Michael@US.FBI.Com
>
>Special Agent Colson,
>I sent you the package connecting the Banderas cartel, the Chinese, LAG, and Perseid. I worked for Rich

Anderson, who I now know as Enrique Banderas, and fled Boston when cartel members were found dead in my cabin and Rich was found murdered.

Your investigation is correct in how it connects all the players. Perseid was a front for a multibillion-dollar money laundering, influence selling, equities manipulation, and industrial espionage scheme. I was an analyst for LAG whose work was corrupted and used at Perseid. Jeff and Deb were on my team. Enrique ordered them killed, and I believe one of the men you found in my cabin pulled the trigger.

Below are the banks and routing numbers for several offshore accounts Perseid had set up for my team as bribery incentives. You will see monies flowed into these accounts, but nothing has ever been withdrawn. It is blood money and should be counted in the forfeitures from your investigation.

I'd like to talk. I think I can help you fill in the gaps. Email me with a phone number at this address within sixty minutes.

Marcus Shea

Disposable email accounts are frequently used by scammers because they can't be traced and disappear once used. Marcus's account would be active for one hour, then it would be wiped from existence. It would be more difficult to mask his location on a live call, but he'd make it as difficult for the FBI as he could. He'd use VoicR, a voice-over IP service. Using his laptop as a phone connection would allow him to secure the line and hide his location temporarily. As long as Marcus was not considered an international crime boss already, the FBI might not have all the resources in place trying to find him. He hoped for enough time to convince Colson he was an asset, not a threat.

Within fifteen minutes a phone number was emailed to Marcus.

"Special Agent Colson, this is Marcus Shea."

"Good morning, Mr. Shea. At least it is morning here. Where might you be?"

"I'm safe."

"You've given us a lot of information, and if you're file is accurate, you've saved me a lot of time."

Marcus could hear Colson flipping through pages.

"Dates, names, transactions. Very thorough." Colson was honestly impressed. "New agents straight from the academy could learn something from you, Marcus."

"I can't take credit for everything in the folder. Most of it was assembled by Enrique as a way to blackmail me and my team into helping Perseid. It's ironic that what he was using to threaten me will be used to annihilate whatever is left of Perseid and LAG."

"Is that why he set up those accounts for you? As blackmail?" Colson had not considered it that way. He was vaguely skeptical.

"For Enrique, it was carrot and stick. He was showing us how much money was available if we helped him. After he set up the accounts, he told me how much jail time I'd face if the FBI found out. He sent those cartel killers after me when I refused." Marcus laid out the case.

"He sounds like an interesting guy. How long had you known him?" Colson asked.

"We have been friends since college. I didn't know him by any other name but Rich Anderson."

"Apparently nobody did," chimed Colson.

"I wish you could have arrested him and his family. They murdered my friends." Marcus's voice quivered. He wanted justice for Jeff and Deb. "But in the end, I guess they got justice."

"I'm sorry for your loss, Mr. Shea. Cartel business is messy. Collateral damage is common. Why don't you fly to Boston and sit down with me to help close this out?"

"Agent Colson, there is nobody left to punish. The people who ordered Jeff and Deb murdered are dead. The cartel leaders are dead. Enrique is dead. You won't be able to do anything to the Chinese government officials, but at least you can stop what they were doing and help the companies they infected to fix their systems. You have all the transactions, banks, and accounts to recover the funds. Their leadership is gone, and they have no money left. The way the cartel and China infiltrated the tech market has been exposed. They can't do it again. There is no need for a prosecuting witness or state's evidence. It's done for you."

"That's a pretty good talk track." Colson sounded like he was smiling.

Marcus didn't reply. He was waiting to see if Colson was going to be an ally.

"We searched your friends' boat and found some interesting files," Colson said. "Everything you sent me is corroborated by what we found on Jeff's computer. He also prepared a letter. He laid it all on Rich Anderson. He specifically says Rich coerced and threatened you. It was pretty flattering, actually. Jeff sounds like he was a loyal friend."

Marcus's eyes started to water. He didn't know how to react to knowing his friend was loyal to the end.

"Still can't get you to come to Boston?" Colson followed.

"There are still lieutenants and members of the cartel who might want revenge on me for shutting them down. They went looking for me at my cabin. I'd be dead if I were there. Good or bad, they killed Enrique in his own home. You can't protect me. I want to disappear."

"Is that so?" Colson knew he had little leverage; the case was basically closed. He'd already been assigned as lead agent into a new political influence investigation.

"Yes. For now, anyway. I'm going to be off the radar. Off yours, off the cartel's, off China's."

Colson waited for his offer.

"How about this, Agent Colson? I'll reach out to you once in a while and check in. You may have questions or loose ends. Maybe another tech crime will arise where I can help. I'll do so, but on my terms. If the US government will let me."

"You've done your duty as a US citizen, Mr. Shea. Contact me in two weeks and I'll let you know if there is anything else we need."

"Thank you, Agent."

"Oh, and Mr. Shea, please say hello to Ms. Rivera for me. You can tell her our agents will not bother her father. Or her mother."

CHAPTER 35
Safety

The global Covid pandemic could not have come at a better time for Solara Advisory (SA). The demand for strategic technology advice was never higher, and global enterprises needed help assessing alternatives to manage increasingly remote and distributed employees and customers. Digital business was accelerating, as was requisite spending on cloud infrastructure, applications, data/analytics, and security. Marcus studied cryptocurrency as an area of specialty too. Covid was a boom for tech and for advisory firms providing CIOs advice and counsel.

Bali, Indonesia, became a popular destination for digital nomads and remote workers due to its affordable cost of living, excellent weather, vibrant culture, and robust internet infrastructure. It was the operational headquarters for SA. Its founding partners, Marcus and Beth Shea, provided written research, strategic inquiry, and consulting, remotely, to a small portfolio of former LAG clients, including the FBI. Only CIOs could be clients. No vendors.

Marcus and Beth were home every day, swam in the warm waters every afternoon, and slept in the same bed every night. Marcus made sure Beth was happy, safe, and healthy.

Their son was due in three months.

About The Author

I dedicated over thirty years to the IT analyst and advisory industry, holding leadership roles in research, consulting, and sales. My teams supported hundreds of vendors and generated over a billion dollars in revenues for the advisory firms I represented. Every day we helped IT vendors build markets, deploy cutting edge technologies, and solve complex business challenges for their clients, the world's largest enterprises.

Every day, I went to work with the conviction we were making an impact. Our efforts were richly rewarded. Under my leadership, my team generated tens of millions of dollars in commissions and incentives, while the vendors we supported amassed trillions in sales. In my tenure, I collaborated with thousands of analysts and witnessed nothing but the highest standards of personal and professional ethics in every interaction. Marcus Shea, and the dubious practices of LAG and Perseid, are purely fictional.

I was blessed. My job gave me a chance to travel to all the locations in Pay-for-Play. It also afforded the flexibility to attend every wrestling match my two boys competed in. From elementary school through high-school, both spent more time on the wrestling mat than any other activity. Their summers were filled with wrestling camps, club teams and matches. Family vacations were sandwiched around big meets. For years, Thanksgiving and Christmas meals were spartan events in an effort to help them stay on weight.

    I was never one of those mat fathers who screamed at refs, argued with coaches, or confronted other parents in the stands. I learned to appreciate the dedication, sacrifice, and honor of the wrestler. It was my sons who introduced me to MMA, and it has become a shared passion for us that endures to this day. We always cheer for the athletes who emerge from the wrestling discipline, appreciating the grit and perseverance they bring to the sport.

    Look for my second novel, *BloodCoin*, next year as Marcus Shea emerges from hiding in Phuket, Thailand, to fight a new and more terrifying enemy inside the US government where dark money and cryptocurrency mix into a toxic cocktail of corruption, murder, and global political influence.

Printed in the USA
CPSIA information can be obtained
at www.ICGtesting.com
LVHW041457200824
788522LV00001B/3